THE SHEPHERD'S HEART - BOOK 2

HIGH DESERT Haven

Ps. 107:30

THE SHEPHERD'S HEART SERIES

by Lynnette Bonner

Rocky Mountain Oasis – BOOK ONE
High Desert Haven – BOOK TWO
Fair Valley Refuge – BOOK THREE
Spring Meadow Sanctuary – BOOK FOUR

OTHER BOOKS BY LYNNETTE BONNER

THE WYLDHAVEN SERIES

Historical

Not a Sparrow Falls – BOOK ONE
On Eagles' Wings – BOOK TWO
Beauty from Ashes – BOOK THREE
Consider the Lilies – BOOK FOUR
A Wyldhaven Christmas – BOOK FIVE
Songs in the Night – BOOK SIX
Honey from the Rock – BOOK SEVEN
Beside Still Waters – BOOK EIGHT

SONNETS OF THE SPICE ISLE SERIES

Historical

On the Wings of a Whisper - BOOK ONE

Find all other books by Lynnette Bonner at:
www.lynnettebonner.com

Lynnette
BONNER

High Desert Haven
THE SHEPHERD'S HEART SERIES, Book 2

Published by Pacific Lights Publishing

Cover design by Lynnette Bonner of Indie Cover Design, images ©
www.istockphoto.com, File: # 9304006
www.bigstock.com, File: # 2561692

Author photo © Emily Hinderman, EMH Photography

ISBN: 978-1-942982-02-9

Printed in the U.S.A.

TO MY PARENTS:

DUANE AND SYLVIA STEWART

A truer example of walking in God's Grace and Mercy would be hard to find.

AND TO MY SIBLINGS:

BETHANY AND HERB,
JON AND PATTI,
MELISSA AND KEVIN

I love you all and am so glad I can call you family twice—once through our own blood, and once through Christ's.

Acknowledgments

Once again, I owe much thanks to my English-teacher mother. I can honestly say I wouldn't be here, writing this sentence, if it wasn't for her encouragement along my writing journey.

Lesley, my crit-partner-extraordinaire, thanks for all your input. I'm so thankful God brought you into my life. I truly appreciate you (even when I'm grumbling through a rewrite).

Psalm 23

A PSALM OF DAVID

The Lord is my shepherd; I shall not want.
He makes me to lie down in green pastures;
He leads me beside the still waters.
He restores my soul;
He leads me in the paths of righteousness For His name's sake.
Yea, though I walk through the valley of the shadow of death,
I will fear no evil;
For You are with me;
Your rod and Your staff, they comfort me.
You prepare a table before me in the presence of my enemies;
You anoint my head with oil; My cup runs over.
Surely goodness and mercy shall follow me
All the days of my life;
And I will dwell in the house of the Lord Forever.

Prologue

California
July 1883

As Dominique Noel Vasquez methodically scrubbed clothes in the tub of soapy water, she listened to the quiet, strained tones of her parents who sat against the shady side of the house.

Scorching afternoon sun shone on the hard-packed, earth yard of the small adobe hut. Heat waves, radiating from every sun-baked surface, turned the landscape into a shimmering sepia blur. Dead brown land lay in every direction; the only hint of green life was the small scraggly plot of corn that would hopefully feed the family for the year to come. Even the wheat struggling to grow added to the dull brown vista. A solitary chicken, scratching for a meager meal, sent small puffs of dust filtering across the yard and a lonely cow, the children's only source of milk, rested her head on top of her split-rail fence and let out a low bellow.

In this heat everyone should have been down for a *siesta,* but on this day only the smallest children of the household were resting.

Tension rode the heat waves.

Dominique plunged harder and glared at the clothes. The creditors had come again this morning. Last year Papa had been forced to borrow money for seed, and now for the second season in a row the rains had failed them. There were no crops; they were down to their last chicken; the one cow's milk was needed by the children; and the creditors were howling for their money like a pack of hungry wolves hot on the scent of lame prey.

Nicki tossed an angry glance at the sky. "Lord, where are You when we need You?" Sweat trickled down her temple and she rubbed it roughly across one shoulder as she shook out a little skirt with more vigor than necessary and tossed it across the line. Gentle conviction washed over her. She was throwing a bigger temper tantrum than two-year-old Coreena did when Papa told her "No."

Nicki's anger eased. "Forgive me, Lord. You alone know and care about our plight. But if there were anything I could do to help Mama and Papa, You know I would do it." She paused in her prayer, thinking, then continued, "What is there to do, Lord? Show me what I can do to help."

Mama called across the yard, interrupting her prayer. "Nicki, you work too hard. Sit! Rest! We will finish the washing when it is cooler."

"Almost done, Mama. Then I will rest."

"That girl!" Mama turned to Papa but the rest of her words were drowned in a dry, hot breeze.

Nicki smiled. Mama often castigated her for working too hard, but with twelve children, nine of whom were still at home to feed and clothe, Mama needed and appreciated all the help she could get.

Silence reigned for a time. The only sounds filling the afternoon air were the soft swish, plunge, and gurgle of Nicki's washing and the giggling of her two younger sisters splashing each other with cool water by the well. Nicki gave the last small shirt a snap and deftly flipped it onto the line where the laundry was drying. Dumping the soapy water in front of the door, which helped keep the dust down, Nicki hung the wooden bucket on its nail and moved to carefully empty the contents of the rinse bucket on the one small rosebush at the corner of the hut.

"Girls, please!" Juanita Vasquez called from the shadow of the house to Rosa and Juna, who were getting a little wild and loud with their splashing game. "I have just gotten Manuel to sleep. Quiet!"

This sent the girls into another gale of giggles. Their mother's voice had been twice as loud as theirs. But when Papa tipped his sombrero back and glared at his two wayward offspring, the giggles ceased immediately.

Nicki shook her head fondly at her sisters' wayward ways and sank to the ground next to Mama, suppressing a groan of satisfaction as she leaned back against the cool adobe wall. She was tired. All morning she had helped Papa haul water from the well to carefully water their acre of wheat and corn. A large enough plot to hopefully get them through another year. Later they would repeat the process, because watering with buckets did not soak the ground like a good rain would, and the crops needed plenty of water if they were to produce well.

Nicki closed her eyes, trying to ignore Mama and Papa's furtive conversation.

"The chicken, Carlos?"

"Mama, the chicken will not bring in enough to get us through one day, much less pay the money we owe."

"Yes. You are right, of course, and it has stopped laying, so we don't even have the eggs from it anymore." Mama sighed. "Ahhh, maybe we should have chicken tonight, *sí?*"

Papa sighed at Mama's little joke. "We could sell the cow."

"Papa, she is the only milk for the children. I would like to keep her if we could."

Hot tears pressed the back of Nicki's eyes, and she leaned back against the wall. What were they to do? Papa would be taken to jail if he didn't come up with the money by next week, and then they would all die for sure. The creditors would take their meager crops to recoup as much of their money as they could. They wouldn't care that they'd be leaving a woman and her nine children to starve to death. Where was Juan when they needed him? Were he here, he'd think of some way to make the money they so desperately needed.

A slight breeze rustled the dried grasses, and Nicki pulled her skirt up around her knees, not caring that Mama would chastise her for such an unladylike action. The small breath of fresh air was worth it. Reaching up, she brushed at the long wisps of black hair that had escaped her braid and rubbed the perspiration from her upper lip. She wanted a drink of water but felt almost too tired to get up and get it. Eventually the thought of the cold water won out. She shifted forward. Mama and Papa could surely use a drink as well.

"Child, you don't sit still for even a minute! What are you heading to do now?"

"A drink, Mama," Nicki said lovingly. "Would you like one as well?" She pushed herself up from the wall.

Mama's voice turned tender. "What would I do without you, child?"

Nicki chuckled. She was hardly the child her mother kept insisting she was. At seventeen she more than carried her weight, but Mama didn't like to see her children grow up. Nicki remembered Mama calling Roberto "my little man" on the day of his wedding! Those had been happier times, Nicki thought as she walked to the well. The rains had been good in those years, and debt had not hung over the little adobe hut and its occupants.

As Nicki cranked the lever that would pull the bucket up from the depths of the well, she scanned the horizon and stiffened. "Papa." Her tone held a soft warning. Someone was coming on the trail.

Papa rose and stood by her side. Nicki pulled the bucket toward her, filling the dipper with cool water. If the creditors had come to take her papa away, he would go having just drunk his fill from the chilled water of his own well. She handed the dipper to her father. He drank, never taking his eyes off the rider heading their way, then handed the dipper back. Nicki filled it and moved toward her mother, who still sat in the shade, tears filling her eyes.

"They said not until next week." Mama's words stabbed a knife of pain through Nicki's heart. Whatever happened, Nicki knew Mama would die a slow death once Papa was taken. Not from starvation, but because the love of her life would be gone.

Fierce determination filled Nicki as she marched with the empty dipper back toward the well. Tossing back a gulp of water, she wiped the droplets from her chin and pivoted to glare at the man coming into the yard.

She froze. He was not the man who worked for the bank.

"Howdy." The man tipped back his dusty, black hat and smiled down at Carlos. The smile didn't quite reach his eyes. His gaze flicked past Papa and came to rest on Nicki. Considerable interest flamed in their depths. He nodded to her, the smile now reaching his eyes, and touched the brim of his hat in a one-fingered salute. "Ma'am." He ignored Papa and spoke directly to her. "I was thinking how nice a cool drink of water would be. I'd sure be appreciating it if I could light a spell."

Carlos stepped between Nicki and the newcomer, effectively blocking his view. "Draw fresh water, Dominique." He stretched his hand toward the man, indicating he could dismount. "Welcome."

But Nicki could hear an edge in his voice. This man could mean trouble.

"Obliged." He nodded and swung from his saddle. The man was tall, had graying hair, steely blue eyes, and a wad of chewing tobacco stuffed in his cheek. He stretched his hand toward Carlos as Nicki pulled up a fresh bucket. "Name's John Trent."

Papa took his hand. "Carlos Vasquez."

Mr. Trent studied her over the dipper as he drank his fill. Nicki averted her eyes but held the bucket for his next dipperful. She had received more than her share of such looks and knew what he was thinking. For although this man would say nothing to her in front of her father, the men down at the cantina showed no such qualms whenever Mama found it necessary to send her there. The thought of their suggestive remarks burned a blush across her cheeks. John Trent lifted the dipper again and raised his eyebrows in amusement.

Papa made small talk about the long hot spell as Nicki pulled buckets of water from the well for the man's horse, but Nicki didn't miss the looks John Trent kept throwing her way.

When he mounted up to ride out, Mama, still seated in the shade, gave an audible sigh. Nicki couldn't deny she felt plenty relieved as well.

Just as he arrived at the crest of the trail, the man paused, and Nicki stiffened. John Trent rubbed a hand across his face and said something to himself, then swung his horse once again toward their adobe. His eyes raked her more boldly this time as he pulled to a stop in their sun-baked yard.

Leaning his arms casually on the horn of his saddle, he spat a stream of tobacco into the dust, turned toward Papa, and brazenly asked, "How much for the girl?"

Nicki and Mama gasped in unison.

The bucket in Nicki's hands crashed to the ground, splashing water over her feet. Quickly she bent and picked it up. She spun on her heel and marched toward the well to return the bucket to its hook. *The audacity!*

Papa spoke with authority. "The *señorita* is *not* for sale."

John Trent's eyes scanned the small house and the scraggly field beyond, then traveled pointedly to seven of Nicki's brothers and sisters who had gathered in a little clump to watch the goings-on. Then he stared into Papa's face before spitting another stream of brown sludge. "I think everything's for sale as long as the price is right."

"My daughter is *not* for sale, *Señor*. I have to ask you to leave us now."

Ignoring him, Trent reached into the pocket of his vest and pulled out a coin. He tossed it to the ground near Papa's feet.

A twenty dollar gold piece! Nicki had not seen Mama move, but the audible click of a cocking shotgun cracked into the afternoon stillness. All eyes turned toward the door of the house to see her there, the gun aimed squarely at John Trent's chest.

Nicki's gaze dropped to the money on the ground. That little piece of gold could save Papa's life. It would get him out of debt and even give them enough to start over somewhere. Remembering her earlier prayer, she started to step forward.

But Papa beat her to it. Picking up the offensive gold, he threw it toward John Trent as if it were too hot to touch. "She is not for sale!"

Trent deftly caught the coin, pulled two more pieces just like it from his pocket, and tossed all three on the ground. "I want that girl. Now I am trying to go about this in a civilized manner, but if I have to, I will take her by force.” He sat up straight and casually rested a hand on his thigh near his gun.

Nicki felt dizzy from the sheer shock of this proposition. Her eyes flashed from Mama, bravely holding an unloaded gun on the man insulting her daughter, to Papa, stooping to pick up the offensive coins, to the hand of John Trent inching toward his holster. She surprised even herself by what happened next.

“Papa, wait!” She stepped forward. *Sixty dollars!* “I will go with him.” Her hands trembled as she smoothed the material of her skirt.

“Nicki, NO!” Mama screamed.

“Mama, *por favor!* The money! You will be free from all this trouble! I will be all right. God, He will go with me, *sí?*”“

Dominique, don’t do this.” Papa’s words were thick with restrained emotion. “We will work something out with the bank. You take too much on yourself for one so young.”

“Papa.” Nicki wrapped her arms around his neck. “You are the one who taught me to be strong, *sí*? Take care of Mama and make Rosa help her now.” Nicki pulled back, gazing deeply into his dark eyes, so much like her own, and rested a hand on his stubbly cheek. “She would have died without you, Papa.”

She spun toward her mother, throwing herself into her arms, before the threatening tears could overflow. “Mama, *te amo!*” The choked words were all she could squeeze past her constricting throat. Would she ever see her beloved mama again?

Nicki hugged her brothers and sisters in turn, giving them each a piece of advice on how to be helpful to Mama and Papa, drying their tears with her skirt and promising she would see them again someday. Going into the house, she ran her fingers across the baby-soft cheek of little Manuel, the only member of the household still sleeping through all the commotion.

And then, head held high, she walked out into the searing sun and allowed herself to be pulled up onto the horse behind John Trent’s saddle.

“Wait!” Mama ran toward her, carrying the family Bible. She pressed it into Nicki’s hands, making the sign of the cross and blessing her daughter one more time, as she had done every day since her birth.

Nicki didn't let her family see her cry, but as she rode away from the only home she had ever known, part of her felt like it died. She allowed herself the small luxury of quiet tears.

They rode north for several days. Nicki was thankful that John Trent seemed to be a kind man. A justice of the peace married them in his dusty office in a small, one-street town that Nicki didn't even know the name of. By evening, they were moving north again.

They had been traveling for more than two weeks, making mostly dry camps at night, when Nicki heard her husband utter an oath of awe. It was mid-afternoon and Nicki, her forehead pressed into John's back, was almost asleep when she heard his exclamation. Lifting her head, she blinked into the sunlight, almost unable to believe the sight before her.

A lush valley stretched before them. A small creek meandered through its center, merging with the Deschutes River at one end. The Deschutes was normally inaccessible due to its steep canyon walls, but here the descent to the river was simply a long, smooth slope. Here and there a cluster of evergreen trees could be seen, but the verdant meadow was what had drawn John's eye.

It was like a vivid oasis dropped in the middle of the high-desert sagebrush they had been traveling through for the last week. The swaying grass was belly high to a good-sized horse.

At that moment, Nicki knew she was looking at her new home. The valley was a rancher's paradise, and John had talked of nothing else since their journey began. He wanted to become a rancher. A rich rancher. And this was where he would make his start.

They made camp early, and Nicki sighed in satisfaction as she waded into the creek for her first bath in a week. She rolled her head from side to side, rubbing her neck, working out the kinks of knotted muscle.

John waded in as well, and she stiffened as he slid his arms around her waist from behind, pressing a kiss to her neck.

Apparently sensing her tension, he sighed. "I'm gonna make you a good husband. You'll see, Dominique. We're gonna have one fine spread across this valley. One day you'll wake up and realize what a good life we've had, and you'll no longer regret the day you first met me."

Nicki bit her lower lip, hoping he was right. She didn't think she'd be able to live with this dreadful despair all her life. She closed her eyes, missing Mama and the family. Willing herself not to cry, she stepped out of his arms and turned to give him a tentative smile, but her heart did not lighten.

They found the soddy later that evening. There was also a run-down barn, a partially erected bunkhouse, and a corral all clustered on the lee side of a knoll just tall enough for the soddy. But the spread had long since been abandoned. The windowless house was dark, and when they lit John's lantern, Nicki saw the spiders scurrying to escape the light. She shivered and went in search of some brush to use as a broom. Soon the room was cobweb-free, and they made a bed on the floor for the night.

It was still dark the next morning when she heard John saddling the horse. She roused herself and set about making coffee. He only took the time for one cup before he rode out with a terse, "I'll be back soon as I can."

He was gone for two weeks. When he came back, he informed her they would be staying.

Chapter One

Shilo, Oregon, in the Willamette Valley
January 1887

The tepid January sun struggled to warm the day, but this winter had been one of the Northwest's worst in a number of years. The temperatures barely reached the teens.

At the knock on the door, Brooke Jordan rose from scrubbing the kitchen floor and dried her hands on a towel. Pressing a hand to her aching lower back and resting one hand protectively on her rounded belly, she moved to see who it was.

"Who do you suppose would be knocking on our door at this time of day?" she asked the unborn child.

It had become her practice to talk to the baby during the day to ease the loneliness of Sky's absence. Since they had moved back to Sky's childhood home from the Idaho territory where they had met, Sky had gone to work as a deputy sheriff for his father and was gone most of the day. She missed him terribly but couldn't bring herself to tell him, knowing how much he loved his new job, even though it kept him away from home for hours at a time.

Swinging the door wide, Brooke gasped. "Jason!" She pulled the blond man, almost the spitting image of her husband, into her cumbersome embrace. "Come in! Sky and I were just talking about you last night, wondering where you might have gotten to."

Jason smiled as his eyes dropped to her midsection. "I see I've missed some news of my own while I've been gone."

Brooke's grin broadened. "This isn't the only news you've missed. Just let me send the neighbor boy to call Sky, and I'll be right in. Make yourself at home."

Brooke waved him inside and headed for the house next door.

Jason entered the little house, noting the bucket on the kitchen floor and the line delineating the clean side from the dirty. Hanging his black Stetson on the back of a chair, he bent down and took over where Brooke had left off.

"Oh, Jason," Brooke said as she came back into the house, "get up off that floor and sit down!"

He grinned at her. "Not on your life. You just plant yourself in that chair right there," he pointed toward the dining table, "and start filling me in on all the news I've missed."

Brooke sank into the indicated chair. "First I want to know all about what you've been doing. My, you've lost a lot of weight."

Jason hated the heat he felt wash his face. "Most of my weight was due to the fact I drank too much. Now that I've given that up, I can't seem to keep the pounds on."

Brooke smiled tenderly. "We are so proud of you, Jason."

He nodded but did not look up. His life had changed because of his relationship with the Lord, not because he was so great a person. There was no reason for Brooke to be proud of him, but knowing she hadn't really meant the words exactly as they sounded, he kept this thought to himself.

"So tell me what you've been up to," she prodded.

"Oh, not much. I've punched a few cows here and there, but I thought it was time I came home to see how all the family was doing. I've really missed Marquis," he said of his sister. "I would have stopped by there first, but your house was on the way, so I wanted to stop and say hello."

"Well, we're all doing fine. As you can see— "

The front door opened. "Jason!" Sky strode in. "Where've you been? Brooke and I were talking about you last night."

Jason and Brooke exchanged amused glances.

"Sky." Jason extended his wet, soapy hand, but Sky pulled him into a manly embrace. Then the cousins stepped back and eyed one another.

"How are things?" Sky asked.

"Fine." Jason grinned. It was good to be home.

"I mean with your relationship with the Lord," said Sky.

Jason grinned at Brooke again. "He sure knows how to get to the point, doesn't he?"

Brooke smiled in response, but her eyes held the same question.

Jason swallowed and fiddled with the scrub brush. "I'm doing good, Sky. I've had my struggles, especially giving up the bottle, but I haven't given in so far. God has given me the strength I needed every time."

"Praise God! We haven't given up praying for you even for a minute."

"Thanks." The one word could never express his deep gratitude. He tapped the scrub brush against his palm. "Brooke told me I've missed a bunch of news."

Sky sat next to his wife and took her hand. "Have you ever."

Jason bent to continue scrubbing the floor, curiosity filling him. "Well?" he asked, waiting.

"Let's see. First, you can see Brooke is expecting. We'll have an addition to the family sometime around the end of this spring."

"Hopefully sooner than later," Brooke said, reaching one hand to her lower back.

Sky continued, "Then there is Sharyah. She's finished her schooling and plans to find a teaching position for this fall."

Jason rocked back on the balls of his feet, letting the scrub brush hang between his knees. "Sharyah. Wow, I seem to only remember her as the little pig-tailed beauty who drove all the boys at the church picnics crazy 'cause she only had eyes for Cade Bennett."

Sky smirked. "Well, she still drives all the boys crazy, but I don't know about her having eyes for Cade Bennett anymore. He's been seeing a lot of Jenny Cartwright."

"Oh, honey!" Brooke voiced exasperation. Turning back to Jason, she rolled her eyes. "Men are so blind! Of course she's still in love with Cade, but he doesn't have a brain in his head where Sharyah is concerned. If he had a thimbleful of wisdom, he would have snapped her up a long time ago!" She emphasized her point with a snap of her fingers.

Sky chuckled. "As you can see, Brooke and my family don't get along very well."

Giving a mock frown, Jason agreed, "Yes, I can see that."

Sky went on. "Rocky is still a deputy in town. He, Dad, and I keep the town running criminal-free." A twinkle leapt into his eyes. "And I guess that's about all that's new."

When Brooke spun, wide-eyed and incredulous, in Sky's direction, Jason surmised that Sky had been teasing her and the largest piece of news would be forthcoming. He swiped his cheek against his shoulder and returned his concentration to the last section of the kitchen floor. *Someday, Lord, if You're willing, I'd like to have someone to love that way.*

After giving Sky a friendly punch, Brooke said to Jason, "Your cousin is deliberately withholding information from you, but maybe we shouldn't ruin her surprise. You'd better go visit Marquis right away, though. She'd be terribly disappointed if you heard the news from anyone else."

"Is she all right?" Jason asked, tension crawling through his chest.

"She's fine," Sky assured.

Jason's shoulders relaxed, but a niggling worry still clung to the back of his mind. "Maybe I'll mosey on over that way." He stood and picked up the scrub water. "Can I empty this for you somewhere, Brooke?"

"Oh, to one side out the back door is fine." Brooke waved him through the kitchen.

As he made his way back to the front of the house, Jason grabbed his hat, trying not to let his worry over his sister's news show on his face. He'd always been a little overprotective of her, since a childhood illness had robbed her of her sight. He had been gone for several years when he headed to the Idaho territory to exact revenge on a man that he blamed for their mother's death. But he'd known that, since Marquis was living with his grandmother, she was in good hands. Since his return to the Lord, finding work had forced him away from his family, but he had faithfully sent Marquis money every month. Now he wondered what news Marquis could have that she wouldn't have told him in her last letter.

"I'll head on over to Gram's, then. It's good to see you both… and congratulations."

Brooke embraced him once more. "Thank you for stopping by. On Sunday everyone is getting together at our place for lunch, so come on by and join us."

"I'll do that." Jason settled his Stetson and headed down the street to Gram's house, which sat on the edge of the snow-bound little town.

The Prineville bank was stuffy and hot. The teller had obviously forgotten to turn down the damper on the wood stove. The heat had felt nice to William Harpster for a few minutes after coming in from the single-digit temperature outside. Now, sitting across from the banker, Tom Roland, he frowned.

Behind his desk, Tom mopped his sweaty brow and tossed an occasional irritated glance at the teller.

William paid no attention to the teller. His eyes were fixed solely on the short, paunchy, balding Roland seated across from him. "I told you it would take some time."

"It's been over two years!" The words were forceful but voiced low so as not to reach the ears of the clerk. "The Association is going to be running *us* off if we don't come up on the good side of this deal. We guaranteed them we'd have the small-timers gone by next month. You said you could get the job done!"

William's eyes narrowed. "Do you think I don't know that? You're the one who said he was the perfect man for our plan! It's not my fault he's welching on his end." His voice became a little too loud and drew a look from the curious teller.

But at that moment a patron entered the building, taking the man's interest off their conversation. When it was once again safe to resume, Tom's pale blue eyes flashed. "Keep it down, would you? This is not my fault. First," the banker held up one short finger, "his wife isn't nearly as timid and withdrawn as you said. She's made friends with over half the country, for goodness' sake! Second, he's no longer willing to go along with our plan. And now…" A third finger joined the first two. "You're telling me you think he might have a herd of horses back in those hills that could pay off his loan?"

William rubbed the back of his neck. "I don't know. Things just don't add up. He's been making his payments?"

"Right on time, every time."

William sighed. There was only one way to ensure their plan would work. "We know what the Association thinks. But how badly do you want your share of that land?"

Tom Roland dabbed at his glistening pate with a handkerchief. Then, leaning back, he lit a cigar and blew a ring of smoke in William's direction. He wanted that land. The original owner had given up on ranching and moved back to Chicago, leaving the land up for sale. Tom had been tempted to buy the land himself, but then John Trent had walked into his bank. The only reason Tom had loaned John the money was that he was almost assured the gambler wouldn't be able to come up with his payments. Then the land would revert to the bank, where Tom could discreetly snap it up at a lower price. That and the fact The Stockman's Association had needed a scapegoat for their dirty work. But then John had developed a conscience. And, on top of that, he hadn't missed one payment.

Tom ran his handkerchief across the back of his neck. Five thousand acres of the finest range land in central Oregon, and half of it was to be his. Well, maybe more than half, but he was careful to keep that thought off his face. Yes. He wanted that land very much. But a couple of things bothered him. "What about his wife?"

William smiled sardonically. "Let me worry about the little woman. Once John is out of the way, she'll give up. There's no way she'll be able to make a go of it. They've only got two hands."

"The Stockman's Association will break loose with all the fury of Hades if this doesn't pan out," Tom warned. "They were plenty upset that I let him buy that land in the first place. And if things don't work out for me, you know they certainly aren't going to work out for you, right?"

"Things couldn't be clearer. Have I ever let you down before?"

Tom blew another ring. "No, William, you haven't. But let's make sure this isn't the first."

William's gaze hardened. "Tom, this better be the last time you need my services. A man's patience can only be stretched so far."

"Just do your job, William. Do your job and let the future take care of itself."

The men glared at each other across the desk. Tom didn't want to be the first to look away. Finally William conceded the battle.

Tom looked down at his desk, pulling in a deep drag on his cigar. "Now, back to the job at hand. I think we both know there is only one way to solve this little problem."

The two men's eyes locked. A silent understanding passed between them.

William stood, straightened his cowhide vest with a tug, and placed his hat carefully on his head. He shook Tom's fleshy hand and said loud enough for the teller to hear, "Thanks. You won't regret making me this loan, Mr. Roland."

With that, he moved toward the door, stepping out into the cold. He took a cleansing breath of the refreshing air, then headed toward the livery, his boots thudding loudly on the boardwalk. He had a job to do back home. And maybe, just maybe, if he played his cards right, by the end of the year he'd be owner of some of the finest range land in Oregon, not to mention the husband of one beautiful, desirable Mrs. Dominique Trent. A smile lifted the corners of his mouth at the thought. Yes, indeed, now that was a dream worth chasing.

Chapter Two

"Sawyer Carlos Trent! ¿¡Que es esto!?" Nicki threw up her hands in distress at the mess on her kitchen floor. Flour, beans, rice, and sugar were all scattered delightfully across the earthen floor, swirled together and crawled through. Baby handprints on a mound of flour and beans showed where the budding artist had patted his creation together.

Clenching her fists at her side, Nicki went in search of her little virtuoso. It wasn't hard to find him; she just followed the flour-white footprints on the dark, hard-packed, earthen floor. He was crouched behind the chest that held their clothes. As she scooped him up and started back toward the kitchen, Nicki found herself wishing for the umpteenth time that she could put the supplies up somewhere higher, but there just wasn't anyplace else to store them. There was barely room enough to stand up straight in the low-roofed, tiny kitchen, much less add higher cupboards.

Sitting the boy down firmly in the middle of the mess Nicki gestured to the floor around him. "Look at this mess you made for Mama to clean up!" She squatted down in front of him, tucking an escaped strand of hair behind her ear, the other fist resting under her chin.

Sawyer's chin dropped to his chest and his lower lip protruded in a calculated pout.

Nicki tried not to give in to the smile that suddenly tugged at the corners of her mouth as she gazed into his sweet face. "Sawyer, Mama has told you not to get into the food. This is very naughty."

Tears pooled on his lower lids, making his huge dark eyes seem even larger. The pout was still in place. "I sowwee, Mama."

"*Está bien*. That's good. I'm glad you're sorry, but we have talked about this before. You are going to sit in the corner while I clean this up."

His rosy lower lip still pooching out, he stood to his flour-dusted feet. Dark head bent toward the floor, he crossed his arms over his chest and did not move.

"Go on, Son. I will come get you when I'm done."

Feet dragging, he made his way to the corner and sat, casting a how-could-you-do-this-to-me look over his shoulder before he slumped forward, resting chubby cheeks on chubby hands.

When Nicki was sure he wasn't looking, she allowed herself to smile. Poor boy. The winter *was* getting long. If only the weather would warm up, then they could go outside and he would have more room to play.

Looking back to the mess, she tossed her hands toward the ceiling in frustration and moved to get the broom and dust pan.

When the mess was cleaned up, Nicki walked over to get Sawyer, only to find that he had fallen asleep on the floor. Stooping, she picked him up and rested his head against her breast. She grinned down at the white print of his bottom on the dark earth floor, then gazed lovingly into his sleep-flushed face. Tenderly she dropped a kiss onto his rosy cheek as tears pooled in her eyes. Blinking, she raised her face to the ceiling.

Thank You, God, for this precious little boy. He has kept me going these past couple of years. You knew just what I needed to make it through this life, didn't You? You have blessed me beyond measure.

Moving to the room's one bed, she laid Sawyer down and smoothed his dark curls. Gently covering him with his favorite patchwork blanket, she moved to add more wood to the stove. Today was exceptionally cold.

She eased herself down at the table, thankful to have a little quiet time. Reaching for her Bible, the one Mama had pressed into her hands that day that seemed like a lifetime ago, she thumbed through the pages. She settled on one of her favorite psalms and leaned back to read. But she only got to verse four. Pausing, she stared at the page. But she wasn't seeing the words, she was hearing them.

"Yea, though I walk through the valley of the shadow of death, I will fear no evil; For you are with me; Your rod and Your staff, they comfort me."

Nicki could remember like it had happened yesterday—Father Pedro from the mission school she had attended as a child, explaining those words. *"The psalmist, he was a shepherd, no?"* The class had nodded. *"And when his sheep were in danger, what did he use to protect them, besides his sling shot?"*

"His rod and staff," the class echoed in unison.

"Good! You sometimes listen when I teach, eh?" He smiled good-naturedly. *"Yes. The rod and staff, and in the same way, when death comes knocking on our doors,"* he rapped loudly on his wooden desk for emphasis, causing several of the girls to jump and a titter of laughter to pass through the room, *"we know that our Heavenly Father, who loves us much more than a shepherd loves his sheep, will come to our aid, yes?"*

Again the class nodded.

"Good! God loves you. He is not going to abandon you to the wolves, and predators of this world. It says He will be with you! Imagine that: God with you, helping you, protecting you. Ahhh, now that is a God worth serving, yes?"

The thunder of horses' hooves in the yard brought Nicki back to the present. She frowned and stood to see who it might be. John was not supposed to be back from checking the ranch perimeter until later this evening.

Jason whipped off his hat, taking the four creaky stairs up to Gram's porch in two strides. The hinges groaned loudly as, not bothering to knock, he opened the door and entered the house where he had been raised. Excitement built inside him. Gram hadn't changed a thing about the house since he'd left. Her rocker still sat by the front window with her worn Bible and spectacles on the table beside it. The woven rag rug that he and Marquis had spent all one winter creating still graced the floor in front of the fireplace. The settee still sported one of her handknit afghans draped across the arm, and the painting he'd done of a wolf pack when he was about thirteen still hung on the wall above the mantle in all its hideousness. He grinned. He'd tried to talk her into taking that down a number of times, but she had never done it. She said it was her reminder to pray for him. Well, he wouldn't argue with that anymore. He could use all the prayers he could get.

He made his way quietly through the house, anticipating the delighted surprise that would dawn on Gram's face when she saw him.

The living room and dining room were at the front, but at the back there was also a small parlor used just for family. It was there Jason assumed Gram and Marquis to be. If they were anywhere else in the house, they would have heard him enter through the squeaky portal.

Jason stepped into the back hallway.

"Jeff, don't!" Marquis' voice drifted through the door from the parlor.

His heart seized in his chest. *Don't what?* Jason had heard that strained tone before. She meant what she was saying.

"Jeff, stop it!"

Jason paused, wondering who Jeff might be. He eased the strap off his pistol and debated whether he should enter the parlor with gun in hand. "Jeff!"

Marquis' squeal sent shivers of alarm racing through Jason's veins and, without further hesitation, he barged through the door.

A man was leaning over Marquis, seated on the settee, about to kiss her! "What in—Marquis!" Jason lunged across the room, grabbed the man by one shoulder, spun him around, and smashed one fist solidly into his mouth.

The man staggered and fell to the floor.

Marquis screamed. "Jeff? What happened?" Hands outstretched, she felt swiftly for her cane.

Before the man on the floor could even blink, Jason had the

barrel of his gun leveled at his head. Never taking his eyes off the man on the floor, Jason said, "Marquis are you all right?"

Marquis, one hand clutching her cane and the other on her chest, asked in a tremulous voice, "Jason?"

"Don't worry, Marquis, I'm here. This man won't be bothering you again, *ever*." The last word he directed at the man on the floor who now gingerly wiped the bloodied corner of his mouth. With a gesture of his free hand Jason directed the man to get up, but the barrel of his gun never wavered.

Suddenly Marquis recovered from her shock. "Jason! Did you just punch Jeff?" Then her voice became truly alarmed. "Jeff! Are you okay?"

"I'm all right, Marquis. Who is this madman? A jilted admirer?" Jeff was now on his feet but kept his hands carefully in sight.

"Well...this is Jason." Then, "Jason, is it really you?"

"Yeah, I came home to see you and Gram."

With more confidence this time Marquis said, "Jeff, I'd like you to meet Jason."

"Well, honey, I know you have a brother named Jason, but this tornado on wheels couldn't be him, could it?"

Marquis smiled. "I'm afraid so, dear."

Jason frowned, perplexed at Marquis' endearment. "Marquis? You know this man?"

At this Marquis giggled. "Jason, I would like you to meet my husband, Jeff Grant."

"Husband!"

Marquis nodded serenely and Jeff, hands now resting on his hips, glared passionately.

Jason glanced down at the gun in his hand and then back to Jeff. A slow smile spread. "Husband, huh?"

Jeff nodded.

Jason holstered the gun and extended his hand. "Sorry."

Marquis, hearing the whisper of metal on leather, gasped. "Jason! Jeff, was he holding a gun on you?"

Jeff wiped the corner of his mouth once more, eyeing Jason's extended hand. "Yes he was, Marquis." Then a hint of a smile showed in his eyes as he spoke to Jason, taking his hand. "I guess you must love her at least half as much as I do."

Jason grinned. "What were you hollering about anyway, Marquis? With you yelling, I just assumed he was forcing his attentions on you."

A blush shaded Marquis' cheeks. And Jeff took a step toward Marquis, resting one hand protectively on her shoulder.

"Jeff was...tickling me."

Jason rubbed a hand across his mouth to hide another smile. Jeff tossed him an unrepentant grin as he gently squeezed Marquis' shoulder.

Irritation flooded in. "Well, you could've at least given me some warning. A guy likes to know when his sister is getting married. Or *is* married."

"Oh Jason, I'm so sorry. We didn't know when you'd be able to make it home. When you didn't respond to our first telegram, we sent Rocky to the Triple J to find you, but they said you had gone to Dodge City and they didn't know exactly when you would be back. So we went ahead with the ceremony. But I sent you a telegram telling you all about it."

"To Dodge City! That was November! How long have you two been married?"

"Two months."

"Two months! Marquis, I left in October. If you've been married two months that means you got married sometime in November and *that* means you couldn't have known this man for more than three or four *weeks* before you got married."

Marquis' unseeing stare was complacent. "Jason you're starting to sound a little paranoid."

Jason opened his mouth to reply, then glanced at Jeff and snapped it shut. This man was his brother-in-law, after all. And he was already glaring at him like a mad bull about to charge.

"For your information, dear brother," there was an icy tension in Marquis' words, "Jeff and I wrote to each other for two years before we ever met."

"You wrote to each other." Jason turned to Jeff. "You know Braille?"

Jeff gave a single nod.

Marquis continued, "Jeff is a professor at a school for the blind in Portland. The school had some correspondence courses, one of which I enrolled in, and that is how we met."

Jason didn't feel like talking about this anymore. "Where's Gram?"

"She went down to the mercantile to get some things," Jeff answered.

Jason spun on his heel. "I'll get you some ice for that cut," he tossed over his shoulder as he stomped toward the kitchen.

In the kitchen, Jason leaned his fists into the counter, hunching his shoulders as he stared out the window in thought. What was suddenly making him feel edgy? He trusted Marquis and knew she wouldn't have rushed into marriage hastily. In fact, now that he thought about it, he remembered her mentioning she was corresponding with a man from a school for the blind. He hadn't paid much attention at the time. But now she was married and he...

He what? He hadn't been there? He was the last to know? He wasn't needed by her anymore? Was that it?

Understanding hit him like a 2,000-pound charging bull. *I'm angry, aren't I, Lord*?

Banging through the back door, Jason headed toward the dugout, where he knew a block of ice would be. As he chipped away some of his frustration on the block resting in the dim, dank cellar, he chastised himself for being so temperamental. He should be happy for his sister; instead he felt a petty irritation over the fact that she no longer needed his support.

"Okay, Lord," he said out loud, pausing to glance out the door, "if you sent this man to Marquis, then he must be what she needed. Just help me to accept him. Open my eyes to his good qualities. And help me to know where I should go from here with my life."

Marquis had a husband. So what was he to do now? Truth-telling, there were virtually no jobs to be found in the little town of Shilo, and he had known it would take some doing to find work. He had planned on having Marquis move back into Gram's room so he could stay in the second bedroom for a while as he searched for a job. But somehow he didn't think that Marquis and her young husband would enjoy sharing a room with Gram.

The thought brought a brief smirk, before he grew serious again.

Marquis would no longer need his financial support…but Gram would. He'd start looking for work tomorrow. The Lord would iron out the housing situation. For now he could sleep on the floor.

Chapter Three

Nicki rose from the table and hurried to the low door of the soddy. She had to stoop to get out the door, and the sun glaring off the snow momentarily blinded her as she exited the dim interior of the house.

Shading her eyes, she squinted to see who rode into the yard at such breakneck speed. Looking past the neglected pole corral, she saw the dark shapes of three horses thundering toward the house. Two men were upright, but the third draped over the saddle, and as the men pulled up in a skidding halt she could see he was severely wounded.

Blood dripped from a nasty, concave gash along his hairline, and one of his arms hung at an odd angle.

Suddenly her neighbor, William, was beside her. "Nicki, don't look. Come with me."

Nicki pulled her elbow from his grasp and did not move. She stared dumbfounded at the wounded man the other rider was easing from the saddle. One hand went to her mouth and she moved forward. "John!"

The man carried John toward the soddy, but Nicki quickly took charge, lifting her skirts and heading for the bunkhouse. "No! Not in there, the baby is sleeping, and he does not need to see his Papa like this." She gestured to one of the spread's two ranch hands. "Ron, go into the house and get me a clean blanket. You," she motioned to the man carrying John, "bring him over here to the bunkhouse. Conner, run clear a place to lay him."

Before they had moved the few yards to the bunkhouse, Ron was back with a blanket and hurried in ahead of them to lay it across the first bunk that Conner, the second ranch hand, had cleared off.

Nicki spoke again as she entered the dim interior of the

freezing cold bunkhouse, "Ron, go back to the house and bring me all the hot water on the stove, then put some more on in my largest kettle. Conner, go get some wood and get a fire going in here. Then ride for the doctor."

The men moved to do her bidding, and all the while the man who had first spoken to her stayed by her side. "Tell me what happened, William." Nicki finally acknowledged her neighbor's presence as she set to work cutting John's shirt away from his broken arm.

He ran a tired hand over his stubble-roughened face and glanced around the interior of the bunkhouse before he replied. "We were out checking the stock, like we always do after a particularly hard storm. John had stopped in town early this morning. I happened to be there and needed to check my stock too, so we decided to ride out together. We had just come around a corner along the Deschutes River canyon…you know, that part along the edge of your place that is so steep." William stopped, rested his hands on his hips, and shook his head. "It all happened so fast. One minute everything was fine, and the next minute his horse shied away from something and John lost his balance and went over the edge of the cliff. If I hadn't had my hand Slim there to help me, he probably would have bled to death right there in the canyon bottom."

Nicki frowned. They had been riding so close to the edge that he fell off? Ron entered with the requested hot water, and Nicki used the opportunity to cast a look at Slim, who sat hunched on one of the bunks watching the proceedings with casual interest. He was a tall man, perhaps the tallest she had ever seen, which explained why he was hunched over the way he was. He was skinny too. Skinny as a corral pole. His boots were run down at the heel, and a drooping mustache completely covered his mouth. Slim nodded, indicating his assent to William's story, solemn eyes meeting hers for only a moment.

"Go on, William," Nicki said quietly as she dipped a rag Ron had thoughtfully brought into the water and washed the deep gash on John's brow. She could see the white of bone where the flesh was missing. He groaned, but he did not come to.

"Well, there's not much else to say. We got a rope around him and pulled him back up to his horse and then rode here as fast as we could."

Nicki frowned. John was a good rider. It wasn't like him to lose his balance in the saddle.

But if Nicki had learned anything in her young life, it was that the west was a brutal place. Accidents happened often here. The year she turned fifteen her brother Juan had lost his hand when he cut it on a rusty hay fork. And just last week at church the Snows had reported that their neighbor's wife had been killed when the cow she was milking kicked her in the head. The family planned to move back east, and their land would revert to the bank. Things happened that could not be foreseen or prevented.

Nicki pushed away her niggling questions about the accident. William had been their friend and neighbor since just after they moved into the valley. She knew he would have done everything in his power to help John.

Conner brought in the wood, but Ron took over building up the fire and soon Nicki heard Conner's horse galloping out of the yard. Looking at the bone protruding from John's arm and the nasty bowl-shaped laceration on his forehead, Nicki prayed the doctor would come in time to save her husband's life.

She gently smoothed his sweat-soaked hair away from his brow and considered their relationship. Although they had been married under unusual circumstances to say the least, she had come to depend on this man. He did not love her, only lusted after her, but he had treated her better than most, she knew. No, she didn't love him, but he was the father of her son, and he had been good to her. She shivered and felt William's warm leather jacket settle around her shoulders. She glanced up. He smiled reassuringly and rested his hand gently on her shoulder. "I'll send for Tilly to watch the boy for you," he said before heading out the door into the late afternoon gloom.

She tended John through the night as best she could, praying that Conner would be able to find Dr. Rike in time. But it was not to be. Nicki had just pulled the sheet up over John's face when Conner and Doctor Rike hurried through the bunkhouse door.

Conner grimaced and snatched his hat off his head in a gesture of frustration.

Without a word Nicki brushed past the two men and headed for the house. She could think of only one comfort she needed at this moment. And it wasn't until she took a sleepy Sawyer from the arms of Tilly Snow, the young girl from church who had come to sit with him, that the tears came. As Sawyer laid his little head on her shoulder she rested her cheek against the soft hair at the back of his neck and let the tears fall. How was she going to raise this precious child alone? His papa had been the world to him, for although John had not loved her, he had doted on his son. and Sawyer was going to be lost without his papa. She rubbed his little back, listening to his deep, even breathing. So innocent and unaware of the gaping, black valley that had just opened up before them.

She allowed herself to close her eyes for a minute, then reality rushed in. Her eyes snapped open. "Tilly, I hate to ask, but do you think your mother could spare you for a couple of days?"

Tilly's tender, brown eyes glistened, and she blinked rapidly. "I'm sure that would be fine, Mrs. Trent."

"I'll send Conner over to tell her. I really appreciate it."

Setting Sawyer into his high chair, Nicki busied herself getting his breakfast. If she worked, she wouldn't have time to dwell on her loss.

"I can do that, Mrs. Trent. Why don't you sit down and rest? You've been up all night."

"Thank you, Tilly. If you will get Sawyer some breakfast, I'll head out and send Conner to your parents' place. And then I need to talk to Ron Hanson about a couple of things. Would you be all right in here with Sawyer for a while?"

Tilly nodded, and as Nicki moved out of the house, she prayed for strength.

Nicki found Ron and Conner standing together next to the jumbled heap of the run-down corral, arms folded against the cold.

Walking up quietly, Nicki tucked a curl behind her ear and fleetingly realized she had not combed her hair yet today. She was still wearing William's leather coat, the sleeves rolled up, and her back ached as though someone had taken a sledgehammer to it.

The two men turned toward her. She stared off into the distance, trying to gather her thoughts and come to grips with the fact her husband was dead.

She suddenly had so many questions and uncertainties. Yesterday when she awoke it had simply been her goal to make it through another day of entertaining a fussy toddler with cabin fever. Now...

What was she going to do?

Should she pack up and head south to California and try to find her parents? What if they had moved after she had left with John? Would she be able to find them?

She could stay here. She glanced around at the run-down ranch. John had been a good rider, and he had known cattle and horses, but it seemed he had known nothing about managing a ranch. Nicki had spoken to him several times about fixing up the buildings and the corral, but he had always said he would get to it in time. He didn't want to spend money that they didn't have.

They had lived here for two and a half years, and John had not made one improvement to the ranch buildings or central holding pens except to finish roofing the bunkhouse.

The bunkhouse was made of logs that had wide gaps between them, but John had refused to chink them when she had suggested it, saying it was an unnecessary expense.

Frosty winds gushed through the gaps, making the bunkhouse bitterly cold on most winter nights. Consequently there was only one hand who had been with them the whole two and a half years they had lived here, and that was Ron Hanson.

Ron was in his late fifties with a deeply tanned leathery face and crinkle lines around his usually smiling gray eyes. His once dark hair was now liberally sprinkled with gray, but it was invariably covered by his gray flat-topped Stetson. He'd had offers from other ranchers in the area but, for some reason, he'd chosen to stay and work for the Hanging T—John's brand. Nicki knew, however, that Ron had not stayed because the accommodations and food were so good. It was his relationship with Christ and a sense of loyalty that had kept him here when there were jobs that offered much more in the way of material comforts nearby.

Nicki's gaze moved on to the little sod shanty that served as the ranch house. Dug back into the side of a hill, all that could be seen of it from this vantage point was the chimney pipe sticking up through the snow-covered dirt, the wooden door, and the one small window that John had consented to on Nicki's behalf. It wasn't much, but it was warm, and for that, Nicki was thankful.

It was the only home Sawyer had ever known. With that thought, her stomach tightened. Could she take her son away from the only home he had ever known in search of her parents, when she had no idea where they were? What if she gave up this place and went to California, only to fail in finding her parents? What would become of them then?

She glanced around the run-down place once more and realized that her mind had been made up even before she had begun this debate with herself. She would stay. It would be so good to see Mama once more, but she couldn't risk it.

Ron interrupted her thoughts. "Ma'am, are you all right?"

Nicki came to with a start. "Oh. Yes." She cleared her throat and glanced at Conner. Her voice was low and raspy when she spoke. "Conner," she cleared her raw throat again, "I need you to ride over to the Snow place and let them know what has happened and ask them if it's okay if Tilly stays here for a couple of days. Um, tell them two, for sure, and maybe three days if we can't get the minister for the…for the…before then."

"Yes, ma'am." Conner touched the brim of his hat as he moved off to saddle up, but Nicki caught the gentle compassion in his green eyes before he turned away. A lump tightened her throat. Whatever happened, she could depend on Conner and Ron.

Conner was young and had only been with them since the summer before, but he attended Sunday services in Farewell Bend with her and Ron every Sunday. She didn't doubt that he truly loved the Lord.

This thought brought another wave of sadness, for try as she might, she had been unable to convince John to join them on Sundays. He had always had something that was more important: a sick cow, a lame horse, a trip around the ranch perimeter to make sure all the fences were intact because he couldn't afford to lose stock to a neighboring spread. There had always been something that needed tending. Something more important than church. Something more important than God.

Blinking back tears, Nicki turned her face away from Ron's fatherly inspection and folded her arms against the bitter wind that had begun to blow. "Ron, I am planning on staying. Now is not the time to discuss things, but I would appreciate it if you would stay long enough to fill me in on some of the things that I don't know about this place. Other than that, you are free to leave anytime you choose. I'm sorry I don't have the money to pay you right now, but if you stop back by someday, I will be more than happy to make it up to you."

"If it's all the same to you, ma'am, I'd like to stay. You will need a good hand and someone who knows a little o' the workin's o' the place."

"I don't know when I will be able to pay you."

"All a man needs is a place to sleep and some food in his belly."

Nicki turned tear-filled eyes on him. "You are an angel in disguise, Ron Hanson." Throwing her arms around the surprised cowhand's neck, she gave him a gentle squeeze. She felt him stiffen before he awkwardly patted her back with one hand while the other hand remained stiffly at his side.

What would I have done if he had chosen to leave? Gracias, Lord.

Holding Sawyer in her arms, Nicki stared bleakly down into the dark hole that waited to receive the body of her husband.

The voice of the minister droned in the background, but somehow she could not bring herself to focus on his words. She felt numb.

All around her friends and neighbors stood in somber silence. Some listened intently to the minister. Others watched her with strange sympathetic expressions. Women held onto the hands of their husbands more tightly. Little boys glanced at Sawyer and then up at their own fathers, stepping closer to wrap small arms around strong, steady legs.

William Harpster stood to her left and Ron Hanson to her right.

Nicki closed her eyes, leaning her forehead against the toddler's. What was she going to do without John? He had been her sole means of support. Could she really run this ranch by herself? *Lord, I don't think I can do this.*

Swiftly the verses she had read only moments before John had been brought in wounded jumped to mind. "*Yea, though I walk through the valley of the shadow of death, I will fear no evil; For You are with me; Your rod and Your staff, they comfort me.*"

Lord, I'm in that valley. Help me to know that You are here with me.

Comfort me. What am I going to do without him, Lord? I never realized that I cared for him so much, but I miss him. Help me, Lord, because I will never be able to make it through this without You. And please be with Sawyer. Don't let this be too traumatic for him. He has already been asking for his papa. Help me to know how to explain to him that his papa's not going to be here anymore.

Opening her eyes, Nicki suddenly felt lightheaded. She shook her head against the dizzy spell, taking a small step backward. She adjusted Sawyer to a more comfortable position in her arms. When was the last time she had eaten? She gave her head another little shake. She couldn't remember.

Out of the corner of her eye she noted Ron studying her worriedly, and William reached out to take Sawyer from her. She smiled at Ron to reassure him, then folded her arms against the chill that seeped into her bones, thankful to be free of the baby and rest her arms.

Exhaustion weighed heavy on her shoulders, even as hunger pangs cramped her stomach. A strange, almost guilty sensation crept over her that she should be feeling anything at all when John lay so cold and still in a coffin only feet away.

Another dizzy spell hit her and she reached out, taking Ron's arm to steady herself. She needed to eat. But when the ceremony ended and Ron ushered her into the small church and set a plate before her, all she could do was pick at it.

The neighbors had rallied together in support of Nicki and an abundance of food graced a long table at the back of the church. Families caught up on news from neighbors they hadn't seen since the last community event, which had been a barn-raising for Jacob and Jenny Ashland. Nicki glanced over to see Jenny proudly showing off Jake Junior's latest skill…walking. He'd been a newborn at the raising. The baby was giggling and smiling at everyone who made eye contact and even coaxed a tired smile out of Nicki herself when Jenny came to express her condolences.

"I'm so sorry, Nicki. If I can ever do anything for you, all you have to do is ask. You know I'm not too far away. I'd be happy to watch Sawyer for you if you ever need someone to watch him."

Nicki nodded. "Thank you, Jenny."

Jenny set a package of home-baked goodies on the table and, with a gentle squeeze to Nicki's shoulder, made her way to Jacob's side.

And that was how it went. Everyone came over to express their condolences and to wish her well, and everyone left something on the table beside her.

The Coles owned a large ranch on the other side of Farewell Bend. Mrs. Cole, who had lost her first husband in much this same way, had tears in her eyes as she gave Nicki a hug and set a basket of food on the table.

Mrs. Pringle had a few choice words to say about Dr. Rike, but the Pringle baby had died the winter before when Dr. Rike hadn't been able to do anything for him, so Nicki let the comments slide and simply thanked Mrs. Pringle for the food.

The next woman to come over was the newest member of the community. Mr. and Mrs. Jeffries had just moved to a small homestead only a couple of miles from the Hanging T. Nicki knew they didn't have much, but Brenda Jeffries, with her six-year-old daughter, May, at her side, set a small bundle wrapped in brown paper on the table.

"I'm right sorry to hear 'bout yer man. I be hopin' that all goes well fer ya. God, He be knowin' all about yer pain. Ya just take it all to Him, now." She reached out and laid a work-roughened hand across the back of Nicki's, giving it a little pat. "If it be all right, I'd like to come in a couple o' days and see if there be anything I can do for ya. That be okay?"

Nicki smiled tiredly. "That would be just fine, Brenda."

"Good. I'll be seein' ya then."

Mrs. Jeffries started to move off, but May tugged on her sleeve. Nicki dropped her eyes to the little girl's pixie-sweet face. Straight blond hair framed a heart-shaped face with a pair of the biggest blue eyes Nicki had ever seen.

May stepped close and whispered, "I'm sorry your daddy died." Nicki blinked back tears and bit her lip, unable to say a word.

"I have a daddy." The little girl brushed a strand of hair behind her ear and held out a finger, pointing out her father across the room.

Nicki glanced at him and then nodded, pressing her lips together to suppress the sob that threatened to escape.

"He's real nice. Ya could borrow 'im sometime if ya need 'im."

The sob escaped and Nicki pulled May into her arms, resting her chin on the little girl's head. May wrapped her slender arms around Nicki's back, and gently patted out a comforting rhythm. When Nicki trusted herself to speak, she pulled back, wiped the tears from her cheeks, and gazed down at May. "Thank you. That's the nicest thing anyone has done for me in a long time."

"I'm sorry I made ya cry. I didn't mean to do that."

Nicki ran a trembling hand over the child's silky blond hair. "Some days are days of crying, little one. But know that you have made me very happy on the inside. If I need your papa, you can be sure I will come calling, okay?"

May nodded, giving Nicki one more quick hug before she turned and took her mother's hand. Brenda Jeffries smiled kindly, blinking to keep her own tears at bay, and then mother and daughter made their way across the room to stand by Rolf, Brenda's husband.

Nicki was just recovering her composure when Suzanne Snow, Tilly's mother, approached and set a large basket full of canned goods on the table. Suzanne pulled Nicki into a long embrace.

Nicki squeezed her eyes against the tears that threatened to overflow once again as memories rushed in.

John had never told Nicki where he got the money, but after he had purchased her, he made a number of extravagant purchases—several fine horses and the ranch being a couple of them—and then the money seemed to run out.

Missing her family, Mama especially, Nicki had been very lonely those first months until she had met the Snows. Ron had brought her to church with him and Suzanne reminded her so much of her own mother that Nicki had immediately been drawn to her. Suzanne had taken Nicki under her wing just as if she had been her own daughter. And now, more than ever, Nicki was thankful for her friendship.

Neither Suzanne's nor Mrs. Jeffries' gifts had appeared out of the ordinary at first but later, when Nicki got home, she found that Mrs. Jeffries' paper-wrapped package was a beautiful lace tablecloth crocheted in the most intricate of designs. *Much too fancy for the soddy.* And in the bottom of Suzanne Snow's basket of canned carrots, tomatoes, and green beans was an unpretentious looking book. The title brought fresh tears to Nicki's eyes. *Ranching in the West: How to Make It Pay.*

Suzanne had known she would stay.

Clutching the little book tightly to her chest, Nicki heaved a shuddered sigh. She had been strong all day, refusing herself the comfort of many tears. Making sure her neighbors knew she was going to be fine. Trying to convince herself she was going to be fine. But now she was alone. Just her and Sawyer.

Tilly had ridden home with Conner after promising to come back in a day or two. William had left for his ranch, promising to check on her often. Ron had gone to the bunkhouse for the evening.

Nicki could finally let down her guard. She glanced around the room at John's few things, still as he'd left them: his rifle on its pegs above the door, his extra pair of boots, a shirt hanging above the bed, the partially carved toy wagon sitting on the mantle that he'd started for Sawyer a couple weeks ago.

How was it that she could miss a man who had walked into her life out of the brazen heat of a California summer and forced her to marry him?

"Papa." Sawyer banged two blocks together and looked at her as he shoved the corner of one into his mouth.

Tears coursed down Nicki's cheeks. She sank down onto the rag rug next to the bed and pulled Sawyer onto her lap. Leaning her head against the quilt, she finally gave in to the deep sorrow. Sobs shook her body as Sawyer happily banged his blocks together.

Chapter Four

A knock on the soddy door awoke Nicki the next morning. She opened her eyes and glanced around the house, momentarily confused. She was on the floor, and her neck was stiff and sore. She groaned and pressed one hand to her forehead. She frowned at the dirt ceiling above her. Why did she feel so spirit-heavy today?

A flood of memory rushed in. The funeral had been yesterday, and she had fallen asleep on the floor.

Sawyer! She sat up quickly, glancing around the dim interior of the house, and couldn't help but smile in relief when she saw him curled up on his side on the bed. Dark curls clung to his head in an angelic halo. His long, dark lashes rested against chubby cheeks rosy from the refreshment of sleep. He must have crawled from her lap the night before and somehow managed to climb up onto the bed.

Poor child, his diaper hadn't been changed for hours. But he was sleeping soundly so she decided to leave him where he lay.

The knock sounded again.

Rubbing the back of her neck, she raked her fingers back through the long, dark tangles of her hair and made her way to the door. A chill breeze swept into the house as she opened it.

"William?" She took in his appearance, wondering what he was doing here so early in the morning. He wore an impeccable long-sleeved white shirt covered by a black and white cowhide vest that gave him a rancher's air of casual confidence. His denim-clad legs ended in well-polished, black boots that were hand-tooled with an elaborate design.

His immaculate attire made her self-conscious. She had fallen asleep in this dress the night before and knew, without looking down, that it was wrinkled beyond imagination. Her hair knotted in a tangled mess around her face, and her eyes felt puffy from last night's crying.

She folded her arms, hoping she didn't look as bad as she felt. A touch of irritation traced its way through her. *Well, he's the one who showed up at this hour of the morning.*

William was not put off by her less-than-friendly stance. He tossed her a smile, though Nicki noticed he clutched his black hat in front of him like it was a lifeline. "Good morning." Nervousness edged his voice. Nicki raised one eyebrow and stepped back, gesturing him into the house. "Come in. I will put on some coffee." She wondered what he wanted. *And why is he acting so strange?* William was always calm and self-assured, so what had set him on edge?

As Nicki stoked up the fire and added grounds to the water in the coffee pot, William pulled out a chair at the table. He glanced at Sawyer. "Little guy's all tuckered out from yesterday, huh?"

Nicki smiled fondly at Sawyer. "*Sí*," she responded quietly. She gazed at the sleeping child for a moment, then turned to find William assessing her, a strange light in his eyes.

She blinked and pulled the coffee into the center of the stove, where it would heat the quickest. "Did you forget something here last night?"

"No."

She looked at him pointedly. Questioning.

"Come sit down, Nicki. I have something I want to talk to you about."

She moved slowly to sit across from him at the table. An apprehensive foreboding gripped her. What could he possibly have to discuss with her? He and John had become good friends in that first year, but recently she had sensed in John a tension whenever William was near. Not that he had ever confided anything to her.

William made small talk with her for a few minutes about the weather and how it might affect the cattle if the snows didn't clear up soon, but Nicki knew that was not what he had come to talk about. Soon the conversation lulled, and she asked, "Why are you here, William?"

William cleared his throat. "Nicki, I've been up most of the night thinking. Ron mentioned you planned on staying here and I got to thinking…" He twisted his felt hat around on the table a couple of times, glanced at her, then back at his hat. He drummed his fingers against the table. "Well, with our spreads sharing one border and all, and you and Sawyer being alone now, I thought—" He stopped again.

The coffee pot started to boil, sending splashes of water out the pour spout to sizzle on the stove top. Nicki realized she had put it too close to the center, so she got up and went over to move it closer to the edge. Behind her, William sighed. What was he trying to get at?

Sitting back down at the table, she rested her hands in front of her. "What do you want, William?"

Reaching out, he laid one hand over the top of both of hers and looked deeply into her eyes. "I want you to marry me."

Nicki gasped and jerked her hands from his as though he had poured boiling water on them. Standing up, she pressed the knuckle of her first finger to her suddenly throbbing temple and the other hand to the small of her back, closing her eyes for an instant. The audacity of his preposterous proposal made her dizzy. "No."

"Nicki, listen to reason. There is no way on God's green earth that you are going to be able to run this place on your own. John has five *thousand* acres here. Do you know how much work it's going to take to keep this place running? And you have *two* hands who stayed through the winter. Two hands." He held aloft two fingers. "You need me, Nicki. There's no two ways about it."

Nicki massaged both temples with cold fingers. She could feel a headache coming on strong. And futility was fast on its heels.

He was right. She did only have two hands. He was right. She didn't know the first thing about managing a ranch and keeping things running smoothly. He was right. She needed help. But she couldn't, *wouldn't*, step into another marriage for convenience's sake. She had done it once to save her family. Now there was just she and Sawyer, and she intended to give it a go on her own. Not to mention, she didn't know where William stood in his relationship with the Lord.

She straightened her shoulders and tried to smile.

A flicker of hope jumped into his eyes.

She spoke quickly, holding up a hand to slow down his assumption. "I see that you are just trying to help me, William, and I know I'm going to need help here, but I can't marry you. Not right now, at least. I need some time."

He rose quickly and came to her, placing his hands on her arms. "I'm sorry. I should have given you more time. I know you are a strong woman and that if any woman can run a ranch, it's you, but I have to warn you. I've already heard talk in town. There are some very big men who would give anything to get their hands on this land. I'm worried about your safety."

Nicki took a step back, looking into his eyes. "You don't think they had anything to do with John's death, do you?"

He stepped close, smoothing her hair, his face contorted with compassion. "No. Shhh. Shhh." He pulled her to his chest. "I was there, Nicki. John's death was an accident."

Tears welled in her eyes. She pushed him away, folded her arms, and stared at the floor, trying to assure herself his words were true.

He touched her cheek and Nicki looked into his face. "You need someone to take care of you, Nicki. You've had to take care of yourself long enough."

Nicki didn't like this assault on her emotions. William was so tender and caring, yet something didn't ring true. She took a slow step away from him, needing distance to think clearly.

He put on his hat. "If you won't consider me for yourself, think of Sawyer. I already love him like he was my own, and he's going to need a father."

Nicki blinked and looked toward the bed where the little boy still slept soundly. She shook her head in confusion and took another step away from him, pressing her fingertips to her temple once more. "I don't know. I'll think about it. I just need some time."

"That's all that I can ask. Meanwhile, I'll send a couple of my men over to help out where you need them. Would that be all right?" His tone was gentle.

"Y-yes. I suppose that would be fine."

He started to turn away. "William?"

"Yes?"

"*Gracias*. Thank you. I mean, for thinking of us." She gestured to include Sawyer. "I know you're just trying to help, and I will consider your offer."

"It will be good forever."

Nicki nodded. "Would you like some coffee?"

"No. I need to be getting back to my spread. It looks like another storm is coming on this afternoon, and I have some things I need to see to. I'll send those men right away, though."

"All right. Would you stop by the bunkhouse on your way out and ask Ron to give me fifteen minutes and then come to the house? I need to talk to him about a few things."

William nodded and ducked out the door.

She hurried to get changed and cleaned up. She was a widow, but that didn't mean she shouldn't look presentable. However, she only had one black dress and that one she was wearing. She settled for the dark blue, noticing that it was a little bigger on her today than it had been when she wore it last week. She had lost weight in the past few days.

She rested a hand on her queasy stomach, closing her eyes against the despair that threatened to overwhelm her. She determined this situation would not get the best of her. With God's help, she would make it through this valley.

Fifteen minutes later Ron tapped on the door and Nicki let him in. "Did you and Conner eat yet?"

"No, ma'am."

"Why don't you go back out and get him, and I'll throw some things together so we can eat while we talk?"

Ron nodded and soon returned with Conner. Nicki put him

to work peeling potatoes. Ron took flapjack ingredients to the table and began mixing while Nicki dashed through the cold to the henhouse for some fresh eggs.

Several minutes later when Nicki stepped back into the house, she paused, eyeing her two ranch hands.

Conner had half-inch-thick potato peelings in the sink and a makeshift bandage wrapped around his thumb. Although he had been working on the potatoes for a good ten minutes, he was just finishing on the fourth one.

Ron had flour on his forehead, in his hair, and on the shoulder of his shirt, and the flapjack batter looked more like a lump of pie dough than anything. Ron looked from the lump in the bowl to the recipe on the table and back again with a quizzical air that showed he had no idea what had gone wrong.

Both Ron and Conner glanced at her when she entered and then turned back to their respective duties. By their unflustered manner, this was not an unusual situation for either of them. When she made no move, both men stopped what they were doing and turned to stare at her.

Merriment traced the edges of her voice. "Well, I can see that the first thing we are going to have to do is hire a cook. How have you two managed to stay alive this winter?"

Ron poked the lump of offensive pancake dough with the end of his spoon and stepped back, eyeing it as though it might crawl from the bowl. "It hasn't been pleasant," he said, picking up the recipe and running a calloused finger from line to line, "but we're gettin' real good at makin' stew."

"Well here." Nicki shooed the men into seats at the table. "The coffee's done, and I will have some food fixed in no time. You two just sit." She poured them both coffee and was just turning to start breakfast when Sawyer awoke.

"*Buenos días*, Sawyer. How is Mama's Sunshine this morning?" Nicki approached the bedside and ruffled his dark curls as the little boy stretched vigorously.

"Mama!" His chubby arms encircled her legs for a split second and then he clambered to his feet, reaching his arms up to be held.

Nicki picked him up, hugged him to her tightly, then placed a kiss on his cheek before she moved toward the table. "Mama is going to fix breakfast. You sit here with Ron and Conner for now, all right?"

The little boy stared wide-eyed at the strange sight of the two ranch hands inside the house. Indeed Nicki could not remember Ron or Conner ever being inside the house before, *other than when I sent Ron into the house for hot water when John was hurt.* She brushed the painful thought aside. The hands had always taken their meals out in the bunkhouse, even in the summer months when the ranch kept a full-time cook.

As Nicki cooked breakfast and watched Conner and Ron play with Sawyer, she knew that God had truly blessed her to have two such men working for her during this time. *Gracias, Jesus, for blessing me with these two wonderful men. Give us wisdom as we discuss what needs to be done around the place. And help us to know what must be done immediately and what can wait for a few months.*

Nicki turned her back on the men as a rush of dismay washed over her.

Taking a deep breath, she reminded herself that God had never yet deserted her and He wouldn't do so now. Wiping her eyes, she set the last plate on the table and then seated herself.

After the meal was over and Nicki had Sawyer changed and playing with some toys on the bed in the corner, she refilled everyone's cups and settled down to talk.

"First of all, I want you both to come to the house for your meals from now on." She raised a hand to stop Ron's protest. "If neither of you can cook, there is no point in you fixing your own meals. In fact, I'm sorry I didn't know sooner, or I'd have done this a long time ago. Besides, it will make meal time more pleasant for Sawyer and me to have some company." She glanced back and forth between the men and saw there would be no further protest. "*Bueno.* It's settled, then. Now..." She took a sip of coffee. "Ron, tell me what some of our immediate concerns should be."

Ron sampled his coffee, staring into the mug thoughtfully

before he lifted his eyes to hers. "Well, ma'am, the first thing I should tell you is that Conner and I don't know enough about the cattle business to tell you too much. Conner here, this is his first job and he grew up in Boston back east. Me, well now, you know that afore I come to work here I was a hard-rock miner down Nevada way for thirty-odd years. We just did what John told us to do. I've learned a few things in the two or so years I've been here, but the first thing you need is a man who knows cows and the cattle business to run this place."

"You mean a manager?"

"Yes'm, I reckon."

Nicki sipped her coffee, thinking. "William was here this morning. He warned me that he's heard there are some men who want this land. Things could get dangerous. I'd hate to bring a stranger into that. In fact, I wanted both of you to know as well. You're free to leave anytime."

Silence hung thick in the room as both men merely looked at her.

Nicki took in their silence with gratitude but decided not to comment on it. Instead, she continued, "William also offered to send over a couple of his men. Do you think one of them might do as a manager?"

Ron cleared his throat and Conner fidgeted in his chair and looked down at the floor.

"I'm not so sure that would work." Ron scratched the stubble on his chin. "I reckon the men William sends will be good help, but they're employed by William, and I doubt we'd be able to pay 'em what they are getting now. Whoever you get would need to be here all the time and will have to be willin' to work for very little pay at first."

Nicki thought for a moment. "Ron, why is William's ranch doing so well when ours isn't?"

Ron didn't reply.

"You can be honest with me."

"I don't rightly know, except that John—he just didn't like to part with his money none too much. Seems to me that improvements have to be made to a place if you want to keep it workin' smooth-like. Not meaning to offend, ma'am, but the only improvements that John made to this place in all the years I've worked here was to fix the perimeter fences."

Nicki nodded and thought back over the past two-and-a-half years.

When she had first met John, he had spent money like it would never run out. First, his unaccountable purchase of her and then this ranch and several horses that even Nicki had been able to see were very fine animals. They had cost a hundred dollars apiece when a good horse was going for about forty. John had kept the horses in the barn for one day. Then he'd ridden off, leading them all in a string, and she'd never seen them again.

After that, John had changed his ways and refused to pay for even the most necessary updates, like the chinking that needed to be done to the bunkhouse. His source of the funds seemed to have dried up.

Where had John gotten the money in the first place? She had never asked him, and he had never talked about it. It was clear now that John did not have the gift for making money. In fact she had suspected him of gambling in the Farewell Bend saloon on more than one occasion. Perhaps gambling was where he had gotten the money. She didn't think he could have earned enough at the tables to buy this piece of property, though.

I don't suppose I'll ever find out now. She blinked back tears. Had his death really been an accident? She shook the suspicion off again. William had been with John. He'd seen the accident happen. It couldn't have been murder.

Her thoughts turned back to the ranch and Nicki nodded to herself, agreeing with Ron's assessment of the situation as she considered its rundown state. Things were definitely falling apart. Yes, things would have to change if she expected to keep this ranch from dying, and there was no time like the present to start. "All right then. Ron if you will hitch up the wagon, I'll just bundle Sawyer up and we'll head into Prineville."

"Into Prineville?"

"Yes. I'll place an ad for a manager in the papers. I need some supplies anyhow. I have a little money from the eggs and butter I have been taking to Farewell Bend every time I go."

Ron nodded, and he and Connor headed to get the wagon. And as Nicki bundled up Sawyer, she prayed that God would send them just the man they needed for the job.

Nicki pushed a strand of hair behind her ear as they finally crested the last ridge and looked down over the sprawling town. Prineville lay thirty miles to the northeast of Nicki's land. The largest town in the county, it was a hard-bitten place with more saloons than horses. *Well, almost.*

She sat on the wagon seat to Ron's right, Sawyer in her lap. Thankful for the mild, windless weather, she took in the countryside around her. Miles of rolling hills stretched to the horizon. Here and there a Juniper tree broke through the white, snow-covered plain like a jagged finger pointing at the sky. She shielded her eyes against the glistening vastness. The sun's reflection glimmered off the snow in radiant beams.

Below them, as they took the black strip of road down the hill, lay the weather-grayed buildings of the town. Smoke wafted in lazy trails from the chimneys, casting a hazy pallor over the valley below.

Nicki grinned at Conner, who took in the sights of the town like a starving man who'd stumbled into a cantina. He had ridden his black-brown-and-white paint mare and now urged his horse to a trot pulling up beside her.

"I see Sid Snow over by the livery. I'll ride over and have a talk with him, if that's all right by you, ma'am?"

Nicki nodded. Sid Snow, Tilly's brother, was the closest friend Conner had. "Sure, Conner. We will be ready to head home in about two hours. Until then, you are free to see who you will."

He tipped his hat at her and urged his mare into a canter, heading for the corral, where several men milled about in seemingly serious conversations.

Sid Snow had one boot propped up on the bottom rail of the corral and a blade of grass protruding from his mouth.

Conner slid from the back of his mare and looped her reins around the top pole of the corral as Sid looked up and gave him a hearty hale.

Grinning, Conner accepted Sid's handshake. "Whatcha doin'?"

Sid shrugged. "Jus' killin' grass."

Conner laughed as he took in the mud beneath Sid's feet. "No grass to kill around here, Sid."

Sid lifted his boots, one at a time. "Guess it worked."

Conner chuckled again.

"You're just the guy I'd hoped to see, though," Sid said.

"Oh?"

"Some of the fellows was thinkin' this'd be a mighty fine day for a race."

Conner's heartbeat quickened. The last time they'd raced he'd beat Sid by head and shoulders only. This time he'd beat him by a full length. "You sure your ego can handle another race against me and my mare?"

Sid tipped his head back for a quick laugh before arching a brow in Conner's direction. "You sure you can handle losing to me in front of my sister?"

Conner swallowed. So Tilly *was* in town. He'd wondered about that.

Hands resting on his hips, he scuffed the toe of one boot through the mud of the street. "Maybe when I beat you, she'll finally notice that I exist." He looked up hopefully at Sid.

Sid chuckled and clapped him on the shoulder. "She knows you exist, pal, believe me. I've seen the way she looks at you and it's not a look she offers to any other guys who've come callin'."

Conner's movements stilled and a rock settled in the pit of his stomach. "Other guys have come calling?"

Sid didn't answer that. "I'll let everyone know the race is on. Plenty of 'em will want to lay money against you."

Conner snorted.

Sid grinned. "Meet me at the stand of spruce trees the other side of the hill. Finish line will be drawn in front of The Bucket of Blood."

Conner nodded and, as Sid walked off, he looked across the street. Tilly Snow stood in front of Hahn and Freid's General Store, her dark eyes drilling into him. He could have sworn a lasso had just snagged his heart and given it a good tug. Standing there in her summer yellow dress, she was the prettiest thing he'd ever seen. He allowed a slow grin to spread across his face and pushed the brim of his hat further back on his head with one finger. She smiled softly, looked down at the boardwalk, then glanced back up at him.

At his elbow, someone cleared their throat. Conner glanced over his shoulder. It was Tom Roland, the banker. He looked back to the store front. Tilly was just disappearing inside. He sighed and turned toward the man. "Hello, Mr. Roland. How are you today?"

"Well now, that will depend a lot on you, son."

Conner's insides curled. What could this be about? There was no doubt that Roland held clout in the area, but Conner was nobody. What could Roland want with him? He waited in silence.

"Odds are three to one in your favor."

That didn't surprise Conner. He'd beat Sid's horse several times, and that news was sure to have made its way amongst the gamblers. He didn't care about the odds. In fact, his dad would skin his hide if he ever heard that Conner had run in a race where bets were being placed. He said nothing.

"Couldn't hurt for you to just slow up a little. Let Sid take this one. Sure would make several of us happy, and I'm sure there'd be a little something in it for you."

Conner felt revulsion coil up inside him. He spit on the ground, glanced up at Roland's fleshy face, and without a word gathered up his mare and stalked off toward the starting line. He didn't care how powerful the man was; his integrity wasn't for sale.

At the starting line, he swung into the saddle and stretched his hand out to Sid with a grin.

Sid arched his brows as he clasped his hand. "Someone told me Tom Roland's got 2,000 dollars ridin' on this race. And he bet it on me. Now ain't that strange? He ain't the only one either. Cox is in town, and word has it he's been braggin' about how he's soon gonna have the money to buy up half the county."

Conner swallowed hard. Neither man was one to make an enemy of. Still, it went against every fiber of his being to give into bullying. And then there was Tilly. He smiled suddenly, decision made. "Don't let her tail hit you in the face now." He bent and patted his mare's neck affectionately.

Sid laughed good-naturedly. "I'll be waitin' for you at the finish line," he said. But there was worry in his eyes.

Conner knew the feeling.

The gun sounded, and he dug his heels into the horse's side, leaning forward with practiced ease. He loosened his grip on the reins and let her have her head. The wind slashed past his face. Oh, how he loved the feel of the power rippling beneath him. His mare's breath puffed out in white clouds as he urged her onward. Heartbeat and hoof-beat pulsed as one.

Sid's horse lagged a full length behind as they rounded the corner onto Main Street and headed for The Bucket of Blood at the far end. The thud of each hoof against the hard-packed ground felt like a shout of victory! Sid gave it his all. Conner could hear him urging his horse onward.

But when they crossed the line, Conner's paint was a full stride ahead.

Conner slowed his mare, his breath frosting the air before him as he laughed with the exhilaration of the win. He turned back toward the crowd gathered at the finish line. Tilly's eyes twinkled as she glanced back and forth between him and Sid. He tossed her a bold wink. Her face reddened and she looked down. A man stepped in front of her, blocking Conner's view. He scanned the rest of the crowd.

Mrs. Trent was there, her lips pressed together, one hand

clutched to her throat. He guessed she was none too happy with him racing.

Ron stood next to her, his arms crossed, an expression on his face that Conner couldn't quite read. He was staring across the crowd. Conner pulled to a stop and followed Ron's gaze. Roland. Face red and fleshy jowls flapping as he snapped at the man next to him. A tall, slim man with a handlebar mustache that Conner remembered seeing with William Harpster on the day Mr. Trent had died.

Conner sighed and glanced back at Mrs. Trent, for the first time realizing there might be consequences to others besides himself because of a little horse race, his cursed pride, and the beautiful Tilly Snow.

Chapter Five

Jason smiled at Gram as he helped her rise from her seat at Sky and Brooke's table. She raised a shaky hand to his cheek and her faded blue eyes glistened as she spoke. "It is so good to have you home, my boy."

Jason pulled her into a gentle embrace, knowing she meant more than just his physical presence. It had broken her heart when he had turned his back on the Lord. She had prayed every day that he would return to the loving arms of his Savior and now that he had, Jason knew she prayed for him still.

It was Sunday, and the family had all gathered at Sky and Brooke's place. Crowded was an understatement in their tiny home, but the fellowship was wonderful. Remembering the long, lonely hours riding herd as the trail boss to Dodge City, Jason felt especially blessed to sit in the company of loved ones.

He dropped a kiss on the top of Gram's gray hair. "It's good to be home, Gram. And it's great to be at peace with Jesus again."

Gram patted his arm and gripped the handle of her cane more firmly as she tottered toward the sitting room where the others had already gone.

"Come on. Let's go sit with the others. You won't be here long, so you better enjoy everyone's company while you can."

Jason smiled as he moved slowly beside her. "I won't be here long?"

"No." She sounded self-assured. "You're young, and there is nothing to keep you here now that Marquis has her Jeff."

"Well, I thought I might stay here and take care of you for a while."

Gram stopped abruptly and banged her cane forcefully on the wooden floor. "Don't you dare waste your life on this old woman!

I can take care of myself just fine." Her mouth set into a stubborn line as she narrowed her snapping blue eyes in his direction.

Worry tightened Jason's chest as he took in Gram leaning heavily on her cane. He wished he could believe her, but it seemed she had weakened even in the last couple of months while he'd been gone. "Well, let's not worry about that today."

Gram waved a hand at him as she continued her shuffling gait into the living room. "Today's as good a day to worry about it as any. Besides, you need a wife, and there is no one in this little town for you."

Jason decided to bait her. "There's Julia Nickerson. She's fine looking." He winked at Sky, who was seated next to Brooke on the couch. Rachel and Sharyah, Sky's mother and sister, had insisted that she sit and relax while they cleaned up after the meal.

Sky grinned while Brooke shook her finger at him as though he were a naughty little boy.

Gram, halfway down onto the couch, struggled back up to her feet. Her pallid eyes sparked a darker blue as she looked up at her grandson. "Don't you even tease this old woman about something like that! I didn't pour my life into you so you could grow up and marry that heathen Julia Nickerson." A twinkle jumped into her eyes as she added, "Poor girl."

Everyone in the room laughed out loud. Julia Nickerson was anything but penniless. Her parents owned half of the businesses in town, and she was just about as spoiled as could be. She'd had her eye on the Jordan boys since they were in grade school. Whenever Jason wanted to get Gram's goat, he would bring up Julia.

"Julia Nickerson, hmmph," Gram huffed as she and Jason sat down. "Hand me a section of that newspaper." When Jason complied, she snapped it open with venom and lifted it to her face, but not before Jason saw the smile she was trying to hide.

Jason eased his legs out in front of him and leaned back, closing his eyes in relaxation. Rachel and Sharyah entered the already crowded room and found seats. Jason listened contentedly to the gentle buzz of conversation around him. Sky and his brother,

Rocky, were discussing the arrest they'd made earlier in the week with their father, Sean. Rachel, Sharyah, and Brooke chatted about the latest dress fashions and whether or not Brooke and Sky had decided on baby names yet. And Marquis and Jeff sat in the corner talking and laughing in whispers. Jason smiled…now able, after having recovered from his initial shock, to be happy for his sister. She deserved someone wonderful in her life.

Slowly the buzz of conversation became a distant murmur and Jason settled deeper into the cushions, intending to take a nap. But Gram took a sharp breath and started mumbling to herself.

Jason slowly opened his eyes and glanced at her.

She pulled the print closer to her face, read something, and then dropped the paper into her lap, staring out the window for a minute.

Jason had just decided that whatever had caught her interest must not be too important and closed his eyes again when she jabbed him with her elbow.

"I've found you the perfect job."

With a sigh of regret over his foiled afternoon nap, Jason sat up, rubbed his face, and stretched his arms over his head. "What?" he asked on a yawn.

"Look here." She jabbed a gnarled finger at an ad in the paper.

Jason took it from her and read the short blurb she'd indicated.

> Spouse deceased. Need ranch manager willing to work for little pay until ranch gets back on its feet.
>
> Contact Nicki Trent of the Hanging T, Farewell Bend, Oregon.

"Farewell Bend? Gram, that's on the other side of the Cascades." The paper rustled as he handed it back to her.

Gram patted his arm. "You pray about it, my boy. If God wants you there, He will make a way."

"What's on the other side of the Cascades?" Suddenly the whole room was listening to his and Gram's conversation.

Gram's voice held a tremor of excitement when she answered,

"There is an advertisement for a ranch manager in the paper today. Somewhere near Farewell Bend. I was just telling Jason that I think he should take the job."

Jason settled back into the cushions, refusing to give up on the prospect of catching a little sleep, yet knowing he was bucking the odds. He spoke with his eyes closed, hoping everyone would get the hint. "I wouldn't be able to go until the spring thaw, Gram. And by then someone from that side of the mountains will already have the job."

Jeff, sitting across the room, cleared his throat. "Maybe not."

Every eye in the room turned on him in question. Jeff glanced at Marquis and put his arm around her protectively before he spoke. "I haven't even spoken to Marquis about this yet, but late last evening I received a wire from the school in Portland. They want me to personally see to it that a noctograph reaches Prineville, which if I remember correctly is only about thirty miles from Farewell Bend."

"Jeff?" Marquis laid a hand on his arm. "You have to leave?"

"I'll try to make the trip as short as possible." Jeff squeezed her hand.

Jason sat back up and cast a frown at the newspaper in Gram's lap. "How are you to get there?"

"The Blind School has its own coach. We would head north to pick up the noctograph and the coach in Portland. From there we would head east through the Columbia Gorge, then south through The Dalles and down to Prineville. That way we wouldn't have to cross any mountain passes. After that, though, you would be on your own." His face softened and he turned to look at his bride. "I have someone to hurry home to."

Even though Marquis couldn't see his face, the two became lost in one another's presence. Jason, noting his sister's contented smile as she reached up to trace her fingers across Jeff's face, felt irritated at their sentimentality.

Jason turned to Gram. "I don't know, Gram. It says, 'Willing to work for little pay until the ranch gets back on its feet.'"

Gram laid a gnarled hand on his cheek. "You're thinking in

the flesh, my boy. Since when have you ever needed anything more than a roof over your head and some food in your belly?"

"Yeah," Sky pitched in helpfully, "I'm sure this ranch at least pays that much. Of course, you might have to live in a cave somewhere and hunt your own food."

Brooke reached over and playfully smacked Sky's arm.

Jason grinned at Sky, but his thoughts turned serious. *Well, Lord, is this the place you have for me?*

There was no answer. But as Jason moved throughout the week, try as he might, he could not take his mind off of the man who had lost his wife and needed someone to help him run his ranch. Every time he opened a newspaper he would see the ad. Whenever Gram looked at him, he could see in her eyes that she thought he should go. Marquis asked him twice if he had made a decision yet. And he even heard some people in the mercantile discussing the advertisement when he went to pick up some sugar for Gram.

Stepping out of the store, he leaned against a post on the boardwalk. Perhaps the Lord did want him there. He'd speak to Jeff and ask when they were leaving. The least he could do was check into the situation. *All right Lord, if the job is still open when I get there, I'll take it. I just hate to leave when Gram seems to be getting old so quickly. Help me to know if I'm doing the right thing.*

As he walked into the house and set the sugar on the counter Gram glanced up at him. "You've decided to go." Jason blinked at her.

"I can see the peace on your face, my boy. I'm so glad." She laid her age-wrinkled hand on his cheek. "I'm so proud of you. You're making the right decision."

Jason grinned at her. "How do you do that?"

She did not give the tart reply Jason expected. Instead she turned to look out the window and answered seriously, "When you've prayed as much as I have, you will be able to see things—spiritual things—that you miss when you're not so in tune with God's Spirit."

Jason hugged her to him and placed a gentle kiss on her gray curls. “I love you, Gram. You take care of yourself while I’m gone.”

Gram stepped away and went back to her painstaking task of mixing cookie dough. “I can take care of myself just fine.”

Jason again found himself wishing that were true. He could have taken the bowl from her trembling hands and had the dough mixed in a quarter of the time it had taken her to get this far, but he would not deny her the freedom of fending for herself.

She’d had to be independent from the time her young husband died to this very day. Raising two boys alone—Sean, Sky’s father, and Jack, his own father—and then raising him and Marquis when their parents died. Before he and Marquis came to live with her, she had become sick and had lived with Sean and Rachel for a while. However, as soon as she recuperated, she had moved back to her own home. No, Jason could not deny her independence. But he would speak to Sky, Rocky, Sharyah, and Marquis about doing some things around the place to help her out.

Reaching into the bowl, he stole a pinch of dough with a wink in Gram’s direction. “I better take some while I’m here. Where I’m headed, I might starve to death.”

As he moved from the room to find Jeff and ask when they were leaving, he heard Gram comment contentedly, “Better to starve while doing the Lord’s will than live high on the hog while not.”

Jason smiled.

William, the last member of The Stockman’s Association to arrive, entered the room and seated himself in an empty chair. The gathering of men quieted. The door was securely shut, and the elite group began their discussion in low tones. It wouldn’t do for what they were about to discuss to get around town.

All seven men owned vast ranches and had a lot to lose as more and more little farms and ranches were set up in the area. But this meeting hadn’t been called to discuss the small-timers; it was to discuss a recent horse race and the blatant disregard, utter contempt even, that a certain young man had shown toward an Association member in good standing. Such actions could not be allowed to go unpunished.

"Gentlemen!" Roscoe Cox, the chairman of The Association, pounded his fist on the table they were gathered around. "Let's get right to it, shall we? Many of you were in Prineville the other day when Conner, who works for the Hanging T, blatantly disregarded the request of Tom Roland to allow Sid Snow the privilege of winning the race. Because of his contempt for our Association, not only did we lose money"—a rumble made its way around the room—"but our authority has come into question! So far we've been able to maintain control, but we all know the potential consequences if we let this act go unpunished."

"I thought they were gonna be off their property by now anyhow! If we don't get rid of these small-timers pretty soon, we're gonna be overrun with them and our cattle won't have any land to graze on."

A grumble of agreement circled the table, and all eyes turned to the two men who were supposed to have this situation well in hand by now.

"Thankfully," Roscoe Cox continued, "Roland has promised to do all he can on his end to prevent that. We all know that he's helped us keep many of the small-timers out of this area, and I'm sure you are grateful for that. I know I am. However," his eyes turned fully on Tom, "I believe I speak for all of us, Tom, when I say we are wondering if things are going as well as you claim."

"Gentlemen," Tom Roland reassured them, "we've had a couple of small problems to take care of since our last meeting, but all is well in hand and we're back on track. And Conner will be taken care of shortly."

"What about that situation we discussed at our last meeting?" asked Rod Signet, owner of a ranch of well over 20,000 acres. "Does the man's wife know anything about our plans? Do you think he spoke to her before—" He glanced around the room at the uneasy faces. "Before his accident?"

William hid a chuckle as several of the men stared downward, fidgeting nervously. At their last meeting the vote had been unanimous that it was time to deal with John Trent, who'd disagreed with their land-grabbing plan of action. The lily-livered yellow-bellies had been prepared to draw straws for the undesirable task, until he had volunteered, much to the relief of everyone.

Yet now there was Nicki, a potential problem if John had spoken to her. All eyes turned toward his end of the table again. William swallowed. It fell to him to keep Nicki out of this. She'd soon be his if he played his cards right.

He leaned forward, tenting his fingers with a smile that he knew would calm even the mother of a kidnapped child. "Gentlemen, she knows nothing, I assure you. The situation is well in control. She will not be a problem. In fact," he grinned, "soon she will be my wife!"

A murmur of relief swept the room, even as Roscoe Cox spoke. "See that it is, young man. I didn't work my hindquarters off to get my fifty-five just so I could lose it when some do-gooder decided some of my plans weren't exactly moral. Just remember: you don't have nearly as much to lose as the rest of us if this goes sour."

William carefully kept his anger hidden. If he had fifty-five thousand acres, he wouldn't trust someone else to save his land; he'd take matters into his own hands. But then he was a man of action, and most of these men had come into their money through inheritance, not hard work. He'd worked hard for anything he ever laid his hands on, and he didn't plan to stop now.

His eyes traveled to Tom. Well okay, there was that one time when he'd been tempted to lay his hands on what he hadn't worked for, and look where it had gotten him. "You have my assurance, Mr. Cox. And since Conner works for Mrs. Trent, I will make sure to convey our displeasure with his rebellion myself." His voice was even, not betraying any of his thoughts.

Roland nodded. "We'll make him wish he'd never bucked us!"

"Good. Then we don't have any more to discuss. I hereby propose that this meeting come to a close."

The motion was seconded and all the men filed somberly out of the room.

Nicki sat up and heaved into the basin she had been keeping by her bed. She had caught some kind of flu bug and, for the last two weeks since the funeral, she had been sick off and on, and tired constantly. Sawyer, his chubby baby cheeks flushed with sleep, turned over with a little moan but did not wake.

Easing herself out of bed, Nicki pressed one hand to the small of her back as she made her way to the stove to put on some water for tea. Picking up the basin and its gruesome contents, she headed outside…and almost stepped on a baby lying in the snow. She jerked to a halt. The baby had a knife protruding from its chest! Horror clawed at her throat, and she almost dropped the basin.

¡Querido Jesús! A scream died in her throat before it had time to escape. The fear left her just as quickly as it had come, taking the strength from her legs.

She sank to the ground, remembering William's warning. "So, it has begun." The "baby" was merely a bundle of burlap, shaped and tied with string to resemble a small child. The handle of a blade protruded from its chest, pinning a crudely written note there. *Get off or pay*. The message was clear.

Nicki rushed back inside to check on Sawyer before she could make herself go out to the creek. The morning breeze chilled her as she rinsed the basin in the creek, but at least the sun was out. She splashed water on her face, trying to ease her trembling. Anger set in. If they thought they could scare her off her land, they had a few things to learn about Dominique Noel Vasquez Trent! She'd go about business as usual.

Today, after feeding the chickens, she would continue her work on the huge pile of wood John had heaped by the bunkhouse. He had hauled in plenty of wood before his passing, but none of it had been cut up. It all lay in a mangled mess by the bunkhouse. Long pieces crossed with logs that had protruding branches, making it almost impossible to separate them from one another for chopping. But she had discussed things with Ron and Conner, and it had been decided that they and the two men William had sent over were needed out in the fields where the cattle were. Making sure no animals were bogged down in the unusually heavy snow, checking fall calves for frost bite, and keeping the fences free of drifts that would allow the cattle to cross them were all jobs that had to be seen to. So the job of wood chopper fell to Nicki. Ron had insisted that he could do the job by the light of a lantern at night but Nicki had nothing else pressing to do and felt that she should carry her share of the weight in this new endeavor. After this morning, she was more determined than ever.

Back in the shanty, after throwing the offensive dummy in the fire, she dressed in a pair of John's pants, cinched at the waist with his old belt. She'd punched an extra hole in it. A shirt she'd bought, which had turned out to be too small for John, and her own riding boots completed her ensemble. Pulling her thick, black curls back and tying them high on her head with a string so they would be out of her way, she glanced down at herself. She looked baggy and rumpled but didn't care. No one would see her dressed this way except for Tilly, who came every day to watch Sawyer, and of course Sawyer, but he loved his mama no matter how she was dressed. By the time Ron and Conner returned from the range she'd be properly dressed and fixing dinner.

She checked the fire. The dummy was nothing but a heap of gray ashes. Good. No one needed to know about this morning's incident.

Tilly arrived minutes later with a basket of freshly baked cinnamon rolls her mother had sent. Nicki thanked her but insisted she wouldn't be able to keep one down. "But they smell delicious."

"Have you not been feeling well?" asked Tilly.

Nicki waved a hand of unconcern. "*No, es nada grave.* It is nothing serious. I just caught a flu bug of some sort. I haven't been feeling well for the past couple of weeks, but I'll be fine pretty soon."

"All right. Don't work too hard out there." Tilly waved her out the door with a smile and moved to wake the still-sleeping toddler.

Jason bought a horse in Prineville, bid his brother-in-law good-bye, and headed for Farewell Bend and the Hanging T. He pulled the collar of his coat up around his ears to ward off the chill wind that swept across the snow-covered knolls. Low hills mounded up in the distance and, beyond them, he could see the vivid purple-shadowed peaks of the Cascade Range against the clear blue backdrop of the sky. Scraggly snow-covered juniper grew along the road, but other than their branches waving in the wind, nothing moved in the vast landscape except his horse.

Even the main street of Farewell Bend was deserted. *Everyone is probably sitting by cozy fires wrapped in quilts with their feet propped on the hearth*, he thought irritably as his breath puffed out in a cloud before him. He was still unconvinced that he had made the right decision.

Tinny music floated across the coldness from the depths of the Main Street Saloon and Jason swallowed against the sudden urge to have a drink. *Lord, You've helped me this far. Don't let me fall back now. Thank You for delivering me from that lifestyle. Help me to be a witness for You in this new place You have brought me to.* He turned, instead, toward the mercantile.

A curtain fluttered in an upstairs window as he pulled his horse to a stop in front of the general store and he glanced up to the curious face of a pretty young woman. Her blue eyes became large for a moment as she looked down at him and then the curtain dropped back into place.

Jason removed his riding gloves as he pushed open the door and entered the spice-scented interior of the store. One glance around showed him that this store was run well. The shelves were neatly arranged, each item in its place, and all similar items grouped together on the shelves. Jason remembered being in one store where he'd had to pick up a shaving brush in one corner, the razor in a second corner, and the lathering bar in still a third area. He glanced around this well-lit, well-stocked room appreciatively. He would buy some supplies before he headed out to the Hanging T. It was the only smart thing to do, especially since he didn't know if he would get the job or not.

Starting down an aisle, he halted, as he encountered the flushed face of the young woman who had just been at the upstairs window. Her face stained to a pretty pink as she asked, "How may I help you, sir?" She was breathless from her apparent headlong rush down into the mercantile.

Jason slapped his gloves into the palm of one hand. "I need to pick up some things; then I'd like directions to the Hanging T, if you can give them."

Her face became instantly serious. "Are you related to the Trents?"

"No."

He could tell by the inquisitiveness in her cornflower blue eyes that she was not satisfied with his answer. "Do you know them?" She followed him down the aisle containing soaps and scented lotions.

"No." He picked up a bar, sniffed it, and put it back.

"You're not going out to repossess their place, are you?" Genuine alarm rang in her voice.

He quirked an eyebrow at her persistence. "No Miss, I'm just after a job."

"Oh." She sighed. "That's good. I was afraid, there for a minute, that you were going to be one of those terrible banking tycoons that come through from time to time. Why, just last month a man came in…he was so handsome! You should have seen him."

Jason tried not to smirk.

"He came through here asking for directions to the Watson place, and I gave them to him just as nice as you please. And do you know that man had the audacity to go out there and kick those poor, hardworking people out of their home? Right off their land! Why, the meanness of some people I never will understand." She inhaled. "But I knew the minute I laid eyes on you from the window upstairs that you wouldn't be that kind of a man. No, sir, I said to myself, you would be a gentleman, plain and simple. I can see it by the way you carry yourself." She paused to take another breath.

"I'll take these," Jason spoke quickly, dropping his selections on the counter at the front of the store.

"Oh dear, I've gone and talked your ear off, haven't I? Ma is always telling me that I talk too much, but it's so fun to talk, don't you think? I mean, we wouldn't be able to really get to know someone if we weren't able to talk to them, so where would we be without talking? Lonely and ignorant, I say, because without talking we wouldn't have been taught anything in school. Of course there's reading, but don't you think that reading is just an extension of talk—" She stopped, evidently noticing the large grin on Jason's face. "Oh, I'm doing it again. Shut your trap, Janice. Next time I run off at the mouth, you can just tell me that. Well, you could maybe say it a little nicer so you don't hurt my feel—"

"Janice!" Jason spoke the one word on a laugh. He found himself suddenly liking this talkative young woman.

Janice looked sheepish, opened her mouth to respond, and then determinedly clenched her jaw. "Three dollars and a quarter," she said, placing his purchases into a bag.

Jason was still chuckling as he counted out the money. "Do I dare ask for directions?"

"Out the door. Take a left. Follow the road for three-quarters of a mile until you come to a fork in the road and take the fork to the left. The Hanging T is about five miles down that road." Her eyes glinted with satisfaction as she ended without adding even one extra sentence. She folded her arms and cocked an eyebrow at him, as though to challenge his perception of her.

"My, but your self-control is amazing," he teased her again, causing another blush to tinge her creamy cheeks watermelon pink. "Thank you." He tipped his hat and moved out the door with a genuine smile.

Janice gave good directions and Jason soon rode under a crooked sign that read *Hanging T* in dim letters. As he topped the rise above the main buildings of the spread, his heart dropped in his chest. The place was even more rundown than he had imagined. He pulled his horse to a stop and surveyed the dilapidated buildings.

The barn roof had collapsed under the weight of the snow and sagged almost to the ground. Splintered beams and boards protruded in all directions from under the mound of snow that covered it. *At least the walls are still standing.*

He didn't see a ranch house, but when he spied smoke rising from the side of a hill across the valley he realized that the main dwelling must be a sod shanty. When he looked more carefully, he could see there was a low door and even what appeared to be a window in the hillside. But even from this distance he could tell that the inside had to be small at best.

The corral was nothing but scattered poles that lay in heaps covered by snow. The bunkhouse, far from inviting, lay to the south of the soddy. Its roof, though in better condition than the barn's, sagged to the point of danger. The door hung awkwardly on its hinges and flapped in the chill wind. Next to it lay a snarled pile of wood. Someone was trying to extract a log from the jumbled pile and, by the looks of things, not having much success. The wood should have been cut, chopped, and properly stacked when it was brought in.

Jason ran a hand over his jaw, the day-old stubble rasping as his fingers scraped over it. *This is really where You want me, Lord?*

The only reply was the moaning of the bitter wind rushing across the juniper, sagebrush, and snow-covered hills. Jason sighed and urged his mount forward through the drifts, heading down the hill toward the run-down buildings.

Chapter Six

Nicki eyed a long thick branch on the top of the mangled heap. The log was the biggest one she had tackled so far, and it lay in such a position that she had to move it before she could get to any of the smaller wood underneath.

She stepped back and rested her hands on her hips, walking back and forth, contemplating the pile in frustration. She blew a loose curl out of her face, cocked her head, and squatted down to see a different angle. "Well I suppose there's nothing to do but just pull and hope it will come out." She grasped the end of the log and pulled.

Snow showered down through the pile, as branches cracked and snapped. Nicki pressed one foot against a smaller log for traction and gave a mighty heave. The log didn't budge.

"Excuse me," a man spoke from directly behind her.

Nicki gasped and spun around. Her mind filled with the same terror she had felt that morning when she'd stepped out her door and caught the first glimpse of the fake baby. The log dropped on her foot and she let out a yelp. Was this one of the men who wanted her off her land?

The rider did not speak, only raised blond eyebrows.

She reached for the ax, gripping the handle with both hands. If this man had anything to do with that burlap dummy, he was most probably dangerous.

The stranger raised his hands, one still holding the reins, indicating that he meant her no harm.

Raising her chin, she eyed him warily, heart pounding in her chest. She licked her lips and tried to take a step back, but her foot was still pinned securely under the end of the log. Keeping her focus on him, she tried to extract her foot, yet keep him from knowing that she would be helpless to escape if he chose to act aggressively.

Irritation flooded her as she suddenly noted that the man before her appeared amused. He glanced down at the ground, composing his features, then spoke quietly. "Sorry to startle you, ma'am. I was wondering if you could tell me where Mr. Trent might be?"

Confusion kept her from answering right away. He had to mean John. A little relief eased her mind. *He must be a business associate of John's and doesn't know of his passing yet.* Still she should clarify just to be certain. "Who?" In her flustered state she spoke the word in Spanish. She leaned the ax against a snowy log, keeping it close to hand just in case. Tucking a stray curl behind her ear, she bent and tried to lift the log off her foot.

The man swung down from the saddle and moved to help her. He lifted the log slightly and she pulled her foot loose. Setting it back down, he stepped back but didn't take his attention from her face. Nicki looked away and then back again. He watched her, hands resting casually on his hips, blue eyes roving over her face as though he were seeing a woman for the first time in his life.

In those first moments of fear she hadn't noticed how handsome he was. Blond hair curled out from under his black Stetson. A day's worth of stubble accented the pleasant angle of his jaw. And there was fire in his ice-blue eyes.

A tingle of heat started at the back of her neck and worked its way up into her cheeks. Annoyed with herself for allowing his stare to affect her, she stepped back and folded her arms.

Like a little boy caught staring at his beautiful, young teacher, he looked away, kicked at a patch of snow, and ran a hand over his jaw. "Do you speak English?" he asked, his voice deep and resonant.

"Sí, Señor." To her chagrin, the words again came out in her native tongue, and he looked up. Her eyes locked with his, and she held her breath.

She'd received her share of admiring looks, but this man....

Something intense resonated between them. Never had she been so affected by a man's attention. Her heart thundered, yet she felt disconcerted. Didn't he know it was impolite to stare? She averted her eyes from his penetrating blue gaze.

Out of the corner of her eye she saw him glance around the yard. He was apparently looking for someone who could understand him, but Nicki couldn't find her tongue.

"Great," he mumbled, "I'm out here in the middle of nowhere chasing a job that is probably already taken and the only person around, beautiful as she may be, can't understand a word I'm saying."

Nicki's heart lurched at his words but she pulled herself together, resting her hands on her hips, throwing her shoulders back and raising her chin. "I can understand you, *Señor*."

He spun toward her. "You speak English?"

The full force of his blue eyes once again made her forget her well-versed command of the English language. "*Sí*." She cleared her throat and stared at his boots, bringing her hands together in front of her in exasperation. "Yes."

He rubbed the back of his neck. "So you understood everything I said?"

She nodded, pushing a stray curl off her forehead and fixing her embarrassed gaze on the side of the collapsing barn several yards away.

"I didn't mean any offense, ma'am. I apologize."

Nicki heard true contrition in his voice and knew that he meant what he'd said. He was definitely not the kind of man who would leave that frightening threat on her doorstep.

She raised her eyes to his, humor tingeing her words. "For calling me beautiful, *Señor?*"

He grinned. Shrugging, he responded in kind. "I don't normally tell a woman how beautiful she is until I've known her for at least five minutes."

"I see." *A lady chaser. I will have to watch this one.* Nicki extended her hand, the smile she felt in her heart not quite reaching her mouth. "I am Dominique Trent. How may I help you, *Señor?*"

The man took her hand. "Jason Jordan."

Nicki quickly pulled her hand from his, trying to ignore the jolt that traveled up her arm at his touch.

He motioned downward. "Is your foot all right?"

"I am fine."

He nodded. "Good. I am looking for your father. Is he around?"

Nicki frowned, her confusion growing. "My father?"

Jason walked to his saddle bag and pulled out a rumpled newspaper. Folding the paper open he tapped the print and handed it to her. "I am responding to this ad. I've come for the job, if it's not yet taken."

Nicki glanced at the paper and then back into his face, realization dawning. "I placed this ad, *Señor*. I am Nicki Trent."

Jason stepped back and examined her small frame, bringing a blush to her face once again. "You run this ranch, ma'am?"

"*Sí*." She again reverted to Spanish and inwardly berated herself for allowing this man to have such an unsettling effect on her. "But not of my own choice, *Señor*."

"Of course." Jason scuffed an arc in the snow with the toe of his boot.

"Well, I've blundered into this rather badly, haven't I?" He raised his eyes to hers.

Nicki smiled.

"Is the job taken?"

She shook her head. Then, folding her hands in the awkward silence that followed, she said, "Why don't we go inside out of the cold so I can ask you a few questions?"

Jason stepped back. "That would be fine. Is there someplace I can put my horse?" He glanced at the barn as though hoping she would not ask him to put the poor animal anywhere near such a death trap.

Embarrassment heated her cheeks. "The barn roof collapsed earlier this year under the weight of the snow. My husband didn't get around to fixing it before..."

"I understand, ma'am. If you give me a couple of minutes, I'll rig something up." He glanced at the sky. "It looks like there might be a snowstorm blowing in, and I would hate to leave him out in it."

"That would be fine. I'll be in the soddy over there. Have you had lunch?"

"No, ma'am, not yet."

"I'll have some waiting then. Come on over when you are done."

"Thanks."

Whap! A bullet struck the side of the bunkhouse not a yard from Nicki's head as she took a step toward the house. The report of the rifle came only after she heard the distinct sound of the bullet shattering wood. Another shot quickly followed.

Jason squelched the curse that leapt to his lips as he dove for cover behind the slot-sided bunkhouse. He hoped a bullet didn't happen to hit one of the large gaps and make its way clean to the other side.

The woman had only been a couple of steps away from him, and he turned toward her. "Any idea who would be shoot—what!" This time an oath did slip out before he could stop it.

She still stood brazenly in the yard. Hands on her hips, she glared passionately at the hill from which the hail of bullets emanated.

Lord, forgive me. And please protect her! What should I do? Fear for her life made his mouth dry as a desert stone. For one frozen second, his alarm paralyzed him.

His only chance was to dive on her and tackle her down behind the partially frozen water trough.

As he lunged out from the relative safety of the bunkhouse, a verse from the ninety-first psalm washed over him. "*You shall not be afraid of the terror by night, nor of the arrow that flies by day, nor of the pestilence that walks in darkness, nor of the destruction that lays waste at noonday.*" Still, he couldn't help but voice a question toward the sky. "Lord, You brought me across the state to work for a crazy woman?"

He hit her torso with a long clean dive, and they landed with a thud on the snow-covered ground behind the trough.

"Are you crazy?" he yelled at her.

She opened her mouth to reply, but his tackle had apparently knocked the wind out of her, and she could only gulp for air.

"Here." He turned her on her side, placing his body on the outside, but scooting as close to her as he could so he couldn't be seen over the top of the trough. For all her seeming bravery, he could feel her body trembling. The bullets stopped a moment later, and thick, ringing silence descended.

His heart rate beginning to return to a more normal pace, a low chuckle escaped his chest. "Last I was told, it's probably best to duck for cover when someone opens fire on you. But then maybe no one ever told you that?"

She tried to laugh with him, but it came out more like a whimper.

He remained silent for a time, allowing her to gather her composure. Then he asked, "Any idea who might be shooting at us?"

"They are trying to frighten me off this land." She told him about the morning's incident with the burlap, child-sized dummy.

"Who's 'they'?"

"I don't know. My neighbor warned me that, since my husband's death two weeks ago, he's heard some talk of men who would like my land."

"And you were standing out there staring them down because...?"

"I will not let them frighten me, *Señor*."

He laid a hand on her still-trembling arm. "But you are frightened."

She sat up quickly before he could stop her, her head and shoulders clearly visible above the rim of the trough. He reached quickly to pull her back down but stopped when there was no shot.

"They do not need to know that, *Señor*." She stood, brushing snow off her clothes. "I will go see about lunch now."

As Nicki made her way toward the house she rubbed her

upper arms and stared up at the hill. Who would be shooting at her? Why not just approach her and offer to buy her out? Her thoughts turned to Sawyer, and she shivered with the knowledge of what her pride could have cost him. *Thank You, Lord, for watching over me.*

Opening the door to the soddy, she slipped inside and wrapped her hands around the warmth of the coffee cup that a shaking Tilly passed her. "I was so worried. What was that all about?"

"Someone wants to scare me off this land."

"God have mercy!"

"I think maybe He already has." Nicki cocked an eyebrow at her over the rim of the cup and tipped her head in the direction of the man outside.

"Are you talking about that man who dove on you?"

Nicki nodded.

"What were you doing anyway, Nicki Trent? I'll shoot you myself if you ever do something like that again! You had me scared witless! If that man hadn't tackled you down, you would have—you could have—Oh! Are you crazy?"

Nicki sipped the dark brew, meeting Tilly's furious gaze with what she hoped was calm assurance.

Tilly sank into a chair, clasping quaking hands in her lap. "I'm sorry. I shouldn't yell at you like that. Just don't do that again, okay?"

Nicki remained silent, intently studying the ebony liquid in her cup.

Stooping, Tilly rubbed a fresh circle on the frosted window, and asked, "Who is he?"

Nicki was unsure how to respond, so held her silence.

"He's awfully good looking!" The gleam in Tilly's eyes indicated she was attempting to lighten the mood.

Nicki smirked and sipped from her cup, following suit. "Not quite as good looking as Conner, though?"

Tilly waved a hand. "Well, that goes without saying." She grinned.

Nicki smiled at her fondly, knowing that her young babysitter had developed a crush on her handsome cowhand since he'd been picking her up in the mornings and driving her home at night. And having seen the way Conner stole looks at Tilly when he thought no one was looking, the feeling was certainly mutual.

"So? Who is he?" Tilly got back to the subject at hand, gesturing out the window.

"He has come to apply for the foreman job."

Tilly peered out the little circle again. "Wait until I tell Janice. He's just her type. She always goes for those blond-haired, blue-eyed men." She spoke of her best friend, the daughter of Ryan and Peggy Sanders, owners of Farewell Bend's mercantile. Then Tilly giggled. "If he stopped in town, I bet she talked him into a corner. She always talks too much when she gets nervous." She glanced at the man out the window one more time. "He does have blue eyes, doesn't he?" Tilly's nervousness over the gunfire was making her own tongue run from the middle.

"*Sí.*" Nicki took another sip of coffee, trying to push the thought of those alluring blue eyes from her mind. "*Pero, no es oro todo lo que reluce.*"

Tilly turned toward her with a puckered brow. "What?"

"All is not gold that glitters. You don't have any idea what he is like. Just because he is fine-looking doesn't mean that he is kind and loving. Nor that he loves our Savior, no?" Nicki spoke the words to Tilly but inwardly realized she was preaching herself a sermon.

Tilly wrinkled her nose. "I suppose you're right." But she quickly returned to high spirits. Her face brightened and she said animatedly, "It will give Janice and me something to talk about, though. It's not often that strangers come through town, much less ones as good-looking as him. And the very day he arrives, you are shot at and he saves you!"

Nicki smirked at Tilly's adolescent romanticism. "Better than me being shot at and him not saving me, yes?"

Tilly chuckled.

Stepping over to the rag rug where Sawyer played with his pile of blocks, Nicki squatted down, ruffling his hair. For a time she closed her eyes, enjoying the feel of his little head beneath her hand, thanking God she was still here to enjoy it. When she opened her eyes he was staring up at her. "How is Mama's big boy this morning?"

The eighteen-month-old grinned at her, banging two blocks together."Mama! Watch dis." He stacked the two blocks on top of each other, adding a third, his tongue held between his teeth in concentration, then joyfully knocked over the tower.

"Wow!" Nicki said enthusiastically. "Can you do it again?"

"No."

Nicki shook her head at his independent spirit. If she hadn't asked for a repeat performance, he probably would have contented himself with doing the same thing over and over all morning. But since it had been her suggestion to do it again, it no longer seemed like fun.

A knock sounded on the door.

Tilly moved to open it as Nicki seated herself at the table, trying to compose her thoughts. *What questions do I need to ask? I don't know the first thing about running a ranch, so how do I know what to ask him? He might not even want the job after what he's seen.*

Jason was taller than John had been. For where there had been plenty of room for John's head, even in this low-ceilinged building, Jason's hair almost touched. He curled the brim of his hat into one hand, tapping it against his leg. Tilly traded him the hat for a cup of coffee, and he thanked her warmly. A blush skittered across her cheeks, but he didn't seem to notice. His gaze was fixed on the little boy playing on the braided rug, a sudden tenderness in his eyes.

Nicki watched as his sorrow-filled glance flickered from Sawyer, to the floor, into his coffee, and then back to the baby, finally settling on her face. "I'm so sorry for your loss, Mrs. Trent."

Nicki could barely speak around the lump that suddenly formed in her throat. "Thank you."

Jason looked back to Sawyer. "I lost my father when I was just a little older than he is, my mother a few years later."

"I'm sorry."

A sad light was still in his eyes as he pulled out a chair and seated himself. "It worked out. I don't know if I would ever have come to serve the Lord if I hadn't been raised by my grandmother."

Nicki heard Tilly give a little gasp from where she stood by the stove. *So the glitter might have a little gold in it.* "Well, I'll be the first to admit that it eases my mind knowing you are a fellow Christian, but tell me what you know about ranching, *Señor*." She hurried on. "That is, if you are still interested in this job?"

"I'm still interested if you'll have me, ma'am."

She nodded. "Fine. Why don't you tell me what qualifies you, *Señor*?"

"First, ma'am, please just call me Jason. You're making me feel old calling me *'Señor'* all the time." His eyes twinkled.

Nicki sipped her coffee as Tilly placed thick sandwiches before them and carried a little plate to Sawyer. They said grace, and then Nicki responded to his comment. "That's fine, Jason." She almost added that he could call her Nicki, but she needed to keep an element of formality in their relationship if the attraction she felt for him was anything near mutual.

Taking a bite of her sandwich, Nicki tried to quash the guilt she felt at being attracted to this man so soon after the death of her husband. True, she had not loved John, but she missed him now that he was gone, and it felt disloyal to be having these unfamiliar feelings.

Her next question came out more caustically than she intended. "So, do you have any experience in ranching, Jason?"

He swallowed his bite of bread and steak and nodded. "Yes, ma'am. I've just come home from bossing a herd from down near Salem, Oregon, to Dodge City. I'd only been home for a couple of days when I saw the ad for this job."

Nicki softened her tone. "Where is home?"

"Shilo, Oregon. Over in the Willamette Valley. Are you originally from around here?"

"No. I was born and raised in California."

"How did you come to be living here, Mrs. Trent?"

Nicki debated between telling him to mind his own business and wondering how much of the truth she should tell him. She settled on, "My husband bought this place after we were married."

"Well, from what I saw of the place, it could be a fine spread. It just needs a little work is all. There is plenty of water and good access to it so the cattle should do well in the spring and summer. I can see why someone would want the place. How many cattle do you run?"

Nicki was chagrined. "I don't know, Señ—" She caught herself. "Jason."

"That's all right." He waved a hand. "There will be plenty of time for counting in the spring. How many acres do you own?"

"Five thousand."

"How many hands work here?"

"Two."

He blinked. His sandwich halted halfway to his mouth. Setting it back down on his plate, he wiped his mouth with his fingers and asked, "Two?"

She nodded. "A neighbor, one of my husband's good friends, has lent me a couple of men to help us make it through the winter, but I only have two hands of my own."

"Has the ranch always run on only two hands?"

"No. In the summer months we usually have up to fifteen, but it gets cold during the winters here and none of the others were willing to—" She felt the blush of regret on her cheeks. Then she threw back her shoulders and raised her chin, meeting his steady gaze. After all, it was not her fault John had let this ranch run into the ground. "None of the others were willing to live in the bunkhouse through the winter."

Jason took up his coffee and sat back. Crossing the ankle of one leg over the knee of the other, he sipped the hot liquid glancing into its depths for a moment before he said, "Well, if you give me the job, I will want to make some specific changes, especially to these central buildings. The workings of a ranch run from the main buildings outward, and if you don't have a functioning barn, corral, or bunkhouse, you don't have a ranch."

Nicki nodded. "I agree with you, *Señor.*" Recognizing her slip, she darted him a glance, then pressed on. "I would have started on the bunkhouse already except for the fact that it is winter and the chinking that needs to be done would never dry."

He went on as though she had not spoken, his concerned eyes drilling into hers. "But the first thing I'll do is ride into town and see the sheriff about this harassment you've been getting."

Nicki didn't have time to ponder the implications of his concern, for Sawyer suddenly pulled on her sleeve. "Mama, come pway."

Nicki looked down and tousled his hair, "I can't play right now, Son. Mama is busy."

Stomping one foot and folding chubby arms across his chest, he repeated, "Come pway!"

"Sawyer. Mama is busy now." When she turned back to resume her conversation with Jason, Sawyer threw his head back and let out a blood-curdling scream, throwing in a few stomps of his feet for good measure. Wide-eyed, Nicki turned to stare at the little tyrant before her.

Tilly set her plate aside and came over, attempting to pick him up, but he arched his back and threw his hands in the air, squirming and writhing and making it almost impossible.

Jason set his cup down and stood, picking up the rest of his sandwich as he hollered over the din, "I'll just go cut and chop some of that wood for you. When you've gotten him settled, you can let me know your decision."

As Nicki attempted to calm Sawyer, she realized with exasperation that Jason had been the one who asked most of the questions.

★

Chapter Seven

An hour later when Nicki had finally rocked Sawyer to sleep, she laid him gently on the bed and made her way outside to finish conducting her interview with Jason.

She stared at the wood pile in amazement as she moved across the yard. He had reduced it by at least half, cutting more in an hour's time than she had been able to cut in the last three days.

Glancing past him, she saw that he had set up a three-sided screen for his horse, using the wind-sheltered end of the bunkhouse and several bales of hay, which she had not even known she had. He must have found them under the collapsed roof of the barn. She could see where he had dug down, removing sections of the roof to get at what was underneath.

She gestured to the animal and then folded her arms against the cold as she spoke. "There might be some feed under that mess." She motioned to the barn. "I haven't been in there since before John's accident. But if you can find some, you're welcome to it."

"Thank you. I'll go look as soon as I'm done with this wood. Where would you like it stacked?"

"Um." She glanced around. They had always had only enough cut up to burn for one day so there was no set place to stack it. "You can put half of it here by the bunkhouse and half over there by the soddy."

He nodded and went back to work chopping as he asked, "So is there anything else you want to ask me?"

"Well, I find myself in an awkward position. You see I don't really know the first thing about running a ranch, so I don't know what questions I should ask you. You said you were the trail boss on a drive, so I suppose that you know something about cattle. Where did you learn that information?"

Jason set another log up on its end, swinging the ax high and chopping it in half before he leaned on the handle and replied, "My uncle's best friend owns a ranch. His name is Smith Bennett, and his son, Cade, and I were pretty good friends growing up. Every summer until I was seventeen I worked on their ranch with my cousins, helping do all sorts of odd jobs. I also sometimes helped my uncle with his work. He is the sheriff back home in Shilo. I learned cattle from Smith Bennett, and I learned about horses from Uncle Sean."

"And organizing and running a ranch, what do you know about that?"

"Well, I'll be honest with you on that. I have never had to run a ranch. But," he glanced around at the rundown buildings, "I have some ideas that I think will work. At least improve your situation."

Nicki was about to ask something else when she heard a rider approaching and turned to see who it was.

"Nicki? I heard there were some shots over in this direction?" William swung down from the saddle, his mouth thinning as he took in Nicki's attire.

She glanced down. She had forgotten about her clothes. Heat warmed her cheeks.

Jason didn't miss the way Nicki's cheeks tinted as she self-consciously smoothed a hand over the front of her baggy pants. The newcomer eyed him in a decidedly unfriendly fashion, then turned his eyes back on Nicki, waiting for her reply.

"Hello, William. You heard right. Your fears the other day were justified. Someone wants me off this land."

"Someone with a .44 caliber," Jason added, his eyes casually taking in the Winchester of the same caliber that rested in the scabbard of William's saddle. He had taken a few moments to check out the rounds that struck the bunkhouse and had even meandered over the hill to look at the area where the shots had originated. The shooter had been on foot, and Jason knew he wouldn't soon forget his tracks.

"Who is this?" The man's accusing tone hung thickly in the air.

Nicki gestured toward Jason. "I'd like you to meet Jason Jordan. Jason, this is William Harpster, my neighbor and friend."

Jason stepped toward William, nodding as they shook hands. Nicki continued, "Jason is my new ranch foreman."

Jason relaxed inwardly, although he didn't let his relief show. After their fiasco of an introduction, he had wondered if she would even consider hiring him, yet somehow even while they were being shot at, he'd known this was where he suddenly wanted to be. He'd ridden down the hill grumbling about this God-forsaken ranch in the middle of nowhere. But one glimpse of his new boss's pretty eyes, and suddenly he felt right at home.

His eyes flickered toward Nicki as he picked the ax back up. She was very beautiful. He suppressed a snort of disgust with himself. He was as shallow as the neighbor who had stepped very close to Nicki in a protective gesture. Nicki folded her arms and stiffened. *Interesting.*

He swiped his cheek against one shoulder, grabbed a log, and set it up on the chopping block. *Lord, help me to serve this woman for the right reasons and not just because she is beautiful.*

Jason eyed the newcomer even as he continued to chop wood. He sensed that this man was not happy with his presence here and wondered what caused his displeasure. His eyes dropped once again to the man's rifle, suspicion darkening his thoughts.

"A ranch foreman, Nicki?" William lowered his voice, "If you would accept my offer, you wouldn't need a foreman." He touched her arm, trailing his fingers from her shoulder to her elbow and looking deeply into her eyes. The hushed words were not meant to reach Jason, but he heard them, nonetheless, and understanding dawned.

She has a suitor this soon after the death of her husband? Something seemed odd about that, but remembering his own reaction to her beauty, Jason was not surprised.

William turned and stared at Jason, who continued calmly chopping wood, his swing of the ax rhythmic and smooth.

"Nicki, I'm afraid I have some bad news for you," he said, his eyes still on Jason, his voice raised a notch.

"You are not going to need a ranch foreman."

Jason heard Nicki give a dry chuckle as she turned on William. "Look around you! This place is literally falling apart. I need someone to help me put it back together; get it organized. I'll not be frightened off this place." There was an edge of iron in her tone.

Good girl.

"Nicki, don't do this. Please. Listen to reason. You aren't qualified to run this place."

"Which is why I've hired a foreman."

William took Nicki's elbow. "Listen to me." He led her a few steps away, paused, then started talking.

Jason, now unable to hear what he said, watched as William handed her a yellow paper that could only be a telegram. Nicki frowned and glanced down at it. Jason's eyes stayed on Nicki as he set another round of wood on the chopping block. She read the telegram, dropped it to her side, and raked the fingers of her other hand back through the dark, loose strands of hair by her face. It was a gesture of defeat. William pulled her into his embrace and Jason saw her shoulders slump as she leaned into his arms.

Lord, help her. Give her the strength to go on. That little boy in there is going to need her. And don't let her fall into the temptation to give up, like Mom did. He swallowed a lump in his throat. *Keep her strong. Show her she needs to keep her eyes on You.*

William and Nicki exchanged some more words, then William turned and mounted his horse. Riding away, he cast one more frown in Jason's direction.

Nicki stood still, staring at the snow-covered peaks of the Three Sisters that could be seen in the distance. Turning, she headed toward the house and then, apparently remembering him, she turned back, the telegram clutched in her trembling fist. She didn't once meet his eyes as she said, "You are welcome to stay for dinner but—" She ended in a choked whisper, "I'm sorry you came all the way out here. I will have Tilly pack you a grub stake for your trip home." With that, she turned dejectedly for the house.

Jason sank the ax deep into the chopping block and swiped his temple against the shoulder of his shirt as he watched Nicki make her way into the house. "Lord?" He spoke the prayer out loud but heard no reply.

Conner and Ron rode toward home as the sun began to set. Conner rolled his shoulders and dropped his head from one side to the other, stretching out his neck. It had been a long day in the saddle. They would have been home by now if it weren't for the heifer and her calf that had gotten bogged down and then tangled in the barbed wire where a drift had mounded up against the fence.

Oh, how he was looking forward to a hot cup of strong black coffee! His stomach grumbled at the mere thought.

Dusk glazed the countryside with a film of gray. Only black shapes indicated trees, bushes, and the strip of trail that lay before them. Off to their right a cow lowed and another responded. The wind picked up and Conner shivered, reaching to adjust his sheepskin coat. Ron's horse tossed its head, the bit clanking against its teeth, and Conner felt the muscles of his mare bunch even as her ears swiveled forward.

"Ron!"

The warning came too late. A lasso sailed out of the darkness toward Ron, a black snake slithering against the twilight sky. Ron's horse reared up, pawing the air, even as the loop settled around his shoulders and jerked him from the saddle. He landed with a thud and a groan against the embankment.

Conner scrambled from his saddle and rushed to Ron's side. He knelt in the snow by him. "Ron!" He was out cold.

A footfall sounded behind him. A blade pricked his throat.

Conner froze, a tingle of fear prickling his tongue with a metallic taste.

The breath from a throaty laugh heated his ear and the stench of stale beer assaulted his nostrils. "Turn around and you're a dead man, boy."

Conner swallowed and kept still.

"You should have tossed that race like Roland wanted you to, son."

Squinting into the darkness, Conner willed his heart to quit beating so loudly in his ears. Did he know that voice? He willed himself to breathe normally and tuned in carefully to the sounds around him, straining to hear if there were any other people with this half-drunk foe.

Off in the distance he could hear the rush of the Deschutes River. And somewhere a cricket chirped happily, uncaring of the drama being played out at its back door. His mare stamped her foot and snorted impatiently. But he heard nothing except the breathing of the man behind him and a soft moan from Ron.

The man chuckled and pressed the knife deeper into his throat, twisting the blade slightly. "Bet you wish now that you'd just slowed up a little, huh?" he whispered. "Wouldn't o' been so hard now, would it?"

Conner swallowed hard but said nothing. He might have one chance to make it out of this alive. And he would bide his time, waiting for the right moment before he acted.

Another chuckle. "You got nerve, I'll give you that much, but it ain't gonna do you a whole lot a good where you're going."

The pressure on the blade eased up slightly as the man raised it for the plunge.

With a feral yell, Conner snapped his head back, smashing it into the nose of the man behind him. He felt the satisfying crunch as it gave.

The man yelped, sprawling over backwards.

Lurching to his feet, Conner spun, then immediately realized his mistake. The blood rushing to leave his head left him blind and light-headed. He stretched his hands out in front of him as he staggered sideways.

A gun cocked and he froze, sure that at any moment he'd be passing through the gates of glory.

"Mister..."

It was a new voice and not one Conner recognized. He held his breath.

The newcomer continued, "I think it would be smart for you to hurry on back to whichever coward sent you out here to hunt down this cowpoke and tell him that if he wants a fight, he should come and get it like a man."

Conner released a puff of air. This man must be an angel sent from God himself! He blinked, realizing that his sight was back, but still all he could see was blackness. Everything was in total darkness now as black clouds obliterated the moonlight, but Conner heard a rapid scuffing and scrambling and then dead silence for a beat.

"You must be Conner and Ron?" the newcomer asked.

Conner was slow to respond, still processing the last few minutes.

"You okay?"

With a shudder Conner finally managed, "Yeah, thanks."

Ron moaned and Conner scrambled to his side. "Who are you?" he asked, as he slipped the rope off over Ron's head.

"Name's Jason. Nicki got worried when it grew dark and you hadn't arrived back home. She hired me today, and asked me to come looking for you." He reached behind Ron from the other side. "Here, let's get him on his horse and back to the house."

Dinner was a solemn, quiet affair. Ron held a bag of snow to his head, and Tilly had fussed over the cut on Conner's neck, making sure it was cleaned and bandaged.

Nicki had prepared a meal of fried chicken, mashed potatoes, gravy, canned green beans, and biscuits, with lemon-meringue pie for dessert. Plenty of hot coffee for the adults and fresh, cold milk for Sawyer accompanied the meal.

Jason did a double-take when Nicki approached the table wearing a dress. If he had thought her beautiful before in the baggy pants and shirt, she was decidedly more so now. His eyes lingered on her face. Quite possibly, she was the most beautiful woman he had ever seen.

She glanced at him, but he did not look away. He could see that she was ready to give up. Whatever was in that wire had convinced her she wouldn't be able to make it and now, with the attack on Conner, she was determined to be done with this place. Stubbornly so. Her look was defiant, daring him to challenge her decision to give up. He had never been one to pass up a dare. He kept staring until she looked away, flustered.

Jason sighed. He wanted to help her; to encourage her; to infuse her with strength. His look had been meant to assure her that she could make it through this time. Whatever had been in that telegram couldn't be all bad. God would help her work through it. Where had her determination of the morning gone?

Nicki broke into his thoughts. "Jason, I know you've met, but I'd like to formally introduce you to my two ranch hands, Ron and Conner."

The men chuckled and looked at one another. Jason had immediately taken a liking to both of them, and he stretched his hand out to each man with a nod.

After a brief discussion about the day's ordeals, they all made light conversation throughout the meal, as if sensing Nicki didn't much feel like talking. When the dishes were cleared, Sawyer was occupied with Tilly, and everyone had a slice of pie with coffee, Nicki broached the unpleasant subject at hand. "William came to see me today."

The men looked at her—Jason with his elbows on the table, Conner over the rim of his coffee cup, Ron still holding the icepack to his head—each slowly chewing a bite of pie, knowing that she had more to say.

"He brought me a telegram. From a bank in Prineville." Nicki glanced at all three men, then turned her eyes back to Ron. "The bank wants the balance of the money they loaned to John when he bought this place. They say I have two weeks to pay off the loan, or they are going to repossess." She sighed. "I didn't even know there was a loan on the place. I wondered where John got the money but never even considered that he'd taken out a loan. Certainly not for this amount."

No one replied. Jason knew that each of them were lost in their own thoughts on how this new information was going to affect them all.

Conner darted a glance across the room to where Tilly played with Sawyer before he raised his cup to his lips. When Tilly met Conner's eyes with an alarmed look of her own, Jason knew there was more brewing in their glance than the desire to keep Nicki from losing her ranch.

Jason broke the thick silence. "How much do you owe?"

Nicki swallowed. "Five thousand dollars. I'm afraid there is nothing I can do. I'm so sorry." She looked back and forth from Ron to Conner. "I will pack up and take Sawyer to California. Maybe I will be able to find my family there if they haven't moved." She shrugged, twirling her fork in the slice of pie in front of her. "There is nothing else to do."

Jason eyed her, savoring a mouthful of smooth lemon sweetness as he contemplated the situation. He had never been one to take defeat lying down. There had to be something they could do to keep this young widow from losing everything she had to her name. "Ron, tell me about the stock."

Nicki blinked at him. "Don't." She raised a hand to stop his line of thinking. "Just don't. There's no way we're going to be able to raise five thousand dollars in the next two weeks."

Jason was undaunted. "Ron, how many cattle would you say John ran here?"

Nicki glared at him. He looked away, waiting for Ron's reply. Ron glanced carefully between Nicki and Jason, then slowly replied, "I'd say 150 or so." He set the bag of snow down on the floor by his feet and took a sip of coffee.

Jason calculated. "Not enough." He drank some of the dark brew, his eyes on Nicki over the rim. "Even if you got twenty dollars a head, you wouldn't be able to raise enough. And that would clean you out of stock, leaving you nothing to repopulate with."

"I figured that, *Señor.*" Nicki glared at him, her slender hands cupped around a hot mug.

Jason raised a forkful of pie halfway to his mouth as he said, "You could sell some of your timber. I saw a large grove of tall pines not too far from here, and lumber is selling for an arm and a leg right now in Portland." He finished taking the bite, wiped the corner of his mouth and raised his coffee cup, sipping.

Nicki shook her head. "I have the contract. John signed something saying we would not sell anything that would decrease the value of the property until it is all paid for or we forfeit all the land."

This last comment struck a nerve. Something didn't sound right about that to Jason. Why would the bank want that clause in there? All they should care about was getting their money back.

Nicki went on. "Besides, we don't have the time to cut them all down, get them to the mill, then haul them to Portland and sell them. Don't you think I've considered all this?"

"I don't think there'd be enough anyhow," Ron said. "Other than that one nice stand, the trees are pretty sparse out here. Just juniper and sagebrush mostly."

Jason nodded. "The cattle need some shelter from the winds on these wide-open places anyhow. We should leave the trees. Just a thought."

Nicki folded her arms and gave him an I-told-you-so look that would have melted butter. Her eyes were black with anger as they bored through him.

Undaunted, Jason went back to considering the problem. He glanced at her, calculating the danger of pushing the she-bear further. The corner of his mouth twitched and he quickly looked down into the inky liquid in his cup.

He'd bet his saddle no one had ever told her how beautiful she was when she was angry. *Who would risk it?* His mouth twitched again, and he spoke quickly before he could reason himself out of it. "I think you are giving up too easily." Jason savored his last bite of lemon meringue and enjoyed the flame of her cheeks and the pulsing of the little muscle along her jaw. "Any other assets besides cattle?" He directed the question toward Ron.

Nicki slapped her palms on the table with an unladylike growl and stood. In his peripheral vision Jason saw Tilly jump. Nicki's voice quavered as she spoke. "*¡Este hombre! ¡Dispense!* Excuse me! Ron, Conner, will you excuse us for a minute?" Nicki glared at Jason, jerking one finger toward the door. "*¡Ben a fuera de la casa!*" She spun and marched outside, not bothering to interpret for him but clearly expecting him to follow.

Jason glanced from Ron to Conner and back again. Both men were suddenly extremely interested in their pie, trying to keep straight faces. Tilly and Sawyer had both stopped playing with the blocks on the quilt-covered bed and were staring at the door, befuddled. Jason took a sip of coffee, eyeing the low door that Nicki had just slammed. He smirked at the fleeting thought that he hoped she wasn't waiting for him on the other side with a loaded shotgun. Then, rising slowly, he removed his hat from its peg and eyed the three adult occupants of the room. Conner and Tilly grinned unrepentantly and humor danced in Ron's eyes.

"A lot of help you three are," Jason said, pushing his hat back onto his head. As he shut the door, he heard a burst of laughter from all three.

★

Chapter Eight

Nicki waited for him, arms folded against the chill, one small foot tapping the snow, her skirts blowing around her ankles.

Seeing she had not brought her jacket, Jason ducked back inside and spoke to Tilly. "Where's her coat?"

Tilly indicated one hanging on a peg by the door and he took it down. Going back out, he held it out to her with a grin—a peace offering.

She snatched it from him with a glare and tossed it around her slender shoulders. "You have no idea what I am going through, *Señor*. If I leave this place, two good men lose their jobs and those who are trying to scare me off win." She turned sparking black eyes on him. "And Conner and Tilly, they have eyes for each other. What is going to happen to them if I leave? I *want* to stay! I just don't see a way. I am *not* giving up too easily! I have thought of every option, yet you think you can come here and, in one day, fix all my problems?"

Jason shrugged. "If that couple is meant to be together, God will see to it. And I wasn't trying to fix all your problems. Just one."

Her black eyes blazed. "Are you implying, *Señor,* that I have other problems you would like to tackle as well?"

Jason shook his head at her rationale, ignoring her barbed comment. "You have two weeks to figure something out. I just think it's a little soon to be putting the horse out to pasture."

Nicki gave an unladylike snort. Her voice was low and dejected when she said, "This horse has been out to pasture from the beginning. It's not too soon, *Señor*. We should have quit this place a long time ago." She gestured. "Look around. We have lived here for almost three years, and this is what we have. The barn." She waved her hand at it, its neglected appearance self explanatory.

"A new roof and it will be good as new," he injected.

"The bunkhouse that is so cold in the winter time that only Ron and Conner will live there."

"Real polar bears those two, huh?"

She didn't smile.

Jason shrugged. "All it needs is a little chinking. For now, we can make some from mud and grass. It's not as good as the store-bought kind, but it will do in a pinch. Soon it'll be so hot in there they'll have to sleep with both the windows and the door wide open."

She ignored his poor attempt at humor. "There aren't any windows."

He glanced at the bunkhouse as he stuffed his hands into his pockets. "You're right. We should put some in."

Nicki threw up her hands in despair. She pointed to the corral and started to say something, but he beat her to it.

"All it needs is some lashing. The poles are all there."

"*Señor—*"

"Jason, remember?"

Nicki sighed. "Jason."

He smiled. "Yes?"

She looked into his face and couldn't say the words she knew needed to be said; couldn't tell him that it would be better for her and Sawyer if he would just go back to where he came from; couldn't tell him that he should stay out of her decisions. Her anger was suddenly gone. She wanted to believe him; wanted to hope. She wanted to save this ranch. Not only for herself but for all involved. For Ron, Conner and Tilly and yes, for herself as well. But mostly for Sawyer. So he would have something to call his own one day. Some days it seemed that only her love for Sawyer kept her going.

Jason seemed to read her thoughts. Taking a step nearer, he

looked down into her face, nodding toward the house. "Do it for your son. Fight for Sawyer, ma'am."

She hunched her shoulders into the wind. Was that the best thing for him? Maybe God's plans for Sawyer didn't include this ranch. "Maybe the best thing for Sawyer would be for me to go to California and find my family."

Jason glanced around the yard. "You've already given up, but I don't think we've explored all your options yet. Just give me some time to look around the place and see if there isn't some way we can save it."

Nicki was thoughtful for a moment before she responded, "No. I don't want to live in limbo for even a little while longer. My world has been turned upside down, and I want to know what I am doing. I will go to California and find my family."

She started for the house, but Jason stepped in front of her. "Think what you could leave your son if you could save this place!"

Nicki pivoted, hands raised in frustration. Bringing tightly clenched fists to her sides, she asked, "What do you care what I do? Do you need a job so badly?"

"Do you believe in God?"

His change of topic took her off guard, taking the anger out of her immediately. She blinked. "*Sí.*" She knew she was not acting in a very godly manner. The stresses of the last weeks had worn her down.

"Do you believe that He loves us and cares what happens in our lives?"

She nodded, wondering where he was going with this line of thinking and said a quick prayer of repentance, asking that the Lord would help her to hear what He wanted her to hear.

"Let's walk while I tell you how I came to be here." He turned so their backs were to the wind and, hands behind his back, began to walk. "My father was killed in a bar room brawl when I was a boy. My mother turned to drugs after that, and it wasn't but a few years later that she overdosed and I found her."

He adjusted his hat. "Grandma Jordan came and got us, my

sister and I. She raised us after that and taught us about the Lord. But eventually I turned my back on Him and went back to Pierce City, intent on killing the man who had sold my mother the opium." He rubbed the back of his neck. "Long story short, God protected me from doing that, but," he cleared his throat, "there were a lot of things I did that weren't right." Turning back to look at her, he shoved his hands deep into his pockets. "I was bitter and vengeful, a womanizer, an alcoholic." He sighed. "I still struggle against the desire for a drink sometimes. But God has faithfully brought me to this place in my life where I can truthfully say, 'I mean to never turn my back on Him again.'"

Nicki examined him quizzically, wondering what that had to do with her situation.

He continued, "I didn't want to take this job. My grandmother is getting up in years, and I wanted to stay close to her. She's very independent, but the older she gets the more help she needs with things. I'd been away for a couple of months on that run to Dodge City and felt like I needed to stay near her for a while.

"That's why when Gram pointed out your classified, I didn't want to take the job. But God wouldn't let me rest. I couldn't get that ad out of my head. Everywhere I went something reminded me of it until I knew I had to at least come check into it, or I wouldn't be obeying God. I told the Lord that if the job was still open when I got here, I would take it. And here I am. I believe this is where God wants me, because I've had perfect peace ever since I rode in and made you drop that log on your foot." He grinned at her.

Nicki smiled gently. "Even when someone started shooting at us?"

His grin turned serious. "That only made me all the more determined to stay. And yes, God gave me peace even then. He brought to mind some verses from the ninety-first psalm, and I knew you wouldn't be killed. Still, I wouldn't recommend staring down the barrel of a gun again."

Nicki didn't respond to his jest and all was silent for a long time. They had stopped walking and merely stood enjoying the cool crispness of the night air. The moon broke through a patch of clouds and glittered brightly off the untouched snow around them, the path they had walked holding the only marred patch in the whole expanse. The wind had stopped, adding to the peaceful feeling that filled the night air. The far-off rush of the Deschutes River could be heard in the evening's stillness.

Finally, Jason turned and looked her full in the face. "I said all that to say, give me a few days, ma'am." He paused. "You remember the story of Esther in the Bible?"

Nicki nodded, knowing precisely where he was going. "Who knows but that you were brought here for such a time as this."

"Exactly."

She angled him a look.

He smiled. "Ten days?"

She shook her head. "One week."

He extended his hand, and they shook on the deal. She started to pull away, but Jason's hand tightened around hers. Her gaze flew to his.

He studied her, his face serious, his thumb caressing the back of her cold hand. His hat shadowed his face, but after a moment she saw his mouth soften into a smile. "You won't regret this."

She jerked her hand back to her side. "I already do," she snapped. But she was chagrined to hear the husky crackle of her voice.

Nicki was at the table finishing her morning coffee and feeding Sawyer his breakfast when a knock sounded on the door.

Tilly, who had been working over the dishes at the wash basin, moved to answer it, a dishcloth in her hands. She pulled the door wide, and Nicki glanced past her to see who it might be.

William stood there, broad-shouldered and well-tailored, the morning sun glistening in his sandy, straight hair. "Good morning." His focus was solely on Nicki. "May I come in?"

Nicki nodded, and he brushed past Tilly without ever acknowledging her presence.

Tilly rolled her eyes at Nicki behind his back and returned to the sink. Nicki averted her gaze, lest she smile and give the girl's annoyance away. William was always thoughtful and gentle toward her, but to others he could be a little difficult sometimes.

"Good morning, William." She placed a spoonful of eggs in Sawyer's wide, waiting mouth and continued, "What can I do for you?"

William ruffled Sawyer's black curls, but his attention was on her face when he said, "Come riding with me today."

She looked at him askance. When she had awakened this morning, for the briefest of seconds she had forgotten all of the terrible things that had befallen her in the last couple of weeks. Then realization had dawned, and a stark depression had gripped her. The last thing she felt like doing was going for a ride.

He quickly amended his demand. "Do you have time?"

Nicki glanced around the already tidy room. She had nothing to do. There were no excuses, and to refuse him without one would seem rude. "I suppose. Tilly was going to go home early today, but I could just bring Sawyer along."

William's face fell a little at this last statement, and he looked over at Tilly, finally acknowledging her. "You don't mind staying a little later than you had planned, do you?"

Tilly's mouth opened, but Nicki spoke indignantly before she could voice her reply. "William, Tilly has worked here from dawn till dusk every day except Sundays for the past three weeks, and I want her to have this day off. If you really want to go riding with me, Sawyer will be no trouble to take along. He can sit on my horse with me."

William glanced at Sawyer and something chilled the warmth in his hazel eyes. Was it anger? But then it was gone and he smiled. "Fine. You're right. I'm sorry, Tilly." His smile turned charming. "I would hate to be the man who took away your day off." He spread his hands and arched his brows with a look that pleaded for forgiveness.

Tilly waved a hand. "Think nothing of it, Mr. Harpster."

He turned back to Nicki. "How long will you be?"

"Give me five minutes."

"I'll be outside waiting with the horses."

Nicki emerged from the house five minutes later bundled to the gills, with Sawyer—looking like a mini snowman in his many layers topped off by a white sweater and knit cap—resting on her hip.

William gazed fondly at them. "I suppose it is a bit chilly for a ride," he said as he walked toward them leading the horses, "but I couldn't stand to be away from you for another minute."

Nicki barely stopped a frown from creasing her brow. Something in his tone struck a raw nerve. She mentally shook herself. William had been a big help to her since John's death and a good friend even before that. He was only being nice. His words held nothing more than friendship. Hadn't he warned her that there might be trouble?

Her mind flashed briefly to his earlier proposal, but she shrugged that off.

He had merely been trying to take care of her as John would have wanted him to.

Refusing to allow her emotional upheaval of the last several weeks to ruin the first outing she and Sawyer had had in months, Nicki forced her thoughts toward more pleasant things. The fact that she was now a widow and her son fatherless was something she could contemplate and worry over at any hour of the many long, lonely nights ahead. She was determined to at least act pleasant for William's sake, even though she didn't really want to accompany him. Her bout of flu had flared up again this morning. But the outing would be good for her, even if she didn't feel that way inside. Besides, Sawyer needed this time out of the house, and he wouldn't relax and have fun if he noticed her tension.

William was just helping Nicki up onto a paint named Patch when she caught a movement out of the corner of her eye. Glancing toward the bunkhouse as she settled herself into the sidesaddle, she saw Jason leaning casually in the doorway, his arms resting on the lintel above his head.

His face was yet rough with stubble, but she knew he had

already been out riding this morning. She wondered what had taken him away so early. It had still been dark when she'd heard his horse leave the yard.

Pushing back off the lintel, he stepped out into the sunlight. He held his black hat in one hand and wore a heavy, wool-lined leather vest over a dark blue flannel shirt. The morning light glinted off his blond curls as he raked his fingers through them, his eyes on her face. Even from this distance Nicki noted the dizzying blue of his eyes. ¡ Qué guapo es ! Nicki caught herself and blushed even at the thought of how handsome he was.

William gave her a strange look as he handed Sawyer up to her. He turned to mount his own Morgan, and Nicki inwardly cringed, knowing he had noticed her blush. Clicking to his horse, William heeled him forward, but Nicki waited a moment. Jason would want to know where they were going.

Jason sauntered toward her, settling his hat on his head and then stuffing his hands in the pockets of his denim pants. He looked directly into her eyes as he approached. Taking note of Sawyer, his eyes hardened to granite blue before he spoke. "Not backing out on our deal, I hope."

Nicki was quick to shake her head. "No. William wanted to go for a ride. I'll be back before noon." She wondered why she wanted his approval so much.

Jason tossed William a hard look, then spoke in a low tone not meant to carry. "I went to see the sheriff this morning. He's aware of the situation now and said he'd send one of his men out later to look around."

"Thank you."

He nodded, removing his hands from his pockets and gesturing toward Sawyer. "Let me watch him for you."

Nicki didn't respond immediately, first of all surprised that he would offer and second, torn between the opportunity to have a few minutes away from the demanding toddler and the desire to let him get fresh air. "I wanted him to be able to get out of the house a bit."

He shrugged and indicated the dilapidated corral. "I need to get to work on the corral. He can stay out here with me." At her uncertain look, he continued, "It's warmer today and you have him bundled up good, but if I notice him getting cold I'll take him inside." Then he added softly, "The break will do you good, ma'am."

"Have you ever watched a little one before?"

"No, I can't say that I have, but I've never let a corral pole drop on a baby's head either." His eyes lit up with humor.

Nicki looked askance. "That's supposed to make me feel better?"

His only response was a heart stopping grin.

"Do you know how to change a diaper?"

Jason scratched his head in pretended befuddlement. Glancing from her to the horse and back, he noted her lack of any diaper-changing essentials before his eyes widened in mock awe. "You can change a diaper and ride a horse at the same time?" Nicki couldn't help the chuckle that escaped as he stepped toward her and asked, "May I touch you, oh talented one?"

"Stop." She pushed him away with her foot. "This is serious. Okay, so he probably won't need to be changed in the next couple of hours, but one never knows." She pulled an extra diaper and a rag out of her coat pocket with a flourish, dangling them before his face, a twinkle in her dark eyes. "I always travel prepared. Maybe I should just take him with me."

Jason dropped to one knee, crossed himself in knightly fashion, and pressed his forehead to her boot. "I will guard your son as if he were my own. And," he added quickly, merriment dancing in his eyes as he glanced up at her, "I'll have Tilly show me everything I need to know about changing a diaper before she leaves."

Nicki leaned over, peering down at the crazy man before her, whispering as much in Sawyer's ear.

The toddler giggled, clapping his mittened hands together and chanting, *"Loco! Loco! Loco!"* His eyes fixed on Jason.

Jason stood, still grinning, but said, "No. Seriously. Take a break. I'll be very careful with him. I'll have Tilly show me everything before she leaves for the day."

Nicki, still somewhat reluctant, handed the boy down to Jason. "What if he falls and hurts himself out here?"

Jason's tone was suddenly very serious as though he knew how hard this was for her. "Do you have bandages in the house?"

"Yes, and ointment."

"I'll remember to have Tilly show me where to find them as well."

"He likes to get into everything, and he's very quick. You'll have to watch him closely. In fact I'm afraid that, with him, you might not get any work done at all."

"We'll be fine." Jason looked at the toddler and jostled him on his arm. "Won't we, pal?"

"Nicki! Are you coming?" William called peevishly from where he sat on his horse several feet away.

"Sawyer, you be a good boy for Mama, eh? *Hasta la vista.*"

Sawyer stared at Jason as though assessing whether he could trust the man or not. And then, as Jason crossed his eyes and made a funny face, Sawyer raised one chubby hand, flopping it from the wrist as he waved his mama out of the yard with a giggle.

As she and William topped out on the first rise, Nicki glanced back and saw that Jason had swung the boy onto his shoulders and was galloping around the yard, his hat already knocked from his head and laying on the snow.

She grinned. Sawyer was in good hands, and she needed to enjoy these precious minutes to herself.

Brenda Jeffries added another stick of wood to the already blazing stove. "John," she spoke to her twelve-year-old, "ya go on over there and bring one o' the quilts of'n you young'ns' bed here. You can all snuggle under it ta keep warm an' I'll tell ya a story whilst I cook dinner."

The shivering boy, did as he was bade, hurrying back to throw the quilt around the shoulders of his younger brother, Bobby, sister, May, and himself.

The walls of their hastily erected summer home were proving to be inadequate, at best, against this harsh Oregon winter. Rolf had promised that before the next snows flew, he would cut sod to stack around the walls outside and that next year they would all be comfy cozy. But that did little to alleviate the shivers of her precious children this year.

If they stayed very close to the stove, they could pretty well keep warm, but both May and Bobby, her eight-year-old twins, had burned their fingers while trying to warm their hands and cooking a meal with the three of them underfoot was next to impossible.

Brenda glanced around the interior of their shack. *Five years.* In order to prove up on this tract of land, they had to live here for five years. The flyers they had seen back home had been so promising. *The best land you've ever seen,* they had promised. Mild winters, dark rich soil, soaking rains when a farmer needed but plenty of sunshine, too. A veritable promised land awaited them in Oregon if they would just pack everything up and move.

The banker they had spoken to in Portland had assured them they would have no trouble lasting out the five years to claim title to their land and in the meantime, kind man that he was, he would be happy to lend them any money they needed.

Of course they had needed money. Two of their horses had expired on the long, hot trip west. And then there was seed that needed to be purchased and some food supplies to last them until they could harvest their own produce. Lumber for the shanty and the crucial wood stove had not been cheap. And two of the children had grown two inches in the six months of travel time, so new shoes and fabric also added a small sum to what they borrowed.

The banker had smiled and told them the amount they requested was just fine. He helped out new homesteaders all the time and almost all of them needed at least this much, most of them considerably more.

They had been given a year to pay the money back. It would be tight what with the crops just coming to harvest as their money was due, but Rolf was sure they would make out all right. “The Good Lord won’t be forgettin’ us,” he’d said.

Brenda flicked her gaze at her shivering children huddled by the stove, and then around the inside of the small shanty again. Could she stand to live in this box for *five* years? Were her arms six inches longer she could stand in this room as it ran the narrow way and touch both walls. The other walls of the rectangular little building were considerably farther apart, but when you detracted the space taken up by beds, a small table, a cabinet and washbasin in the kitchen area, the room was very crowded indeed.

Now, Brenda, she mentally chided herself, *the Good Lord be knowin’ all about yer troubles. Ya just leave things up to him.*

“Mama, will ya tell us a story now?” May asked, her large blue eyes pleading as she scooted from under the blanket and wrapped her slender little arms around Brenda’s waist.

Brenda smiled and suddenly knew true contentment. She had been blessed beyond measure by her loving Savior, and the blessings were right before her. A tow-headed girl who looked just like her and two brunettes with physiques identical to their papa’s.

“Let me see...” She tapped her chin with one forefinger. “Have I told ya the story o’ the Knight and his Lady of late?”

“Yes!” May scrambled back to the blanket, inserting herself snugly between her brothers.

“That one. I like it!”

“It’s my favorite.”

Ten minutes later, when their papa entered the house, none of the children even noticed, so engrossed were they in their mama’s story.

Chapter Nine

As they pulled up in front of Farewell Bend's mercantile, Nicki patted the shiny brown splotch on Patch's neck. She glanced over at William as he dismounted his Morgan and came around to help her from the saddle. His face showed the tension of their riding conversation.

The ride to town would have been a pleasant diversion were it not for the discussion that had marred the morning's serenity. And she could tell by the look on William's face that he wasn't through. If she had thought this morning that William's interest in her was mere friendship, she now knew better. He seemed sure he could convince her to marry him.

She sighed.

Looping Patch's reins around the hitching post, he reached up, slid his hands around her waist, and pulled her into his arms. Her heart seized with an unexplainable uneasiness at his touch and she tried to step away. With a horse on either side of them, shielding them from the view of the town, the situation felt far too intimate.

He tightened his grip, holding her close to him for a moment as he looked deep into her eyes. "I love you, Nicki."

She expelled a quiet breath of exasperation. "I'm sorry, William. I can't say the same to you. I need more time." She tried to loosen his hands even as she searched his rugged face. His grip remained firm, and rather than make a scene, she gave up and looked away.

Could I ever learn to love this man, Lord? He has been so good to me since John died. It would be so nice to let him take care of me, but I know that I don't love him now. And I don't know where he stands with You. Show me what to do, Lord. Please.

Looking toward the door of the mercantile, she tried again to take a step back, but his grip tightened even more. "This is where you belong, Nicki."

She arched a brow skeptically. "I've always liked Farewell Bend, but I much prefer living out on the ranch."

He chuckled, a dry unpleasant sound, and let her go so abruptly that she had to take a step back to catch her balance. "I have to go to the telegraph office. Is ten minutes enough for you?"

She nodded and watched him stalk into the building next door to the store. Ryan and Peggy Sanders not only ran the local mercantile but the telegraph office as well so the two buildings were connected.

She shook her head at his retreating form, lifting her skirts and moving up the steps. She never would understand William. One minute he was ready to lay his coat across every puddle and the next he was stalking off in a fit of temper.

As she stepped through the jangling door of the mercantile into the spice sweetened warmth of the interior, Nicki rubbed her aching lower back, hoping that William would want to go directly home after this. *If this flu doesn't go away soon, I'll have to pay a call to Doctor Rike.*

Janice Sanders came out of a storage room at the back wiping her hands on her apron. "Oh hi, Mrs. Trent. How are you doing?" Her tone softened into one of sympathetic question, her cornflower blue eyes showing genuine concern.

"Hello, Janice. I'm doing as well as can be expected, thank you."

"I'm so glad that Till has been able to help you out. How is she doing? I haven't gotten to chat with her in just forever!"

Nicki smiled fondly. "She is doing fine. She has been more of a help to me than I can say."

"Are she and Conner still getting on?"

Nicki remembered Conner's lingering touch on Tilly's waist as he had helped her out of the wagon just that morning and the blush that had shaded Tilly's cheeks as she entered the house. "*Sí.* I'd say 'getting on' is a good description."

Janice beamed. "Good! I'm so happy for her. Till has had her eye on him ever since he came to work for you and started coming to church." Janice heaved a great sigh as she stared at a shelf of ammunition, not really seeing it. "Do you ever wonder if there is one certain person in the world for you? Like someone God made with just you in mind?" Not waiting for Nicki to answer she went on, "What happens if you're supposed to meet one day but, say, you lose a button and have to take time to sew it on, so you're not at the right place at the right time and you don't meet him? Or you happen to be looking in the other direction when he walks by?"

Nicki chuckled. "Don't you think, *señorita*, that if God made the perfect man for you, He could orchestrate it so you would meet?"

Janice smoothed the front of her apron. "I suppose you're right, Mrs. Trent. I just wish that God would get on the ball and send him my way, you know?"

Nicki chuckled again. "Your turn will come, Jan. And if you never meet the man for you, then you have to trust that God has something better in mind, *sí*?"

Janice's eyes widened. "Oh, I hope that's not what God has for me! I sure—" The loud clearing of Peggy Sanders' throat could be heard from the storage room. If possible, Janice's blue eyes widened even more. "Oh listen to me prattling on so! I do declare God gave me two tongues instead of one, Mrs. Trent. Do you suppose that's why I haven't met Mr. Right yet? Because I talk so much? Oh, if only I could be quiet and—"

"Janice!" Peggy Sanders' laughing voice echoed from the supply closet and Janice snapped her mouth shut mid-sentence. "Hello, Nicki," Peggy called again, still not emerging from the little room, "I would come out and be civil, but I'm boxed in—literally."

Nicki called, "Don't worry about it. I always love to talk to Jan." She gave the young woman a sly wink.

"Did you need anything in particular today, Mrs. Trent?" Janice wore the determined look of someone on a diet trying very hard to ignore a plate of cookies, as she worked at using a bare minimum of words.

"Actually, no. I'm just in town with Mr. Harpster." Nicki didn't miss the romantic gleam that leapt into the eyes of the young idealist before her as she continued, "and he needed to go into the telegraph so I thought I would come in to see if you had anything new while I waited."

"We got in some lovely soaps the other day. There's one I particularly like that smells like cinnamon and honey. They're on that shelf back there. Why don't I let you look around and you can holler at me if you find anything you can't live without?" She laughed. "I'll go and help Mom unbox herself."

"That would be fine. Thank you."

Janice swiveled to head for the storeroom, then paused midstride and turned back. The girl stood in indecision for a moment, her mouth opening and snapping shut as she tried to decide whether to ask the question that was on her mind.

Nicki hid her smile. She knew exactly what would be forthcoming.

"Did you recently hire a new hand, Mrs. Trent?"

"*Sí.*" Nicki nodded and then shook her head in mock pity, "Too bad he is so homely, eh?"

Janice's eyes bulged and her jaw dropped before she caught the twinkle in Nicki's deep brown eyes. "Yes. Too bad." Jan blushed prettily. "Do you think he will be coming to church with you and your hands?" The hope infiltrating the question was unmistakable.

An image of Janice flirting with Jason in the church yard flashed through Nicki's mind and she cringed inwardly at the bolt of jealousy that shot through her.

Janice waited, the question still in her eyes.

Nicki shrugged. "I think there is a good possibility. He mentioned that he has a relationship with the Lord. But I haven't had a chance to ask him if he would like to attend services with us yet."

Janice sighed. "So good-looking and a Christian, too? What more could a girl ask for?"

Nicki chuckled. "If anyone could think of something, it would be you, Jan."

Janice gave a mock curtsey. "Someone has to keep those men on their toes." With a wink she pivoted on her heel and made a jaunty retreat toward the storeroom.

Nicki headed down the nearest isle. The truth was, Janice would be a very good catch for Jason. Much better than a widow with a—

With a small shake of her head, she focused on the items stocked on the shelf, refusing to allow her mind to go any further down that path.

When William came in to fetch her, Nicki was ready to go, having just finished paying for the bar of cinnamon-and-honey scented soap that she, too, had found irresistible. She noticed that William clutched a telegram in his fist as he ushered her out the door.

The ride home was stony with silence. Nicki knew she had irked William by her resistance to his proposals but didn't know how she could have handled the situation differently. He would just have to get over it.

As they crested the rise above the ranch buildings, he turned toward her.

"I have to be gone for a couple of days...about a week, really. I'll come by and see you when I get back."

"All right."

He gave her a hard look. She could tell that he wished she would say something more, but she had no assurances to offer him.

The silence stretched out until he finally said, "I'll leave you here, then. See you in a few days."

"Have a wonderful trip." Nicki smiled, genuinely hoping he would.

He nodded tersely and pulled his horse roughly around, spurring it in the direction of his spread.

Nicki urged her mount forward, heading down the hill toward home. She was pleasantly surprised to see the corral all but finished. Conner and Ron were lashing the last of the poles into place, but Jason was nowhere to be seen, and neither was Sawyer. *They must be in the house.*

Ron glanced up and smiled, coming to help her down from the saddle.

"The boy's just fine. Jason took him inside a few minutes ago. He's been going hard all morning and was about droopin' when Jason took him inside to rest a mite. He sure did have fun. That Jason is right good with the lad."

Nicki felt relieved. She headed for the house, removing her riding gloves as she went. She had imagined all sorts of horror stories on the way home, knowing how quick her young son could move. Quietly opening the soddy door, she eased her way inside so as not to disturb Sawyer if he was sleeping. She expected to find Jason chomping at the bit ready to get back to work.

Jason, pillow propped against the wall behind his head, was lying down on the bed with Sawyer sprawled across his chest. His black boots, crossed casually at the ankles, hung over the end of the bed. One of Sawyer's little fists clutched the first finger of Jason's big hand as though the child was afraid Jason might disappear while he slept. Both man and boy were sound asleep. She stepped closer and saw that Sawyer was sleeping so soundly he had left a large patch of drool on the front of Jason's shirt. She grimaced, debating whether she should wake Jason but decided to let him sleep. His early morning ride had probably cost him some sleep the night before.

Instead, she hung Jason's heavy vest, which he had laid across the table, beside his black Stetson on a peg by the door. That done, she put away Sawyer's scattered wraps and sank into a chair at the table, only now realizing the toll the morning's ride had taken on her. *What is wrong with me?*

She was bone tired and her feet ached. Her riding boots were pinching her feet, which had been a little swollen lately.

Raising her skirt to her knees she bent over to loosen her boots.

"A man could get used to waking up to a sight like that, ma'am."

Jerking upright, Nicki flung the hem of her skirt to the floor, her eyes widening in indignation. Drat that man! Why did he always have to fluster her so?

Jason rose from the bed in one fluid motion and laid Sawyer down, carefully extracting his finger from the little boy's grasp and tucking the blanket around him to ward off any chill. "He did just fine, but I'm afraid I might have let him run himself into a frazzle. He's plum tuckered out."

Nicki looked away, trying to keep her eyes off of the distinct drool stain on the front of his muscle-taut, navy shirt.

He stretched, one hand going behind his head and the other gliding over his chest and coming into contact with the wet patch. The grimace on his face reminded her of the time that Papa had taken too big a swig of Dr. Dan's Cure-All Elixir, which was composed mostly of vinegar and lemon juice.

Nicki looked away, covering her mouth to hide a smile, but his low snort brought her eyes back to his face. She tried not to grin but didn't quite succeed.

His eyes darted from the stain on his shirt to his hand and back. "Ah, the dangers of sleeping with a toddler on your chest are now quite apparent. I don't recall you warning me about that this morning when you went off on your little jaunt with Mr. Harpster." His twinkling blue eyes belied the disgust in his tone as he took in her amused face and wiped his hand down his pants.

Nicki moved her hand away from her mouth. "Yes, I suppose I did forget to mention that hazard. But be glad it is only drool." She arched an eyebrow for effect and watched the light dawn on his face.

He nodded. "Yes, I can see there are a great many things to be thankful for in this situation." He glanced over at the innocently sleeping toddler and shuddered. "Things could be worse. Much worse. But still," Jason rubbed his palm across the wet patch again, his frown deepening, "things could be better, too."

Nicki couldn't help the chuckle that escaped as she rose to hand him a towel. "Thank you for watching him. And," she indicated the spot he was vigorously rubbing with the towel, "I'm sorry."

"Hey, I had fun. Really. He wasn't a big help in putting up the corral, but we had fun nonetheless." He grinned at her with a wink that sent a tremor racing down her spine into her boots.

"Yes, I can just imagine. I was surprised to see Ron and Conner putting up the last pole when I rode in. I had pictures of the three of you in the house trying to determine which end of the boy to diaper."

"Hey! We would have at least known that. Tilly told us."

She smirked and sank back down at the table, her weary legs not wanting to hold her up for another minute. At that moment, she would have liked nothing more than to fall into bed with Sawyer. Instead she said, "I really appreciate you watching him. We had a nice ride."

His head snapped up and he looked deep into her face, all traces of humor gone. "You did, did you?" There was more than a little inference in his tone, and Nicki felt herself blush to the roots of her hair.

"It's not what you think. William has simply been a good friend to me since John's passing." She carefully omitted the fact that William had been pressuring her to marry him.

"So…you and William? There's nothing between you?"

"Not that it is any of your business, *Señor*, but no. We are just friends. He has helped me a lot since John's death."

He studied her for a long moment, holding her gaze as he moved across the room and dropped the towel on the table next to her. She started to look away, but he reached out with one finger and touched her chin, his eyes still searching her face. Her heart pounded uncontrollably at the undisguised fire in his eyes. She couldn't help but meet him, gaze for gaze. She felt the need to say something witty to expel the sudden connection between them, but with him looking at her that way, she couldn't breathe, much less put two coherent thoughts together.

A smile twitched the corner of his mouth before he dropped his hand and said, "Good."

He spoke the one word with such finality that Nicki wondered what he meant by it. Good that William had been a friend to her, or good that they were only friends?

His next words explained. "I don't like the man."

She tightened her fists, suddenly annoyed. Why would anyone dislike William? "You don't even know him."

"I know his type. He wants something from you. I'd watch myself around him if I were you."

Her anger flared. William had gone out of his way to help her since John's death. He'd done nothing to make her question him or his reasons for helping her. He had even warned her that there could be trouble over her land.

What about your questions over John's death? She shoved the thought aside. Those had merely been passing doubts that had evolved out of the stress of John's injuries. William wouldn't do anything to harm anyone. He and John had been friends, for goodness' sake.

And she certainly didn't need this know-it-all telling her who to trust. Why, if he had his way, she supposed he would have her fall into his arms and beg him to take care of her for the rest of her days.

Would that be such a bad thing? She tossed her head, refusing to acknowledge the answer to that thought, and took out the brunt of her frustration on him. "I don't need you telling me how to handle myself or my relationships!"

He arched a golden eyebrow in her direction. "I wasn't trying to tell you how to handle anything. Just that I would watch William Harpster closely where my stock and money were concerned if he were buddying up to me."

"Well, he's not buddying up to you, is he?" She folded her arms.

"No. Of course not. I don't own five thousand acres, and I'm not beautiful."

Her eyes were riveted to his.

His face serious, he reached toward her.

She held her breath, steeling herself against the desire to lean closer.

His fingers were almost touching her cheek when he must have thought better of the action and dropped his hand back to his hip. "All I'm asking is that you watch him closely. If he does anything that makes you uneasy, be doubly careful. All right?"

She sighed in resignation, wondering at the disappointment that coursed through her when he decided against touching her again. "Fine. I'll watch him." *Whatever that means.* "Are you happy now, *Señor?*"

"*Sí.*"

She blinked, his Spanish answer taking her off guard.

He continued, putting her off balance yet again, "You look tired. Ron said you haven't been feeling well since the funeral. Are you all right?" He squatted before her and gently took one of her feet in his hands, unlaced her boot, and eased it off. Then did the same with the other.

All anger at his outspoken brazenness fled. Nicki nodded. She couldn't find her voice.

Looking up into her face he asked, "You're sure?" She nodded again.

"Why don't you lay down with Sawyer? I'm going to ride out and scout your land. I'll be gone for a few days."

Nicki's heart constricted, and she wondered that the same words from two different men could have such contrasting effects on her heart. When William had spoken those words to her, she'd felt something akin to relief.

But now, with Jason, she felt only...what? It certainly wasn't relief. She couldn't quite unscramble her tangled emotions and wasn't sure if she wanted to. But a thought occurred and she started to rise. "You'll need food."

"That's all taken care of." He took her by the arm and led her over to the bed. "I had Tilly pack me some grub before she left."

Nicki sat on the edge of the bed as he moved to put on his heavy vest, pulling his black Stetson from the peg beside it.

Opening the door, he turned to look at her one more time. "You take care. I'll be back in a couple of days, hopefully with some good news."

She nodded. "I'll pray for you."

He pulled on the brim of his hat as he dipped his chin. "Thanks." With that, he eased out, shutting the door quietly behind him.

Nicki lay back, wondering where the empty feeling had come from.

Tom Roland, the banker, tapped the ash from his cigar into the crystal ashtray as he eyed his wife across the elaborately decorated room. He had come back to his Portland residence for a while and had decided to send for William to meet him here. It wouldn't do for Prineville's residents to see them together too often.

His gaze narrowed as Vanessa provocatively sipped her drink. She knew the eyes of every man in the room were on her. Her dress, low-cut as usual, showed off her voluptuous figure to the fullest, and she used this fact to her advantage as she floated from one cluster of chatting socialites to the next.

Tom sighed as he watched her giggle flirtatiously with the town mayor. She leaned over provocatively to whisper something for the mayor's ears alone and then stood, sipping her sherry as though nothing were out of the ordinary.

And nothing was. This was how Vanessa always behaved.

Someone cleared their throat. Tom turned to see William dressed in the height of fashion. His black suit coat hung casually open to reveal a matching black vest. Across the expanse of his broad chest dangled the intricately woven gold chain of an expensive pocket watch. The lights from overhead caught the chain, glittering off it like the sun's reflection on still water. At his throat, the high collar of his pristine, white shirt just turned down at the points accentuated the coal black of a very thin bow tie. His perfectly tailored slacks ended in highly polished, black snakeskin boots that added at least two inches to his height. The man cut a striking picture.

Tom cast one more glance in his wife's direction before he

spoke around the cigar in his mouth. "Glad to see you made it. You got my message?"

William scanned the room as though their conversation were not important. "Yes. I need to get back, though. Let's make this as brief as possible."

Tom nodded. "My office. Eleven o'clock tonight."

William didn't reply, but Tom knew he would be on time. Whether or not William would like what he had to say was yet to be determined. He watched as William straightened his coat and made his way over to a beautiful young woman who was batting her cobalt eyes boldly in his direction. Bowing over her hand, he smiled up at her and said something, gesturing to the dance floor. The young debutante fanned herself coquettishly, allowing him to lead her onto the floor with an exhibition of reluctant embarrassment. Tom's eyes scanned the girl from head to toe, and a small smile played across his mouth.

William knew how to pick them.

"Really, Tom." His wife's quiet but strident voice made him jump a little. "Must you gawk at the girl so? It's embarrassing."

Tom turned to her with a snort, making sure to keep a false smile on his face. They must keep up appearances. "Really, Vanessa," he mimicked her, "the way you have been throwing yourself at every man in the room tonight, I would think that my looking at another woman wouldn't cause you to worry about your reputation. Any damage that could be done has already been inflicted by you." He patted her cheek gently, as though the quiet words he spoke were tender endearments, but he couldn't keep the spark from his eyes that told her maybe she had gone too far this time.

Her tone changed immediately. "Oh, Tom, I'm so sorry. I didn't know you still cared so much. Why, you're jealous!" She smiled coyly up into his face, placing one hand across her breast. "That positively makes my heart flutter. We really need to get away. It's all the pressure of this city living. We don't have time to spend together anymore. You know what we need? We need to spend some time at our place in the country. We can go just to spend time with each other. Maybe next time you need to go to your Prineville bank. Wouldn't that be nice?" She tucked her arm possessively through his.

Tom eyed her, wondering. Some of the anger left his eyes as he looked down on her. Had she meant what she said? He could hope so. Yet he often wondered whether she stayed with him because she loved him or his money. It wasn't the first time she had made the comment about getting away to their place in the country. Yet she rarely came with him when he visited their 30,000-acre ranch, managed by Ted Koerling near Prineville. Thinking of his ranch caused his mind to wander to William, and he glanced at his pocket watch.

He still had some time.

He glanced back into his wife's emerald eyes. He knew Vanessa loved to flirt. It gave her existence meaning.

There had been a time when she had suffered from deep depression. She had even tried taking her own life once, but he had been there to stop the flow of blood. He gave an involuntary shudder as he remembered the deep red in the bottom of the claw-foot tub upstairs. He had been shocked. Hadn't he given his young wife everything she asked for? Yet he had come home to find her leaning against the tub, both wrists slit, and a trail of blood leading from the knife on the floor beside her, up into the white bath. He had staunched the blood and pulled her fiercely into his arms, begging her never to do that to him again. It was soon after that she had begun her little games.

For a time he had ignored her debauched sport as it had seemed to renew her vigor for life. After all, she kept him happy, too. Without him, there would be no money for her little parties, and without her parties there would be no men to toy with. Vanessa was walking on a fence. Below her were a pack of hungry wolves, each wanting her to please them. And she loved every minute of being the center of attention, dangerous though it might be.

It wasn't until recently that Tom had realized how much Vanessa's little game had hurt their relationship. Yet he was still trying to please her. If it weren't for her, he would care nothing about ranching in the high desert of central Oregon. He was a banker, not a rancher. But Vanessa liked to brag to her friends about their property in the country. He kept it for her, to keep her happy. Insurance that she wouldn't try to...leave him again.

He glanced at his watch once more and patted Vanessa's hand resting on the crook of his arm. "I have a meeting I need to see to, dear. We may take that trip to the country before you know it."

"Really?" Her eyes sparked with interest. "Oh, Tom, that would be so nice. It really would." A glint of mischief flickered in her green eyes, and she leaned forward to whisper in his ear, "I'll bid the guests farewell and then be waiting for you in my room." Her breath wafted warm on his ear, and Tom's body heated with the remembrance of why he cared. At times she really could be very pleasing.

Chapter Ten

His office felt a trifle chilly, but Tom didn't build a fire in the fireplace. He only had a couple of things to discuss with William. Their meeting would be brief. Pulling his watch from his vest pocket, he examined it. Five after eleven. William was late.

Just then, a tap sounded on the door, and William stepped into the room. He was out of breath. Inhaling deeply, he shook his head as he glanced at Tom, a slight twinkle in his eye. "You give a woman one dance, and she thinks she can claim you for them all!"

Tom chuckled dryly. "Had a hard time getting away from Miss Stubben, did you?"

William nodded in exasperation.

"Well, I trust it wasn't too unpleasant for you."

"I'll live to see another day." William made an hour-glass gesture in the air, rolling his eyes in pleasure.

Tom's laugh was hearty this time. "I'll just bet you will!"

William sat in the leather wingback chair across from Tom's desk and crossed one ankle over the other. "So, what did you want to see me about?"

Tom glanced at the door to make sure it was shut before lighting himself a cigar and extending the box toward William.

William shook his head. "No thanks."

Tom took several puffs on his cigar, then propped his boots on the corner of his mahogany desk. Reaching into the top drawer, he withdrew a paper and shoved it toward William across the desktop.

William eyed the paper for a beat, then leaned forward and picked it up. After a moment he blinked up at Tom in surprise. "You're not serious."

Tom had never been more so. He did not reply, only took a pull on his cigar and watched William's face through the cloud of haze.

William glanced again at the paper in his hands. It was a plot map of Crook County. It showed all the sections of land in the county and who owned what. Outlined in the center of the county was not only the five-thousand-acre spread of the Hanging T but also many other spreads around it, large and small.

He looked up at Tom. "And what did these others do to deserve the eye of the Association?"

Tom shrugged. "The Jeffries fellow was talking about going into sheep the other day. We all know how sheep graze the grass to the dirt, leaving nothing to grow back."

"And the Snows?"

Tom tapped his cigar against the ash tray. "He's a friend of Rolf Jeffries.

Besides, he's running sheep already. We have to give them some incentive to try their operations somewhere else."

As William stared in rapacious incredulity at the paper in his hands, he realized that greed, like a stray dog once fed, had come back for more. Even as he looked at the properties, he realized this plan must have been laid well ahead of time for almost all the owners of the properties indicated, for one reason or another, owed Tom's bank money. It irked him that The Association often made decisions without consulting him, but that was the price he'd known he would pay even before he was accepted onto the board. He wouldn't even be a member were it not for Tom. But because of his past and what Tom knew, he was a member. The lowest one.

Shoving aside his irritation, he glanced up, caught Tom's eye, and allowed a slow smile to spread across his face. His day would come, and then they would all be sorry they hadn't treated him with a little more respect. Especially Tom. William hated doing another man's dirty work. "Same deal as before? Equal shares for all?"

Tom nodded. "The Association has agreed."

William sat up straight and stared down at the paper in his hands once more. "We might be biting off more than we can chew."

Tom stubbed his cigar out. "We never have."

William scratched the back of his head in a sudden quandary. He wanted his share of the land represented before him. His ranch was meager compared to some of the ranches in the valley, and he could certainly use the boost in income. Yet he was afraid that if they scared too many people off their land it would become quite obvious what they were up to. He had no desire to spend the last minutes of his life with the scratchy feel of a hemp rope around his neck.

But if the plot map in his hands was correct, he would stand to receive at least twenty-five-hundred acres more. That was not counting the lush acres he would get when Nicki finally decided that she should quit her ranch—her ranch with the only easy access to the Deschutes River for miles along the canyon. His cattle wouldn't lose so much weight traveling to water then. Fatter cattle meant better prices at market, and better prices meant he would reach his goals that much sooner.

He stared at a spot on the floor, seeing acres and acres in his mind's eye. All of them lush and green, dotted with thousands of fat, well-watered cattle. Twenty-five-hundred acres were to be his from the small-time settlers they had previously discussed, twenty-five hundred of Nicki's acres would be his when she married him, and now twenty-five hundred more from this new proposal. Seven-thousand-five-hundred acres in total! Added to his own three-thousand acres, that would make quite a sizable ranch. He would be that much closer to his aspiration. The one thing that grated on him was that he got stuck with all the grunt work.

He glanced at Tom.

Tom's mouth twitched.

"All right, I'll do it."

"I thought you would. The Association has agreed to make it worth your while, in addition to your share of the land." He tossed a heavy bag of coins on the desk in William's direction. Tom stubbed out the end of his cigar in the crystal ashtray before him. "You'll have to start slow. And every place will have to be done different."

William nodded.

"Well then, I'll see you next time you're in town."

Acknowledging his dismissal, William stood, picking up the bag of good fortune. He would have done it even without the money. "I best be going anyway. I promised Miss Stubben I'd walk her home." He tossed Tom a lewd wink.

"William."

The hardness in Tom's tone froze William in his trek toward the garden door and he turned with raised brow to see what the older man wanted.

"Marry that woman or finish her. Either way The Stockman's Association wants her off that land with the insurance of silence."

William contemplated the statement, knowing that Tom was not referring to the pretty Miss Stubben. "I don't think she knows anything, but I'm working on it. She was ready to quit when I delivered your telegram to her, but she has a new hand working for her now. He changed her mind, I think."

"Well then, maybe he should be dealt with first." Tom dropped the words like a boulder falling from a cliff-top, but his air was casual, his feet still propped on the corner of his desk, his cigar held lightly in one hand.

William stared at him for a moment. Then, turning with a thoughtful air, he walked toward the door leading into the garden and, with a casual lift of his hand, stepped out into the darkness. He was already taking care of that, but Tom didn't need to know everything.

Standing well back from any light, he turned to study Tom. With a curl of smoke drifting from his mouth toward the ceiling, Tom crumpled the plot map, placed it in his ash tray, held his lighter to it, and watched it disintegrate into a pile of ash. William clenched his teeth. The day would come when Tom would regret lording it over him. He would make sure of that.

But that would come another day. Now he had other plans to carry out. He jingled the heavy weight of the coins in the pouch. Yes indeed, he had plans to take care of Nicki's new hand, and this money would come in handy.

William rode straight for Nicki's spread when he got back, silently cursing the wiggling mutt that lay across the saddle in front of him. After Tom's ultimatum, he had decided that marrying Nicki Trent was infinitely more appealing—and challenging—than simply eliminating her. He had known that for a long time but couldn't seem to get through to her. Now it was imperative that she come around or she was going to have to be taken out of the picture. He didn't want that. He wanted the satisfaction that would come when he convinced her that she needed him now that John was gone. So he had decided that he would make it impossible for her to refuse his proposal. He would woo her heart. And what better way to the heart of a woman than through her child? Sawyer was going to love this ugly mutt. He hoped. And Nicki would be one step closer to agreeing to marry him.

The puppy yipped, startling his horse into a sidestep, and he cuffed it hard across the head. "Shut up, you stupid mongrel!"

It whimpered, cowering and scrambling to get away from him. He smacked it again. "STAY!"

He pulled his horse to a stop just before he topped the hill that would lead down to the Hanging T. Rubbing a hand across his face, he made an effort to compose his features. He had to get a hold of his emotions before he saw Nicki. He didn't want her seeing the stress he was under.

He sighed. Tom Roland might be the death of him yet. Why had he ever let the man blackmail him into this deal? If he had just copped to that bank robbery, he would have been done with his time by now and free to live as he chose. But no. He had let Roland control his life instead.

Stealing people's land was a dangerous business, but what else was he to do? If he refused now, he was too big a liability for

Roland, and his life would be over…literally. While he was sure he could take Roland in a head-to-head fight, he knew Roland wouldn't play fair, and he didn't want to live out the rest of his days looking over his shoulder.

No, the best thing to do was what he had decided last night. Take care of the new hand and then marry Nicki. That prospect alone would be worth the danger. But added to it there was the land… He snorted. Ah yes, with the land added in, he was within grasp of a very sweet pot, indeed.

Throwing back his shoulders, he glanced over himself, brushing off the trail dust and straightening his vest and tie. He adjusted his hat and deliberately adopted a smile. After all, he was going to see the woman that he hoped to one day make his wife; he should be happy. She needed to think he was happy. He *was* happy.

He reached for the dog, but it cowered away from his hand. Annoyed, he grabbed it by the scruff of the neck, shoving it into the front of his coat. His voice was low and controlled when he said, "Come on, pup. Let's go make a good impression, shall we?"

With a click of his tongue, he started his horse down the hill.

Jason had been gone for six days when Nicki glanced up from where she was taking down the wash she and Tilly had done earlier that morning. William was riding into the yard, a huge smile stretching his face. She sighed. He was back and by his expression, her refusal had not deterred him one bit now that he'd had some time away. She snapped a pillowcase and folded it carefully. Could she learn to love William?

"Hi, beautiful," he drawled, as soon as he was within range.

She bent and put the last sheet into the basket, lifting it to her hip. "Hi. I wasn't expecting you back until tomorrow."

His eyes raked her from head to toe. "I had someone to hurry home to."

She grinned cheekily. "I'm sure your men will be happy to know you rushed home to see them."

He threw back his head with a laugh that somehow sounded hollow. She frowned slightly as she headed for the house. He jumped down and followed her asking, "Is the boy around?"

"Sawyer?"

"Yeah."

"He's inside with Tilly, taking a nap."

"Could you wake him up a little early?"

She turned to stare at him, not remembering the last time she had seen him show an interest in Sawyer. At the innocent grin she saw on his face, she couldn't help but smile. "Why?" Her voice was leery.

He shrugged, doing his best to maintain an innocent expression, but Nicki saw a light of mischievousness glinting in his eyes. He only said, "It's a surprise."

She watched him for a moment, but when he didn't volunteer any more information, she turned toward the house. "I'll go get him up. Do you want him out here or in the house?"

"Better bring him out here."

"All right. Give me a minute."

She emerged into the bright sunlight shortly with the still-sleepy Sawyer in her arms. The toddler buried his head in her shoulder to shield his eyes from the sun.

Nicki glanced down.

Sitting at William's feet was the cutest, golden puppy she had ever seen. She gasped with surprise at the sight.

Sawyer's head popped up to see what had caught her attention.

The puppy looked up at them with soulful brown eyes, settled itself more comfortably on its haunches, and gave a little yip.

"Puppy!" Sawyer squirmed out of her arms in a flash and gathered the little dog into his chubby arms, trying to pick it up.

William chuckled. "Hold on now, boy. Don't pick him up. We don't want him to get hurt."

Sawyer obliged and set the puppy back on his feet, choosing instead to pet his fur the wrong way. William squatted by him. "Here. Like this." He took Sawyer's hand and showed him how to pet the dog from head to tail. The pup ducked away from

William's hand, scooting in closer to Sawyer and licking his face with a long pink tongue that sent the toddler into a fit of giggles.

William stood and looked over at her with a contented grin. She smiled in return, blinking back emotions she was unwilling to show. This meant more than she could say. "Thank you for thinking of him."

He nodded, satisfaction in his eyes.

"Would you like to come in for some coffee?"

"Yeah." He smiled. "That would be nice."

"Sawyer, come get your hat and mittens. Then you can play outside with the puppy for a while."

"Okay, Mama." The toddler raced for the house and was back out again even before Nicki and William made it to the door, one mitten on the wrong hand, hat tucked under his arm, and the other mitten gripped firmly in his teeth as he hurriedly tried to put it on his opposite hand.

Nicki and William chuckled, and William bent down to help. "Here boy, let me help you with that."

Nicki moved on into the house to pour their coffee, shaking her head.

William. What a good neighbor he was.

The ride from one corner of Nicki's property to the other, skirting every nook and cranny, had taken longer than Jason had hoped. And for all his searching, he'd found nothing. He was discouraged and was now on his eighth day, even though their deal had been for seven. There had to be some resource here that would help Nicki save her ranch.

All was just as it had been described to him. The cattle would live, although this hard winter was taking more than its toll on them. He made a mental note to recommend that Nicki plant several acres of hay in the spring to increase the winter feed supply. From what he had noticed, none of the ranches in this area supplemented winter feedings since the winters were usually mild. Still, even in a mild winter, the cattle would benefit from the extra nourishment.

He had also gone back to look over that stand of timber he had noticed on his way into the ranch. It was substantial, but Ron was right. There wasn't enough of it. And there was no way they could cut, haul, and mill the timber in the allotted amount of time, which was dwindling fast. Not to mention that strange clause in Nicki's loan contract.

He needed to find a solution to Nicki's problem soon. So far he had found nothing.

His mind went back to a conversation he and Ron had had that first night after he had convinced Nicki to let him stay and search for a way to help her.

Ron had mentioned that just after he had come to work for John, the man had bought some of the finest horses he had ever seen.

"I'm not much of an authority on horse flesh," Ron had said, "but those broncs looked to have some good blood in them. And John told me he paid a hundred dollars apiece for 'em. He rode off with 'em the next mornin' and I haven't seen hide nor hair of 'em since. I don't know what he done with 'em." He shook his head. "If he sold 'em, then we don't have a hog's chance on sausage-makin' day of saving this place, but if he didn't...." He had shrugged meaningfully.

Their only hope of saving the ranch was to find those horses, and so far, Jason hadn't seen even a tail hair of a horse out here.

Yet, skepticism persisted in his mind. What could four stallions do for them? Bring in about four hundred dollars... that was, if they were worth as much as Ron said they were... and that wasn't nearly enough to pay off Nicki's debt. Still, if they sold the stallions and all the cattle for top dollar they might just break even. They would have to start over from nothing, but they would be debt free. It was this thought that pushed him on.

But his luck did not change.

The sun was descending toward the western horizon when he swung down from his saddle in disgust and lifted his canteen to his mouth. Pulling the collar of his long, warm coat up around his neck, he stared off at a snow-whitened saddleback ridge on the horizon, wondering how he would explain his failure to Nicki. Her deep brown eyes, full of sorrow and uncertainty, swam before him and he rubbed a hand across his face, wishing there was something more he could do. He fixed his eyes on the horizon again, *Lord, you brought me here for a reason, didn't You? What was it? Isn't—*

He never finished the prayer. Reaching into his saddle bag for his field glasses, he trained them on the ridge in the distance. "Lord, please let that be what I think it is." This time his prayer was spoken out loud. He replaced his binoculars, mounted up, and headed in the direction of the ridge across the valley.

His horse, a good mountain-bred mustang, was used to traveling in thick snow, a fact for which Jason now found himself extremely thankful. As he made his way up into the small hills surrounding the ridge he had seen through his binoculars, the snow got deeper. The horse was jumping through drifts sometimes up to the stirrups and Jason reached down, making sure that his snowshoes were securely fastened in their lashings. It would not do to lose them now. If his horse mired down, he would need them. Coming to a windblown level plain, he stopped to let the horse catch his breath. He raised the binoculars to his eyes once more.

This time, as he lowered the binoculars and scrutinized the ridge with his bare eyes, he turned full circle, eyeing the countryside all around him and checking his back trail.

Several times in the last few days he had felt someone watching him, and had even, on one occasion, seen a rider disappear over the skyline of a knoll just as he had turned in that direction. Someone was trailing him, and he didn't like it. It wouldn't do to lead them right to what he hoped would be the salvation of Nicki's ranch.

He hadn't realized how exceptional Nicki's spread was until he had spent this time inspecting the place. None of the ranches around for miles had the excellent water access that Nicki had from her property.

The Deschutes River, the main water source for the Hanging T and any other ranches in this area, ran along the bottom of a canyon with steep sheer walls, but at some points the canyon walls seemed to lean outward, forming easy, slanted descents instead of sheer drop-offs. Nicki's land had the only easy descent to the river bottom that Jason had seen for miles, and he had taken the liberty on his first morning out of riding up and down the river for several miles in each direction.

Nicki's land also had a seasonal creek that ran with several inches of water.

Cows walked off much of their weight trying to find water. Using the narrow trails that hugged the canyon walls the cattle on the nearby ranches would lose a lot of weight just getting to and from the crystal clear Deschutes River. In the winter, some would slip to their deaths from the icy, narrow paths.

Many a man would do just about anything to have this acreage!

Jason had learned, from his years in law enforcement, that patience often saves a man's life. He was itching to search out the small crevice he had noted in the ridge just across the valley, but his instincts held him back. Why hadn't the person following him made a move against him yet? If they were friendly, they would have approached him openly. And he had only been in the area for a few days, so he had made no enemies.

Of course he couldn't rule out the possibility that an outlaw from his past—maybe someone he had helped capture—had gotten free and come after him, but he didn't think that was likely. No. This was someone who didn't want him finding information that would help Nicki. So why hadn't they simply made their attack on the first day? Unless they were under orders to wait for something.

He sat, waiting. He would have his answers sooner than later. He flexed his gloved hands, bringing first one fist to his mouth to blow on his fingers and then the next.

His horse stamped impatiently, its ears pricking in the direction of a knoll off to his right. Jason turned, scanning the hill for any signs of movement. A snow-white jack rabbit dashed down the hill, ears laid back flat against its head. That was all the proof he needed. Jason slid to the ground, pulled his snowshoes loose, and slipped them on.

He dropped the reins on the ground, knowing that his well-trained steed would not move from his spot. Shucking his rifle from its scabbard, he eased off around the lee side of the hill. There was no cover to speak of, only sagebrush and scraggly snow-dusted junipers, but his years as a lawman had trained him well in the art of keeping out of sight.

Slinking through several gullies, always being sure to stay below the skyline, Jason made his way around to the back side of the hill the jack rabbit had just descended and was not surprised to see a tall, lanky man doing a belly crawl toward the crest of the hill, a long-barreled rifle in one hand.

Jason made no immediate move. Instead, he hunkered down as best he could behind a small bush and scanned the area for any other accomplices. He saw no one.

Standing then, he cocked his rifle, the sound shattering the stillness of the evening like the first roll of thunder in a gathering storm. The man on the hill froze just a fraction of a second before Jason spoke. "Put that rifle down nice and easy."

The man carefully eased his rifle away from his body and raised his hands off the ground.

"Mister, you get to your knees real slow and clasp your hands behind your head. You and I are gonna get to know each other tonight." The steel in Jason's tone was unmistakable, and the tall, lean man moved ever so slowly to comply as Jason trudged cautiously up the hill behind him.

Pulling a strand of rawhide out of his pocket, he cinched the man's hands tightly behind his back and retrieved his weapon. Jason shoved him forward over the crest of the hill and down to the small level plain where his horse waited patiently. Pushing the shivering man to the ground, Jason set about starting a fire to warm the captive, whose clothes were soaking wet from crawling up the hill.

"Who are you?" Jason took in the man's face. He had yellow

patches under both eyes. It appeared that not too far in the past he had had two black eyes. His nose was crooked and swollen. *Black eyes from a broken nose?*

The man grunted and glared at him, trying not to shiver so noticeably.

"You got a horse?"

A jerk of his chin indicated the direction from which they had just come, but other than that there was no reply.

Motioning toward a log with his rifle, Jason used his lariat to tie the man's hands, still cinched behind his back, to a thick sturdy branch that could not be broken. The top of the short limb had a burl on it so the rope could not slip off the end. Unless his captive dragged the huge log with him as he went, he wouldn't be going anywhere.

Jason retrieved the horse and brought it back to the fire. Finding a blanket in the saddle roll he unfurled it and settled it around the stranger's frame.

The man looked a little surprised at this kindness but still didn't speak.

Instead he looked away.

Jason cocked an eyebrow. "Why are you following me?"

Another guttural sound from the disgruntled captive. He was obviously put out at having been caught so easily in his own game.

Jason grinned suddenly. "Not a talker, huh? Well, that's fine. But I have some business to take care of."

Adding another stick to the fire, Jason mounted up. "Hopefully I'll be back before you freeze to death." Spinning his horse, he trotted off in the opposite direction than he intended to go. As soon as he was out of sight he circled around and went to check out the little crevice he had noticed earlier.

Just as he had hoped, the crevice was deeper than it appeared from a distance, or even from close up to a casual observer, and it formed a little steep-sided trail that led deeper into the hills.

When Jason topped out above an expansive valley he sucked in a deep breath of awe. At one end of the valley lay a good sized pond, now ice-covered except for the end closest to a small stream that cut a snaking black strip across the snow-blanketed basin. Not even the dimming light of the setting sun glistening off the thick blanket of covering snow could conceal the heavy grasses that would be a lush green come warmer months. This sight in itself might have been enough to take his breath away, but what affected him was what the valley contained: for spread across the white expanse of the basin was a herd of wild mustangs—the most beautiful sight he'd ever seen!

Below him, where the trail he was on spilled into the valley, a rock-slide blocked the path, effectively making a huge corral out of the basin.

As he swung down, pulling his binoculars to his eyes, a stallion lifted his head, nostrils flaring in the slight breeze that descended into the valley, and gave a sharp whinny. The heads of the rest of the herd snapped to attention, the last rays of a red-gold sun glimmering off their hides. After a moment of suspended stillness, the herd began to mill about nervously. He couldn't get an exact count, but Jason guessed that there were at least two hundred head, most of them yearlings and two-year-olds. All marked with the Hanging T brand.

It was amazing to him that no one at the ranch knew about them. He considered, his eyes following the lead stallion. John must have brought those four fine-blooded broncs he had purchased and left them here in this natural corral with a herd of mares. For the past two years the herd had been left to run free and multiply. And hidden as they were back in this huge valley, which had plenty of shelter along one end where the brow of a hill jutted out to form a covered area, Jason could see how no one had known. Especially since John Trent apparently hadn't told anyone of their existence.

There had to be suspicions, however, because many people had known that John had purchased four excellent horses. That might explain why the man who had been following him hadn't made a move on him earlier. Maybe he'd been hoping that Jason knew something he, and presumably his boss, didn't.

Who had sent the man? Jason mounted back up. He wasn't likely to get that information from his uninformative captive. But the face of William Harpster sprang to mind and Jason contemplated on that. He hadn't liked William from the first moment of their meeting but he couldn't quite place his finger on why.

His thoughts turned to Nicki. He was honest enough to admit that his dislike of the man could stem from the fact that Nicki seemed to like him so much. Yet there was something deeper in it. Something rippled under William's calm exterior, and Jason didn't like it. He would keep his eye on William.

Suddenly the tawny stallion gave another piercing whistle and the herd shifted as one. Rippling muscles launched into a smooth rhythm and the herd, manes and tails flowing behind them, cantered to the far end of the valley. A mass of glistening blacks, whites, tans, browns, and reds.

Jason let out the breath he had been unwittingly holding and tipped his hat at the sky in a salute of gratefulness for God's guidance. The answer to his prayers had just arrived.

Chapter Eleven

Brenda Jeffries finished putting the warm, heavenly scented bread rolls into the basket on the kitchen sideboard, covering them carefully with an extra towel so they stayed hot. Smoothing her apron, she glanced around the small space, making sure she hadn't forgotten anything.

Rolf eased up behind her, slipping his arms around her waist. "Ya aren't gonna leave any o' those for me?" He sniffed appreciatively.

Smacking his hand playfully, Brenda stepped out of the circle of his arms and faced him. "I can't feed ya more'n you can work off in a day! If ya gain any weight, we won't be able to move around in this palace." She gestured magnanimously around the room.

Rolf laughed uproariously. Placing hands on his trim hips, he waggled his dark eyebrows. "Woman, I think yer askin' for a takin' down!"

From their place on the bed in the corner, where they had been huddled under a blanket reading a book, the children giggled, apparently excited by the knowledge of what the next moments would bring.

"Rolf," Brenda shook an authoritative finger in her husband's face, "don't you do it! You'll muss my dress and me just headin' off a-visitin'!"

"Ahhh, Bren. No one's gonna notice a few wrinkles on yer dress when they can look into eyes the likes o' yours." And with that, he lunged for her, a grin splitting his face from ear to ear.

"RoLLFFF!" Brenda's squeal of mock alarm was accompanied by the excited cheers of her traitorous offspring.

"Get her, Papa!"

"Look at Mama run!"

"Around the table, Papa! The other way! Go!"

With a final lunge, Rolf had her cornered and Brenda threw up her hands in surrender as Rolf's hands eased around her waist, settling threateningly just below her highly ticklish ribs. He cocked his head, winking at her. "Now, what were ya sayin' 'bout my weight?"

Brenda pulled an innocent face. "Did I say somethin' about yer weight, Love?"

"Yes, I believe ya did, *Love*," he mimicked with a jab to her ribs that produced a squeal.

"Oh! Wait now." She giggled, grabbing his hands and trying to move them away from her ribs. "I be rememberin' a mite." She scrunched up her face, biting her upper lip as though in deep concentration. His fingers moved toward her ribs. "Yes!" she spoke quickly before he could make contact, "I apologize, Love fer havin' offended yer manly pride."

"Mmm." He stepped nearer, his face not losing its smile, but his voice dropping to a tone that only a wife would recognize. "Well," he whispered, "mayhap I'll let ya make it up to me when ya get back from visitin'." His eyebrows pumped twice just before his lips settled over hers and Brenda heard three distinct giggles from her brood, although she knew that they couldn't have heard their father's deliberately low words.

As soon as Brenda left the house for her visit with the widow Trent, Rolf turned to his children. "All right ya passle o' rascals. I have some work I need to be finishin' in the barn, and you three have been cooped up in this house all winter long. Why don't ya come out and join me? I daresay it might be warmer out there than 'tis in here. What do you say?"

A chorus of "Yes" greeted him, and he smiled as he held the door for them to precede him.

Satisfaction slid onto William's face as he watched the little cabin through his binoculars. This was his chance. He had been waiting patiently since early that morning for the little wooden shack to empty of all its occupants so that he could begin his task, and now the opportunity was finally here.

He scanned his route of escape once more through the lenses, memorizing every twist and turn he would have to take to stay out of view. Another glance at the barn confirmed no one had come out.

He picked up the small can of kerosene and the box of matches and headed down the hill.

The squeak of saddle leather and the crunch of horse's hooves in the crisp snow of the yard brought Nicki's head up.

Diablo, the puppy, set to yapping by the door. She jumped up from the table where she had been darning a pair of Sawyer's little socks and rushed to the window, hushing the dog. She hoped Jason had finally returned. She had agreed to give him a week. And this was the afternoon of the eighth day. All day she had been watching for him to come and had finally sent Tilly home early so she wouldn't have to put up with any more of her knowing looks.

As she reached the window and rubbed a spot free of frost, she laid a hand across her chest, trying to still the racing of her heart. It wouldn't do for him to see that his tardiness had caused her concern.

But it wasn't Jason. It was Brenda Jeffries come for the visit she had promised at John's funeral.

Nicki brushed aside her disappointment. She was just excited to find out if Jason had discovered anything that would help her save the ranch, not longing to see the man himself....

Glancing at Sawyer to make sure he was still sleeping soundly, Nicki eased her way out the door, puppy at her heels, to greet her friend.

"OW!" Bobby Jeffries whirled on his sister. "PA! May just bit me!"

"May Ann Jeffries! What have your mother and I been tellin' ya 'bout bitin'?"

May hung her head, large tears forming in her blue eyes.

Eyes so much like her mother's. Rolf sighed. May tugged so at his heartstrings that he often had difficulty disciplining her like he knew he should. But this biting had gone on long enough. He cleared his throat pointedly, waiting for her reply.

She tucked a strand of straight white-blond hair behind her ear and mumbled, "No bitin'."

Rolf scratched his bearded face, reminding himself not to smile, as she turned the full force of her blue eyes on him, using her tears to full advantage.

"He took my doll, Pa!" She tossed an angry glare at Bobby. "And he wouldn't give it back!"

"No! I—" Bobby's protest fell dead at the searing expression Rolf turned on him.

Satisfied to have their full attention, Rolf looked back to his daughter. "May, I don't care what he did to ya; it's never all right to bite. Ever. You've been told this afore and now I'm tellin' ya again. No bitin'!"

Her lower lip trembled. "Yes, Pa."

"Now you need to go say sorry to your brother."

She sighed. "Yes, Pa." Feet dragging and her doll dangling by one arm, May walked over to Bobby. "I'm sorry, Bobby. I shouldn't a bit ya."

Bobby folded his arms and looked at his father.

"Go on, son."

"Fine. I forgive you. But it better not happen again!"

"Bobby!" Rolf dipped his chin, indicating his displeasure.

"Sorry," Bobby mumbled.

"Right. Now you two go on and play nicely together."

"Can we go back inside, Pa? I could read to May. An' we could wrap up in the quilt."

"Sure, just be careful that you don't get too close to the stove. And no adding any more wood until I get in there. I don't want you to get burnt."

"Yes, Pa!" Both children ran for the door, their fight immediately forgotten.

Rolf watched them in wonder, shaking his head over the ease with which children forgave. "We could all learn a lot from the forgiveness of children, John," he told his other son.

John nodded thoughtfully, watching his siblings as they raced across the yard to the house.

"Nicki, hello," Brenda greeted as she dropped from the saddle, wrapping her mount's reins around the top rail of the newly erected corral.

Diablo sniffed at the horse's hooves, shying away with ears laid low when the horse stamped one foot.

"Brenda, it's so good to see you," Nicki responded warmly, truly meaning her words.

"I'm right sorry it's taken me so long to make it over for that visit we talked about. I been meanin' to get here for a couple o' weeks now. I see you have a puppy. Bobby and May would just love to have one, but Rolf put his foot down." She chuckled, "I have to say I was pretty thankful he did. The last thing I need is one more thing to take care of."

Nicki stooped to scoop the puppy into her arms. "Yes, he was a gift to Sawyer from William." She ruffled the pup's ears roughly. "And he is a menace! We named him Diablo after he dug a hole through the wall of the soddy not once, but twice!"

"Oh, my." Brenda reached out to pet the puppy on its head. "Be ye a little devil, mite?"

Diablo glanced up at Nicki and then swiped at her cheek with a long pink tongue.

Nicki chuckled as she dodged the doggy kiss. "Trust me when I say, yes, he is. Please come on in. I'm so glad you could come."

Brenda looped her arm through the handle of her basket as the two women made their way indoors.

"My, it's so nice and warm in here," Brenda commented as Nicki set the puppy down and put water on the stove for tea. "Our house be so bloomin' cold that the young-uns huddle right around the stove all day long. I can't seem to get a thing done without steppin' on one o' them."

Nicki knew how small Brenda's place was. "I can't imagine living in a house this size with *three* children. Some days I wonder if I won't go crazy before spring gets here. And I only have one, plus a puppy." She cast a teasing glare at Diablo, who'd flopped down in front of the stove. "A very devilish puppy."

Brenda chuckled and set to pulling out her freshly baked gifts. She waved a hand in Nicki's direction as she responded, "The size don't bother me so much, but the *cold is* gettin' to me. I feel for the children. We didn't know 'twould get so cold in these parts. When we built, everybody we spoke to told us that winters here were fairly mild, so we built with that in mind and now...." She shrugged. "Well, winter's almost over and come spring first thing after we plant our crops I'm gonna hold Rolf to his promise o' soddin' the outside o' the house. Next winter we will be warm!"

Brenda's enthusiasm tugged the corners of Nicki's mouth upwards. "*Sí.* This winter has been uncharacteristically cold. I think we've all been surprised by it. Ron just told me yesterday that he hasn't seen our cattle looking this poorly since he's been working for us."

Nicki picked up her darning as they continued to talk, and the rest of the afternoon passed in pleasant conversation. Nicki relaxed for the first time in several days, temporarily forgetting her worries about the ranch and Sawyer's future.

Sawyer had long since awakened and was playing with his few toys in front of the stove when Brenda glanced out the window and gasped. "Oh my, look at how late it is. Why, it be most dark. I must hurry home, Nicki. If the poor children have to eat somethin' that Rolf cooked, I'll have a mutiny on my hands."

Nicki rose to hug her friend. "It's been so good to visit with you. I didn't notice how late it was, either. I need to get Sawyer some dinner, although," she chuckled, "you brought enough food with you to feed the whole town, so I won't have to fix much."

Brenda smiled, waving a hand, indicating it had been her pleasure, and headed for the door.

"Brenda, wait." Nicki hurried to pull a large quilt from under her bed. "I want you to have this. It isn't much, but maybe you could hang it on the wall and it would help keep the house a little warmer. I wish there was more I could do."

Tears pooled in Brenda's eyes. "Thank you," was all she choked out, but Nicki knew that a mere thanks did not accurately express what was in the woman's heart. She would feel the same if Sawyer was cold all the time, and someone had done something similar for her.

"De nada." Nicki blinked back her own tears as she hugged her friend once more. "Come again when you can."

"Ya can count on that. It's been so nice to visit with another woman."

At that moment Nicki realized just how good she had it with Tilly coming every day. She waved as she watched Brenda mount up and ride out of the yard, thankful for the woman's friendship.

William had just finished dowsing the back wall and a portion of the roof with kerosene when the door to the house squeaked on its hinges as someone entered the little cabin. He froze and suppressed a groan of aggravation as he glanced in both directions. There was no cover here. If someone should come around the side of the house there would be no place for him to hide. Yet there was nothing they would need back here and he could tell by the expanse of untouched snow that no one had been behind here since the last snow, which had been several days ago. It wasn't likely he would be found if he just stayed put.

He debated what to do. If he just did it quickly, surely whoever had entered the cabin would be able to get out. Yet with them this close, he would have less chance of escape. Everyone around these parts knew everyone else, and it wouldn't suit for him to have to explain why one of the Jeffries thought they had seen him running away from their house right before it burned to the ground.

He glanced again at his escape route. He had to run a

hundred feet before he would have any cover at all, and even then he would need to make it to the road before he would be safe, for in the snow his trail would be clearly visible. Anyone who came to the back of the house would be able to see it and follow him. And not until he got to the road, where many people and carriages passed every day and his footprints blended into the slush, would he feel safe.

Sinking down to wait for whoever was inside to go back to the barn, he sighed. It wouldn't do for him to get caught. He had come too far for that. His neck itched, and he scratched at it, trying not to imagine the prickly feel of a noose.

He sat for a long time. Standing up every now and then he paced quietly, rejuvenating circulation to his numbing extremities, his patience wearing thin.

It was getting dark when he heard a horse trot into the yard. He decided that he was tired of waiting. Maybe in the chaos of the new arrival and surprise of it all, he would be able to get away. Besides, it was almost totally dark now and that would help to hide his trail.

He struck a match, tossing it up onto the roof, and hesitated only a fraction of a second to watch as the flames licked greedily at the dry wood and kerosene. Then he vanished into the night.

Brenda pulled her horse to a stop and slid to the ground, leading it into the barn. Rolf glanced up from where he was mending a harness, and Brenda smiled. "Hello, Love."

He stood and gave her a quick kiss. "Did ya have a nice visit?"

"Wonderful."

Taking the reins from her, he led the horse into a stall.

"Where are Bobby and May?" she asked John, who sat mending a separate harness.

"May bit Bobby and they fought. Then Pa made them 'pologize. Then they got cold and wanted to go read in the house and Pa said they could, so long as they din't mess with the stove none."

Brenda turned to Rolf, who busied himself with checking her horse's hooves. "Did you spank her this time?"

Rolf looked sheepish. "It's those eyes o' hers, Bren. I can't hardly take it when she looks at me the way she does. I tell you I'm gonna have to get me a buffalo gun when the girl comes to age. The boys won't be able to keep away!"

Brenda winked at him. "Well, first we have to stop her from bitin' every boy that upsets her, or none will be wishin' to court her 'tall."

Rolf chuckled, a slow rumble that started in his chest and worked its way into a full-blown laugh. He paused, wiping his eyes, as he glanced out the barn doors toward the house. His face transformed into a mask of horror. "Dear Lord, have mercy!"

Brenda's heart seized in fear at Rolf's cry of terror.

He lurched out of the stall and sprinted toward the house. She spun around.

Dancing eerily on the snow outside was the orange-yellow glow of fire! "Lord God Almighty, help us!" She clutched at her throat, her words coming out in a choked exclamation.

"Brenda! Buckets! Water!" Rolf was already halfway across the yard before Brenda could make her feet move. But as she launched into action, her mind was frozen on one thought alone: *My little ones! Jesus! My little ones is in there!*

Rolf plunged through the door of the house. Smoke billowed out in a thick cloud, and vivid orange sparks painted streaks against the black velvet sky.

Her heart stuttered, then resumed in quadruple time. "Dear God, help him!" she prayed as she snatched up the watering buckets that hung by the door.

John tumbled out of the barn behind her, and she shoved two buckets into his hands, pushing him toward the orange reflection of the watering trough. She ran after John with her own buckets, all the while praying that Rolf would make it out of the house with May and Bobby alive.

A lifetime seemed to pass as Brenda and John filled up their buckets and raced toward the blazing house. The flames were now starting to lick at the front of the dwelling, and a sob caught in Brenda's throat. There would be no saving the house. But the house was the least of her worries.

Bobby stumbled out the door, and Brenda cried out in relief. Dropping her buckets she ran and clutched him to her chest in a fierce hug. "Be ye okay, son?"

He nodded, his breaths coming in ragged gulps. "I tried to get her, Ma. She fell asleep while I was readin' to her, and I couldn't lift her." Tears marked white trails through the grime covering his face.

"Hush, now. Papa's gonna get her. He'll be out any second now." Her eyes remained fixed on the door, as she prayed her words would not be a lie. "Dear God, Dear God, Dear God..."

John threw his water on the roof and headed back for more. Still the door remained empty. The house was fully engulfed in flames. What mattered now was to see Rolf and May coming out the door. But it had been too long. She lifted her face to the heavens. "Oh God!" The cry was a guttural scream.

Rolf stumbled out of the house with May clutched to his chest. May's arms flopped limply behind her, and something in Rolf's expression chilled Brenda to the core. He staggered a few more steps, then sank down onto his knees. "Forget the house!" His voice was hoarse. "Help me with her."

Brenda knelt down at May's head, feeling more than seeing that the boys were huddled over them. Her heart hammered in her throat. Her hands fluttered helplessly around the still form of her child. What should she do? "Jesus! Jesus!" She couldn't decide where to settle her hands.

"May, honey! MAY!" Rolf's voice was terror-edged. There was no response from the little, pale, limp form. He pressed his cheek close to her mouth. "She's not breathin'!"

"May," Brenda pleaded, pressing down panicked sobs, "wake up, honey. We need you to wake up!" Her hands fluttered helplessly to a stop, cupped around the little blond head. What should she do? "John, there be a blanket. The saddle roll." She gestured toward the barn. "Get it. Quick!"

"May! May, honey. It's Papa. Can ya hear me, darlin'?" Rolf shook May's unresponsive shoulder. Her head flopped over to one side, and even in the macabre glow of the shimmering flames, Brenda could see her face was ashen gray.

She gasped and sat back onto the cold ground. "Oh God, dear God. No! Not my May. Please, Lord don't take her from me now. Jesus! Jesus!" Brenda clutched her head and rocked back and forth, silent sobs shaking her body.

The flames crackled hungrily, devouring the remaining walls of the little shanty in a final spray of orange sparks.

"Dear Jesus! What have I done?" Rolf lifted his face to the sky. His shoulders heaved, but he made no sound. Hands clasped behind his neck, he rocked forward and let his head fall gently on May's little chest. But quickly he lifted his head, again patting her face and shaking her unresponsive shoulder.

Helpless anguish flooded Brenda's soul as she watched, one hand pressed over her mouth.

John returned with the blanket and, through the haze of slow motion around her, Brenda noticed things she would never forget as long as she took breath.

Rolf finally giving up his useless attempts to revive her baby. The way John's chin shook as though with palsy as he meticulously laid out the blanket and gently lifted May's lifeless little body onto it. The way Bobby sat, forearms resting on his knees, staring blankly at the engulfing flames, silent tears coursing down cheeks that reflected the flickering, golden-orange horror. Rolf on his knees, face buried in his lap, his shoulders heaving with wracking sobs, but making no sound whatsoever. And May. Her sunshine in winter. Blue eyes closed forever, face ashen gray, lying unmoving on the brightly colored quilt, the breeze gently lifting her white-blond hair as the raging flames danced eerily on the snow all around them.

Brenda turned and retched onto the snow. She would never forget that, either. The terrible, gut-wrenching pain that engulfed her. Pulling, tearing, and ripping at her heart.

★

Chapter Twelve

The scent of smoke alerted him first. Jason raised his nose, testing the air, and frowned. This was not just the smoke from a cookfire. It was too acrid, and there was too much of it. He turned to face the wind and began to follow his nose, leading his prisoner's horse behind. It wasn't long until he could see an orange glow tinting the night sky and he stopped, quickly lashing his prisoner to a tree far enough back from the fire that if the brush caught flame, he would be able to make it around and rescue him. After securing the man's horse, he mounted back up and hurried forward.

Something crashed through the brush in the darkness to his right and his horse shied, snorting and pawing. Jason pulled up for a moment, listening, but heard nothing but the angry cursing of his captive. Attributing the sound to a rattled buck racing to escape the fearful scent of the fire, he turned and moved on toward the glow.

Coming out of a small stand of evergreens, Jason took in the scene at a glance and urged his mount into a gallop. A hundred yards ahead of him flames engulfed a cabin and as far as he could see, there was no one fighting it. They might all be trapped inside!

He wracked his brain, trying to remember from his conversations with Ron who might live here.

He pulled his horse to a skidding halt in the yard, but even as he started to slide to the ground, he could see the reason no one was fighting the fire. A family clustered around the still form of a child. *Dear Jesus, give them comfort*. The prayer came to mind even as he launched into action, picking up the buckets scattered in the yard and running for the trough he could see by the barn.

He had made two trips from the trough to the cabin before any of the family seemed to notice him. The older boy joined him at the trough, filling up two buckets of his own and heading for the house. His movements were stilted, and Jason knew from experience that he was acting mechanically. His mind was somewhere else, but he felt the need to be doing something.

They were fighting a losing battle. Jason could see that, but he knew that the boy needed to keep his mind occupied for a while longer, so he continued on with his rhythm, moving from trough to cabin and back again, the boy following his lead.

It was well after midnight when they poured the last bucket on the smoldered ruins of the clapboard cabin. They had long since emptied the trough and had been pumping water from the well. Jason stepped back, wiping the perspiration from his forehead. The boy's mother and father had not moved from their places in the snow and Jason knew that he had to get them up and moved to someplace warm. The temperature had dropped quickly after the sun went down, and both of them were shivering visibly, although neither seemed to notice.

The younger boy had finally gotten up and ever so carefully folded the blanket over his sister's body, tucking it around her as though to keep her warm. He had then set to work helping Jason and his older brother douse the fire, tears still streaming quietly down his cheeks. He wasn't strong enough to carry more than half a bucket at a time, but Jason could see the determination on his face and understood his need to help put out the fire.

The looks on the young boys' faces took Jason back in time. There was no fire in his memories and the corpse was that of his mother, not his sister, but the similarities were there. He wanted to pull the boys into a comforting embrace but knew that comfort from a stranger was not what they needed now. They needed their parents.

He approached the couple, who sat lifelessly staring into nothingness all around them. Hat twisting in his hands, he spoke. "Sir, ma'am, my name is Jason Jordan. I work for the Widow Trent just down the way a spell. I'll take you and the boys to her place where you will at least be warm. From there you can make the decisions you'll need to be making in the coming days.

I'm..." He struggled for the right words to convey his sympathy to them. "I'm so sorry." It didn't express the depths of his feelings, but what else was there to say?

Neither spoke for a moment, but then the woman's eyes darted to the blanket. "We can't just leave her here."

Her words were so low Jason almost missed them, but he reassured her quickly, "No, ma'am. We won't leave her here. If you'll just come with me, I've sent your boys in to hitch up the wagon."

The father didn't say anything but stood to his feet, helping his wife up. Then he shuffled toward the barn, with a final glance over his shoulder at the smoldering heap of charred rubble. The mother stood unmoving, her eyes on her husband's back, an unfathomable pain etched into her face.

Jason left the yard and headed back to where he had left his captive.

Gone! He glanced hurriedly around but knew there was no way of finding the man in the dark. On closer inspection Jason could see scarring on the bark where he had lashed the man's hands to the trunk, but there was something else as well. There was a thin vertical mark from a knife being inserted under the ropes. His prisoner had been cut free.

He stood for a moment debating what to do. It was too dark to track the man and whoever had rescued him now. He would have to come back tomorrow and see what he could find. He didn't like the fact that the man was gone, for he definitely had some questions that he wanted answers to, but there was nothing he could do about it. He would simply have to wait.

Mounting up, he headed for the ranch, hoping he wasn't destroying any of the tracks he would need to follow on the morrow.

When they reached Nicki's ranch, the sky was just beginning to lighten.

Jason saw to it that the family was ensconced in the shelter of the bunkhouse. He instructed Conner to put more wood on the fire and put on some coffee. Then, after quickly changing out of his soiled shirt, he headed for the house to give Nicki the sad news of the neighboring family's tragedy and see about moving them to the soddy, which would be much warmer.

Ron stepped out the door after him and asked, "Jason? What happened?"

Jason shrugged. "I smelled smoke and followed it. They were all just sitting there." His voice cracked. He cleared his throat. "In a circle around the little girl. I stayed. Put out the fire just to have something to do. It was already too late when I got there. Looked like it was set on purpose. Who are they?"

"The Jeffries." Ron shook his head. "Why would someone want to set their place on fire? They just had their homestead. A hundred and sixty acres. That's it. A hundred and sixty. You sure it looked like arson?"

Jason nodded, trying to stretch the kink out of his neck. "Not only arson. Murder."

The sky gleamed with the first stages of pale morning light when Nicki awoke. She glanced frantically around for her bucket, realizing even as she did so that she had forgotten to put it by her bed the night before.

Her long nightgown momentarily tangled up her feet and, throwing back the covers, she almost tripped over Diablo as she hurried out the door. Her bare feet stung painfully as she rushed through the snow to the edge of the creek but she paid no heed, the queasiness in her stomach taking momentary precedence. She fell to her knees and held her hair out of her face with one hand as she lost the contents of her stomach.

"Lord," she groaned the prayer in Spanish, "why can't I seem to kick this flu? I am going to need all my strength to travel with Sawyer to California and find Mama and Papa." On the heels of this prayer came the realization that she had no faith that Jason was going to be able to save her ranch...or that he was even coming back. Her heart sank. Much as she wanted to stay here, she knew that was an impossible hope.

Her stomach momentarily settled, she moved up-current a little ways and scooped a handful of the icy water to rinse her mouth and wash her face. A thought seeped into her consciousness. Her head jerked up, and she stared at the far bank. *What if I'm not sick?* She braced her hands on her knees and shook her head. *I didn't have one day of sickness, carrying Sawyer.*

She sat still in concentrated thought. It couldn't be. She mentally calculated. Her shoulders slumped. She did the math again. Yes. It could.

I can't do this, Lord. Not without support. She suddenly felt helplessly inadequate and underqualified. The pink sunrise glinted off the snowbank across the creek as she knelt, staring at nothing in particular.

"Yea, though I walk through the valley of the shadow of death, I will fear no evil; for You are with me; Your rod and Your staff they comfort me."

The verse came to her as though whispered on the gentle wind that had begun to blow.

Bowing her head, she gave her burden to her loving, Heavenly Father. *Father, You have never yet let me down. I don't understand why You let some things happen, but I know that You always work things out for the good of those who love You. Help me through this, Lord. I'm scared. I was daunted by the thought of having to raise one child alone, but now two? Thank You for Your promise to be there for me. Help me to keep my eyes on You, Lord.*

When her prayer ended she felt lighter. Somehow she knew she would make it through with God's help.

Suddenly she felt stinging pain from the freezing snow on her bare feet and knees and pushed herself up, spinning to rush back into the house. She collided with the firm, solid chest of a man. A terrified squeak escaped her mouth. She had not heard him approach because of the rushing creek, and it took her a moment to realize who he was in the pale morning light.

Jason took her gently by the upper arms and set her back away from him just enough so he could look down at her. Her hands rested against his chest as she studied his face. At the concerned look in his eyes, she swallowed, willing the desire curling through her to ease. His week-long growth of beard only added to his rugged good looks. His warm hands on her arms sent little streaks of fiery heat across her shoulders and up her neck into her hairline.

"Do you have to always sneak up on me?" She tossed the words in his face, her anger stemming more from her physical reaction to him than anything else. He blinked at her, and her tone gentled a little as she hastened, "You were supposed to be here the day before yesterday." As soon as the words left her mouth, she regretted them. It wouldn't do to have him thinking she had missed him.

But seeming to ignore her comment, he angled a glance to where she had been kneeling in the snow, then looked deeply into her face with a worried frown. "Are you all right?"

Under her long, floor-length nightgown Nicki began a little dance, picking up first one foot and then another, attempting to warm her now aching toes. "I'm just fine."

But her teeth chattered, causing him to step back and look down the length of her, his eyes widening in alarm. "You don't have any shoes on, do you?"

She started to answer, but all that came out was a startled gasp, for before she could form a reply, he had her scooped up into his arms and was heading for the house.

As soon as her feet were solidly on the floor, she stepped away from his unsettling touch. "What were you doing out there so early?" she snapped. Even she recognized the irritation in her voice. *Este hombre! This man! He doesn't show up for days, and then he sneaks up on me at first light! I have a right to be cranky.* Moving to the lamp, she held a match to the wick, her hands trembling with chill.

Jason pulled a warm shawl from a hook above the bed. Easing her into a chair at the table, he handed it to her. "I just got back about fifteen minutes ago. I was headed to the house to talk to you when I saw you run out and head for the creek."

He glanced at Diablo, who had stood to his overly large feet and was stretching, his hindquarters poking up in the air, his front paws pushed out before him. "Where did you get the pup? He's cute."

"William gave him to Sawyer when he came back from Portland."

Jason's mouth pressed into a thin line as he set about searching for coffee ingredients. "You're still not feeling well? How long has this been going on?"

Nicki didn't reply. His tone alerted her to the fact that something was wrong. The shawl now wrapped around her shoulders, she brushed a stray curl of hair out of her eyes and simply watched him.

When she didn't speak, he gave her a searching look. "How long?"

Still she made no reply. She tore her gaze from his and fussed with the shawl. Somehow she knew that if she told him she'd been sick since John's funeral, he would overreact. And she certainly couldn't just out and tell him the truth about her condition. It wasn't seemly.

She grew more annoyed as she felt herself blush at the mere thought. Why did her emotions always betray her whenever this man was present?

She tossed him a glance to see if he had noticed, and his upraised eyebrow told her he had. Turning back to the stove, he put the pot on to boil. Then, coming to stand before her, he planted himself like a grizzly bear guarding its den, his head just brushing the ceiling. He fixed her with a steely blue gaze and repeated, "How long?"

She knew he wasn't going to budge until she answered. "I'm not sick." She skewered him with a glare. "And while we're interrogating people, what are you hiding from me?"

He snorted, ignoring her question. "I just saw you lose last night's dinner in the creek. You were so sick that you didn't even bother to put shoes on before you ran outside." A sudden pained look crossed his face and he squatted down before her, resting his hands on her knees and looking directly into her face. "Nicki, are you all right?" It was the first time he had called her by her name and she liked it. Too much.

The touch of his hands sent her reeling, and she stood quickly to her feet, almost knocking Jason over backwards. But he was quick to recover. Standing, up, he folded his arms over the broad expanse of his chest and gave her a look that told her he wasn't going anywhere until she explained.

She tried to smile, tried to reassure him. But her senses were swaying, and she couldn't remember any English. Her heart couldn't take the pulse-quickening scrutiny anymore. Looking away, she squeezed the words out of her tightened throat in a whisper. "*Sí. Estoy bien.*"

Suddenly she realized how much it meant to her that he would worry about her. *When was the last time someone showed this much concern for me? Not since Mama.* It wasn't only his physical looks that attracted her to this man. It was his heart. He had come here to help her without even knowing her. He stayed even when it was obvious there was danger in doing so. He had insisted there would be a way even when she had been ready to give up. And now he was worried about her. Turning back, she looked into his anxious face once more.

God had sent Jason here to help her at just the right time. Thankfulness washed over Nicki. And along with the thankfulness came a desire stronger than any she had ever felt. She wanted to lose herself in the strength of his arms. To tell him all that was on her mind and let him advise her on what she should do.

Jason cocked an eyebrow, not having understood her words.

Momentarily giving in to her heart, Nicki leaned toward him, resting a hand on his cheek. "I am fine. Stop worrying about me."

He looked deeply into her eyes, as though trying to assure himself that she spoke the truth, his bristly jaw tensing under the gentle pressure of her palm. She let her hand drop, but Jason caught it in the warmth of his own and Nicki's body trembled with the fervency of the emotions rushing through her.

Jason's gaze dropped to her mouth, and Nicki's eyes widened

at the blatant desire she saw reflected in their depths. Sucking in a short breath, she stepped back quickly, looking down, but he did not release her hand. Nicki knew she was on dangerous ground. She didn't know if she would have the emotional fortitude to resist him. Or even if she *wanted* to. His thumb trailed a hot path across the back of her hand, and her eyes shot up to his. His voice was thick as he asked, "Why do I get the feeling that you're not telling me everything?"

"I am not sick, *Señor*." She deliberately inserted the formality to remind him, and *herself* of their relationship and tipped her head, eyes still on his face, as she gently tried to extract her hand from his.

But he tightened his grip, a slow grin starting in his eyes, then spreading to the corners of his mouth. He spoke in a whisper. "You are a stubborn woman, Mrs. Trent."

She smiled slightly and responded in the same low voice, "Somehow I don't think I am the only stubborn one in this room, *Señor*."

"Jason," he reminded softly. Reaching out with his free hand, he tucked a curl behind her ear, his thumb tarrying on her cheekbone.

As his thumb traced a searing course from her cheek downward and then gently trailed across her mouth, she swallowed convulsively, unable to form his name on her lips and correct her deliberate mistake. The heat she could see blazing in his eyes rendered her speechless, churning her insides like fresh skimmed cream.

The coffee pot boiled over, hissing and sputtering. Jason flashed an irritated look at the stove and slowly pulled away from her, leaving her suddenly cold again. Taking the pot off the stove, Jason set it down heavily and leaned his fists onto her little table, hunching into his shoulders as though the weight of the world rested there.

She pulled the shawl tighter and waited for him to speak. Something was troubling him.

"I have some bad news." He looked up at her with pain-filled eyes. So…he was going to tell her there was no way to save the ranch.

"The Jeffries' cabin burnt down last night."

Nicki's heart plummeted as she sucked in a gasp.

"That's not the worst of it. The little girl was...she was in the house and didn't make it."

Jesus, Jesus, Jesus! The prayer filled her mind even as she sat heavily at the table.

"Brenda was just here last night." Tears coursed down her cheeks. "They must come here. I will make room for them. Will you go get them? Bring them here? Dear God. Brenda...how did it happen?"

"They're here already, out in the bunkhouse. I was coming to tell you when..." He gestured to the creek outside and Nicki understood. If she were, in fact, sick it wouldn't be good for the Jeffries to stay here.

"I'm not sick, Jason." He glanced at her sharply and she looked away. "Not in the way you think. The Jeffries will be fine here. Please show them in."

"Nicki—"

Suddenly Sawyer sat up with a whimper. "Mama?" The word turned into a sob as he saw that she was not in the bed with him where she usually was when he awoke. "Mama!"

Nicki was already moving before the second cry had even formed on his lips. "I'm right here, honey. *¿Cómo estas tú?*" She picked the boy up, cuddling him to her chest.

Sawyer didn't answer her question but merely let out a contented little sigh as he laid his head on her shoulder and nestled closer to her, already back to sleep.

Nicki met Jason's eyes above the baby's head. "Just give me a moment and then send them in." She nodded to reassure him that he had done the right thing in bringing the Jeffries here.

Pushing his hat back on his head he moved out into the dawning day.

Sighing, she laid Sawyer back in the bed and quickly dressed, praying that she would have the words of comfort she needed for this family of friends.

★

Chapter Thirteen

The untouched coffee in the cups Nicki had poured for Brenda and Rolfe wasn't even cold yet when horses thundered into the yard and Diablo started barking.

It was William.

Nicki moved to greet him, but he was already rushing toward the house. "Nicki! I was out riding early this morning when I smelled smoke and went to investigate. That couple that lived just a few miles down the road, their house is gone! Burnt to the ground! Have you—" He cut off as he stepped into the house and saw Brenda leaning dejectedly against the kitchen table. "Oh good, you're here. When I couldn't find anyone around the place, I feared the worst." Silence filled the room. "You...is...is everyone alright?"

Nicki placed a hand on William's arm, touched by his concern for these people he barely knew. "William."

There was a note of warning in her voice as she turned him back toward the door, but he didn't seem to notice. "Everyone's all right, aren't they?"

"William." Nicki's voice brought his eyes to her face and she nodded toward the door.

Outside, away from the family, she drew a shaky breath and spoke. "The Jeffries had a little girl, William. She was eight. And she was killed in the fire last night."

William blanched and took a stumbling step backwards. "Dear God!"

Nicki grasped his arm to steady him.

"Dear Jesus!" His eyes glazed, and he stared at the door to the soddy, horror etched into his face.

He's praying? Maybe he does know the Lord, after all. What a kind man to be so affected by the news of their loss.

"I'll get you some coffee." She ducked back into the house. When she re-emerged, William was trembling from head to toe and staring vacantly across the yard.

Jason approached. He had been to the bunkhouse for a shave, she noted. "Everything all right?" Concern edged his voice as he eyed William.

"I was just telling William about the Jeffries' loss." She pressed the hot cup into William's hands.

Jason eyed the man, taking in the ashen color of his face and then looked at Nicki. "How are they? Did you get them to eat anything yet?"

Nicki shook her head. "They are still in shock."

He nodded, prodding the snow with the toe of his boot. "Find out where they want to bury her, and Conner and I will dig the grave."

She nodded, resting a hand momentarily on his arm before she headed back into the house.

Nicki tried to ease Brenda's sorrow the only way she knew how, with an embrace accompanied by prayer. Tears stung her eyes. This was exactly the way May had comforted her only weeks ago after John's death. Brenda's trembling lessened as she leaned into Nicki's embrace, and for that Nicki was thankful.

They had buried little May earlier. It had taken Jason, Ron, and Conner all day to dig the grave in the frozen soil. She had stood arm in arm with Brenda while Ron had said the words. And when they had lowered May into the hole, Nicki had felt the tremor that raced through Brenda's arm.

Now they were all back in the soddy, and there was no room to move.

Tilly had come and volunteered to take Sawyer home with her for a couple of days, which Nicki was deeply thankful for. But all the rest of them were crowded into the warmth of the little house. Conner and Ron leaned against the wall in the kitchen area. Rolf, William, and Jason were seated at the table, and the boys sat bleary-eyed on the bed in the corner, Diablo curled up between them.

Nicki had been supporting Brenda's weight for a good half-hour and was beginning to feel the strain in her lower back. She shifted her feet.

Jason must have noticed, for he suddenly stood. "Mrs. Jeffries," his voice was soft, "you've been standing for a mighty long time. Why don't you come sit for a spell?"

Brenda moved out of Nicki's embrace, woodenly taking the chair Jason offered her, and Nicki took a couple of steps, trying to work some of the kinks out of her back. It took every ounce of her willpower not to rub the small of her back. Yet she would have stood there for the rest of the night if Brenda had needed her to.

Jason poured Brenda a steaming cup of coffee, and Nicki was pleased to see that Brenda sipped it without seeming to notice.

Silence hung heavy in the room. Nicki had just started to tuck in Bobby, who had fallen asleep on the bed, when William's angry voice broke the stillness.

"Jordan, where were you last night when this fire started?"

Jason, who was just refilling his own cup of coffee, stopped mid-pour, blinking at William.

Nicki gasped and stood erect. "William! What are you saying?"

Every eye in the room suddenly fixed on Jason.

"I'm saying Jordan, here, only rode into town at the first of last week! I want to know where this stranger was when the house of one of our own burnt to the ground, killing their little girl. I took a good look at that house after the funeral today. The back of the place burnt hotter than the front, and we all know what that means. That fire was set."

Nicki swallowed. Could Jason have done such a thing? He *had* told her that before he came to the Lord, he'd attempted to kill a man. How much did she really know about him, anyway?

"How 'bout it, Jordan?" William snarled. "Care to tell us where you were?"

Jason quietly set the coffee pot back on the stove, his thoughts racing with the speed of a wild stallion. His gaze automatically sought out Nicki's, and air left his lungs at the doubt and confusion he saw on her face. He could almost hear the thoughts running through her mind. He *had* been gone longer than their agreed amount of time. He hadn't said a word to her about the horses since he'd gotten back; there hadn't been time. By her expression, she was wondering how well she really knew him. After all, William had been her friend and closest neighbor for the past three years, not to mention the fact that the man had been courting her since the death of her husband.

He turned from her bewildered face and looked at William, angry with himself for underestimating the man.

He had taken a look around the Jeffries' place for himself after the funeral this afternoon and what he had seen had chilled him.

A single set of tracks led away from the back of the cabin and directly into the brush he had traveled through the night before on his way to the fire. Could the sound he had heard in the brush and attributed to a scared animal have been the arsonist himself? The tracks had led him to the tree where he had tied his captive the night before, so whoever had set the fire had also loosed his prisoner. Had it been William? But why would William want to burn down the Jeffries' cabin? It didn't make sense unless—

"Jason?" Nicki interrupted his thoughts.

He turned his eyes back to her, taking a sip of his coffee and trying to remain calm. He wanted to reassure her, to tell her about the herd of horses that was going to save her ranch. But he knew he couldn't do that in front of William. He knew beyond a shadow of a doubt that the man could not be trusted.

"He come an' helped us," Brenda spoke up. "He come and put out the fire."

William snorted. "How *convenient* that he just happened to be in that area at the right time!"

Jason made no reply, knowing that anything he said in this atmosphere would only sound like a lie.

"Ron," William spoke again, "did you smell any smoke from where you were working?"

Ron's lips thinned as though he didn't like being roped into William's accusations. He glanced at Jason for a moment but finally shook his head no.

"Conner?"

"No." Conner's answer was also reluctant.

"Yet Jordan here, who works the same spread as both of you, just happened to smell the smoke and run to the rescue. Isn't that nice?" William's meaning was clear.

Rolf and Brenda stared at him, questions in their eyes.

"I didn't start that fire," Jason said. The words sounded empty even in his own ears.

William turned to Rolf. "Do you know this man from somewhere, Mr. Jeffries? Does he have some reason to want to hurt you or your family?"

Rolf studied him, then shook his head. "I don't...I don't think so."

Suddenly, there was the sound of horses in the yard outside. William smiled faintly, and Jason had the feeling that a noose was being tightened around his neck. "I sent one of my men into Farewell Bend for the sheriff. I believe he's had a look around the Jeffries' place. That must be him. Why don't we all go out and see what he has to say?"

Jason swallowed. Whatever the sheriff had to say, he had a feeling it wouldn't be good.

Ron's head was reeling as he headed out the door. Could he have misjudged the man so badly? He had liked Jason the moment he laid eyes on him. Had he really set that fire? On the other hand, William Harpster had always made the hair on the back of Ron's neck stand up like a dog on alert, and Ron would be the first to admit that the man generally put him in a fighting mood. But would he stoop so low as to accuse someone of arson and murder without proof?

The memory of what Jason had said just after he came back with the Jeffries flashed through Ron's mind. *"Not only arson. Murder."* Jason's face had been troubled. Had he meant to set the fire but not to kill the little girl?

Ron glanced at Jason again. The man seemed calm enough. Maybe too calm. He stood now with his thumbs casually hooked in his belt loops, waiting to see what the sheriff would have to say. Ron wondered what would be forthcoming.

Sheriff Dan Watts was an older man with a drooping walrus mustache that hung down on either side of his mouth below his chin. He had the habit of twisting the ends with his thumb and forefinger as he talked, and he was doing that even now.

The sheriff addressed Rolf and Brenda, "Sir, ma'am. I'm right sorry to hear 'bout yer place and yer girl."

Rolf and Brenda nodded.

"Been out to yer place. Seems that there fire was set a-purpose. Know anyone who'd want to do y'all harm?"

Both shook their heads.

"Could smell kerosene distinct-like on a patch of snow just behind the cabin. None o' yer kids would have been playing with the lamp, would they?"

Brenda looked at Rolf. Rolf looked at Bobby.

"I weren't, Pa! I was readin' to May, and she fell asleep. Then the back wall started on fire. I never touched the lamp."

Rolf's voice cracked. "When I found May she was...sleeping on the bed in the house. I can't say for sure, but I think the lamp was still on the table where we kept it."

Sheriff Watts gave his mustache several more twists. "Figured as much. Anybody recognize this?" He held aloft a button.

Ron watched Jason's face but couldn't tell what he was feeling when he spoke. "That looks like it came off my shirt. It's in the bunkhouse. I'll go get it."

The sheriff watched him take several steps before he nodded

at Ron to follow him and turned toward the Jeffries to ask some more questions.

Jason heard Ron enter the bunkhouse behind him, but he did not turn around. He was still holding the shirt he had changed out of that morning. Someone had splashed kerosene on it. He knew it hadn't smelled like this when he rode in earlier.

"Ron, I'm in trouble, and I'm going to need your help." He swiveled and fixed his gaze on the older man as he made the impulsive decision to trust him with his life.

Ron blinked and rested his hands on narrow hips. "Son?"

"We've got about two minutes before that crew out there comes busting in here, wondering what's going on. I need you to listen carefully, but first I need to know if you believe me when I say that I did not start that fire."

Ron stroked one hand down his wrinkled cheek in thought, but it didn't take him more than a second to reply. "I reckon I do, son. I reckon I do."

"Fine. Remember those horses you told me about? Well, I found them. And a whole lot more than just four of them. He must have left those stallions in that valley with a herd of at least fifty brood mares. There are at least two hundred horses in there."

Ron let out a low whistle.

"Ron, I don't know who set that fire last night, but it looks like someone wants me to take the fall for it. Smell this." He handed the shirt to Ron, who promptly lifted it to his nose.

"Kerosene."

Jason nodded, then grimaced at the doubt that leapt into Ron's gray eyes. "Think back. You talked to me right after I came in with them. Did you smell even a whiff of kerosene? Why would I set the fire and then go back to help them? I was at least a quarter of a mile from that cabin about the time the fire must have been set."

"I believe you, son." Ron sniffed the shirt again with a frown. "But you're in a heap o' trouble. What are we gonna do?"

"First, don't mention a thing about those horses. Someone

was following me out there. I was bringing him back here to get some answers out of him when I came on the fire. Something crashed through the brush, and I thought it was just a scared animal, but it wasn't. After the funeral today, I went down to have a look around. There were footprints. I missed whoever set the fire by a couple of yards in the dark. And whoever it was set my captive free. I followed his tracks to where I had tied him up and could see the mark where someone had cut the ropes."

"Your guy have a name?"

Jason shook his head. "He wouldn't talk. Tall. Real skinny. Dark hair. Droopy mustache. Looked like he might have recently broken his nose. Sound familiar?"

"Could be Slim. He works for William. Conner said he thought he mighta broke the nose o' whoever attacked us last week." Ron's tone held a note of something Jason couldn't quite put his finger on. Was Ron doubting that William would have him followed? Or was he beginning to have questions of his own about Nicki's neighbor?

There was a commotion outside. Jason could hear the crunch of footsteps and knew he was running out of time.

He lowered his voice. "I want you to send a wire. Rocky Jordan. Deputy Sheriff in Shilo, Oregon. Tell him everything. Tell him to bring Cade." Jason fleetingly wished he could send for Sky, but Brooke was due to have her baby any time now, and Rocky was just as capable. He had never been more thankful for the strong bonds their family shared. "And get to those horses, Ron. Southwest corner. I brushed my trail, but if they have a good tracker they may have already followed it. You'll have to hurry."

Sheriff Watts stepped through the door and swung his eyes from Ron to Jason and back again. He gave his mustache a twist. "Ya find yer shirt?"

Ron handed it to him.

The sheriff's nose twitched, and he cast Jason a glance before examining the buttons. Jason hadn't even bothered to look at the buttons; he knew one would be missing. Whether he had lost it last night while fighting the blaze or whether someone had ripped it off and planted it by the cabin was immaterial, though the latter was probably the case. With the kerosene smell on that shirt, he knew he would be spending at least one night in jail. Probably more.

The sheriff found the missing button and then held up the one in his hand to make sure it matched the others on the shirt. Jason would give him credit for the fact that he appeared to be checking out all the evidence and not just trying to haul someone in for the crime.

Watts' face was grim when he spoke. "Jordan, I'm afeard yer gonna have ta come with me."

Jason thought of something. "Sheriff, I went and had a look around that cabin myself after the funeral today. There was a set of footprints there that don't belong to me. They led directly into the brush behind the house. Someone else was there besides me."

"Well, now, ain't it just amazin' that from the time ya was there to the time I got there those footprints just disappeared? I been out there myself, Jordan, and the only set o' tracks I seen were yours."

William, who had stepped into the room behind the sheriff, spoke up. "I'd have to concur, Sheriff. I went down there after the funeral myself and the only tracks that were there were Jordan's. He's just trying to think fast and save his hide."

Jason cast a look at Ron. *Get going.*

Ron gave an imperceptible nod, then eased himself out the door.

Jason could only hope he was heading out after those horses. If they didn't get to them before the others, Nicki's hope of saving this ranch was gone forever.

The sheriff spun Jason around and roughly tied his hands behind his back. As he was pushed out the door of the bunkhouse into the swirling snow that had begun to fall, he experienced a moment of satisfaction as he saw Ron and Conner disappearing over the crest of the hill. Good. *Dear God, let them be on time.*

The sheriff left Jason standing and walked over to saddle up his horse which was in the round corral.

Nicki looked at him, her large, dark eyes fixed directly on his face. Jason's eyes never left hers as he rubbed his cheek against his shoulder. He wished he had the words to convince her that he hadn't done this terrible thing. He wanted to assure her that everything was going to be fine; that he would be back to take care of everything as soon as he could.

But he had no assurances to offer her. Murder was a hanging offense, and unless Rocky was able to find something that would clear him, he probably wouldn't set foot on Hanging T soil again. Ever. He swallowed the lump that formed in his throat at the thought. His only consolation was the fact that if Ron and Conner got to the horses on time, Nicki's ranch would at least be saved.

His gaze flickered to Mr. and Mrs. Jeffries. They stood just outside the entrance to the soddy, seemingly oblivious to the swirling snow, Rolf's arms around Brenda's shoulders. Jason felt his heart grip with compassion for them. What would it be like to have your little girl healthy and happy one day and gone the next?

His thoughts turned to prayer. He had no other recourse. *God, help them. Help us find out who really did this and bring them to justice. Be with Nicki. Keep her safe. And Lord, if you could work it out, could you please get me out of this situation? Bring Rocky quickly and guide him in the right direction once he gets here. Help him know what needs to be done.*

He turned his face back to Nicki, and she came and stood before him, looking up into his face with compassionate, questioning eyes.

"Ma'am." He cleared his throat. The word was too formal in light of the emotions pumping through his heart. He traded it for her name. "Nicki, I didn't do this. I need you to trust me."

She searched his face before she asked, "Where were you, Jason? Where were you when that fire started?"

He licked his lips, debating what he could tell her. Could she be trusted to keep the information about the horses from William? At this point Jason didn't know for sure how the man was involved in this situation, but he had learned long ago to listen to his instincts. And every instinct he had screamed foul whenever that man was around.

He tossed a glance at William and noted that he was striding toward them from where he had been by Sheriff Watts near the corral. Jason made his decision. Stepping closer to her and lowering his voice, he said, "I don't have time to tell you everything right now. Talk to Ron. And please don't trust William with any information. I can't prove it yet, but I think he is somehow involved in all of this."

It was the wrong thing to say. What had been compassion on her face hardened into granite distrust.

He sighed, wishing he hadn't told her quite so much about his past.

"Nicki—"

There was no time to say more. William was suddenly by her side, his hand resting protectively on the back of her neck, his hard gaze fastened on Jason's face.

Jason stepped back, still watching her face, pleading silently with her to believe him. Trust him.

Anger sparking in her dark eyes, she deliberately took a step closer to William. Jason felt the air vacate his lungs, as though a steer had just kicked him in the brisket. Her message was clear. She believed William.

William's eyes glinted in triumph as he slid his arm gently around Nicki's shoulders, pulling her even closer to his side.

Jason looked down at the ground, working to compress his anger. His jaw clenched as he fought the urge to hurl himself at the man. There was nothing he could do while his hands were tied behind his back.

He turned the full force of his gaze back on Nicki, praying that she would open her eyes to the truth before it was too late. Hoping she would change her mind even now. But she lifted her chin defiantly, daring him to challenge her decision.

Sheriff Watts took his arm and directed him over to his mount. Jason did not look her way again as he was led out of the yard. It was too painful. He was more than a little perturbed with her constantly taking up for William. Couldn't she see the kind of man he was?

As for seeing her in William's arms, well, that brought about another unpleasant emotion all together. One he wasn't yet ready to face.

William felt his satisfaction rise as Jason was led away by Sheriff Watts. It looked like his spontaneous plan was coming together better than he'd thought. How lucky it was for him that Jason had stumbled onto that fire and stopped to help. His presence there had raised just the right amount of suspicion.

He regretted the death of the little girl, but he couldn't have planned Jason's demise any better if he'd had all year. The thought of Slim's failure momentarily left a bitter taste in his mouth, but this was just as good as Jason's death. A bolt of inspiration jolted through him. Maybe even better. Ever since he'd cut Slim free, he'd been trying to figure out how this could work to his advantage. Maybe he just had.

He glanced down at Nicki. Who would have thought that she would believe his insinuations so easily? Perhaps she hadn't been as attracted to Jason as he'd at first feared. It looked like the last two years of cultivating her friendship were going to be well worth the effort it had taken.

He tightened his grip on her shoulder, doing his best to look sympathetic to her plight. She had, after all, just lost the man she had been putting her hope in for the salvation of her ranch—a ranch that would shortly be his.

Yes indeed, things couldn't have worked out better. And he was standing by the woman who would soon be his wife. He caught himself before a whoop of delight escaped.

"Come on, Nicki." His voice was appropriately sober. "Let's get you inside out of this snow."

She didn't move but stood watching until Jason and the sheriff disappeared over the crest of the hill.

William experienced a moment of dread. He quickly forced

his emotions to calm. Let her watch to her heart's content. The day was soon coming when she wouldn't be able to stand the sight of Jason Jordan.

His plan had only just begun.

Nicki sighed as Jason disappeared over the horizon. William's hand around her shoulders suddenly grated on her nerves. She stepped away from him and headed toward the house. Had she made the right decision? She paused before moving through the door and turned to stare at the spot where she had last seen him.

What would Jason have to gain from setting fire to the Jeffries' place? She couldn't think of anything, yet it had irked her to have him telling her not to trust William. William had been there for her from the moment of John's death. And it flew in the face of all she had ever believed in to turn against an old friend on the whim of a new one. But was it a whim?

Her eyes flicked to William and she rubbed her temple as she turned to head into the house. She could feel the beginning of a stress headache.

The question remained: if Jason hadn't set that fire, who had? Again her eyes flicked to William as she shook the snow from her shawl and hung it on a peg over the bed. Could he have done such a thing? She shook her head. No, she couldn't imagine William ever doing something like that. But neither could she see Jason doing it. What would be the motive behind such an act?

She would talk to Ron like Jason asked and see what he had to say. Suppressing the tears that threatened to overflow, she moved to join Brenda and Rolf at the table. She couldn't shake the feeling that she'd just made the biggest mistake of her life.

★

Chapter Fourteen

Rocky Jordan, Jason's cousin, leaned his shoulder into the post and hunched his coat up closer to his ears, tilting his hat further back. The February sun shone, but the day was more than a little nippy. He shoved his hands into his pants pockets, pleasure curving his mouth as he watched Victoria Snyder talking animatedly to the little boy down the street. She and the boy had just emerged from the bakery, her basket now empty. They were coming his way and he really shouldn't stare, but he couldn't seem to turn away.

If possible, she was even more beautiful than the last time he had seen her, which had been yesterday. Her red hair was pulled into its usual bun, wisps framing her face. The basket she always carried to deliver her mother's fresh-baked goods to the bakery down the street swung easily by her side. Her step was just as light as always. All in all, he surmised, she didn't look much different than she had yesterday. *Still, she's more beautiful than ever.*

He exhaled, his breath frosting the air before him in a cloud of frustration. Glancing around to make sure no one had caught him looking, he chuckled to himself, then swung his eyes back to the woman and child approaching. He had it bad. He should just ask her to dinner and be done with it, but somehow he could never bring himself to voice the question.

He and Victoria were good friends…had been since childhood. Through the years she had courted a few boys, including Rocky's older brother, Sky, and Cade Bennett, but she had never turned her attentions on him. Ever since she had dated Sky, Rocky had sworn himself to silence over his attraction to her. Perhaps it had something to do with not being the first one she had been interested in, nor even the second for that matter. After all, a man had his pride. More to the point, it had to do with the fact that Victoria had broken it off with Sky because he'd become a lawman.

Rocky fingered the cold metal of his badge. It was the reason he'd never asked her to dinner.

Victoria glanced up and smiled at him. He dropped his hand into his pocket, willing his heart not to thunder out of his chest.

"Hi, Rocky. How are you?"

He dipped his chin. "Just fine, Ria. How's your mother feeling today? Any better?" His smooth voice betrayed none of his inner turmoil.

She sighed. "She says she is, but I'm not convinced. If you see Doc Martin, would you ask him to meander by the house? If he just stops by for a cup of coffee, she'll be more likely to confide in him than if I drag her into his office."

He grinned at her. "Are you conspiring behind her back?"

She returned his grin with a nonchalant wave. "I'm always conspiring to get her to do *something!*"

Rocky chuckled.

Victoria and her mother were close. They had been alone in this world since Victoria's father passed away. She had been eight at the time if he remembered correctly. Victoria's mother hadn't been feeling well for the past month, and Rocky knew how worried Ria was about her. "If I see Doc, I'll pass your request along." Rocky's eyes dropped to the little boy by Victoria's side.

"Oh." Victoria rested a hand on the boy's shoulder. "Rocky, I would like you to meet a new friend of mine. Trevor, this is my friend Rocky. He's a sheriff in town. Rocky, this is Trevor. He just moved in down the street."

Rocky caught her meaning even as he squatted on the balls of his feet so he would be at the young boy's level. The little man before him was a new resident at the town's orphanage. Victoria volunteered some of her time there every day. He extended his hand. "I'm pleased to meet you, Trevor. How do you like our town so far?"

Trevor's smile, minus one tooth, was impish. "It's nice." He leaned forward and, in a stage whisper, added, "I especially like the ladies." His large brown eyes angled in Victoria's direction and Rocky turned his surprised gaze toward her just in time to see her blush a pretty pink that went perfectly with her red hair.

He grinned and ruffled Trevor's brown curls. "Yes. We do have our share of pretty ladies, don't we?"

Trevor stepped toward him and whispered conspiratorially, "Ria's more than pretty; she's fun too!"

Rocky widened his eyes in mock awe. "Pretty and *fun* too? Well now, it *is* rare to find both of those qualities in a woman, isn't it?" Rocky tossed Victoria a broad smile even as he stood quickly to dodge a blow from her basket.

"I'm going to marry her when I grow up. Then we can play hide-n-seek all day long! It will be so much fun!"

"Yes. I'm sure that being married to Ria would be fun indeed." The words slipped out before he thought, and his eyes flashed to her surprised face as he quickly added, "After all who could resist playing hide-n-seek all day long?" He winked at her and her face darkened another shade, deepening her freckles so that he wanted to reach out and touch them. He settled for shoving his hands back in his pockets.

"You could have her for a while 'til I get growed up. Then you could find somebody new, and I could have Ria."

Victoria gasped at the audacity of the little boy's proposition. "Trevor! A—"

Rocky quickly touched her elbow and spoke before she could embarrass the boy. "Well now, that's just not the way things work, Trev. And besides, we shouldn't make plans about the lady as though she isn't even present. If we act like that, Miss Snyder won't have either one of us." He leveled a look at the little boy. "What do you think? Think maybe we should apologize?"

Trevor's face sank and he looked down at his feet, shuffling them back and forth. "You first," he mumbled.

Rocky glanced at Victoria, who was giving him a look that warned him not to make too much of this in front of the boy. "Ria, I'm sorry."

Trevor glanced up at her through his bangs. "Sorry."

She bent at the waist and pulled the little imp into a one-armed hug. "You're forgiven. Now run along and get the things Ms. Johnston needs and don't dawdle on the way back. I need to speak to Mr. Jordan for a moment."

The relief on Trevor's face was palpable. He turned and started hurriedly for the mercantile but had only gone a couple of steps before he spun back in their direction. "Aren't ya gonna forgive Mr. Jordan?"

Ria's mouth quirked as she swung her eyes to Rocky's face. "You're forgiven, Mr. Jordan."

Rocky swept off his hat in a deep bow. "Thank you, ma'am."

Trevor swung sparkling eyes to Rocky. "She must like me better. She gave *me* a hug!"

Rocky threw back his head and laughed as Victoria once again used her delivery basket as a weapon. The basket connected solidly with Trevor's backside even as he tried to scamper out of the way.

"Go!" she laughed, her green eyes sparkling with delight. "I'll deal with you later."

Trevor jauntily strode down the sidewalk, turning to wave at them before he disappeared into the mercantile with his list from Ms. Hannah Johnston.

Victoria turned back to Rocky, noting once again how handsome he was when he smiled, as he was doing now. He really was a lot of fun and all the children at the orphanage adored him. He stopped by often to help Ms. Hannah with the constant repairs that needed to be made to the old building that housed the precious orphans.

Victoria often found herself wondering if Rocky knew the real reason she had dated his brother and his best friend. Her mouth turned up at the corner. No, he wouldn't know. He was much too humble to suspect that she'd had her eye on him for years. During school she'd drawn the interest of several boys, but never Rocky. She had tried in an untold number of ways to get his attention but he'd always treated her like she was a little sister.

She'd agreed to see Skyler in hopes that if she dated his brother, she might get his attention. It hadn't worked; neither had her relationship with his best friend, Cade Bennett. She had become fast friends with both Sky and Cade, but it hadn't gotten her any closer to a relationship with Rocky. She really liked both Sky and Cade, but it had always been Rocky she'd had her eye on.

Lately though, she had begun to realize that she would have to settle for just being his friend. He wasn't interested in her, and she was finally learning to deal with it. Wasn't she? Then again maybe one day she would get up the courage to ask *him* to dinner. She giggled at the unconventional thought.

"Ria?" Rocky's voice penetrated her thoughts, sounding more than a little worried.

She came out of her reverie and realized that she had been staring at him with a silly smile throughout her contemplation of their relationship. Her face blazed hot, and she silently berated herself for an idiot. She was always blushing like a school girl when Rocky was around.

Her mind scrambled for something coherent to say. What had she needed to talk to him about? Oh yes. Her words tumbled out before she could make an even bigger fool of herself. "Rocky, the roof at the orphanage is leaking badly with all this rain we've been having lately, and Hannah wondered if you could find time on your next day off to come by and fix it?"

He shrugged. "Sure." But his bewildered gaze was almost more than her composure could stand. He obviously couldn't figure out why she'd been giggling about the orphanage roof leaking. She felt another giggle coming on and quickly turned away so he wouldn't suspect.

Waving over her shoulder she said, "Thanks," and moved off quickly before he came to the conclusion that she had totally lost all her senses.

At the corner of the building she cast one more glance over her shoulder. He was standing in the same spot she had left him, but he was talking to the telegraph operator, Mr. Sinclair. As he frowned down at the telegram in his hands, he unconsciously reached to touch the badge on his chest.

So, he was being summoned for something. Victoria sighed as she thought of her father. Yes there was definitely one drawback to Rocky Jordan. One very big drawback.

Jason lay back on the cot, hands clasped behind his head, and stared at the ceiling of the jailhouse. His booted feet, crossed at the ankles, hung over the end of the too-short bed. Today was Sunday. Nicki, Ron, and Conner would be coming into town for services at the little church. Maybe they would stop by with some hopeful news, because as things stood, they did not look good for him.

The sheriff busily scratched his pen across some forms at the desk only a couple of feet away. The only thing separating them was the wall of metal bars. Jason had slept the night through in exhaustion, not having slept since before he discovered the horses, and now found he was thinking a little more clearly.

His thoughts turned to the fire at the Jeffries' place. Whoever had set it had a connection to the man he had apprehended.

Someone had crashed through the brush just yards from him that night, then gone straight to his prisoner and cut him free. He had seen the tracks with his own eyes and recognized them. Each man has his own way of walking, standing, turning, and striding. If a man's shoe was cracked along the sole, it showed in his tracks. If it was worn more on one side or the other, that showed, too. There were any number of ways of telling one man's footprints from another, and Jason had learned, early on, working for his uncle in Shilo, that it was wise to take note of and remember everyone's footprints. You never knew when the knowledge might come in handy. And the tracks left in back of the Jeffries cabin were the same tracks left by the man who had shot at Nicki on his first day.

Had he recognized them as William's, he would not have been surprised, but William's pricey hand-tooled boots had a very distinct deep heel print with the outside edges on both feet worn down just a little. Whoever had made the tracks he had followed from the cabin back into the woods had been wearing a worn-at-heel pair of boots that had obviously seen better days.

But if a man were smart and planned to commit a crime, he might think to put on a pair of shoes that he didn't normally wear. Jason sighed. He would have to find that old pair of boots and their owner to prove who had been at that cabin, and who had shot at him and Nicki. A near impossible task.

His next thought wasn't any more comforting than the last. He had told the sheriff about his captive, even risked telling him about the horses, but the lawman hadn't believed him. He'd said he would check into it, but so far he hadn't been in any hurry. There were no tracks at the scene to back up his story, and the sheriff thought he was just trying to give himself an alibi.

That left another question. Who had gone back and cleaned up the evidence? They had to have done a pretty thorough job because the sheriff was an observant man. Jason snorted at the thought, tossing the man a glance. *Not observant enough, or he'd know I wasn't guilty.* There had to be something at the scene that proved he hadn't been the only one there. Jason didn't really blame the sheriff for suspecting him. After all, he had only been in the area for a few days. A stranger was always the first suspect when a crime was committed.

The door to the outer office opened, and Jason swung his legs over the side of the bed, sitting up to see who had just entered. Sheriff Watts looked up from his paperwork.

It was Nicki and Ron.

Jason's pulse jumped. Had she seen reason and come to apologize for doubting him?

Nicki held a basket in her hands, her worried dark eyes immediately searching him out. But it was Ron that his eyes fixed on. The man's face showed no emotion whatsoever. Had they found the horses?

Jason stepped forward, gripping the metal bars in his hands. "Morning."

Ron nodded. Nicki did too, swallowing as she did so.

The sheriff stood, reaching his hand out to each of them. "Mornin'," he echoed Jason's greeting. "What can I be doin' fer ya?"

Nicki lifted the basket slightly. "I've brought Mr. Jordan some breakfast, if that's all right."

Jason's mouth watered. He hadn't eaten since just after the funeral yesterday.

Sheriff Watts rubbed a hand across his cheek. Eyeing the basket, he extended his hand for it. Nicki gave it to him, and Jason wanted to grin at the anger he saw darken her eyes as the sheriff began to methodically search it, even going to the extent of breaking her muffins in half and then again into quarters.

She lifted her chin. "Sheriff, I assure you that if I planned to try and help Mr. Jordan escape from jail, it wouldn't be by hiding something so small that he might choke on it while eating." She pointedly looked at the small pieces he had broken apart.

The sheriff only looked at her and shoved his finger into the scrambled eggs, stirring them around. Nicki crossed her arms, and Jason heard her mutter something in Spanish. This time he couldn't keep the smile from his face. He might be facing a noose by the end of the week, but she was worried about his breakfast getting ruined. He liked that. It renewed the hope he'd lost when she'd sided with William the night before.

Sheriff Watts finally finished with his search and nodded that it was okay for her to give it to Jason. She snatched it from his desk with a glare that would have made a lesser man step back. Jason had to admire the sheriff for standing his ground. He quickly wiped the smirk from his face as she looked his way, but he could tell by the way she arched one slim, dark eyebrow that she had noticed it.

Behind her, Jason saw Ron step over to the sheriff and speak in low tones.

Then Sheriff Watts stepped toward the door and looked back at them. "I'm steppin' out to talk to Ron. I won't be more 'n a minute, so don't try nothin'."

Jason nodded and turned his attention back to Nicki as the two men walked out the door. "Thank you," he said, as he accepted the basket she angled through the bars to him.

"Sí. De nada."

She was speaking Spanish again, and it gave him pause. She only reverted to her native tongue when in highly emotional moments of anger, surprise or confusion.

"Nicki?" He waited until she looked him full in the face. "Are you all right?"

She gestured to the bars and then the room in general. "You are here, but you're asking if *I'm* all right?"

He shrugged not knowing what to say to that. "Feeling any better?" He saw her cheeks tinge with a blush and suddenly he *knew*. His eyes dropped to her stomach and then snapped back to her face. He saw her eyes widen as she recognized he understood. He stepped closer. "Nick?"

She curled her lips together, looking down and away as she nodded slowly, her face grave.

He banged the heel of his hand against the bars in frustration. Nicki's gaze jumped back to his face in surprise.

The sheriff opened the door and poked his head inside. "Everythin' okay in here?"

"Everything is fine, Sheriff," Nicki assured, but her eyes were still fastened to Jason's.

He leaned heavily against the bars, his arms locked at the elbow, and took in her calm expression. She was pregnant! Pregnant! And someone wanted her off her ranch. Someone who was most likely guilty of murder—at least an accessory to one—and willing to go so far as to set fire to a house. He glanced at the floor. *Someone* ...probably William. Even though the pieces didn't fit, he couldn't shake that suspicion. Hadn't Ron said that a man who fit the description of his captive worked for William? He wanted to caution her once more about the man, yet he knew he dared not warn her away from William again.

He glanced over at the sheriff, who nodded and pulled the door shut, leaving them alone for a second time.

Fear and worry for her safety clenched a tight fist in his stomach as he turned back to study her. He chewed one side of his lower lip, trying to decide if there was a way he could caution her about William that wouldn't send her into a fit of anger.

"I'm just fine," she assured him, touching his hand where it clasped the bars separating them. "Why didn't you tell me you'd found the horses?"

He wiped his mouth on his shoulder. Maybe this was his opening. "You won't like my answer."

"Try me."

"I didn't want you to tell William about them."

She opened her mouth, and he hurried on before she could voice her irritation. "I think it would be better if you sold some of those horses quickly and paid off the loan before anyone knows you have the money to do so. And then I think you need to hire several hands that are good with a gun. You're going to need them."

"Why?" Ice traced the edges of her tone.

"You haven't had any more threats recently. Someone thinks they've won; that you won't be able to come up with the money. Maybe they plan to buy the ranch from the bank or maybe the bank's in on this deal. But when you pay off that loan, they'll have to rethink. Who else knew about the bank calling the loan, besides me, Ron, Conner, Tilly, and William?"

Nicki's eyes narrowed as she tumbled to his logic. "No one." The words were clipped.

He raised his eyebrows to emphasize his point. "Have you told him about the horses yet?"

She smoothed a hand across the front of her skirt, refusing to meet his eyes. "No."

The corner of his mouth quirked. Maybe she had taken more stock of his words than he thought. "Don't. He wants your land, Nick. He wants it bad, and he'll do anything to get it. Sell the horses, pay off the loan, and don't tell anyone until it's done."

"Word travels fast. I wouldn't be able to sell them without everyone in the county knowing about it."

"I've sent for my cousin, Rocky, and a friend, Cade. Trust them. They'll know what to do. Cade's father owns a ranch, and he's going to want every one of those horses that you're willing to part with. They can arrange it so the money goes directly to the bank without even passing through your hands. *No one* has to know you've sold them."

Instead of the anger that he expected, her shoulders slumped. "Why don't you trust him?"

"I don't know."

"I've known him for three years, and you for a little more than a week, but you want me to take your word over his?"

His face softened. He raised his fingers, meaning to capture her hand in his own, but she pulled away slightly. Her hand paused midair and started to come back to his before she changed her mind and dropped it to her side. She turned toward the door, not waiting for him to reply.

Jason's heart plunged as she walked away. He wished she would trust him a little more. And yes, he hoped she would take his word over William's. He could only pray that God would help her make the right decision.

Ron came back in. Clearing his throat, he turned to look at Nicki, where she waited by the door. "Ma'am, I'll just be a minute if you want to wait for me to walk you down to church."

"No." Nicki shook her head as she fiddled with the strings on the reticule that hung from her wrist. "I'll be fine. I'll be late if I wait for you men to quit gabbing. I'll see you there." Her dark eyes darted to Jason. "I'll think about it," she said, then hurried out the door.

Ron turned back to Jason. "We found the horses right where you said."

Jason sighed in relief. "How many?"

"Two hundred and nine."

Jason let out a low whistle.

Ron continued. "I hired Sid Snow to guard 'em. I didn't think we'd be able to drive 'em back to the ranch just the few of us. 'Sides, the corral wouldn't hold 'em all."

"Good. Any news on who started that fire?"

Ron grimaced in sympathy, shaking his head. "Nary a trace."

Jason squelched the curses that came to mind. *Forgive me, Lord.* He banged his hand against the bars with a fierceness that made them vibrate in their sockets.

"Good news is, I was just talkin' to the sheriff, and he's inclined to think you didn't do it, despite the evidence to the contrary. Watts is a good man. He smells the barn afore he gets there if you catch my meanin'. Nicki, on the other hand..."

Jason frowned, waiting.

"Well, Harpster's been around every spare moment since you were arrested. Tryin' to prove he's the man o' the hour—a little too hard if you ask my opinion. He's been fillin' her head with all the reasons you can't be trusted. I don't cotton to that man. Never did."

"I don't either, and with things turning out the way they are, we're going to need some help. You know of any trustworthy men we could hire? I think whoever wants Nicki off that land thought calling in this loan would do the trick. Now that she's going to be able to pay if off, I'm afraid we might have trouble again."

Ron lifted his hat and raked a hand through his hair. "I'll see what I can do."

"Good. Rocky and Cade should be here within the next couple of days. I'll feel better when they get here. In between time, see if you can't get someone out there with you two."

Ron nodded and turned for the door.

"And Ron? Maybe you could talk to Nicki about William? I tried. Maybe if it comes from you, too, she'll listen. He really has the wool pulled over her eyes."

"I'll talk to her. But she's pretty convinced that he isn't involved."

Jason dropped his chin to his chest and shook his head.

"If it makes any difference, she doesn't think you did it, either."

Jason looked up, hope surging through him. "Really?"

"Sure. She's claimin' she don't know what to believe, but I can tell she knows you didn't do it, in here." He thumbed his chest.

Jason exhaled. He'd been hoping for more evidence than that. "Keep an eye on her, Ron." A thought occurred to him. "How are the Jeffries holding up?"

Ron shrugged. "Good as can be expected, I guess. They're staying in the house, and we have an area in the bunkhouse blanketed off for Nicki to sleep in. Sawyer's still staying with Tilly for now."

"Give her my blankets. They're warm, and it gets cold in that bunkhouse at night."

"She's using them. She didn't have anything else to use. She insisted on leaving all the blankets in the house for the family to have." Ron put on his hat. "Well, I'll let you get to breakfast. We'll be back tomorrow. And don't worry, son, we ain't gonna let you hang."

Jason picked up the basket of food Nicki had handed him earlier and moved to sit on the cot, hoping that Ron would be able to keep his promise.

The church members crowded into the pews, the lamps overhead casting a warm glow throughout the room. Nicki eased into the third row back and sank down with a soft sigh. It felt good to be here in God's house after the stress of the last few weeks.

"Mommy!"

Nicki twisted toward the sound just in time to catch Sawyer as he launched himself into her arms.

Tilly smiled as she scooted onto the bench after him. "'Morning. How are the Jeffries?"

Nicki reached to squeeze her friend's hand. "They're not coming this morning. Brenda couldn't face church yet without May. She so loved being here."

Sawyer snuggled under her chin and stuck a chubby thumb in his mouth.

Tilly pressed her lips together as she methodically pulled off her gloves, one finger at a time. She glanced up and Nicki saw tears pooled in her large brown eyes. "I still can't believe that little May is gone."

Nicki blinked back her own tears and rested her chin on Sawyer's head after a quick nod of agreement. So much death and sadness. Was God really somewhere in all of this?

Pastor Saunders stepped up behind the pulpit as Conner and Ron slid onto the bench beside Tilly. "Stand with me as we open in prayer, would you?"

The congregation stood and Nicki took the opportunity to settle Sawyer more securely in her arms.

After prayer and some congregational singing, Pastor stepped forward to stand behind the pulpit once more. He set his Bible on the surface, opening it and flipping some pages without looking up. His voice rang out sure and strong. "*Yea, though I walk through the valley of the shadow of death, I will fear no evil; For You are with me; Your rod and Your staff, they comfort me.*"

Nicki's heart lurched at the text he'd chosen.

He looked out over the congregation, his face serious. "Those words are found in the twenty-third psalm, verse four." Pastor Saunders paced several steps to one side of the pulpit and surveyed the congregation. "Do you believe them?"

Nicki squirmed uneasily in her seat. Where had God's comfort been for her and the Jeffries these past weeks? She'd thought Jason was God's answer, sent to help her, but now he was in jail.

Pastor cupped his chin and paced to the other side of the podium. "Make no mistake. We have evil walking our hills these days." He held out a hand in Conner's direction. "When a man can't even ride out after dark without being assaulted, we have evil walking in our hills!"

Conner looked down and fidgeted with his hat where it rested on his knee.

"So what are we to do?" Pastor asked. "Let's think for a minute about what fear makes people do. Fear usually causes one of two reactions. We either run and hide and pretend that what is happening isn't really there. Or we get angry and fight back to get rid of the object causing the fear. Both of those reactions are us trying to take matters into our own hands." He paused behind the pulpit just long enough to fiddle with a paper that marked his place in his Bible and then paced to the very corner of the platform. “I was in town the other day.” He cleared his throat. “It was a couple weeks back, and God had laid this sermon on my heart already. I was thinking about fear and what it causes us to do. I walked into the mercantile and,” he blinked hard and cleared his throat again, “I bumped into the Jeffries.”

A collective murmur rippled through the congregation.

Pastor blinked back tears. “I stopped little May and I asked her, ‘May, you ever been afraid?’ She nodded. And I said, ‘What do you do when you are afraid, May?’”

Nicki swallowed hard and pressed her eyes shut to prevent the tears from falling. But in the silence that followed, she finally opened her eyes. Pastor was trying to regain his composure, but at last he gave up and let the tears fall. He pulled a hanky from his back pocket and wiped his eyes. “You know what she said to me? She said, ‘When I’m afraid, I run to my daddy.’”

In the back of the room someone blew their nose, and off to her left, Nicki heard several people sniffling.

“Now that is the right response, my loved ones. Times are hard, right now. Evil presses in on some of you. Will you run to your Daddy?” He pointed at the ceiling. “He might not take the evil away, but His Word says He will comfort you.” He paced back the other way. “One of the ways God comforts us is by putting other people into our lives.”

Nicki’s mind immediately went to Jason, and her pulse quickened.

“My granddaddy used to say, ‘Sometimes people just need to see Jesus with skin on.’”

The congregation chuckled.

Pastor looked right at Nicki, and she felt herself squirm. Jason had been wonderful to her, and she had been awful to him when he was being hauled off to jail.

Pastor’s next words made her even more uncomfortable. “We have one lady in our congregation who has seen some particularly trying times this past couple weeks.”

All eyes turned to see who the pastor was looking at, and Nicki buried her face in Sawyer's hair. Why was he pointing her out? Others had had trouble, too.

"Well this past week the board members and I had a meeting, and we've decided to be Jesus with skin to that lady." Nicki lifted her head.

Pastor smiled at her. "Mrs. Trent. We would like to help you put a new roof on your barn. We've talked it through as a board, and it looks like the first weekend in April would be a good time for all of us to come help you. Would that work for you?"

Nicki blinked and looked over at Tilly, Conner, and Ron. Tilly smiled nodding her encouragement.

Nicki looked back at Pastor. Her mouth opened and closed. Opened. Closed. Finally she blurted, "I…I…I don't know what to say. That would be wonderful. But—"

Pastor raised one hand to still her protest. "Jesus with skin, Mrs. Trent, just as you are being to the Jeffries by allowing them to live with you during this difficult time in their lives."

Nicki pressed her lips together. She didn't want thanks for that; it was only what any decent person would do.

Pastor Saunders clapped his hands together. "Good. It's settled then. Let's close in prayer, shall we?"

As the congregation shuffled to the door, saying their good-byes to one another, Nicki had only one thought. She hoped she still had a ranch come the first weekend of April, or there would be no barn to put a roof on.

★

Chapter Fifteen

William leaned his forearms across the top rail of his corral and glanced at Slim. The tall lanky man, leaning in a similar fashion beside him, blew a smoke ring and turned to face his boss.

William's mouth thinned. "I need you to have a chat with Sheriff Watts.

Give me two days and then tell him something believable to let him know that Jason was otherwise occupied when that fire started. He's already told the sheriff that he was with someone who looked like you. Confirm it, without making it look like you were following him. I still want him under suspicion, but I need him out of that jail."

Slim's gaze was expressionless as he blew another smoke ring, but he appraised William carefully.

William chuckled without humor. "I know it doesn't seem like the smart thing to do right now, but trust me, he's gonna wish he never set foot outside of that jail when I'm done with him." He started away, then paused. "And Slim?"

Slim looked at him.

"Fail this time, and your broken nose will feel like a feather pillow compared to what will happen."

Slim tossed his cigarette down and ground it out with the toe of his boot. William nodded in satisfaction. *Soon Nicki will be all mine.* The thought brought a smile to his face. Yes, indeed, things were going well.

Brenda wrapped her hands around the mug of hot coffee and stared across the table at her husband. They had not felt up to attending services in town this morning. Rolf stared into his cup, rubbing one finger around the rim listlessly. She had never seen him this way before. His guilt was killing him.

She sighed. He was impossible to talk to since May's accident. She reached across the table and stilled his hand with her own. "'Twasn't yer fault, Rolf."

He didn't say a word, only lifted pain-filled eyes and tilted his hand so that hers slid off and down onto the table.

She slammed her cup down so hard that the hot liquid shot up into the air and came down all over the table and her hand. Rolf jumped back. She ignored the pain. "Do ya think yer the only one feelin' pain and guilt, Rolf? Don't ya think I lay 'wake at night just a-wonderin' what I should o' done different thet night? If I hadn't stayed so late here at Nicki's…or if I hadn't come at all. If I had just brought May with me, stead o' leavin' her home." She lost her control then and couldn't keep the tears at bay any longer. Covering her face, she allowed the sobs to shake her, giving in to the grief.

Rolf came to her slowly and wrapped his arms around her, pulling her up until she stood in the comfort of his embrace. "'Twern't yer fault, Bren." They were the first words he had spoken directly to her since the tragedy. She buried her face in his shirt and cried until her knees became so weak she could no longer stand even with his support. She sank down onto the floor, the wracking sobs still shaking her. Rolf squatted next to her, running his hand gently over her hair, his eyes still dry. "Ah, Bren. What're we gonna do without our angel?"

She didn't reply. The thought was simply too agonizing.

The door to the sheriff's office opened. Jason stopped pacing in his cramped quarters and turned to see who was coming in. It was the morning of his third day in jail and his patience was wearing thin. If there was one thing that drove him crazy, it was being cooped up and unable to do anything to prove his innocence.

Jason blinked in surprise as the man walked in. It was his escaped captive, the man who had followed him. The man pulled his hat from his head and twisted it around in his hands. "Sheriff, I been talkin' to my boss, and he said I should get down here and talk to you since what I got to say might save that man's neck." He jerked his chin in Jason's direction.

"What it be, Slim?"

Slim. Jason remembered Ron telling him that a man named Slim worked for William. *What a surprise*, he thought dryly.

"Well," he turned his hat another quarter turn, "the night that fire started out at the Jeffries' place," Slim gestured to Jason, "he couldn't have started it."

Watts glanced at Jason and then back to Slim. "And ya know this how?"

"He was with me," Slim replied.

Jason raised one eyebrow, knowing the real truth was not going to be forthcoming. He folded his arms and leaned back into the heels of his boots, wondering what kind of story he was about to hear.

"With you?" asked the sheriff.

Slim nodded and gave his hat another twist, dusting the crown. "I'd caught him passin' through Bar H Slanted land and stopped him to have a chat and find out why he was there." He shrugged. "He didn't have a good reason, but he was too far away to have started that fire."

Watts turned to Jason. "You were on Bar H land?"

"No."

The sheriff frowned. "This man comes in with a story that might set ya free and ya deny thet what he says be true?"

"Sheriff, I didn't start that fire. I've never balked on that point from the beginning, but I wasn't on Bar H land. In fact it was quite the opposite. Slim here was following me across Hanging T land, and I detained him for questioning. I just wanted to know why he was sneaking up on me with his Winchester shucked, but he didn't seem to want to talk to me then." He raked Slim with an assessing gaze. "I find it curious that he is here trying to free me, unless of course his boss has something to gain by it." Jason kept the full force of his glare on Slim, who glanced at the ground and fidgeted with his hat some more.

"I just come to tell you what I know, Sheriff. And that is he couldn't have started the fire. He was too far away."

"Well Slim, I've known ya fer a long time, and I never knowd ya to lie. And if William sent ya, then I guess he must believe ya, too. So..." The sheriff walked across the room, removing a ring of keys from a peg. "Jordan, I guess you be free to go, but I'll be askin' ya to hang around and not be goin' far in case I have some more questions I need to be havin' answers fer."

"Don't worry Sheriff, I won't be going anywhere. Not until I have some answers of my own." He cast one more hard glance at Slim before the man turned, placed his hat on his head, and exited the building.

It only took Jason a moment to gather his guns and knife from Watts.

Settling his black Stetson on his head, he nodded at the sheriff and stepped into the bright March sunlight. The winter wouldn't be lasting much longer, even this year with the snow and cold loath to give up their quarter.

What would William have to gain by freeing him from jail? He couldn't figure it, but he would break that bronc in its own time. At least, now that he was free, he'd be there to protect Nicki.

Nicki paced back and forth in the bunkhouse. Ron was out working on the barn as the snow had begun to fade in the last couple of days. Even though the nights were still very cold, the days were getting warmer and warmer and the snows were fighting a losing battle.

The first weekend in April was just a couple weeks away. Many families from the community had stopped Nicki after church to say they would come and help fix the structure. Nicki was so thankful for the blessing of good friends. Ron was preparing for the event—removing the scattered debris from inside the structure and making sure the walls would be braced properly so that on the day of the roofing things would go smoothly.

She rolled her head from side to side, trying to ward off the oncoming headache.

Jason. The name hung in her mind like a torment. She almost wished she'd never laid eyes on the man. She didn't want to think about what he was accusing William of, yet Ron concurred with him.

Could William really be as deceitful and conniving as they were making him out to be? She just couldn't picture it of him. Yes, he was abrupt with people sometimes; didn't always look at things from another's position before he spoke or acted. But toward her he had never been anything but a gentleman. To believe that he was trying to steal her ranch, *lying* to her, she would have to believe that all he had ever done for her had been done in pretense. In deceit. She rolled her shoulders to ease the tension. No, there had to be another explanation.

She turned her thoughts to the Jeffries. Who would have set fire to their house? Perhaps it had been an accident that merely looked like it had been set on purpose?

She was halfway across the floor for the umpteenth time before she realized that she was worrying about something she had no control over.

Father forgive me. Help me not to take on things that I cannot figure out. I need Your help, God. I don't know what to do. William has been so helpful to me since John's death, and now Jason is accusing him of conniving to get my land. I don't know about these accusations, but You do, and in Your word You have promised to be a husband to those who need one and a Father to the fatherless. My family needs You now more than ever, Father. I pray that You will work this out. Help the truth to come to light. If William is innocent, then help me to know.

Her thoughts turned to the other man that seemed to occupy her thoughts constantly lately. *And, Lord, I pray that You would help Jason. I know he didn't start that fire. Help us find who did.* She sighed. *Lord, am I even supposed to be here? I don't know. I need some assurance. I need to know what to do with my life now. I never had a choice before. There was just John…and Sawyer. But now there is just me and Sawyer and this new little one.* She laid a hand on her stomach. *And I don't know what to do. I could go back home if I wanted, but I want what You want. Send someone to show me what to do. Lord, I want to be used of You. But if I'm going to stay here, You're going to have to work out this money situation. The money from the horses will get us out of debt and maybe leave a little extra, but with all the repairs that need to be done…well, I don't see how it will last. I can't keep asking Ron, Conner, and Jason to stay on for no pay. And now there are these three new hands that Ron hired.*

Nicki rubbed her temples, realizing how thankful she was for someone to give all her burdens to. Her headache was lessening already. Just knowing that God loved her more than words could say and would be there to help her because she'd asked removed some of her tension.

Her prayer continued as she thought of the Jeffries and all they had lost. *Help them turn to You for their strength, Lord. Help them know that You are with them even during this terrible time. Use me, if You can, to be a comfort to them, but mostly I pray that you will give them the strength to make it through the coming days and still cling to You.*

Thoughts of the Jeffries' little May saddened her, and she suddenly wanted to see Sawyer more than anything. She headed toward the door, intending to ask Ron if he would mind running her over to Tilly's for a while. *Maybe I should ask Conner. There's no way he would pass up a chance to go to Tilly's.* A slight smile crossed her face at the thought.

She was just reaching for the door handle when it opened. Startled, she stepped back.

It was Jason, with his saddle slung over one shoulder. He started to step into the room but paused upon seeing her. Their eyes met and held for a long moment, then his mouth softened into a barely perceptible smile.

Her heart soared but she was careful to keep her face blank.

"Hi." His one word was tentative.

He obviously wasn't sure if she was going to welcome him back. Well, he *should* be wondering after what he had accused William of. *He's out of jail?* "Hi. What are you doing here?"

He nodded, rubbing one hand across his jaw. "You're right. I'll just find a place to stay in town. But I'm not backing down. I'm telling you the truth, and until you figure it out for yourself, you need someone to watch your back for you. So don't expect me to go far." He started to turn away.

"Wait. That's not what I meant. I meant, how did you get out?" He told her, his words clipped and to the point.

"Slim was the man who was following you?"

He frowned even as he nodded, knowing he hadn't told her about Slim.

She smiled slightly. "I've been talking to Ron."

"And did he convince you that I was telling the truth?" He shifted the saddle to get a better grip.

"Oh, goodness, come in. I didn't mean to keep you standing at the door." He hesitated briefly but followed her back into the room, dropping the saddle into the corner.

"I never thought you were lying," she said.

He contemplated her for a moment, then evidently chose to ignore that line of conversation. "You were going somewhere?" He gestured to the door.

"I was going to see if I could talk Ron or Conner into taking me to see Sawyer. He's at Tilly's."

"I'll take you. Just give me a minute to hitch the buggy."

She nodded. "Thank you."

Minutes later they were seated in the buggy, with his blanket tucked snugly around her legs.

The silence grew heavy as they jostled across the snow-rutted road. Nicki sensed Jason's tenseness. His words had been deliberate and controlled for the past hour.

"Something bothering you?" she asked.

His jaw clenched, but his hands remained loose and steady on the reins. The horse trotted on, and he made no reply.

She chuckled dryly. "You're mad at me and acting like a spoiled little boy!"

He cast her a sideways glance and then pulled the buggy to a stop by the side of the road. He stared across the fields. "A little." He turned and casually draped his arm across the back of the seat. "Mad—not acting like a spoiled boy," he clarified with a slight smile.

The point of contact where his arm brushed her shoulders sent shivers of pleasure down Nicki's back, and she leaned forward, not daring to allow herself to linger in that pleasure. She had to keep her head about her if she was going to figure things out. She searched his face but found no answers in his frank gaze. "Why?"

He lifted the arm draped behind her and trailed his fingers across her temple, tucking a strand of her hair back. "Because I'm worried about you. Especially now that I know you're pregnant." His eyes gentled.

"Worried?" she whispered. The word almost stuck in her throat as she tried not to think about the intimacy of his last statement.

He nodded, but no twinkle leapt into his gaze as she had hoped. He was angry.

"And worrying about me makes you angry with me?"

A twinkle did show in his eyes then. "No. *You* make me angry with you."

She shook her head. "You're not making sense."

He looked past her, staring out across the white fields around them again. Nicki followed his gaze and could see several of her cows dotting the crests of the hills on the horizon. He didn't respond for a long time.

Nicki was just opening her mouth to speak again when Jason laid the finger of his free hand across her lips and she stilled. "I'm frustrated that you won't listen to the facts. And worried about you because you might be in danger. And yes, a little angry with your stubborn insistence to stick by William. But mostly worried about you. I'm sorry I was short with you." He let his hand drop back onto his knee, but his other hand still played distractedly with a strand of her hair. Tingling darts of fiery heat ran down her spine.

She fought to churn the Spanish words floating in her head into English. "Don't. Worry about me, I mean."

"You're right. I shouldn't worry. But with the money coming in from these horses, I can't help but think there will be more threats."

"Yea, though I walk through the valley of the shadow of death, I will fear no evil; For You are with me; Your rod and Your staff, they comfort me,"

Nicki quoted quietly as she gazed across the fields surrounding them. "I don't know who wants me off my land. But I know God will be with us, Jace." She blushed at her inadvertent use of a more intimate version of his name and fiddled with an invisible speck on her skirt, but he didn't seem to notice. She hurried on. "I owe you an apology, too. Pastor said something in his sermon on Sunday, and I realized that God sent you to me to help and comfort me during this time and I wasn't very pleasant to you when Sheriff Watts arrested you." She turned to look at him. *"Lo siento."*

He swallowed, his throat working visibly, as he turned from looking at her to scan the horizon. He dipped his chin once, indicating his acceptance of her apology. Then he spoke. "Yes, I know God will be with us. I'm still learning to leave things in God's hands. But I think it would be wise to be a little more careful over the next few weeks. And no more glaring down bullets, all right?" His blue eyes pierced her, a demand for compliance shining in their depths. "Promise me you'll run for cover if shooting starts?"

She smiled. "I guess that was pretty stupid. I just didn't want them to think they could bully me."

"Promise?"

She rolled her lips together and nodded. "Promise."

"Good." He sat up straight and gave her mouth a gentle tap

with one finger. "You've got to stop doing that." He faced forward and once again took up the reins in both hands.

She frowned even as she realized he meant her habit of pressing her lips together when she was in deep contemplation. "Why?"

With a click of his tongue he started the buggy down the road. "It makes me want to kiss you."

She sucked in a startled gasp and turned her face away so he wouldn't see the heat washing over her.

He chuckled. "Consider yourself warned, Nick." He bumped her gently with his shoulder.

She groaned inwardly but found that a tingle of anticipation couldn't be vanquished.

Dusk was just falling when Tilly Snow opened the door and stepped outside to call the dog in. She froze, horror dropping her jaw.

Cutter, their sheep dog, hung by his back legs from the weeping willow tree in the yard, his throat slit, a pool of blood darkening the ground underneath his body.

Tilly glanced around. Terror pounded through her fast and furious, taking the strength from her legs. She collapsed to the ground, staring at the horrible sight, her mouth gaping. Who would do something like this? And then everything inside of her broke loose.

Her scream brought her family running.

"Oh, sweet Jesus." Mama sank to the ground beside her.

One word had been carved boldly into the bark of the tree. "Leave."

Mama wrapped her arms around Tilly's shoulders, tears coursing down her cheeks. "Oh, honey. Come inside. It will be okay, now. Patty," she spoke to Tilly's younger sister, "put on some water for tea." The last thing Tilly wanted was tea.

"I'll be all right, Mama." She climbed to her feet, stepped away, and started for the barn to get the shovel.

Behind her, she heard her father pull his rifle down from its pegs above the door and check his loads.

"Jim?" Mama asked. Tilly glanced back.

Daddy laid one hand on Mama's arm. "It will be okay, Suze. Don't worry. I'm just going to town for the Sheriff."

Tilly's eyes were drawn once again to the gruesome scene, and she couldn't seem to make her legs work.

With purposeful strides Papa stepped past her and into the barn to saddle his horse.

Sid galloped into the yard just as Papa led his horse from the barn. "Pa! The sheep've been slaughtered. More'n thirty of 'em!"

Jenny Ashland smiled at her husband, Jacob, over the top of their son's head. They both held one of Jake Jr.'s hands, swinging him between them. They had taken the opportunity to enjoy the warm weather and had gone for a family walk.

"Ready?" Jacob hollered. "One...two...THREE!" They swung the boy high in the air, laughing as the child squealed in glee.

"FEE!" Jake giggled, when his feet were back on the ground. "'Gain!"

Jacob's eyes dropped to her slightly rounded belly and then took in her face. She knew there were tired circles underneath her eyes. She hadn't slept well the night before.

Jacob glanced down at Jake. "One more time, son, and then we have to get home so Mama can get dinner and I can finish the chores." His eyes held a little worry as they traveled back to her face, and Jenny smiled to assure him that she was all right.

"Ready?" Jacob asked, "one...two...THR—" Jake's swing died before it had even begun.

"Oh, dear Lord!" Jenny gasped at the sight before them as they crested the low rise just south of their farm. One wall of the barn was on fire, and someone had shut the doors so the livestock couldn't escape.

Jacob immediately launched into action. "Jenny, stay here with Jake. I'll put out the fire and call for you if there's no danger."

"Be careful, Jacob." Jenny reached to touch the back of his shoulder as he hurried down the hill.

"Uh-oh," Jake uttered, pointing at the burning building.

"Yes, honey." Jenny squatted down and pulled the toddler into her embrace. "Uh-oh." *Lord, if only this* was *an accident.*

But it was obvious the fire had been set on purpose.

The note was pinned to the front door of the house with an arrow: *Move on, or next time it will be worse.*

★

Chapter Sixteen

The evening sun was sinking low as Rocky and Cade swung down from their saddles in front of Farewell Bend's mercantile and looped their reins over the hitching rail. Rocky sighed and stretched. It had been a long trip. They had pushed themselves hard to get here as quickly as they could. After all, this was Jason they were talking about. He would have done the same for them were the situations reversed.

Sky was back home, literally pacing a worn path in the floorboards of the sheriff's office. Rocky smiled. Sky had wanted to come with them, but Brooke was coming into her time any day now. And Sky's pacing wasn't even half due to the fact that Jason was in trouble.

Rocky glanced down the street and saw the sheriff's office and jail. He and Cade wanted very badly to go straight there and see Jason, but Ron's telegram had informed them that it might be better if they showed up without making it known they were here to help Jason out of this fix.

The town was not very large. Most of it stretched out before them on the one main street, although he could see a few buildings behind the others. Much of Farewell Bend's patronage probably came from outlying farms and ranches.

They pushed open the door of the mercantile and stepped inside to the jangling of the bell overhead.

"I'll be right there," the voice of a young woman called from a storeroom behind the counter. A moment later she emerged, carrying a stack of small crates that towered above her head. "Is that you, Mrs. Hamilton? We just got in that shipment of shoes that you were asking about last week." She peeked around the stack, let out a startled squeak, and dropped all the boxes, sending shoes, lids, and crates flying in all directions.

Rocky glanced at Cade and laid a hand of sympathy on his shoulder. Women were always falling all over themselves when they saw his good-looking friend. Cade's black curly hair and blue eyes were apparently enough to send even the most collected of women into a titter.

Ever the gentlemen, both bent to help her pick up the scattered mess but when they were done, Rocky was convinced that several of the boxes had shoes of different sizes in them. He was also surprised to note that the young woman was not staring at Cade but at him.

The pretty girl who apparently had lost her ability to speak for a moment suddenly found her voice. "Oh dear, I'm so sorry. I was expecting Mrs. Hamilton. You see, she always comes in on Wednesdays about this time. She's been wanting a new pair of shoes, and we just got in the shipment yesterday." She blushed and gestured to the once again neatly stacked crates. "As you can see. Well, when I looked around that stack and saw you two, you can imagine..." She giggled. "Well, you're definitely *not* Mrs. Hamilton. She's not nearly so—oh goodness!" She blushed to the roots of her hair, her eyes flitting from Rocky to the ground and back again. "I can't believe I almost said that. It's just that—" She stopped once again and Rocky saw her literally bite her tongue.

He decided to rescue her. "Ma'am, we need directions out to the Hanging T."

She jumped on that lifeline. "You're here to work for Mrs. Trent, aren't you? I heard that she was hiring. At least you look like ranchers." She paused. "Well," she gestured to Cade, "he does. You," she turned back to Rocky, "look more like a lawman."

Rocky pushed his hat back on his head and scratched his scalp before he replaced it. "Ma'am, can you tell us how to get out there?"

"Sure I can. It's not difficult to find. Why, once you've worked here for a time, you'll be able to ride the trail with a blindfold on." She giggled. "Not that you'd want to. That's just how easy it is to get there from here."

Cade sauntered down an aisle to browse. Rocky glared at

his retreating form, promising himself that he would lock horns with Cade later for leaving him to deal with this chatterbox.

"Ma'am?" he paused, waiting.

"Oh my! I've gone and done it again. I'm always talking too much, people say. It's really a bad habit. I tend to talk too much when I'm nervous. I'm not always like this, you know. It's just—oh! Never mind. Okay." She took a calming breath. "Head out of town that way." She gestured to the left. "Go about three quarters of a mile and you'll come to a fork. Take the fork to the left and the Hanging T is down that way just a couple of miles. You won't be able to miss it."

Rocky and Cade started toward the door.

Rocky tipped his hat. "Thank you, ma'am. We're much obliged. You have a good afternoon." The words almost tripped over themselves, he rushed to say them so fast. Turning, he hurried to the door, hoping that Cade would quickly follow suit.

He did, and when they were clear of the building, Rocky glanced at him. "That woman needs a man to temper her tongue."

Cade laid a hand on his shoulder. "Just so long as it's not one of us, Rock." He gave a mock shudder, and both men grinned as they mounted up. Cade's grin turned devilish. "'Course, it was you she had her eye on, and she wasn't bad to look at. Maybe you'll have to try your hand at quieting that tongue before we leave town."

Rocky snorted. "Not in this lifetime, Cade. I'll leave the flirting to those who are good at it." He gave his friend a pointed look, and Cade threw back his head on a laugh. Rocky knew that would keep Cade quiet for a while. He had been needling Cade lately about the number of girls he had taken out over the past two years. And Cade wouldn't want to touch that subject with a thirty-foot cattle prod.

Janice sighed as the two men rushed out. Sinking down onto one of the crates, she folded her hands on her lap.

"Lord," she whispered, "If You're going to send me a husband,

You'd better make him ugly as a cow's backside. I can't seem to hold my tongue around the good-looking ones You send my way. But my, I can't say that I'd mind if You'd just send one handsome man that liked to hear me talk. I would greatly appreciate it."

She leaned back into the wall and stared with starry eyes at the door. She was still sitting just so when Mrs. Hamilton came in a few minutes later.

"Janice! Are you all right?" the woman screeched.

Janice grinned. "The shoes you've been waiting on came in, Mrs. Hamilton. I was just going to put them out." She turned away before the woman could pry further into her state of airiness.

Jason glanced up when Nicki entered the barn. He was in the back corner clearing out the last vestiges of rubble. Jacob Ashland had ridden over to let them know what had happened at his place last night. And Tilly had arrived this morning with the news of what had happened to their dog and their sheep.

Nicki's face held vague disquiet, and he wondered what was troubling her now. They had brought Sawyer home with them the day before, and he knew she hadn't slept well last night with the boy in her bed. He'd heard her up a couple of times in the night. Perhaps she was just tired.

Sunlight poured into the barn's interior, since the roof was off, but he was in a back corner shaded by the hay loft, which miraculously had escaped too much damage when the roof caved in, and she hadn't noticed him yet. Glancing over himself, he grimaced. Shirt off, dirt smudged, and glistening with sweat, he would be quite a sight when she did notice him. But there was no help for it. Tapping his hat onto his head, he reached for his blue shirt, wiping his grimy hands on it before he swung it on and stepped out of the shadows. "Hi," he said, beginning to do the buttons.

Gasping, she spun toward him.

"Sorry. I didn't mean to startle you."

She smiled faintly, her eyes darting uneasily over his exposed chest. "You seem to be good at it, though."

He couldn't stop a grin as he finished with the last button and casually rested his hands on his hips. "Yes, I suppose I have given you more than your share of surprises by showing up…or waking up," his gaze dropped to where her legs were concealed under her skirt, "when you least expected." He enjoyed the blush that skittered across her cheeks.

She looked away. "*Sí.*"

That one little word sent his heart racing, because he suddenly knew she was feeling some of the same life-changing emotions he was. Could it be they'd only known each other for a few weeks? It felt much longer than that. He swallowed, trying to ignore the stampede taking place in his chest. *Breathe, Jordan. Breathe!*

He bent and slapped the dust from his denim-clad legs. "Nicki—" He frowned. "You've never said I could call you that. Do you mind?"

She shook her head and whispered, "No."

Not allowing himself to take the step toward her he longed to take, he continued, "We'll ride out and bring the horses here. They will need to be broken a little before we can hope to transport them to Bennett's ranch. But Cade can wire to have the money paid to the bank as soon as he sees the horses and determines what they are worth."

She tucked a black curl behind her ear. "That's fine."

There was a long silence as she stared at the ground, refusing to meet his gaze, and he simply enjoyed watching her. At length, she looked up. "What do you think we'll get for them?"

His heart rate spiked yet again. He liked the sound of that "we'll." She'd used it a couple times lately. "I could only venture a guess at this point. Cade knows a whole sight more about horses than me, and he'll give you a fair price for them."

"I'd like to be able to pay off the loan on the Jeffries' place too, if that's possible."

He smiled. "Jesus with skin? Ron told me about Pastor's sermon."

She nodded.

"I think it likely. We'll know soon. I expect Rocky and Cade any day now."

Her eyes suddenly glistened with unshed tears, and she spun away from him, starting out of the barn. Probably hoping he hadn't seen them.

"Nick?" He spoke her name before she could step through the door. She stopped but did not turn to look at him. Waving a hand over her shoulder, she shook her head to indicate she was all right. He knew better.

Stepping up behind her, he took her elbow and turned her to face him, stooping to look into her face. And when she tried to evade his scrutiny by twisting her face away, he finally gave in to the impulse that had been pounding at him from the moment he saw her walk in the door. Pulling her gently to him, he smoothed a hand over the back of her head. "Shhh, it's going to be all right."

She began to sob and he simply held her, allowing her the release of tears. Finally she was silent, but she didn't pull away. After a moment he asked, "Want to talk about it?"

Nicki knew she should step away from him but chose to stay right where she was. *"No sé. Estoy cansada."*

Pulling back slightly, he tipped her chin up, forcing her to meet his eyes and waiting for an interpretation. Reaching up, she straightened his skewed collar as she explained. "I don't know. I'm tired. The Jeffries, the Snows, the Ashlands, the ranch, William." She waved a hand, taking in a 360-degree scope of their surroundings. "You." The word was out before she could stop it. If ever there was a time Nicki wished that her words were tied to string, this was it. She wanted to pull that one little word right back into her mouth and swallow it.

But Jason didn't seem to notice. Bending toward her, he pressed his forehead to hers briefly and then pulled her head back onto his chest. "You're not forgetting your verses, are you? We're in the valley, Nick, but God has not left us. He's here. Sometimes we just don't feel like He is."

"Why did he take John, leaving Sawyer fatherless? And now this little one, too?"

"I don't know why John died, but God promises to be a Father to the fatherless."

"What about the ranch? What am I supposed to do? I don't even know if this is where God wants me to be."

Jason sighed. "That decision will have to be up to you. But I believe that God has provided for your needs at the moment. At least you aren't going to lose the ranch because you don't have the money. If you're to give up the ranch, God will help you know it. If not, I think you'll know that too. We just don't always get our answers immediately."

"Why did He let little May die?" Nicki could barely squeeze the question out past the deep anguish cinching her throat.

Jason's muscles tightened. "I don't know. I don't have all the answers, Nick. But I'm *'persuaded that neither death nor life, nor angels nor principalities nor powers, nor things present nor things to come, nor height nor depth, nor any other created thing, shall be able to separate us from the love of God which is in Christ Jesus our Lord.'"*

Nicki recognized the verses from the end of the eighth chapter of Romans.

Jason continued, "Those verses were a great comfort to me after I came back to the Lord. At first I was afraid that I'd done too much wrong for God to ever forgive me again, especially since I knew better. But Sky showed me those verses." He stroked the back of her head with his palm. "I don't know, Nick. We don't always understand God, but the Bible promises us that He loves us. We simply have to have the faith to believe what The Word says."

"I just wish I could take some of their pain."

He settled his chin on the top of her head. "Only God can do that now. You're trying to take too much on yourself."

Nicki allowed herself to relax in his arms. It felt so comforting to be here.

This embrace brought none of the disquieting sensations

she always experienced when she was with William. Jason was stable, whereas William always carried a volatile air, like he might explode with one emotion or another on a mere whim. And she still wasn't sure about his relationship with the Lord.

She thought back over her relationship with John. He had never held her this way, just to comfort her, showing her he was thinking of her needs above his own. To John, she had been a servant—there to meet his needs and nothing more. Toward the end maybe, he had softened a bit, but John's main purpose in life had been to gratify his own flesh.

Jason struggled with this as well—she had seen it on more than one occasion—but she never felt threatened by him. She had always been a little afraid when John returned at the end of the day. And William...she was never sure how to feel when she was with him, and it bothered her that his faith wasn't more evident.

She settled more comfortably into Jason's embrace, feeling his hand come up to cup the back of her head. As she thought back over the men in her life, she realized she had never been in love…until now. The sudden realization hit her with such a staggering force that she gasped and buried her face in his chest.

"Hey." His tone was worried, and he bent down, trying to glimpse her face. "You okay?"

Her cheeks burned hot. She nodded, her forehead still firmly planted against his broad chest.

"I thought maybe...you know...you were having some pains." She shook her head.

Jason settled his weight more comfortably, leaning back into his heels, and she relaxed again, simply enjoying being near him. Finally, when she thought she couldn't stand another minute in his arms lest she burst out with her newfound knowledge, and in Spanish nonetheless, for she knew she would never get all the words out in English, she giggled. Imagining the look on his face when she launched into a passionate speech in her native tongue, she lifted her head and started to pull back. He tightened his grip slightly and she sensed that he was reluctant to let her go. She glanced up quickly and the contented pleasure on his face gave her pause.

Eyes twinkling with obvious curiosity over her giggles, he stared down at her in question. "From crying to laughing in less than ten minutes. You really must have had a stressful week." One strong hand began to massage the tight muscles at the base of her neck, but Nicki refused to close her eyes and give in to the groan of pleasure the sensation elicited. Instead she studied his face. Could he be feeling some of the same things she was? She wondered at his feelings as she rolled her lips together and pressed tight.

One golden eyebrow arched. His gaze dropped to her mouth, then rebounded quickly, a devilish glimmer leaping into its depths. Her heart lurched as she realized her mistake. But a slight smile couldn't be vanquished and she waited expectantly, her heart rate increasing with every passing beat. This time she wanted him to follow through on the desire she could see reflected on his face.

For a moment he merely looked at her, and she thought he wouldn't do it. Disappointment surged through her.

But then his eyes dropped once more. "I believe I gave you fair warning," he whispered, just before his lips found hers.

He kissed her lightly at first, and Nicki trembled with pulse-pounding tranquility. She leaned gently into the kiss, her hands inching their way up his chest and reaching around his neck to pull his head down toward hers. The kiss deepened, and Nicki tapped the toe of one foot on the ground to make sure she was still solidly on *terra firma*. Two years of marriage and she had never felt this way. His kiss left her breathless, yet she could feel his restraint and that only added to her sense of well-being. She knew without a doubt that she could trust this man with her heart.

Jason finally pulled away, pressing his cheek to hers. He drew a ragged breath and cupped the back of her head, easing it down onto his shoulder. He spoke into her ear. "Well, I better go see to the horses."

She jerked back, stunned, but stopped at his innocent expression and jabbed him playfully in the ribs with a smile.

He grinned. "Come here." He pulled her back into his arms. They stood in silence for a time, each lost in their own thoughts. Finally he spoke, leaning back to look into her face. "God is good, Nicki. I don't have the answers to all your questions, but I know that you can trust Him."

"I know."

"And I'll be here for you." He let the back of one finger trail over her cheek. "You can count on that, Nick. I'm not going anywhere." He kissed her again, quickly this time, and then took a small step back, pressing his thumb across his lips as he put some distance between them. "The Jeffries still having a really rough time of it, huh?" His thumbs hooked into his belt loops.

She stepped back slightly as well, turning to look at the soddy door. "Yes. It's to be expected, I guess. I just wish there was something I could do."

"We'll have to pray for them. That's something we can do."

She nodded. "I have been."

"So have I." Taking her hand, he led her out of the barn.

He walked her to the door of the house and then reluctantly released her hand. "I really *should* go see about those horses." He gave her a sheepish smile. "I'll take Ron with me and, with Conner's help we shouldn't have any trouble getting them back here. We've set up a temporary holding-pen using the coral and the barn walls. All the stalls needed to be stripped out of the barn anyway. They were ruined when the roof fell on them, but we've pretty much got it cleaned out in there now. If we just close off the one end and make sure they have plenty of feed, they'll be fine for a couple of days until Rocky and Cade can get here." He backed away from her slowly. "We'll probably sleep out there tonight and start for here early in the morning. Could you pack us a little grub?"

She nodded.

He started to walk away but then turned back with a grin and winked at her, his appreciative gaze taking her in from head to toe.

Her eyes widened, but with a shake of her head she spun around and opened the door to the house before he could see her blush. *Won't be long and I'll be as big as the barn. We'll see what he thinks then.*

Jason couldn't believe his good fortune when he stepped out from the barn leading his horse and saw Rocky and Cade riding up. A grin split his face. "If you two aren't a sight for sore eyes, I don't know what is."

Rocky and Cade swung down. Jason clasped Rocky's hand, pulling him into a manly hug and clapping him on the back. "Cade." He turned to his friend, doing the same. "It sure is good to see you guys."

Rocky said, "I see you managed to finagle your way out of jail without our help."

Jason tipped back his hat and raked a hand through his hair before he replaced it. "Strange thing, that. I'll tell you all about it. But I bet you two could use a cup of coffee."

Cade grinned. "Now there's a man I like. Knows just what to offer a fella at the end of a long trip."

Rocky gestured to Jason's horse. "Heading somewhere?"

"I was heading out to round up the horses, but now that you two are here, I'd like to fill you in first."

As they approached the soddy, the door opened and Nicki stepped out. "Hello." She extended her hand. "I saw you ride up a moment ago. You must be Cade and Rocky. I'm Nicki Trent."

The men whipped hats from their heads and clasped her hand. "Yes, ma'am."

"Come in. Coffee's on." She stepped aside, and the three men filed into the house, each ducking to avoid hitting his head on the lintel. "Please, have a seat." Nicki motioned to the table where Rolf and Brenda were seated, then introduced all the adults in the house ending with, "Everyone, this is Rocky and Cade."

The men nodded, and Tilly smiled pleasantly. "Pleased to meet you."

"And this," Jason scooped Sawyer up into his arms, giving him a whirl before settling him against the crook of one arm for the men to see, "is Sawyer. He's the man of the house."

Sawyer grew suddenly shy and buried his face in Jason's neck. Tender love tightened Nicki's throat as she took in the sight.

Jason met her gaze for a moment before he ruffled Sawyer's hair and placed him back on the rug in front of the stove. Then he seated himself at the table.

Rolf stood. "Best we go fer a walk, Bren, an' let these folk talk business." He stretched a hand toward his boys. "Boys, come along."

Nicki reached out. "Please don't feel like you have to leave."

Brenda patted her arm. "Fresh air will be some good fer us, I reckon."

Quietly the family gathered their wraps and shuffled out the door. Nicki wondered if they would go up to May's grave and prayed this would be one more step in their healing process.

While Nicki poured coffee, Jason filled Rocky and Cade in on the details of their situation.

As she took her seat, thankfulness once again coursed through her. God had sent a wonderful man to her aid. *Gracias, Jesus.*

Rocky and Cade listened intently without interruption until Jason finished.

Then Rocky clarified, "So we have until Tuesday evening to get the money to the bank in Portland?"

Jason nodded. "Right."

"That gives us four days."

"It's gonna be tight," Jason agreed.

"And you said there are 209 horses?" Cade asked.

"I haven't seen them up close. But that's the number Ron said they counted. Four of our—" He cleared his throat. "Four of *Nicki's* hands are out there with them now."

Nicki's heart warmed at his slip, but she sipped her coffee casually.

She noted that Cade and Rocky exchanged an amused glance.

Jason looked up, meeting her gaze over the top of her cup. She put her cup on the table, wishing she could lean over and slide her hand into his.

Cade chuckled, evidently taking in the way they looked at each other. He placed a hand over his heart and looked directly at her. "Ma'am, if this man is bothering you in any way, you just let me know, and I'll be happy to put him in his place for you."

Rocky grinned and swallowed a mouthful of coffee, his eyes darting back and forth between Nicki and Jason.

Nicki smiled softly. *"Para amigos, todos; para enemigos, uno solo."*

The men all looked at her with blank expressions. Jason, humor filling his eyes, sipped the dark brew, his gaze never leaving her face as he waited for her interpretation.

"We have a saying. 'One enemy is too many; and a hundred friends too few.' I believe that Jace is in exactly the place God meant for him to be. He has been a true friend, and I am glad to have him here." She turned her frank gaze directly on Cade. "We have another saying, *La serpiente no está muy lejo de la casa de las gallinas*. 'The snake is never far from the hen house.'" She raised an eyebrow at him and took a saucy sip.

Jason, Rocky, and Tilly burst out laughing.

Cade did his best to look hurt but couldn't help but join in the laughter. "Hey, when it comes to a pretty lady, I can't help but try."

Rocky shook his head. "Ain't that the truth." Another ripple of laughter circled the room.

A moment of silence followed and then Jason asked, "So Cade, how do you think we should handle this situation?"

Cade's face immediately turned serious. "I agree with you that if someone is set on getting this land, we should keep the existence of the horses as much a secret as possible until I can wire Dad to take the money to the bank. I set that up before we came. Dad is waiting in Portland for my wire. He'll go straight to the Portland branch once we settle on a price and I wire him about it."

Jason ran a finger around the rim of his cup with a worried frown.

"Time's short. You think we can pull this off?"

Rocky tossed back the last swallow in his cup. "Why doesn't Cade come out and look at the horses? You two can decide on the price, if that's all right with Nicki. And then we can herd them back here while Cade rides to town and wires Smith."

"That's fine with me," Nicki said.

"Sounds good to me, too." Cade drummed his fingers on the table, apparently eager to get on with the mission.

The stiff line of Jason's shoulders softened slightly, and Nicki hated to mention her next question, knowing it would bring back some of his tension. "The reason someone might want my land, I can see. It is good land. But what about these others who were threatened? They each only had 160 acres. So why them?"

Jason tipped back in his chair, folding his arms and Rocky and Cade toyed with their cups.

"How many people have had trouble now?" Cade asked.

"Four, including Nicki." Jason replied. "Thing is, the other three were just small homesteads."

Tilly spoke up from where she'd been playing with Sawyer on the rug in front of the stove. "Mom and Dad don't know what to think of it. There is no reason someone should want our land so badly. It just doesn't make sense.

Daddy says he's not going anywhere without a fight."

Jason nodded. "Jacob Ashland said the same when he stopped by earlier. I'm afraid if someone doesn't figure this out soon, we're going to have a bloodbath on our hands."

Nicki's heart pounded with dread at his words. Would there ever be an end to the trouble? Only God could help them all. If ever there was a time when people needed His comfort, it was now.

The men pushed back from the table and reached for their hats.

Quickly, Nicki stood. "Can we pray, please? There are so many people who need God's help right now."

Jason nodded and his face softened. "Sure, let's do that." Tossing his hat back on the table, he gripped the back of the chair in front of him and bowed his head. The others did the same. "God," Jason's voice was sincere, "we really need Your help right now. There are so many people who have been threatened and just a lot of questions, Lord. First I pray that You would bring whoever is responsible for all of this to justice. Reveal who they are, Lord. Second, we pray for Your favor for these innocent, hard-working people. We know You are a God of comfort even when we are going through a difficult time, so make Yourself ever closer to them now. We also ask, Lord, that You would allow Nicki to keep her ranch. Help us to be able to get the horses back here and the money to Portland with no further complications. We ask these things in Jesus' name. Amen."

Nicki looked up, eyes misty, and met his gaze. "Thank you."

He nodded and reached for his hat as Cade and Rocky headed for the door. "We should be back by this time tomorrow."

She followed him, wishing he didn't have to go. "I'll be looking for you."

He stepped out the door, then faced her and reached for her hand, squeezing it gently. "Don't worry about us. We'll be fine."

"*Si*." She pressed her lips together.

His gaze flicked briefly to her mouth, and he grinned. "*Si. No preocuparse.*"

Her eyes widened. How had he learned to say "Don't worry" in Spanish? He chuckled and stepped back, his hand lingering on hers so their arms stretched between them.

"How—?"

He held up his free hand, stopping her question with a wink. "A man has to have some secrets."

"Really?"

He nodded, grinning like a cat lapping cream.

Across the yard Cade led two horses from the barn and cleared his throat loudly. "Jordan, the horses will all be dead by the time you quit staring like a schoolboy with a crush at Ms. Trent!"

Rocky grinned as he swung into the saddle.

Jason squeezed her fingers one last time. "I gotta go. We'll be back tomorrow."

She nodded, wishing she could throw herself into his arms. But Rocky and Cade waited.

He stepped back, breaking the contact between them, and Nicki felt bereft. She gripped the doorpost with both hands, leaning into it as she watched them ride from the yard. *Jesus, bring him back to me, please.*

★

Chapter Seventeen

Brooke rose to clear the dishes from their late lunch. Sky had just left to go back to work, and she missed him already. Her belly preceded her as she stood from the chair and she giggled at her own bulk. It seemed she couldn't do anything these days without her tummy getting in the way.

She reached to pick up Sky's plate and sucked in a gasp. "Ohhh." She closed her eyes and waited. The pain eased, and she let out her breath. She would do the dishes and wait to see if she really was in labor. The dishes were in the hot water when the next contraction seized her. She waited for it to pass and calmly finished the chore.

That was how she spent her afternoon. Doing little chores here and there, making sure the house was in perfect order, and in between halting as a contraction demanded.

She was in the rocking chair, darning one of Sky's socks, when he came in the door that evening. He took one look at her face and rushed to her side, squatting down by her chair. "Brooke honey, are you…?"

She bit her lip. "Sky, I think you should go for the doctor."

He bolted to his feet. "The doctor!" Spinning back toward the door, he opened it so fast that it hit the toe of one of his boots, bounced back, and smashed his fingers against the jamb. Brooke winced, hearing his yelp of pain as he bolted outside, not even bothering to retrieve his hat from its peg. But he'd only been gone for a couple of seconds when he burst back through the door and took her by the elbow. "Up. I'm not leaving you sitting here in the living room."

"Sky—," Brooke began to protest but the iron in his gaze stopped her.

"Come on. Into bed." He helped her climb the stairs, remove

her dress, and get into her nightgown. Even brought her a cup of hastily made tea. "How long have you been—?" He rolled his hand around in the general area of her stomach but included her head and toes in the gesture.

"I think since lunch time." She sipped the tepid tea calmly.

"Lunch!" He bolted to his feet again and, as he rushed out the door, she heard him mumble, "Lord, don't let this child be as headstrong as she is!"

She smiled tiredly, knowing she was in the best of hands.

Sheriff Watts ran a tired hand down his face. He was trying to wrap his mind around the cases. He stood and moved to the woodstove, picking up the coffee pot and pouring the thick black liquid into his still half-full cup. It was an act of habit; his mind was not on the drink.

Jason Jordan had been out of jail only a couple days and already several more families had been threatened to move off their land. Could he have misjudged the man? He'd been in this business a long time. Long enough to know that sometimes even the most likable of men weren't what they appeared to be.

His mind went back to Slim. He had come in and said that Jordan couldn't have set the fire out at the Jeffries' place. Could they be in this together?

No. He shook his head, staring out the window as he took a mincing sip of the hot coffee. Slim had been in this area for years. He didn't think they were together on this, so that left only two options. One, Slim was lying for some reason and Jordan did set that fire. Or two, Slim had been telling the truth and Jordan was innocent. So why had the threats started again as soon as he was freed?

Clomping back to his desk, Watts pulled out the chair and sat down heavily. There was a third option, he suddenly realized. Someone could want to make it look like Jordan was doing this. But who would that be?

He twisted the end of his mustache. Perhaps he should have

another talk with Slim. Maybe he could shed some light on this. Shuffling through the papers on his desk, he located the county plot map. He added two more squares to the page, one around the Snow place and one around the Ashland's. Two squares already encompassed the plots indicating the Jeffries and Trent places.

He stared at the page, thoughtfully. What did these pieces of property have in common? Absentmindedly, he slurped his coffee.

A thought occurred to him. Jordan couldn't have been the one shooting up Mrs. Trent's spread; he'd been there, Nicki had told him so when he questioned her. Could the incidents be separate?

"Blazin' saddles and cactuses! I got me more questions than rattlers in the Deschutes canyon!" Slapping his hand on the papers he stood, reaching for his hat. He needed some answers, and he wasn't getting any sitting in the office.

Sky paced the living room. Ma was here, up in the room with the doctor. Marquis and Jeff had also come over, and the scent of coffee now wafted from the kitchen, where Jeff had disappeared on arrival. With a huff Sky sank down into a chair. He rested his elbows on his knees and clasped his hands behind his head. He sat there motionless for just a moment, then scrubbed his hands through his hair and looked up.

Marquis, seated on the couch, head cocked slightly to one side, wore a gentle smile as she listened to his movements. "Sky? She is going to be just fine. Doctor Martin is really good."

He grimaced, praying she was right as he looked toward the stairs. "I'm sure you're right. Just wish it wasn't taking so blasted long!"

Marquis covered her mouth, but her mirth was plainly evident.

For a moment irritation flooded his veins; then he grinned. "Been pacing like a caged bear, haven't I?"

She nodded.

"I've never been so excited and so worried all at the same time."

A rustle on the stairs drew his gaze, and he jumped to his feet in anticipation.

Ma, skirts lifted, hurried down the last couple steps and across the room toward him. Tears streamed down her face and, without a word, she pulled him into a tight hug.

His excitement guttered and died. His arms went around her slowly, and he rested his chin on the top of her head. Something had gone wrong. His eyes slid shut. "Ma?" The word was barely audible.

She stepped back, brushing away the tears on her cheeks with both hands and straightening the front of his shirt.

He stood waiting, hands hanging limply at his sides. Knowing he wouldn't be able to bear whatever she was trying to tell him.

She looked up, meeting his gaze, and a slow smile parted her lips even as more tears coursed down her cheeks. "You're a daddy," she whispered.

Relief flashed but was quickly followed by another plunge into dread.

He glanced at Marquis. Her face was taut, mouth slightly open, one hand pressed to her chest.

Dear God, not Brooke! He took a step back. "Brooke? Is she…?"

Ma brushed away more tears and blinked in surprise. "She's fine, dear. Go on up and see for yourself."

The strength left his knees and he plopped back down into his chair, his own eyes filling with moisture. He ran his fingers back through his hair. "You just took ten years off my life, Ma. I thought something was wrong." He looked up at her.

She covered her mouth, eyes widening. "I'm sorry. It's just that I'm a grandma and you're a daddy and….it's all too much. God is so good."

He grinned, surged to his feet, and headed for the stairs with long strides. "Yes, He is."

Quietly he pushed open the door to their room. Brooke was sitting up in bed, her back to the headboard, hair in wild disarray, cheeks flushed, and tired bags under her eyes. She was the most beautiful thing he'd ever seen. Her concentration was on the swaddled baby resting in the crook of one arm as she talked to it softly. But when he entered she looked up and smiled, resting her head against the headboard. "Hi," she whispered.

He blinked back tears as he padded to the edge of the bed and sat down, looking into the face of his child for the first time. "Hi." He never took his eyes off the baby.

"Do you want to hold her?"

"Her?" His voice was gravely, and he cleared his throat. He had a daughter!

Brooke smiled and placed the baby in his arms. "Her."

He felt like a peasant who'd just been handed the crown jewels. He swallowed, still blinking back tears. One man didn't deserve so much blessing.

All he could see was the face of the swaddled little bundle. A small tuft of black hair pulsed in time with her heartbeat at the top of her head. Long black lashes rested against small round cheeks. And when he stroked her cheek with the back of one finger her tiny pink mouth automatically turned in that direction, looking for something to latch onto.

He chuckled tenderly and looked at Brooke. "She's beautiful."

Brooke smiled, eyes sliding shut. "I want to name her Sierra Dawn."

He looked back at his little girl. "That's a fine name. Hello, Sierra Dawn."

Doctor Martin approached, drying his hands on a towel. "Best to let them sleep for now," he whispered.

Sky stood, helping Brooke, who gave no protest, slide down under the covers and snuggle the baby securely in her arms.

His heart soared as he stood back, arms folded, and took in the sight of his wife and daughter. Yes, indeed. No man ever was so blessed.

The next morning, Nicki was checking the barn over one last

time when she heard a rider enter the yard. Diablo began to have a conniption.

Rolf looked up from where he was huddled in one corner mending harnesses, but Nicki waved him to stillness as she moved to see who it was.

"Diablo!" Nicki stepped out of the barn. "Quiet!" The pup lay down and put his head on his huge paws with only a whimper of protest.

It was William. He swung down from the saddle with practiced ease and emerged into her vision holding a huge bouquet of wild irises.

He held them out to her with a smile. "I thought you might like these. There are hundreds of them in the little valley at the back end of my property. When I saw them, I thought of you and couldn't resist bringing you some."

Feeling slightly uneasy, Nicki took the flowers. "They're beautiful, William. Thank you." She buried her nose in the blossoms.

"You named him Diablo?" William gestured to the puppy, but his eyes took in the barn, stripped of everything but the walls. A frown formed.

Nicki rolled her eyes at the puppy, ignoring William's obvious interest in the barn. "Trust me, he earned the name. The first night we kept him in the house and he dug himself a hole to the outside, right by the door there." She gestured to a place at the base and to the left of the door that had obviously been patched recently. "Ron fixed it. And the next night we decided to tie him outside. He proceeded to redig the hole to the *inside*." She gestured to the same spot. "He's a little devil, but Sawyer loves him, and for that I thank you."

William smoothed one hand down the front of his cowhide vest. "I see you are cleaning out the barn. I heard in town that the church members are going to help you with a barn-raising."

Nicki nodded, her unease growing. Jason, Rocky, and Cade could be back with the horses at any minute. It wouldn't do for William to be here when they arrived. She grimaced inwardly.

Had Jason convinced her, then, that William wasn't all that he made himself out to be? She shuddered. Could he really have set fire to the Jeffries' cabin? Shot at her? Maybe even killed John? She buried her face in the bouquet to hide her thoughts from him. What would be his motivation for those actions? Just to get land? Surely not. Still…*better safe than sorry.*

"What can I do for you, William?" She wanted to hurry him on his mission, whatever that might be, and get him out of here.

His face softened. "Come riding with me."

Nicki looked up. What should she do? Could she keep him riding long enough for the men to get the horses back to the ranch undiscovered?

William cleared his throat.

Nicki sighed. No. Better get him on his way as soon as possible. "I can't go riding with you. Sawyer has had a runny nose, and I don't want to take him out in this cold."

His face hardened. "Tilly can watch him."

Nicki shook her head. "No. It's just about time for her to head for home. And something awful happened at their place two nights ago. I don't want her riding home in the dark."

William folded his arms. "Yes, I heard. Interesting that things started happening again as soon as Jason got out of jail."

And just like that, Nicki knew. Like a kick in the chest from a mule, the truth hit her. It was William. He was trying to set Jason up. Jason had been with her the whole afternoon and evening when the Snows and Ashlands had been threatened. He had a rock-solid alibi. Fear clenched a fist around her heart, and she stepped back.

William nodded. "Yes, I can see the truth dawning on your face. Where has Jason been lately?"

Jesus! Help me remain calm. "I—I don't—he hasn't been here for several hours."

Satisfaction washed his features. "I thought so." He almost smiled. "I'll let the sheriff know."

"Yes, well. I best be getting inside so Tilly can go home." All she wanted was to get away from him as fast as she could. She started toward the soddy.

He fell into step beside her. "How about Mrs. Jeffries? She could watch the boy."

Nicki hated it when he referred to Sawyer as "the boy." She turned to look him full in the face. "Mrs. Jeffries is still grieving the loss of her murdered daughter. She does not need to be babysitting Sawyer." Did his face pale slightly at that remark?

William cleared his throat. "Fine, then have Tilly wait. Come riding with me, and I will escort her home when we get back."

Nicki scrambled for something to say. "William, nothing more can ever come from our relationship. I thank you for being a good friend and neighbor, but that is all we can ever be—friends and neighbors."

"Nicki." His tone was cajoling, and she felt her skin crawl as he took her elbow. "Give it some time." He pulled her to a stop. "You've only been widowed a little less than a month. There is a future for us. After things settle down, you will see things differently."

Just get him to leave! That was her current goal. She smiled thinly.

"Maybe so. But I don't feel right about making Tilly wait. Can we go riding another time?" She desperately hoped he couldn't hear the revulsion in her voice.

He sighed. "Fine. I should probably head into town to talk to the sheriff anyways."

Nicki nodded. She didn't care what he told Sheriff Watts. She knew Jason had an alibi for yesterday's events. And town was in the opposite direction from where Jason would be coming with the horses. She lifted the bouquet and opened the door, stepping inside. "Thanks for the flowers, William."

William smiled. "Things are gonna get better, Nicki. And when they do, you'll see that you and I could have a great future together."

Nicki felt like her smile was chiseled out of ice. "Bye."

He tipped his hat, spun on his heel, and almost tripped over Diablo, who was skulking just behind him.

The pup yipped and scuttled toward the door. Nicki let him

in and then clicked the door shut. She leaned against it, tipping her head back in relief.

Brenda and her two boys sat before the stove weaving rags into braid to later be used for a rug. Tilly sat at the table mending clothes. Everyone looked up, but then Brenda and the boys immediately resumed what they were doing.

Tilly paused in her sewing and eyed her. "What?"

"De noche todos los gatos son negros. Un gato verdadero negro es revelado por la luz."

"Un-huh."

Nicki smiled, opened the door to the woodstove, and threw the flowers inside. A satisfying hiss sizzled through the room.

Tilly gasped at the abrupt action. Brenda and the boys made no indication of even having noticed.

Nicki shut the door and dusted her hands with satisfaction, smiling at Tilly. "We have a saying, 'At night all cats are black. A true black cat is revealed by the light.' Today the light has turned on in my heart."

Tilly huffed. "If you had asked me, I could have told you William was a black cat a long time ago."

Nicki sighed. "I should have asked."

"Fwowers gone?" Sawyer asked, studying the stove intently.

Nicki and Tilly chuckled. Nicki swung him up into the air and spun him around in a circle. "Flowers gone!" she acknowledged, tickling his belly.

Sawyer giggled, then waved at the stove. "Bye, Bye," he said, bringing a fresh round of laughter.

Nicki settled Sawyer on her hip, then nodded toward the door and spoke to Tilly. "You better get home. Today was your day to only work a half day. You need the break, and I'm sure your mother could use the support at home."

Tilly's face fell, but she put the mending back into the basket and stood. "You're probably right."

Nicki knew she had been hoping Conner would arrive in time to escort her home. The young couple hadn't seen each other for several days. She pulled Tilly into a one-armed hug. "He'll be here when you get back in the morning."

Tilly groaned. "Am I *that* obvious?"

Sheriff Watts swung down from his horse in front of the Snows' place. Suzanne opened the door as he wrapped his reins around the corral rail. She dried her hands on her apron. "Sheriff. Glad you stopped by. Jacob just came over a short while ago. Won't you come in?"

"Oh, Jacob's here? Good. That'll save me a trip o'er to his place." He removed his hat as he stepped over the threshold and both Jim and Jacob stood from the table.

The men extended their hands.

"Jim. Jacob. Good to see ya both. I had a few more questions about what happened t'other night an' wondered if I might impose, so to speak. It be pure providence that Jacob is here today."

Suzanne poured the sheriff a cup of coffee as all three men settled themselves around the table.

Sheriff Watts shifted uneasily. "Some o' my questions may seem a mite personal. But I want ya both t' know that it's only my intention to find out who's causin' all the ruckus 'round these parts." Jim and Jacob nodded.

"First off, do either of you have anyone that you know as your enemy?" Both men shook their heads.

"Do you have any money tied up in your place? An equity loan of sorts?"

Jim nodded. "We don't owe anything on our land, of course, since we're homesteading. But we had to borrow some money from the bank for seed and supplies last year when things got a little tight. Nice banker in Prineville, name of Roland gave it to us."

Jacob agreed. "Yeah, same for us. We'd already proved up, but we had to borrow for a woodstove and some hay last year. Must be the same banker. Nice guy. He made us feel real comfortable, not like some o' the bankers do these days. He's a rancher too. Owns a ranch just south o' here. Something like twenty thousand acres. So he knew what it was like to be in the business. He doesn't get down here much, though, since he has a bank in Portland and one in Prineville. He has a man managing his place down here."

Sheriff Watts twisted the end of his mustache. "And what did you put up for collateral on these loans?"

Jim made a circular gesture with one finger. "My land. All of it. Seemed like a lot of collateral to me, but he assured me that was how banks did things now. And I knew I would get it paid off, so I didn't worry overmuch about it, until our sheep were slaughtered. Now I'm not sure what's gonna happen to us."

Jacob nodded. "Same for us, Sheriff. We put up all our land as collateral. We don't get that loan paid off, our land reverts to the bank. Now that our barn has burned, and the horses didn't make it…." His shoulders slumped with the weight of his burden.

Sheriff Watts twisted his mustache for another minute, staring up at the ceiling and muttering under his breath. Suddenly his hand came down on the table with a loud crash. "Blazin' blue-bellied bulls!"

Suzanne gasped from the living room where she'd been sewing on a quilt piece.

Sheriff Watts looked chagrined and lowered his voice. "Sorry, ma'am." He stood and snatched up his hat. "I believe we done caught ourselves a varmint, boys. I got to get me out to the Trent place and talk to the Jeffries. I'll be seein' ya."

With a touch to the rim of his hat he dashed out the door.

Tilly had only been gone for a couple minutes when Nicki heard a rider enter the yard. Picking up her skirts, she hurried to the door. Maybe the men were home! But it was only Sheriff Watts. And, to her dismay, William was with him. She hurried over and met them by the corral.

"Ma'am." The sheriff tipped his hat as he faced her.

"Sheriff." She eyed the horizon, hoping against the odds

that Jason and the horses would be later than she expected. She brought her gaze back to the men before her as they started toward the house. Had they detected her worry? "William," she acknowledged.

He nodded. "I bumped into the sheriff on my way into town. He said he was coming here, so I accompanied him. I figured you'd need to verify that your new hand hasn't been around for several hours anyways. Isn't that right, Sheriff?"

Nicki's heart pounded as she waited for his reply.

Sheriff Watts cleared his throat. "Well, let's not git the cart afore the horse. I ain't so sure that this here Jordan fella is our man."

Nicki sighed with relief. Sheriff Watts was no head-hunter. He was after the truth.

William ran a hand down the front of his vest. "Really? Why ever not? Things started happening again right after he got out of jail."

The sheriff paused midstride. "Yes, sir, I guess you'd be right on that count." His gaze narrowed, and he caressed one end of his mustache. "You know a fella by the name o' Roland? Banker down Portland way who owns a branch in Prineville, too?"

Nicki gasped and put one hand to her collar. That was the banker John had borrowed the money from! She fixed her gaze on William.

The muscles in his face tightened and he blinked. "Yes. I do. He…he holds a loan of mine. Why do you ask?"

Sheriff Watts stilled. He didn't respond for a minute. Then, like the hands on a clock that had just been wound, he started for the soddy again. "No reason. Just a hunch o' mine. If you owe Roland money, though, I'd watch things around the home place real careful like o'er the next couple a days. Ms. Trent, you seemed surprised a moment ago by the name o' Roland. You know him?"

The trio paused in front of the soddy door.

"Yes, sir. Well, I've never met him, but my husband owed him quite a substantial sum of money. If I don't have it paid off by Tuesday, my land reverts to his bank."

Sheriff Watt's huffed. "Figured as much. Are the Jeffries here?"

"Yes. Do come in." Nicki reached to open the door.

William fiddled with the edge of his vest. "Well, Sheriff, it appears you don't need me here. I'll be heading home now, but keep Jordan in mind. He's still a prime suspect in my book." He tipped his hat to Nicki, then strode purposefully toward his horse and rode out of the yard in the direction of his own spread.

Nicki sighed in relief as she watched him disappear over the horizon. Following Sheriff Watts into the house, she poured him a cup of coffee, praying that William would ride home and not come back today.

William clenched his jaw. Curse it all! Something was not right. Why would the sheriff be asking about Roland? And Nicki certainly had been acting strange today.

Once out of sight of the Hanging T and Nicki, he paused to contemplate his next move. He'd better stick around and see if his worries were justified. Spitting on the ground, he turned his mount and circled to a small cluster of Junipers. Leaving his horse there, he belly-crawled up the hill until he could peer down into the valley. He settled down to wait. He intended to find out what was going on at the Hanging T.

Half an hour later a sharp whistle pierced the air, and Nicki hurried to the door, scanning the horizon.

Jason, Ron, two of the new hands, Conner, and Rocky rode into view, herding the most magnificent lot of horses Nicki had ever seen.

Covering her mouth with one hand, Nicki blinked back tears of joy and amazement. Another sharp whistle pierced her reverie. Dashing across the yard, she opened the corral gate, yelling for Rolf to come out of the barn. He stepped out beside her as she watched the herd coming down the slope. She clutched her throat, the tears falling freely. They had done it! *Gracias, Jesus!*

"Well, I'll be!" Rolf whispered in wonder.

The lead stallion, a beautiful white creature with the longest cornsilk mane Nicki had ever seen, arched his neck. His head bobbed this way and that, the whites of his eyes clearly visible as his nostrils flared wide, and he searched for a means of escape.

Rocky, riding at the back of the thundering mass, gave a sharp whistle. "Ho! Get on there!" His whip cracked just to the outside of a mare trying to dart away from the herd and she shied back into line.

The white stallion dodged, trying to lead his pack away from the looming trap, but Jason and Ron rode on either side of him, giving no quarter. He had nowhere to go but into the corral. He darted in. Snorting and pawing, he cantered a quick circle. For one moment Nicki thought he would leap the fence. Then shaking his head, mane flying, he trotted into the barn, his milling brood of mares following right behind.

Rocky urged the last horse into the pen, then reached down and latched the gate.

Swinging down from his horse, Jason tipped back his hat, grabbed Nicki by the waist and twirled her around in a wide circle. "We did it!" He grinned.

"I can see that." She laughed, clutching the lapels of his coat for dear life. He set her back on her feet and tucked her close.

Her heartbeat raced as though she'd been sprinting right alongside the herd. He swallowed, his blue eyes roving over her face. "God is good."

"*Si.*" She swallowed. "William was here a little while ago," she whispered.

His eyes never left her face. "Don't worry about it." He tapped her nose. "He won't have time to make any trouble now. Cade rode to town to wire his father. We settled on fifty dollars a head. I picked out nine of them for us to keep. The rest he bought."

Nicki quickly did the math and then gasped at the price. "That gives us extra money to work with even after we pay off the land and the Jeffries' place!"

He nodded.

Gracias, Señor.

Both realized at the same moment that they were the center of attention.

Jason let go of her waist and stepped back, settling his hat straight on his head.

Rocky grinned and clapped him on the shoulder. "Come on, let's go get some coffee."

The men headed for the soddy, but Nicki was transfixed. She couldn't move. She could only stare at the horses. They were beautiful—the most beautiful thing she'd seen in a long time.

She wiped tears from her cheeks with the flats of her fingers. Freedom. A home for Sawyer and the new little one. A bright future. All milling around in front of her in a collage of blacks, browns, reds, and creams.

She climbed onto the bottom rail of the corral to reach over and pet one of the animals.

The sound of a pistol cocking made Nicki look up. Her awe over the horses dissipated like fog touched by the first rays of the sun. William stood at the corner of the barn; his head and gun arm all she could see.

He centered the aim of the pistol on her chest. "Don't make a sound, or you are going to leave one little boy all alone in this world."

★

Chapter Eighteen

Tom Roland was not usually home at this hour of the day. But he'd received the shock of this life this morning and so, for the first time in weeks, he headed home for lunch instead of to the Boarding House Café. He needed a stronger drink than was socially acceptable for this time of day. Maybe two.

The money had come through to pay off the Trent property. Not only that, but the loan he'd made to the Jeffries had also been paid off. And this morning he'd received a wire from his ranch manager. Something had stampeded his herd at the ranch, and over half his cattle had been killed when they tumbled into the Deschutes canyon.

His jaw clenched. His plans were crumbling before his eyes. The Stockman's Association was not pleased with the job he'd done, and he knew there would be more repercussions to come. That's what he got for hiring his work done, instead of just doing it himself. William had obviously failed.

He slammed through the front door and stormed into the foyer. Voices filtered down the stairs. He stilled. Paused to listen.

Vanessa's laughter. And a man's response.

Tom ground his teeth. Not again. He'd thought they'd made it past all this. Rage started to rise somewhere around his knees and made his legs quake as he took the stairs three at a time. "Vanessa!" he bellowed as he rounded the banister on the top floor. The pearl-handled Colt, still in its holster, felt cool to his palm. He launched himself against her bedroom door. "Vanessa!"

The door to the bedroom splintered inward, and he crashed through the portal.

Vanessa gasped and snatched for her robe.

He took in the scene, fury blinding him to everything but the two people in the room.

"Tom."

That was the voice she used when she wanted to calm him. He pressed his lips together and scanned her from head to toe. It was not going to work this time. She'd picked the wrong day to betray him again. Blasted woman! He should have washed his hands of her years ago. Fury made him quake. He spun in a wide roundhouse, sending his foot through the panel of the door.

The wall rattled as the door crashed against it and bounced back.

The man, still snatching for his clothing, jumped straight up and froze, wide eyes fixed on Tom, his pants clutched to his chest.

For one electric moment they stood looking at each other and then, suddenly, a gun appeared in the man's hand.

Tom blinked. "Who are you?"

A hard smile split his opponent's lips. "Name's Jonas. The Association sent me. Seems they ain't too happy with the job you done over Prineville way. I'm the clean-up man."

Tom clenched his jaw. "What are you doing with Vanessa?"

Jonas smirked. "Had me some time on my hands, whilst I waited for you ta git home. She's a passing pleasant diversion. Don't suppose I'll be able to leave'er alive, though, once I'm done."

Vanessa screamed and curled her head into her arms, trembling like a wind-blown leaf.

Fear coiled in Tom's belly and he spread his hands, down by his hips, but wide enough to offer no threat. There was only one way to deal with this situation—to take the man out while he wasn't expecting it. *Talk to him; that will throw him off guard.* "Let's be calm now, we can work this—!"

In that moment, when his words were still a slight distraction, he threw himself down onto one knee and palmed his gun.

Jonas pulled the trigger a hair too late. The bullet grazed harmlessly over Tom's right shoulder and sank into the wood of the door frame.

Tom's bullets did not miss. Two holes appeared in the fabric of the pants Jonas had clutched to his chest and with a strangled grunt he fell to his knees.

Tom eyed the man, swaying there on his knees, blood pumping from the wounds in his chest in spurts, and let loose the breath he'd been holding. He relaxed his aim, his Colt dropping to his side. He had no desire to watch the man die, whoever he might be. Turning, he leaned his arms against the lintel of the door.

When he heard Vanessa get shakily to her feet, he glanced over his shoulder. She stood trembling at the foot of the bed, eyes wide with disbelief.

"Get dressed, Vanessa."

"No!" Vanessa screamed.

At first he thought she was screaming at him. But even as he turned, he heard the gunshot.

Vanessa crumpled at Tom's feet. Her eyes glazed lifelessly. Tom stumbled back a step, looked up.

Shock spread across Jonas' face as he gaped at Vanessa. His bullet obviously hadn't been meant for her.

Tom blinked once, and then his bullet took the man through the forehead.

Jonas toppled, his gun sliding across the room and thudding to a stop against the bureau.

Tom stared at it in stunned silence. Resting there. A snub-nosed derringer. So oddly out of place against the beautiful grain of the oak flooring.

Reality slammed home, and he sank to his knees at Vanessa's side. The blood drained from his face at the sight of her body, cocked at an odd angle, lifeless eyes staring at the wall.

"Dear God! What did they do?" Tom clutched his head, his eyes darting about the room in wild panic. He couldn't live without Vanessa. "Vanessa!" He reached for her, pulling her against his chest as he buried his face in her hair.

This was his fault. He should have taken care of things himself instead of trusting to William!

"Vanessa, forgive me." He choked on a sob as full realization of what had just happened penetrated. He held her for a long time, until finally his shock hardened into brutal anger.

Hands shaking, he laid her back down, covering her carefully with a blanket. He had some revenge to take.

Nicki glanced from the gun to William's face and stepped down from the corral fence, her fists clenched by her sides. *Dear Jesus, dear Jesus, dear Jesus.* She was holding her breath, she realized, and slowly let it out, lifting her hands. "William, whatever this is about, we can work it out."

"Shut up! Just shut up. Get over here, now!" He gestured with the gun, his eyes flicking back and forth between her and the door to the soddy.

Nicki trembled even as she moved to comply. How had she thought she knew the man so well?

"Up on the horse!" he commanded, jabbing the barrel of the gun painfully into her ribs as soon as she was out of sight of the house.

Heart thundering, she climbed into the saddle. In a flash, William swung up behind her and kicked the horse into a gallop. The horse dashed up and over the hill—only visible to the house for a few seconds as they crested the rise.

They rode hard for 10 minutes. With each passing moment Nicki expected to hear her rescuer's hoofbeats behind them. But none came. None.

William reined the horse down into a little gully and leaped down, roughly pulling her after him.

Her foot caught in the stirrup and she almost fell but was able to maintain her footing. She blinked back tears, refusing to give him the satisfaction of seeing her cry, even as fear slammed through her chest.

He took her by a shoulder and squeezed, the fingers of one hand digging into her flesh like fiery daggers. The point of the gun bit painfully into the soft flesh under her chin. His voice shook. "Blasted, confounded woman! Why didn't you just let me marry you and have done with it! I was trying to protect you! Now—"

He jerked her after him down a barely visible trail. Her arm flung backwards and she stumbled several steps before settling into a jog behind him.

"Now, there's just me to worry about. I have to protect myself, you see. With you out of the way, and me offering to run the ranch until Sawyer comes of age, well, you can see how that will work for my good, now, can't you?" He stopped at the base of a small hill and swiveled toward her so quickly that she smashed into his chest with a whimper. His voice softened. "Why wouldn't you just marry me?" He laid the barrel of the gun alongside her temple, his eyes roving over her face with odd detachment. He swallowed thickly and his grip tightened. The point of the gun dug into her temple.

Nicki closed her eyes. Her body shook like the last leaf of fall in a windstorm. She was going to die. She and her baby. Who would take care of Sawyer? Mama? Papa? Would Jason even know how to find her family? Had she said enough about them for him to be able to find them?

"Answer!" His hot breath slapped her in the face.

She flinched.

"Yea, though I walk through the valley of the shadow of death, I will fear no evil; For You are with me; Your rod and Your staff, they comfort me." The words whispered through her soul as though Jesus Himself were right there, with His arms around her, His mouth pressed to her ear. Blocking any threat that could come from William.

And with sudden clarity, like a pinprick of light that shows the way in a dark cavern, she knew peace. She had been searching for peace ever since John Trent had ridden into her life from the brazen heat of a California summer. And now, like refreshing water in the desert, it filled her soul, bubbling over and spilling into her fingers, cascading down her legs, giving them strength. It didn't come from being in control; it came from letting go of control to the only One who had any control in the first place. Her trembling stopped, and she opened her eyes.

She studied his face and saw there a curious mix of emotions. Anger. Fear. Pride. Humiliation. And disquiet.

"Nothing you do to me will bring you happiness, William. Complete surrender to Jesus is the only thing that will do that."

He huffed a breath of disbelief. "You going to turn this into a Sunday school lesson? Save it, Nicki. Turn around." He pivoted her to face away from him and pulled her arms behind her, lacing her wrists together tightly. Then, gripping her elbow, he pushed her down the trail ahead of him.

To their right was a short cliff no more than 15 feet high. They passed a scrubby pine tree whose branches overhung the trail and William pulled her to an abrupt halt. Cut into the base of the cliff was a small notch with just enough of an opening for a person's body to fit through. The inside of the small cavern dipped into the ground and was dark. Nicki couldn't tell how deep it was. She raised her chin, refusing to look at him.

"Sit!" He shoved her down onto the cold ground and bound her feet together, then turned her onto her belly and tied the lashings on her wrists to the ones around her ankles so she could not straighten her legs.

Her heart beat faster. She clung to her promise and repeated the verse over and over to herself. Her hair fell forward into her eyes, but she was helpless to remove it. Any moment now Jason would come thundering around the pine tree and lay William out with one solid punch. *Please, Lord.*

Stripping off his bandana, he squeezed her cheeks together and stuffed it into her mouth.

She gagged and the cloth moved just far enough forward to stop triggering her gag reflex.

Two rawhide strips cut into the crease where her lips met as he tied them tightly at the back of her head.

Eyes closed, and cheek pressed into the cold ground, she concentrated on breathing in and out through her nose and tried to ignore the cloying press of the cloth in her mouth and the bite of the rawhide at her wrists.

Finally, he squatted down beside her. "You should have taken me up on my offer, Nicki." Without another word he pushed her toward the black depths of the crevice.

Nicki's eyes widened and she struggled, but he cuffed her hard at the back of her head, momentarily stunning her as he pushed her belly down, and then forced her, head first, into the dark hole.

The ceiling of the cave gave way to a black void above her as the ground continued to slope away, sucking her deeper into the heart of the earth.

Blackness wrapped around her like a damp mist, and a bone-penetrating cold shivered through her as she slid down a shale incline deeper into the darkness.

Heart thundering and head reared back, she heaved short quick breaths through her nose as she slid. *Dear Jesus, save me and my little one. Come to our rescue now in this darkest hour. If ever there was a valley of the shadow of death, this is it. I felt so much peace a moment ago. Where is it now?*

At any moment she could hurtle off a ledge and fall into never-ending darkness! Or she could meet some wild animal. *Or maybe I'll just keep sliding and never stop!*

The incline beneath her grew steeper, and she started to slide faster.

Her whole body trembled, and her heart threatened to lodge in her throat until she wouldn't be able to breathe at all. She willed down her panic with a long inhale and a slow exhale.

Rocks cut into her, slicing through the bodice of her dress. Debris bounced up and pinged off her face. She could feel the bulge of her baby pressing back into her, and tears stung the backs of her eyes.

She leaned to the left to take the weight of her body off the little one nestled in her womb. Her left arm took the bulk of her weight. Bits of shale ground into her elbow as the material of her dress gave way. Then the rope that stretched taut between her wrists and her ankles snagged on something hanging down from the ceiling, and she was jerked to a halt!

A loud pop penetrated the darkness, and pain burst into

flame in her shoulder. She cried out and dropped her head to the ground as pulses of agony coursed through her, radiating in ever-enlarging circles from her shoulder.

Another moan escaped as she tried to adjust to a more comfortable position, and realized there was no such thing.

Don't move. Just don't move.

After spending the day riding the cold range, all the men had gladly crammed into the small soddy to wrap their hands around a warm cup of coffee. Ron had done a good job in his selection of the new hands. The two that were here had proved their worth on the drive back with the herd.

Jason grinned as he thought of the third hand Ron had hired. Jason had sent him to California to locate Nicki's family and at least bring her some news of them, if not bring them here. He couldn't wait to see the look on her face when she found out. That man was the one who'd taught him how to say "Don't worry" in Spanish.

Jason took a sip of coffee as he scanned the room. The two new hands, with Ron and Conner, sat squeezed around the table. In the corner, Sheriff Watts had talked with the Jeffries in quiet undertones before taking his leave.

Jason had remained standing in the kitchen with Rocky. It had been good to hear some news from Shilo.

He rubbed his jaw, realizing he hadn't thought of Shilo as "home." He thought of this as home now. How had that happened in such a short amount of time? Nicki's face came to mind, and he lifted his head. "Where's Nicki?"

Conversation stopped, and everyone looked around the room.

Ron was the first to stand. "She was outside looking at the horses when I came in. I'm sure she's still out there somewhere. I'll go check on her."

Jason downed the last swallow of his coffee and followed him out the door.

The yard was empty.

His heart started pounding harder.

Conner and Rocky sauntered out behind him, followed by Brenda.

He glanced at them as Ron headed for the bunkhouse. "She might be down by the creek. I'll check there."

Moments later they all were standing in front of the soddy again.

Brenda's voice was quiet when she said, "William was here earlier. 'Bout a half hour ago. He left but…"

Sick dread dropped into Jason's stomach like a stone. "Conner, ride after Sheriff Watts. Rocky, I need you circling and finding tracks while I gather our horses. Ron, can you tell the others?" He tipped his head at the house. "We may need every man we've got before this is over."

Everyone jumped into action at the same time.

As Jason sprinted toward their horses he prayed fervently. Thankfully, all their horses were still saddled as every man had been in a hurry for some warmth. Gathering the reins of several mounts he noticed that his hands were shaking. *Lord, just help me to find her. Please keep her safe.*

Ron and the ranch hands came barreling out of the sod shanty.

Jason looked at Ron. "Where's Sawyer?"

"Brenda's gonna watch him for a while."

"All right everyone, listen. Nicki is not here. We don't want to jump to any conclusions." *It was obviously Harpster, that dirty rat.* "But we are all going to ride out and look for her. Rocky's a good tracker, and he's out scouting a circle now. As soon as he finds a trail, we'll let him take the lead." *And when I find Harpster, I'm going to kill him!*

Rocky gave a shout from behind the barn, and every man mounted up and trotted that way.

Rocky looked up. "I've got a trail here. Looks like one rider came in on this horse, but two riders went out on it. The hoofprints are deeper leaving than they were coming in."

Jason nodded. "Let's follow it. Howard," he turned to the younger of the two new hands, "can you let Brenda and Rolf know which direction we're headed so they can let Cade, Conner, and the sheriff know when they get back? Then catch up to us."

Howard nodded and reined his horse back toward the house as the other men moved out to follow the trail Rocky was tracking.

Jason drummed his fingers against one thigh. He hated following a trail. It was always such slow work. He grimaced. Why hadn't he kept a better eye on her? She'd been worried about William when he'd ridden in with the horses, that much had been clear. In the night and a morning he'd been gone, what had happened to change her mind about the man?

William watched Nicki's body slide down the shale floor of the steeply slanted cavern until the darkness swallowed her. He pressed his lips together.

He probably should have shot her before he sent her sliding into the depths of that cavern, but the sound of a gunshot would alert anyone out looking for her where they were. No. She would just have to suffer the long, slow death that now awaited her. She deserved it anyhow.

He snorted.

Life would have been a lot easier if he'd just taken care of her at the same time as John. He should have found a way to do them together, but he'd held out hopes that Nicki would agree to marry him. He spat on the ground.

"Always was a fool for a pretty woman," he mumbled.

He glanced around. He needed to hide the mouth of the cave, and he didn't have much time. It didn't take him long to find enough of the plentiful tumbleweeds to pile against the opening so that it wasn't visible from the small path he had taken. Satisfied, he led his horse a good ways up a hill in the direction of his home, then returned to the tree by the cave. He broke a branch from the scraggly pine and strode fifty yards down the main trail. Bending and walking backwards, he carefully dusted out any signs of his and Nicki's presence on the trail. He continued past the cave all the way up the hill to his horse.

Straightening every so often, he checked his work. Only the most experienced of trackers would be able to tell anyone had been here. And that would only last until a gust of wind came along, then all traces of the trail would be gone. He tossed the pine branch on the ground, dusted his hands, and mounted up, cutting across the hills toward home.

Later, once it had been discovered that Nicki was missing and everyone, including himself, had been given a chance to grieve, he would step forward and offer guardianship to Sawyer.

He rubbed a hand down his vest and stared out across the juniper-studded landscape. He would miss her. But seeing her in Jordan's arms this morning had confirmed that she had betrayed him and fallen in love with another. He exhaled. They could have had such a wonderful life together. Now it would just be him and Sawyer.

Sheriff Watts knew William had been of great help to Nicki since John's death, so he was a shoo-in for the position of guardian. And even if Sheriff Watts might have suspicions about him, William knew The Stockman's Association would back him, even to the point of "replacing" the Sheriff, if necessary.

His thoughts flitted to Tom, and his jaw clenched.

Tom Roland wouldn't be so easy to convince. But maybe it was time for Tom to have an accident of some sort. He was tired of that man looking over his shoulder and always pointing out his mistakes.

A whispered word in the ears of certain members of The Association should do the trick. All he had to do was convince them that all the failures had been because of Roland.

He shifted in the saddle comfortably and chuckled, thankful for the day that he'd decided to throw in his lot with The Association.

The secret, emergency meeting of The Stockman's Association

convened in Rod Signet's barn. The men filed in silently. Two members were noticeably absent.

Roscoe Cox was the last to arrive. He stalked in and slapped a newspaper down on the barrel serving as a makeshift table. "Tom done killed the man we sent after him, but not afore his wife, Vanessa, was killed."

Thick silence filled the room. The timbers groaned when a light breeze wafted by outside and feet shifted uneasily. Each man knew he had now become a living, breathing target.

Finally, Rod Signet leaned into the heels of his boots and folded his arms. "I heard Roland used to be a gunman before he became a banker."

Each man stared at the floor as they contemplated that information. "What are we going to do now?" one finally asked.

Roscoe Cox cursed violently and threw his hat on the ground. He paced toward a stall, and then back again, looked up and met each man's eyes before he spoke. "I've known Roland for years. And you're right—he used to be a gunman and a blasted fast one, too. Tom won't take something like this lying down. He is going to hunt each one of us down, and we'll be lucky if he kills us quickly. Slow and painful is more his style. So…" He made eye contact with each man again. "I suggest we all watch our backs, gentlemen."

"What about Harpster? Don't we need to," Rod cleared his throat, "take care of him?"

Cox chuckled dryly. "We won't have to worry about taking care of him. He'll be the first one Tom goes after because he failed to do the job Tom told him to do. As for me? My place is for sale. Every lock, stock, and barrel on the place. Any of ya'll interested in buying, you come on by. But I won't be staying around these parts to be hunted down like a Muley."

With that, he scooped up his hat and, pushing back his hair, jammed it onto his head and walked out of the barn.

The other men shuffled restlessly, no one speaking. Finally, one by one, they trickled out of the barn the same way they'd come.

★

Chapter Nineteen

A groan rumbled through Nicki's chest and woke her. She gasped as a knife of pain stabbed through her shoulder. Her eyes opened to complete darkness. Something poked hard into her cheek and she lifted her head to ease the pressure. Stark pain shot through her arms in white hot streaks and she cried out, but the gag blocked the sound and it came out more like a muffled moan.

With a whimper she rested her cheek on the ground again. A low sound vibrated through the cavern. Like a stiff wind blowing through ripened stalks of grain. She listened intently, trying to determine where it was coming from, but it was all around her, filling the cavern and coming seemingly from every direction.

She couldn't move her legs or the string pulled agonizingly at her dislocated shoulder and she was starting to get a cramp in her right thigh.

Her tongue felt like a stick in her mouth. *So thirsty.* She pressed against the rag with her tongue and gagged, the involuntary movement clenching her shoulder in a vice. Immediately she let up the pressure and tipped her face forward so the rag would gravitate to the front of her mouth. If she threw up it would mean the end for her, she knew. But if she could just get rid of the gag, she could breathe easier. She closed her eyes in concentration. The rawhide strips that kept the gag in her mouth were tied tight enough that she would never be able to push the rag past them. But maybe she could chew through them? She bit down hard and felt the leather give just before she gagged again.

When the waves of pain had dulled and she was calm once again, a butterfly of hope fluttered in her stomach.

She repeated the gesture and ground her teeth from side to side.

Finally, on the fourth agonizing try the rawhide broke, and she spit the rag out as a satisfying rush of cool air filled her mouth.

She cried for sheer happiness, feeling the sweet moisture of saliva soften her taste buds. She took a full breath and rested her cheek on the damp, soft cloth. In a moment she would see what else she could do, but for now it was enough to be able to breathe easily.

Jason clenched his teeth and pounded a fist against his saddle's pommel as Rocky scanned the road and embankments ahead of them for the third time. The trail had gone cold.

Rocky looked at him apologetically. "He's brushed the trail. I can still find it, but it's going to take me a little longer."

Jason rubbed the back of his neck.

Hoof beats sounded, and he turned to see Cade, Conner, and Sheriff Watts riding up.

Cade cocked an eyebrow at Jason.

Jason sighed. "Trail's been brushed. But Rocky will find it."

Sheriff Watts surveyed the countryside. After a moment he harrumphed and said, "Any of ya'll ever see'd a polecat?"

Blankly, Jason and Cade eyed each other, but both turned back to nod at the sheriff.

"Heard tell one time o'er in Nevada that a polecat won't spray anywheres near its den." The sheriff smirked. "I don't know if it's true or not, 'cause I was never crazy enough to track one so's I could find out."

Several of the men chuckled. Cade's horse shifted, and he stared down at a spot between his horse's ears. Jason's hands tightened on the reins and he focused on Watts, sensing the man was about to get to the crux of what he was saying.

Watts spat into the dust of the roadbed. "Point is, closer ya get to a skunk's den, the cleaner it is." Jason's head snapped up and he scanned the horizon, looking for anything that might be a hideout. Already it had taken them far too long to get here. Nicki could be somewhere injured, hurting. Dead.

His heart threatened to stop.

He made a split-second decision. "Rocky, Cade, and I will ride out wide and see if we come across a trail. We'll each form a half circle and meet you down trail fifty yards."

Rocky never lost concentration on the road before him. He raised a hand of acknowledgment without looking up.

Jason gestured for Cade to go left, and he took the side of the road to the right. He leaned forward in his saddle as his horse took the embankment and then studied the ground for any signs that someone had recently ridden this way. He was three-quarters of the way through his half of the circle when he spotted the pine branch and pulled up short.

His pulse quickened.

He leapt down and circled the area, carefully studying the ground. A few paces away the tracks of a horse could clearly be seen heading down the hill and across the valley.

He gave a loud whistle that he knew Cade and Rocky would recognize, and when they both looked up he waved them over. His part of the circle had led him to much higher ground, but just ahead, the ground sloped down again quite steeply, and a narrow wildlife track led back to the road that Rocky was searching. Off to his left the ground had broken away sharply sometime in the past and formed a small cliff that was probably fifteen feet high by thirty feet long.

Both Rocky and Cade urged their mounts forward and cantered his way.

After just a moment's rest, Nicki lifted her head again. No matter how badly her shoulder hurt, she had to try and work her way back to the top of the cave. Whatever had snagged the rawhide rope and stopped her slide had to be above her somewhere.

She lay sideways to the slope now, her left shoulder lower than her dislocated right.

Her right arm had no feeling in it now except for at the shoulder. And every time she so much as breathed, the joint sent thorns of pain shooting down through her body. Her left arm was tingling, and she guessed that soon it too would be totally numb.

She needed to move immediately, before it was too late.

She took a deep breath and held it, then tried to push off with her left shoulder and begin the process of getting her head pointed uphill. With the movement, white-hot shards shot through her shoulder and she cried out. But after a moment of recovery she forced herself to repeat the gesture and began to rock herself around so that her head was uphill.

The shale under her gave way, and she started to slide again.

Fear jolted through her, and she whimpered in the darkness. She dug her knees in with all her might, and her slide eased to a stop. But the pain pulsing from her shoulder was so vivid that she threw up. She was afraid to try again. If she started to slide again, she might not be able to stop herself. The rushing sound grew louder the further she slid into the cavern.

"God!" she whispered in despair, tears dampening the ground beneath her face. "Where are you now?"

There was no audible reply. She stilled her breathing. No voice as she had heard earlier above ground whispered her verses in her ear. Simple silence engulfed her and a thought penetrated. Something Mama had told her once while they were rolling out tortillas and Nicki had lamented about God having abandoned them.

"Dominique, when you can't feel God's presence, you have to go back to the Word. Feelings are fleeting. They come and they go. One minute we are happy. The next we despair. Through it all, we trust in the Word that never changes because it is Truth. And the Truth sets us free. God says He will never leave us, or forsake us… and so…we trust. What else can we do? Like Peter we say, Who else has the words of life, eh?"

Nicki sighed. "I know You are here, Jesus. Your Word says You will comfort me in the valley of death. But please, I don't want to leave Sawyer with no one to watch over him. If it is my time to come to You, please lay it on Jason's heart to raise him. He is a good man, who knows you and would be a good example to Sawyer." A peace settled in her heart. "Thank you, Jesus."

Rocky and Cade swung from their saddles, and Jason handed Rocky the broken pine branch. "Found this right here and these hoofprints leading away. Are they the same ones we've been following?"

Rocky stooped to examine the trail and after a moment he stood with a grim set to his lips. He lifted his hat and ran his fingers through his hair, then settled it back on his head. "Same tracks. The ground is a little softer here than it is out on the road so it's a little hard to tell, but I think these prints would be deeper if the horse were holding the same amount of weight it was on the road."

Cade cleared his throat. "So she's got to be around here somewhere."

Jason looked at the pine bough in his hands again. Then gave another piercing whistle and waved over the group of men still waiting on the road.

As they all came to a stop, Jason held up the branch for everyone's inspection. "We're looking for the pine tree this branch came off. That's the best place to start searching. Everyone spread out and let's find that tree."

Five minutes later Jason rounded a bend on the wildlife trail at the base of the hill and saw a pine tree just ahead, near the section of cliff wall. Heart thundering, he kicked his horse into a faster trot and hurried toward it. He spied the broken branch on the tree before he'd even slid from the saddle. Leaping down, he matched the broken ends together with trembling fingers.

It fit. This was the tree.

He spun in a circle looking for Nicki, even as he let loose with another whistle to signal Rocky, Cade, and the others. His horse shied and sidestepped, bobbing its head in protest of the loud sound. Jason put a hand on its neck to calm it, then led it to the tree and wrapped the reins around a low branch.

Rocky and Sheriff Watts rode into view.

"I found it!" Jason called. "She's got to be near here somewhere!" *Dear God, please let her be all right.*

Rocky stepped up beside him. Sheriff Watts kept all the others back until Rocky determined if there were any tracks.

Jason's hands were trembling like they had when he used to drink, so he shoved them deep into his pockets and studied Rocky intently.

Rocky scanned the ground.

Jason forced himself to study the area. There was not much here in the way of hiding places. Just juniper-covered hills, with tumbleweed-filled valleys. He looked at the pine tree. Peered up into its branches. Nothing.

A thought occurred, and he swallowed hard. "What if he buried her?" He kicked a stone violently. "Why didn't I keep a better eye on her?"

Rocky laid a hand on his shoulder. "He wouldn't have had time to bury her. Besides, I don't see any evidence of that, do you?"

Jason rubbed the back of his neck with one hand. "I don't see her around here either. Just Russian thistle." He gestured to the mangled pile of tumbleweeds in a heap at the base of the cliff. "And sagebrush." He stretched a hand toward the hills.

"We'll find her, Jason."

"I just hope it's not too late when we do."

"Then stop hoping and get to praying." Rocky squeezed his shoulder. "That's what Gram would tell you."

Jason's countenance softened. "Been doing that, too."

Sheriff Watts approached. "Find anything?"

Rocky shook his head and stepped away from Jason, folding his arms across his chest. "Winds have been gusting a little. When that happens a brushed trail disappears pretty fast."

As if to prove the truth of his statement, a tumbleweed rolled by, followed by a stiff wind. The pile of tumbleweeds at the base of the cliff shifted. One fell away from the tangle and rolled down the game trail.

Something tugged at Jason's consciousness for attention and he paused, having learned long ago, that when tracking a criminal, the smallest details can be what give them away. He turned to study the pile of tumbleweeds heaped against the base of the cliff.

They just didn't look right, somehow, the way they were all stacked on top of each other.

His heart began to hammer like a blacksmith.

He took two swift strides and began tossing them aside like a man gone mad, ignoring the sharp barbed thorns that sank into his fingers.

The mouth of a small low cave appeared and elation bubbled up, but he didn't let himself react. This could be nothing. Simply some tumbleweeds that had piled up of their own volition against the cliff.

Then he saw the marks just inside the opening of the cave and his hope disappeared. He sank to his knees. "I think I found her." The words were a choked rasp. He bent down and peered deep into the cavern as Rocky, Cade, and Watts stepped up behind him.

Dear Jesus.

He cleared his throat. "The floor angles down steeply. I can't see her.

We're going to need some rope and a torch."

Nicki heard a faint sound above her. Far away and muted. She lifted her head so that both ears were free to listen. The rush of sound all around her made it hard to distinguish any other sounds, but she thought she could hear men's voices.

"I'm here," she tried to yell. But her mouth was so dry only a rasp came out. She closed her mouth and swallowed, moistening her throat. "I'm here!" Louder this time, but loud enough?

A thought occurred. What if it was William coming back to finish the job? A low moan escaped and she pressed her face into the ground beneath her. Her whole body trembled, and she forced herself to whisper the psalm. *"Yea, though I walk through the valley of the shadow of death, I will fear no evil; For You are with me; Your rod and Your staff, they comfort me."*

"Nicki? *Nicki…Nicki…Nicki…*"

Someone called and she lifted her head. Her name echoed around the chamber, bouncing down to her from several directions. She could not distinguish the voice other than it was male.

Rocks trickled past her, bouncing and pinging as they cascaded toward her. She closed her eyes, and pressed her cheek to the ground, willing down her pounding heart. She could do nothing but trust in Jesus now. If Jesus wanted her on this earth, He would save her. If not, then she knew that it was for the best. Sawyer was in His hands now.

"Nicki?"

The voice was louder now, and it sounded like Jason.

Joy trilled through her heart. He had come for her! A faint orange glow dusted the air above her head. "I'm here!" she called.

"Oh, thank You, Jesus!"

More rocks cascaded past her head, and now she could see the flame glowing at the end of a torch. Shadows shifted on the walls, eerily swaying this way and that.

"She's down here! Let down more rope!"

She sighed in relief. Soon she would be free of these bonds, and they could fix her arm. More scrabbling and she could feel the vibrations of his movement in the floor under her cheek now.

Jason sucked in a sharp breath. "Nicki, I'm coming! Don't move!" A strange note tinged the edge of his voice, one she'd never heard him use before.

He was right there, his boots right above her head as he lay sprawled out on the cave floor, a halo of light emanating from the torch in one hand, his other firmly clasping a rope. His face was in shadow.

Oh, how she longed to see his face. To trace the stubble along his jaw. To lose herself in the depths of his blue, blue eyes. To feel his lips pressed to hers with *life* coursing between them.

"Jason." She tried to scoot up closer to him but cried out when her shoulder protested, and she slid a little further down into the cavern.

"Nicki!" Terror laced Jason's voice. "Honey, don't move. You can't move!" A metallic prickle of fear started in the back of her throat and danced toward the tip of her tongue. She lifted her head and licked her lips, glancing back.

Behind her the floor of the cave gave way to a gaping, black canyon. She was only inches from the edge!

Terror sizzled through her and she pressed her face back to the ground, wishing she hadn't just seen that.

Jason called up to where the others held the rope. "More rope!"

"That's all we got," came back the faint call.

Jason huffed a breath of impatience and turned back to evaluate his options. *Okay Lord, what now?*

He studied the scene below him in the flickering light of his torch. Somewhere far below he could hear the rush of an underground river. Above him, sharp spears of pointed rock hung from the ceiling. Some had grown so far down as to meet the ground and formed a pillar of sorts.

Fear thrummed through his chest as he noted just how close she was to the edge. One more slip on the shale and she would go over for sure. Nicki was mere inches from falling to her death.

He moved his torch so he could study how best to pull her up. Her hands and feet were bound and then tied to each other behind her so that her legs, bent at the knees, could not be straightened. One shoulder bulged, oddly misshapen, and his stomach curled. "Nicki, it's really important that you don't move, Honey. Don't even nod or lift your head, just answer quietly. Your shoulder's hurt, isn't it?"

"Yes," she answered softly.

Assessing the situation, he only had one option. He propped the torch against a rock to one side of the cavern and worked his way far enough up the rope so that he could form a slip knot. Kicking off one boot, he slid his foot into the loop and cinched it tight around his ankle. The last thing he needed was his boot slipping off just as he was about to pull her to safety. Flipping over on his stomach he crawled down the incline toward Nicki once again.

A tremor buzzed through his body. He just wanted to have her in the comfort of his arms, safe.

He felt the rope go taut and stretched his body full length, reaching down as far as his arms could go. His fingers grazed the top of her head. The rope cut into his ankle.

Frustration zinged through him. "It's okay, Nicki. I'm going to get you out of here. Everything's going to be all right."

He stretched again and bumped the torch. It toppled and bounced toward Nicki's face.

Instinctively Nicki jerked away from the flame. She started to slide.

"No!" Jason lunged for her.

William stared down at the newspaper lying on his table at home. One of his hands must have bought it in town and left it here for him to read. Arms stiff, he leaned heavily on clenched fists planted on either side of the article. Tom's wife was dead. He felt a curious mix of dread and jubilation at the news.

Jubilation, because Tom would be suffering now, and it was about time the man felt some torment.

Dread, because he now had other problems to tie up. The Association had to have been behind this. And if they were going after Tom…

He slammed a fist into the table. Just when he thought he had things back under control! Would they be coming for him next? Or would Tom himself come for him?

At that instant the window next to him shattered. The first bullet hit the wall beside his head with a strange *thwap*.

He turned and looked at the hole. For one moment his heart stopped, and then he was somersaulting across the tiles toward the entry, away from the windows.

A second bullet splintered the logs just behind him and above his head.

He grabbed his rifle resting in the corner and pushed his back to the log wall beside the door. He pressed his head against the swell of a log, and clutched the rifle, chest heaving, mouth dry.

So it had come to this. He had failed, and now his payment for failure loomed on the horizon.

"I know you're in there, William!"

It was Roland. William cursed the fact that all his hands were branding in the south pasture today. Even Hank, his cook, had gone since it was a sun-up to sun-down process.

So he was here alone. Trying to think his way back to life.

The scent of smoke spiked his heart rate. "No, no, no, no. Come on! Think!" He drummed his fingers on the barrel of the rifle. Tom and probably an accomplice or two would be waiting for him if he tried to go out the door or one of the windows. Burn to death in the house? Or get shot trying to escape the flames?

"I'm not gonna shoot ya! Come on out." Roland called. "Just take this as a warning, so to speak. You got work to do!"

William ground his teeth. He wasn't an idiot.

Tom was silent for a few moments, then, "You ever wonder what that little girl felt just before she left this earth? You don't have to find out. Just come on out. I want to talk to you."

William cursed under his breath. Where was his voice coming from? The crackle and hiss of hungry flames obscured the direction of the voice. Smoke stabbed his nostrils. His eyes started to smart and water. He glanced to his left and crawled toward the window, rifle clutched in one hand. There was a steep, shale hill on the east side of the house, making it the least likely place for Roland to be waiting.

Smoke curled down the walls, slithering toward him in a death march. He stripped off his shirt and tied it around his mouth and nose, then eased up under the window, still clutching his Winchester. He pushed up against the wall and peered out the window. Tears streamed from his eyes, making it hard to see, but it didn't appear that anyone was stationed on this side of the house. He lifted his head higher. Smoke filtered across the yard in thick clouds. Someone could be hidden by it, but he would just have to take his chances. If he couldn't see them, they would have a hard time seeing him, too.

Behind him he heard a window burst. Several more windows shattered in succession. *The heat must be causing that.* Pure providence.

"Here goes," he muttered. Clutching the rifle by the barrel, he shoved the butt through the window. He could only hope the sound of this window breaking would be mistaken for the same. Quickly, he reamed out the glass and dropped his rifle onto the ground. In one swift leap he was out the window and sliding down the steep hill, cursing the shale and juniper prickles that immediately sought out any bare inch of his flesh.

He slid several feet, scrabbling for purchase to no avail. Finally, to stop his descent, he plastered himself flat against the hill, spreading his weight as much as possible and grabbing for anything that rose by, gritting his teeth against the rocks grinding into his bare chest. Dust rose in a cloud around him and caked the inside of his mouth. At last, he came to a stop clutching a hand-full of bunch-grass.

Hands, knees, and chest sliced and bleeding, he pressed his cheek to the dirt gasping. He took in a lungful of dust. Racking coughs threatened to start his slide again and he curled onto his side, digging in one foot and not daring to let go of the clump of grass. He'd lost his shirt somewhere above. But he was alive.

For now.

He was remarkably cold, for just having escaped a fire. A shiver coursed through him as wind gusted across the landscape. He could still see a patch of snow here and there clinging to the shady side of a juniper bush. He looked for his flannel shirt, spied it up and to his right, and belly-crawled toward it. Warmth would help him think. He wasn't out of danger yet. Unless Roland assumed he hadn't escaped the fire and had left already, which wasn't likely.

Shirt in place and clutching a juniper bush, he rolled so that he could look up the hill. Smoke billowed in great gusts above his head. Bright orange sparks and ash floated down through the air. He groaned. His place was gone!

Jaw clenched, his free hand fisted around a handful of dirt and he growled under his breath. *Roland will pay for this.*

Determined, he started the climb, one clump of bunch-grass at a time. Handhold after handhold, his anger growing with every inch he moved.

He came on his rifle several feet above and slung it across his back as he continued up the hill skirting wide to the right. If Tom was still up there, he intended to catch him by surprise.

He heard the muttered curses and the sound of pacing before he crested the ledge and was thankful for Roland's incautious stupidity.

Keeping below the crest of the hill, he moved a ways off, scrambled into the yard, and ducked behind the watering trough next to the barn. Carefully he scanned the surrounding hills and plains. Smoke drifted in a lazy haze across the scrub brush, but he didn't see anyone else with Tom.

His house was a heap of burnt logs and ashes. Tom was treading the perimeter, one hand held to his eyes warding off smoke as he peered into the charred rubble and muttered to himself. *Apparently looking for my body.*

William cocked his rifle, the sound loud in the stillness.

Roland froze, his back still to William, then lifted his hands to shoulder height.

William grinned. "Lookin' for something? Or, should I say, someone?"

Tom didn't move. "I told you I wasn't gonna shoot ya. Think of this as a little lesson learned, that's all."

"If you think I'm fool enough to believe that, you don't know me too well. I heard you used to be a gunfighter before you became a banker."

Tom nodded, hands still raised.

"So what happened? I saw the article in the paper."

Tom sighed. "The Association was not happy with the job we

did. They sent a man to kill me." He sniffed. "They weren't happy with the job he did either."

"So, what now? We just part like old friends?"

Tom shook his head. "I want you to help me go after them. We can—" He started to spin around, his hands dropping.

William pulled the trigger. The blast was deafening in the afternoon stillness.

Tom blinked, took a step forward, and looked down at the hole in his side as blood spilled onto the ground. Then he collapsed.

William ground his teeth. If The Association had sent someone after Roland, he would probably be next. He was finished here. He would have to move onto some other part of the country. His eyes narrowed. *All because of a stupid woman and a nice piece of land!*

★

Chapter Twenty

Jason's heart nearly stopped as the torch bounced past Nicki and flipped flame over handle into the maw of the canyon.

Nicki whimpered and pressed her body hard against the floor, but to no avail. She was slipping away from him.

He grabbed for her but caught nothing except a thick strand of her hair. He seized it like a lifeline and her slide slowed to a stop. Thankfulness coursed through him. They were in total darkness now, but she had slipped far enough that he knew her knees had to be jutting over the lip of the canyon.

With grim determination, he wrapped the strand of hair around his hand and pulled hard. Nicki cried out, but he kept tugging until he felt her move toward him. Feeling around on the ground he found more of her hair and grasped another handful. He heaved her toward him again and only stopped when he surmised he'd pulled her several inches closer to him.

Pausing, he let her catch her breath. When he spoke, he deliberately kept his voice soft. "I need you to try and scoot your way up toward me a little."

"I can move now?" The words were no more than a whisper.

"Yes, I've got you, and I'm not going to let you slide further down."

"What if the men let go of the rope?"

"The rope is tied to a tree outside the mouth of the cave. Everything is going to be fine." *Lord, let it be so.*

She lay still for a moment, as though judging whether she could trust him or not. Then she asked, "Is William out there?"

The fear he heard in the question pierced his heart. "No, honey. William is not up there. Just Sheriff Watts, Rocky, Cade, and the ranch hands."

"Okay." With that she lifted her head and pushed off with her knees.

The shale tumbled over beneath her, cascading away behind her into the canyon and crashing into the torrent below. But with him pulling on her hair, she actually moved a few inches closer.

He wrapped her hair in both hands. "Again."

She tried again, with a muffled cry of pain as her jostling legs yanked against her arm.

"Almost there, Honey. Try one more time. On three. Ready? One. Two. Three!"

She pushed one last time and he pulled hard, and then she was close enough for him to grasp her good arm and he tugged her even higher. "Thank you, God!" He placed a quick kiss against her hair. And then he hauled and scuffled and scraped until they were high enough that he could loosen his foot and turn his body around.

Reaching into the boot he still wore he removed a knife and sliced through the rawhide strip that tied her hands and feet together. He heard her feet, numb from being in the same spot so long, thud to the ground and she groaned. Quickly he sliced the bonds at her wrist and her arms flopped to her sides in the same manner. She screamed.

His heart lurched and he grimaced. *I'm an idiot*. "Sorry, Nick. We'll get that arm popped back in as soon as we get you into the light. We're almost done." A quick slice freed her feet from their bonds and then he rolled her gently over her left shoulder onto his chest and clasped her to him with one arm. His other arm he wrapped several times around the rope and grasped it firmly. "Ready!" he yelled. The rope tightened and they started to slide upwards.

Only when they were steadily sliding upwards did he realize that he'd left his boot at the base of the cave.

It didn't matter. He had all that mattered clutched to his chest.

He tightened his grip on her in the darkness and pressed a kiss to her temple. "I thought I'd lost you. I'm so glad we found you." He kissed her again and couldn't suppress a shudder at the memory of the gaping maw of black that had almost swallowed her whole.

She sighed. "I thought I was going to die."

When the men pulled them out into the light, Jason carefully laid Nicki on her good side and gave her a drink. He stood and gaped down at her, hardly able to believe his eyes. She lay there, eyes closed, head resting on her good arm, hair tangled around her face. Her other arm lay cocked at an odd angle, the shoulder bulging grotesquely. Her dress was torn to shreds, and her face had numerous cuts and contusions. Her wrists and ankles were ringed with bloody circles.

Jason scrubbed his jaw and suppressed a growl as he gimped away. He felt like a half-shod horse with one boot on and the other somewhere in the darkness below.

Cade took one look at his feet, grabbed a second torch and the rope, and disappeared into the mouth of the cavern.

Rocky stepped up beside Jason. "We need to set that arm, Jace."

Jason clutched his head and scrubbed his fingers through his hair. "I know. Just give her a minute." he glanced around. "Where are Sheriff Watts and the others?"

Rocky stilled and looked at him. "He recognized the hoofprints. Said they were Harpster's. He went after him. I sent the others back to your ranch when you called out that you had found her."

Hatred pulsed in blinding waves across Jason's vision. If it wasn't for the woman lying on the ground who needed him, he would be galloping across the hills toward William's place with gun drawn and only one thing on his mind.

Nicki stirred and moaned.

Jason pulled off his belt and folded it in half. "Let's do this. I'll hold her. You deal with the arm." He squatted beside her. "Nicki, we need to fix your arm."

She tipped her chin in acknowledgment.

"Here, I need you to bite down on this." He slid the double thickness of leather between her teeth. Then he sat down and eased her onto his lap with her good shoulder pressed into his chest, her head resting on his shoulder.

Wrapping one of his legs over top both of hers, he slid his hands carefully under the dislocated arm and pinned her tightly to him, then nodded at Rocky.

With grim determination lining his face, Rocky placed both strong hands on Nicki's upper arm and rotated the joint upward, so that her arm pointed at the sky.

Nicki cried out and her whole body convulsed, but both men held onto her tightly, wanting this to work right the first time.

Jason laid his face against hers and pressed her head into his shoulder, tightening his grip even as tears pressed at the backs of his eyes.

Rocky placed his palm on the ball of bone that protruded at the front of her shoulder and pushed hard, pulling firmly on the arm with the other hand.

Nicki moaned through the leather clenched between her teeth and pressed her face hard against Jason's neck.

Sweat beaded on Rocky's forehead. He pulled and pushed on the protruding bone again.

A satisfying snap and the joint was restored.

Jason released the breath he'd been holding.

Nicki slumped against him. He smoothed her hair away from her face in relief. "There. It's done, now. It's done." He rocked her gently like she was a little girl.

Rocky stepped back, took a deep breath, held it for a moment, and then sank down onto the ground as he let it out.

Cade reappeared at that moment carrying Jason's other boot and glanced back and forth between the two of them sitting on the ground. "Well, if you two don't make a sorry pair." He grinned and tossed Jason's boot in a long arc so that it landed beside him. "Come on, we've got a bad guy to catch!"

Jason met Rocky's eyes over the top of Nicki's head as he placed a kiss against her temple. They blinked at each other and then Rocky smiled and both of them chuckled. Jason stood, helping Nicki to her feet. She swayed and he took a moment to steady her. Bending down he peered into her face. "Ready?"

She nodded but her face could have rivaled flour for color.

"Come on. Let's get you home."

She looked up at him, pressing his belt into his hands. "It was William." He nodded and slid his belt on. Then as he stripped off his bandana and gestured for Rocky to do the same, he said, "Sheriff Watts already went after him. We'll get him." He fashioned a sling as he talked and gently rested her arm on it, then tied it around her neck. He was careful to keep the rage from his face and voice, but it pulsed through him nonetheless.

He looked over at Cade and Rocky, both of whom were already mounted.

"Go on ahead. I'll get her home and then meet you over there."

They nodded and rode off as Jason stooped to pull on his boot and then turned and helped Nicki into the saddle.

He wouldn't be far behind them.

Sheriff Watts rode southeast, his horse running hard. Despite the clear skies and sunshine, the day was cold and his horse's breath fogged the air with cloudy puffs.

Watts sighed. So it had been William who was helping Roland.

He grimaced. He had carefully pieced together a timeline of Tom Roland's last few months and had come to the conclusion that he'd had an accomplice in the area. Maybe more than one. May Jeffries had been murdered at a time when Roland definitely was in Portland, so someone else had to have set that fire.

William had said he knew Tom Roland; that he owed him some money. But when Watts had reviewed the loans held by Roland's bank, there had been no note on William's place. Still, he'd been reluctant to believe that William could be such a man.

Watts shook his head. Perhaps if he'd followed reason instead of his heart, Nicki Trent wouldn't have had to go through what she did this morning.

Well, he was headed to the Bar H Slanted now, and William wouldn't be going anywhere this time.

He pulled up as he crested the rise before him and saw a huge column of black smoke stretching for the sky.

With a muttered oath, he set his heels into his horse's side once more and set off at a gallop. That fire was no burn pile.

A shot rang out when he was still a three hundred yards off. When he skidded to a halt in the yard of William's ranch a few moments later, a man was lying on the ground. He snatched his canteen from where it hung on the saddle and rushed to the man's side. "Roland! What in thunderation happened?"

He surveyed his injuries and with a sinking heart realized he would be witness to the man's last breath. "Here." He pressed the canteen to the man's lips, but Tom pushed him away weakly.

"Listen!" The word was barely audible, a strangled whisper.

Watts bent closer. "I'm here, Roland. Whatever ya need to say, just say it."

"B-b-bank." Moisture bubbled at the back of his throat, and Roland swallowed convulsively.

"Yer a banker. Yeah, I know 'bout that."

Tom grasped his sleeve, clutching at him as he labored to take in a breath. "Stockman's Association didn't want s-small timers to ruin our rangeland."

"So you were tryin' ta scare 'em all off and make sure the land turned o'er to yer bank when they left or forfeited."

Roland nodded. "W-W-William." He gestured weakly at the still smoldering house.

"He the one's been working with ya an' causin' trouble fer the homesteaders?"

Another nod. This time he closed his eyes and seemed to relax a little.

"Did he set fire ta the Jeffries place?"

A short nod.

"Was he in his house?" Watts eyed the ruins of the smoldering building with a shudder.

Tom shook his head, sputtered one last time as though he was trying to say something, and breathed his last.

Watts twisted the end of his mustache with grim realization.

William Harpster was still at large. Not only that, but there were several members of The Stockman's Association to arrest for accessory to multiple charges.

He sighed. It was going to be a long day. He stood to his feet.

A bullet sank into the ground by his foot, and he heard the report as he dove for cover, realizing even as he did that had he remained squatting by Roland for even a second longer he would now be a dead man.

He tucked into a roll and came up on the other side of a still partially smoldering section of log wall that hadn't burned completely to the ground. His gun nestled snuggly in his palm as he came out of the roll, and he spun to face the barn, cowering behind the wall. But he didn't fire a return shot yet.

He'd known a man once that shot his wife in the dark as she came back in from the outhouse, and he'd made it a policy ever since not to fire unless he knew who he was firing at.

He twisted his mustache and studied on the situation a bit.

Rocky heard a shot as they galloped toward William's place, and the column of smoke on the horizon was not a good sign. His jaw hardened. He and Cade pressed their horses to go faster.

Seconds later another shot rang out, and he glanced over at Cade. "We might be too late," he yelled.

Cade didn't reply, just kept bent low over the neck of his horse as they raced forward.

They pulled up on the ridge above William's house to study the layout. All was now quiet. From here, they could see Sheriff Watts ducked down behind a portion of still-smoking wall, his gun drawn, and a body sprawled in front of the house.

He glanced up at them and gestured toward the barn, holding up one finger.

One man in the barn. Rocky rubbed his face. William Harpster? Or someone else?

The barn, a large building, stood just off to their left. From this angle they could see there was a door in the side as well as in the back.

He turned to Cade. "We need to settle this before Jason gets here. I don't want him doing something he'll regret, and he was plenty angry."

Cade nodded. "Noticed that." He studied the situation a moment. "Sheriff's got the front of the barn handled and has pretty good cover. From this direction you can see the back and the right side. I'll swing around wide and cover the left. If the sheriff keeps his attention on the front and we both move in when I get into place and whistle, we should have this done in no time."

Rocky nodded and gestured for the sheriff to wait for a minute. Cade turned and rode swiftly for the other side of the barn as Rocky shucked his rifle and swung down from his horse, leaving it ground tethered.

It was only a moment before he heard Cade's bird-call whistle and gestured for Sheriff Watts to keep William's attention on the front of the barn.

Rocky lay down and started to belly-crawl toward the barn from one sage to the next. *Lord, keep us all safe and help us to apprehend this guy.*

From the corner of his eye he saw Sheriff Watts remove his hat, place it on the end of his pistol, and then raise the crown above the top of the smoldering wall. The loud crack of a rifle split the air, and he quickly dropped the hat down. A second later the sheriff returned fire, placing the bullet into the ground a good five feet in front of the barn door.

That was good thinking. Then there would be no chance of a bullet piercing a wall and accidentally hitting either Cade or himself.

He was out of sight of the sheriff now, and there was only open ground between him and the side barn door.

A movement to his left caught his eye. It was Cade gesturing that he would go in the back door. There must not be a door on the other side of the building then.

At the front of the barn another shot rang out from the sheriff's pistol, followed by return fire from the rifle.

Cade held up his fingers, counting up, and on three both men broke cover and raced for their respective doors.

Rocky hoped this would be over in a matter of seconds.

At the soddy, Jason carried Nicki inside and laid her on the bed, leaving her in Brenda's care. He sent Conner off to find Dr. Rike and then switched his saddle to a fresh horse.

Ron stepped up beside him. He chewed on a piece of hay for a moment and then spat on the ground. "Anger can make a man do some pretty stupid things, sometimes."

Jason stilled, recognizing the warning in the older man's tone. His jaw hardened, but he nodded his acknowledgment as he tightened the cinch and swung into the saddle.

He was coming into William's yard from the west when he saw Rocky break free from crouching behind a juniper bush and rush for the side door of the barn. Off to his right Sheriff Watts had just returned fire to the barn. The house smoldered, a heap of charred rubble.

He calculated the scenario. Rocky would have to pause to open the side door before he could move inside to apprehend William. The sound of the door opening might give him away. There needed to be a vivid distraction to keep William's attention on the front of the barn. He swallowed. He might have a chance of rushing in from the front, but there was a long space of open area between him and the barn.

Rocky was only five steps from the side door when Jason made his decision and kicked his horse past Sheriff Watts, galloping for the front door of the barn.

"Son!" he heard the sheriff call from behind him.

Rocky glanced up, his eyes going wide, but kept on toward the door, gun in hand.

From the front of the barn Jason heard a shot.

Felt his horse stumble beneath him, then catch itself.

And then he leapt out of the saddle, pistol nestled against his palm, and took the last six steps in a zigzag sprint, energized by sheer anger.

He felt searing heat burn along his jaw as he burst from the sunlight into the darkened interior of the barn. He tucked his head and somersaulted across the floor at an angle to where he presumed Harpster might be. At least as a moving target he would be harder to hit than one standing in blatant contrast to the sunlight outside. A loud crash reverberated in his ears and echoed all around him. *God, I'd like to live through this, please.*

Rocky shouted from somewhere in the shadows toward the back, pulling Harpster's attention away from Jason.

No! Jason blinked, his eyes just beginning to adjust to the interior.

Toward the middle of the barn he could see William swinging around toward Rocky.

Jason raised his gun. "Put down the gun, Harpster!"

The man kept moving, ignoring Jason's command, raising his gun toward Rocky.

Three shots rang out, one echoing on the heels of another. The two men in his vision both collapsed.

"Rocky!" Jason's heart was in his throat.

"Rocky!" That was Cade's voice.

Two bodies lay sprawled on the floor—Rocky, near the side-door, and William, in the center of the room. Jason rushed toward Harpster to make sure he would be no more of a threat.

The man sprawled, unconscious, on the floor.

Jason bent and felt for a pulse. It was there, but faint. One bullet had taken the man low and on his right side, and the other had cut a furrow along his scalp that oozed blood. Jason kicked the rifle away from the man and then stooped to pat him down for other weapons.

Sheriff Watts came through the front door just as Jason heard Cade's exclamation from where he'd squatted near Rocky. "Rocky! You trying to take ten years off my life? Or are you just aiming to get some nice attention from the pretty Victoria Snyder when we get home?"

Stark fear laced Cade's tone, and Jason's blood washed cold.

Watts stooped to turn William over on his belly. "I got 'im. Go see ta yer friend."

Jason stood and started to turn toward Rocky when something caught his attention. An old, worn-at-heel pair of boots was tossed in the corner of one stall. He'd bet his bottom dollar the print they made would be familiar.

"Jason, a little help!" Cade called.

Jason pulled his attention from the boots and rushed to Cade's side. A puddle of blood was pooling under Rocky's right shoulder and Cade, stripped to the waist, pressed his shirt to the front of the wound. Jason immediately stripped off his own shirt, noticing that it was already slick with blood across one shoulder. He blinked at it and swiped a hand across his cheek. It came away bloody.

He snorted and swiped the blood onto his pants. Carefully folding the bloody patch to the inside he pressed his wadded up shirt to the spot where the bullet had exited Rocky's back, then eased Rocky back down to lay on the ground. His weight would keep pressure on the makeshift bandage.

Thankfully the bullet had only gone through the thick muscle along the top of his shoulder. Since there didn't appear to be any broken bones, it would heal quicker.

Rocky grimaced. "Wouldn't you know I'd get shot when there wasn't even a pretty gal around to lessen some of the sting of it. All I've got is your ugly mugs to look at." He took a breath and squeezed his temples with one hand's fingers and thumb. "Did we get him?"

Jason nodded. "Yeah, Sheriff is cuffing him now. You did good."

"You saved my life." He looked hard at Jason, pain glazing his eyes. "He had the drop on me. I was having trouble adjusting to the dim light. He'd stacked a couple bales of hay right inside the door, so it took me a bit to get in. When I heard all those shots, I was sure your next job was gonna be as a sieve, and just came in yelling to get his attention off you."

Jason grinned. "It takes more than a couple of bullets to take down a Jordan…you know that."

Rocky attempted a grin.

Cade eyed Jason seriously. "It looks like you came close."

Jason gingerly felt his jaw as Cade stripped off his bandana and handed it to him. Jason took it and pressed it to the cut. A twinkle leapt into his eyes. "Guess God's still got plans for this old hide of mine."

Cade sighed and scrubbed a hand down his face. "I'm so glad you two are all right. I came running in the back door and stepped on a rake that was lying there. It sprung up and smacked me so hard I was seeing flashes of light. Next thing I know bullets are flying, and everything is over." He glanced toward Sheriff Watts. "I'm gonna go see if the sheriff needs any help."

Jason and Rocky stared at each other. As Cade walked away, both burst out laughing, then grimaced in pain and settled into quiet chuckling.

Chapter Twenty-One

Nicki smiled as she placed the last warm tamale in its cornhusk shell into the pan with the others. Her heart felt as light as the mists that rose from the white waters of the Deschutes.

Her arm was healing, although it was still quite painful and she couldn't lift heavy things or rotate her arm in a full circle yet. She'd been able to give up the sling several days ago, however, so that felt like progress.

She thought of William and shuddered. Sheriff Watts had taken him to the jail in Prineville to await his trial. It had been pushed to the front of the court's docket because of the nature of his crimes, and Nicki had already been to town to testify. Between her testimony, Sheriff Watts' testimony, and the evidence of the pair of boots found in William's barn, there had been no chance that he'd go free. William had been found guilty and sentenced to hang—a verdict that had been carried out the next morning. Nicki hadn't gone, but the men had, and all of them had come home with solemn faces.

The first day after the hanging Jason and the men had spent the day creating a temporary corral for the horses. Since then, they had spent a week and a half gentling the creatures so they would be easier to handle on the long drive they would face. Cade planned to drive the herd up to Canada, where he expected to get more than double his investment.

Today the men would take a break from the horses to help put a roof on Nicki's barn. And tonight would be Rolf and Brenda's last night at her place. Nicki had talked to Pastor Saunders and he was more than happy to agree that building a home for the Jeffries should be the next "Jesus with skin" act the congregation performed. Several men said they were available, so tomorrow would see a snug, warm soddy constructed for the Jeffries on their homestead.

Today people would not only bring food for today's work, but also items to donate to the Jeffries for their new home. Nicki had been working at sewing the rag braids Brenda and the boys had woven together into a rug she would give to them.

A wagon clattered into the yard, and Nicki picked up the towel and headed outside, calling for Sawyer to follow. She would send someone back in for the heavy pan of tamales and come back in a moment for her pies.

Two long tables had been set up in the yard and were already laden with food. Fried chicken, ham steaks, and beef of all kinds graced the meat table. Potatoes, boiled eggs, pickles, canned vegetables, breads, and desserts filled the remainder of the tables.

Suzanne Snow stepped up beside her, and concern for the woman who had been like a mother to her since she arrived here filled Nicki's heart. "Oh, Suze! How are you? Are you all going to make it?"

"Well, Jim and Sid were able to save the wool from most of the sheep that were slaughtered. And we had Sid ride from ranch to ranch to try and sell some of the meat. We were able to sell quite a bit of it. So I think we are going to make it." She smoothed her skirts. "I heard that Jason helped out Jacob Ashland with a couple horses?"

Nicki smiled. "Yes. He sold him the horse he bought in Prineville when he came here. It took all their savings to buy it, but at least they had some savings to use. He also gave them a pregnant mare from the nine horses that we kept, on the condition that this foal would be given back to us once it's weaned. I think the Ashlands are going to be fine, too."

Suzanne grinned and studied her face with motherly affection. "You say 'us' like you are planning for him to stick around for a while."

Nicki felt herself blush. Coming from anyone else that would be construed as prying. But coming from Suzanne she didn't mind so much. "Um…well…he has said nothing to me, but already I cannot imagine life without him. I've never felt that way before."

The women's eyes traveled to where Jason worked with several men to nail the trusses together. Sawyer lolled on Jason's back, arms wrapped firmly around his neck and Jason bent to the work for a moment as though the boy wasn't even there. Then he stood and set Sawyer on his own two feet, ruffling his hair and squatting down to his level. He said a few words to the toddler, then watched with a tender light in his eyes as Sawyer scampered off after Jake Ashland. Jason stood and caught Nicki's eyes on him. He smiled, his blue gaze drawing her like a compass needle to north.

Suzanne's words were soft. "He's a good man."

Nicki sighed, lost in the magnetic current that kept her gaze fixed on Jason. "Yes. He is," she whispered.

Jason's smile stretched into a grin, and he tossed her a bold wink before bending to his task once more.

"Oh! My pies!" Nicki's hands flew into the air, and she rushed toward the house, Suzanne's chuckle following her across the yard.

She heard another wagon trundle into the yard as she pulled her pies from the oven. She noted with satisfaction that she'd had the coals just right this time. The crusts were a perfect golden brown.

The door opened and Jason stood there with an odd expression. "Nick, can you come outside for a minute?"

She looked at him, wondering what he needed her for. "Can it wait a moment? I have—"

"No." He motioned her toward him. "Come on. It won't take more than a minute. Just come outside." He stepped back and held the door for her, a distinct twinkle glittering in his eyes.

Her curiosity was piqued. "What are you up to?" She stepped outside, shading her eyes with her hands.

Standing next to a wagon was her family. Mama, Papa, and all her younger siblings.

With a gasp she closed her eyes, one hand going to her mouth, the other to cover her heart.

Jason chuckled. "I sent the third hand Ron hired to California to find them."

Opening her eyes, she looked at him. "*Muchas gracias.*" He nodded, and then she was running forward and wrapping her arms around Mama, Papa, Coreena, and little Manuel. Juna and Rosa were young women in their own right, now. My, how they'd all grown! Her brothers were taller than she was! Papa's hair was a little grayer. Mama's wrinkles a little more pronounced, but they were here!

Mama was the last one she pulled into her embrace. "Oh, Mama, *te amo!* I have so much to tell you, I don't know where to start. I have a son, and—Sawyer!" She spun to search the crowd for him, but Jason was there, just behind her, with Sawyer sitting on one arm. He handed the toddler to her.

It felt so right to have Jason there in the midst of her family. She grabbed his hand and swiveled back to her parents. "This is your grandson, Sawyer, and this," she pulled Jason forward, "is the man responsible for bringing you here. This is Jason."

Without hesitation Juanita pulled Jason into a hug, kissing him on both cheeks. "Thank you. You will never know how much it means to me to be here with my Dominique once more."

Jason nodded.

Papa reached for Sawyer, and suddenly everyone began talking at once. Jason stepped back, looking a little lost and confused standing in the center of the chaos that was her family.

Nicki wrapped her arms around Coreena again and met Jason's eyes over the top of the little girl's head. She wished he could see into her heart and understand the happiness he'd given her. Resting her cheek on the top of Coreena's head, she mouthed, "Thank you."

He nodded again and backed away, his gaze locked with hers. Rocky approached his side, taking his attention, and handed him a letter. He said something to Jason, clapped him on the shoulder, and walked away. She watched as Jason slid the letter from the envelope, read it, and then tucked it into his shirt pocket, a strange emotion etching his face. Her focus flicked to his pocket and then back. What could it be?

She started toward him, but just then Mama clutched her arm with a demand to know everything that had happened to Nicki since she'd last seen her. Nicki turned to answer the barrage of questions. She could talk to Jason later. For now, she was thankful to have her family here.

The day went quickly after that. With so many people there to help, the roof was completed before the last rays of the sun disappeared below the horizon. Then everyone moved inside the newly roofed structure for the dancing that was to follow.

Men brought forth fiddles and harmonicas and guitars and the music began.

Women lifted their skirts and sashayed to the lively tune, petticoats flashing white lace in the lamplight.

Janice passed by in a splash of jade, twirling in the arms of Jacob, one of Nicki's new ranch hands. Janice's mouth moved a mile a minute and Jacob listened so raptly that he missed a beat and stepped on her toes. Nicki grinned as they both laughed, and Janice limped off the dance floor to sink onto a barrel, Jacob right by her side.

Nicki tucked her hands behind her back and leaned against one wall, her mother and sisters flanking her. Sawyer leaned against her legs and clapped his tiny hands totally off-beat to the music. Nicki grinned, loving the sight of him enjoying the music.

She tipped her head back and closed her eyes, wondering how it was possible to have so much joy bubbling up inside her. She listened to the sounds of life flowing all around her and almost felt giddy from the sheer blessing of it.

Tanner, the ranch hand Jason had sent to California to find her family, stopped before them and asked Rosa if she would dance with him. Juna giggled as Rosa agreed, and the couple moved out onto the dance floor. To her right, Mama sighed and Nicki smiled.

Someone cleared their throat in front of her, and she opened her eyes to find Jason. Her heart skipped a beat. The bullet scratch along his jawline had healed, but there was still a scar there. She knew it would fade, but it would forever be there to remind her of all that he had done for her.

His face serious, he studied her for a moment, then turned to look out over the dancers. "Could I talk to you for a minute outside?"

Nicki's throat constricted. After she had watched him read the letter, he had been quiet and pensive all day. She had talked to him several times. Even tried to coax a smile from him once, but always his face had remained serious, thoughtful. Why couldn't he talk to her right here? There was something in his eyes she couldn't quite read, and that scared her.

A thought suddenly hit her. What if he wanted to leave? After all, he'd done what she hired him for. He'd gotten the ranch back on its feet, and she could take the reins from here. He'd done more than she hired him to do. He'd brought joy back into her life, made her last weeks bearable. What if the letter was an offer for a job somewhere else?

Tilly stepped up beside them with Conner just behind her. She squatted down to Sawyer's level. "Sawyer, do you want to come and dance with Conner and I?" She held her arms out to him, and he gladly reached up chubby arms to allow her to lift him. With a meaningful look from Nicki to the door, Tilly sauntered onto the dance floor with Conner's hand at her back.

Nicki turned back to Jason. His eyes were once more on her face, waiting for her reply.

She couldn't seem to form an answer. Her heart lodged in her throat making it hard to breathe.

He arched his brow. Mama elbowed her.

She wet her lips. "*Si.*"

He seemed to release a breath and took her hand, leading her out into the dusky night.

She followed him up the trail past the soddy and onto the ridge above. The music from the barn grew faint and blended in with the crickets and the bull frog that croaked nearby. Could she let him go if that was what he wanted? She inhaled slowly. He'd come to mean so much to her in such a short time.

From the crest of the hill they could see the last rays of the sun caressing the sides of the Three Sisters, their snowy nightcaps aglow with crimson. The sky behind them was fused with saffron, tangerine, and jade.

Jason took in the sight for a moment in total silence as he interlaced his fingers with hers. He never took his eyes off the sunset. "Nicki…"

She waited quietly, drinking in the beauty of the night.

The silence stretched long, and she turned to study him. This brooding silence was not like him. She'd never seen him this way before. Something surely was wrong. Her heart thundered in her chest.

His eyes turned back to study her face, and he stepped closer, wrapping one arm around her so that their interlaced fingers rested at the small of her back.

Her confusion grew.

"I got a letter today that made me realize I want to move on with my life, and I…"

Blood drained from her face. He really was leaving.

"Nicki." He watched her intently, his free hand caressing the hair at her temple. His throat worked. "Will you marry me?"

She gasped and felt her knees go weak.

He grimaced and looked toward the mountains again. "I know. We haven't known each other that long, and you've only been a widow for a short time. I've been talking myself in and out of asking you all day. I probably should have wait—"

She covered his mouth with the fingers of her free hand, and his gaze snapped back to hers. She couldn't hold her tears at bay. "I thought you were trying to work up the courage to tell me you were leaving."

He blinked.

"What was in the letter?"

"My cousin Sky and his wife, Brooke, just had a baby girl." He kicked at the ground. "Are you going to answer my question?"

She closed her eyes and let all the love she felt for this man pour into one little word. "*Si.*"

Total silence greeted her.

She opened her eyes.

He wore a look of stunned confusion. "Yes, you are going to answer? Or yes, you will marry me?"

She grinned. "I will marry you, Jason Jordan. Yes, yes, yes."

His face cleared. He let go of her hand and cupped her face, lacing his fingers back through her hair. A slow smile spread across his face. "You've just made me the happiest man in the world."

He dipped his head and his lips touched hers softly, like the caress of a butterfly's wing. He eased back, but she leaned after him, unwilling to live with such a brief bit of bliss. Wrapping her arms around the back of his neck and pulling his head back down to hers, she whispered, "*No pares todabia.* Don't stop yet."

A rumble escaped his chest and when his lips settled on hers once more, she felt a tremor race through him. He slid one hand down her back, tucking her firmly against him.

She cupped his face, her thumbs caressing the corners of his mouth as he kissed her. Standing on tiptoe and leaning into the solid strength of him, she reveled at the love she felt for this man. For the first time in a long time, she felt safe.

With a ragged breath he pulled away, looked at her, leaned back in, trailed a line of kisses from her mouth to her earlobe and then pulled her head to his chest and rested his chin on the top of her tangled hair.

She pressed her ear against him, clutching handfuls of his shirt in her fists. She could hear the wild hammering of his heart…or was it hers?

From this vantage point Nicki could see out over her ranch, *their* ranch.

Smoke drifted lazily from the soddy chimney, a soft gray column against the dimming sky. Light spilled from the barn door in a happy golden rectangle, and laughter and music floated on the cooling air. Off to the right the milling herd of horses mingled, feet stomping and heads bobbing as if they themselves were dancing to the music.

She sighed. So much had happened here in such a short time. So much death and destruction, but through it all, God had kept His promise to her. His promise to be a comfort to her. And much of that had come about because of the man holding her in his arms.

"Jason?"

"Hmmm?"

"I'm glad God sent you to me. You have taken this valley of death," she gestured to the spread stretched out before them, "and turned it into a haven for me."

He dropped a tender kiss against the top of her head, and Nicki closed her eyes, simply relaxing in the safety of his arms.

Dear Reader,

The saying is true that reality is stranger than fiction. Historical records show that the Ochoco Livestock Association was much more violent than I have depicted here. Most people of that day simply referred to them as "The Vigilantes." Their desires were enforced upon the community with hemp rope and bullets. The Association's mission was to keep the range free of settlers, and anyone who opposed them was in danger of losing their life. One man made the mistake of announcing that he'd found an underground river on his property. Since that was viewed as something that might attract settlers to the area he was "asked" to move on. Being a smart man, he did. Others who weren't so lucky were simply in the wrong place at the wrong time, or were of the "wrong" lineage. For further information about this time of turmoil in Oregon's history, I recommend Thunder Over the Ochoco—And the Juniper Trees Bore Fruit, by Gale Ontko.

Also, of note is the fact that most of the terrible reign of The Vigilantes ended in 1884. Those who are history buffs, please forgive me for fudging the timeline of history to fit my story.

Don't Miss…

He's different from any man she's ever known.
However, she's sworn never to risk her heart again.

Idaho Territory,

Brooke Baker, sold as a mail-order bride, looks to her future with dread but firm resolve. If she survived Uncle Jackson, she can survive anyone.

When Sky Jordan hears that his nefarious cousin has sent for a mail-order bride, he knows he has to prevent the marriage. No woman deserves to be left to that fate. Still, he's as surprised as anyone to find himself standing next to her before the minister.

Brooke's new husband turns out to be kinder than any man has ever been. But then the unthinkable happens and she holds the key that might save innocent lives but destroy Sky all in one fell swoop. It's a choice too unbearable to contemplate…but a choice that must be made.

A thirsty soul. Alluring hope. An Oasis of love.
Step into a day when outlaws ran free, the land was wild, and guns blazed at the drop of a hat.

Find out more at: www.lynnettebonner.com

What People Are Saying About Rocky Mountain Oasis

The perfect blend of suspense, drama, and romance. Best keep your eyes on Lynnette Bonner. She's a gifted storyteller.

—SHARLENE MACLAREN, Through Every Storm, Long Journey Home, Little Hickman Creek series, The Daughters of Jacob Kane series

A tale with a unique twist that keeps your attention from the front cover to the back. Based upon actual events, people, and places, this story will linger with you long after you've read the last line.

—BRUCE JUDISCH, Katia, A Prophet's Tale series

A delightful step back into the Wild West. A touching, fulfilling, strong message of redemption.

—L.D. ALFORD, Centurion, Aegypt, The Chronicles of the Dragon and the Fox series

Full of wonderful scenery, excellent character development, and intense emotion. I read many books a week and am happy to say I will be reading this book over and over. The message is simply STUPENDOUS. I loved every minute of it and was quite sad when it was over.

—ANNDRA, Amazon reader

I love this story. I couldn't put it down. I kept it in my hands until I was done. The story line was well-written, and the use of historical facts made the story all the more fascinating for me. Thanks for such a great book! I can't wait for the next one!

—KRISTA, Amazon reader

I enjoyed every word of Rocky Mountain Oasis! I really related to Brooke's feelings and emotions. Lynnette does an excellent job making you feel each aspect of her life. Plus the suspense part keeps you on the edge of your seat! This is a great historical mail-order-bride read. I highly recommend it!

—MARTHA, Amazon reader

Also Available...

She's loved him for as long as she can remember.
But can she trust her heart to a man haunted by constant danger?

Shiloh, Oregon, April 1887

Victoria Snyder, adopted when she was only days old, pastes on a smile for her mama's wedding day, but inside she's all atremble. Lawman Rocky Jordan is back home. And this time he's got a bullet hole in his shoulder and enough audacity to come calling. Since tragedy seems to strike those she cares for with uncanny frequency, she wants nothing to do with a man who could be killed in the line of duty like her father.

But when an orphan-train arrives at the Salem depot, Victoria is irresistibly drawn toward the three remaining "unlovable" children...and stunned by a proposal that will change all of their lives forever.

Can she risk her heart, and her future happiness, on someone she might lose at a moment's notice?

Two stubborn hearts. A most unusual proposal. Persevering love. Step into a day when outlaws ran free, the land was wild, and guns blazed at the drop of a hat.

AN EXCERPT

Fair Valley Refuge

Prologue

New York City, July 21, 1867

Thick black clouds covered the moon and stars, blocking out even the pretense of light. God had, at least, granted that favor. Ignoring the pain that emanated from every pore of her body, the woman clutched the baby to her chest and took Zeb's hand, allowing him to help her from the coach. "I'll only be a moment."

"Yes'm."

Darting a look around, she scuttled across the cobblestone street.

The Foundling Hospital lay just ahead now, all its lights extinguished. Hannah had told her to expect that. She trembled as she stepped onto the walk. Pausing, she swiped the tears from her cheeks and glanced both ways, and then behind her, straining to glimpse any movement or change of shadow. No one was there, as it should be at this hour of night.

Clutching her precious bundle tightly, she hurried on towards the hospital. Mercifully, the babe slept. At least her last memory of the child would be one of peace and contentment.

The door loomed ahead, its pointed arch only a lighter shadow outlining a darker center. Her steps faltered, now that safety was so near.

Easing back into the dark shadows next to the door of the hospital, she pressed against the wall and lifted the baby touching her damp cheek to the child's small soft one. A silent sob parted her lips, shook her shoulders, and stole the strength from her legs.

Sliding down, she laid the babe across her lap and wrapped the blanket tightly around her so she wouldn't get cold in the night. She dashed more tears from her cheeks with quick, angry swipes and tucked the note carefully into the folds of the blanket making sure the rag doll was there too. It was not right, this travesty.

Yet love compelled her. One last time, she trailed the back of her first finger over her daughter's soft cheek. "Ahh Lambkin, the good Lord He be knowin' I'm only tryin' ta save ye. 'Tis His forgiveness I'll rest on. I ken not another path to take."

The baby took a soft shuddering breath and turned her face towards the finger, searching even in her sleep for something to latch onto.

Quickly now, lest she change her mind, the woman opened the outer door of the hospital and stepped into the vestibule. Standing still, she let her vision adjust to the soft candlelight, searching first for anyone who might be lurking in the room. It was empty. She sighed in relief even as her heart sank at being so close to this oh-so-final act.

There across the room, tucked into a small alcove she could see the candle-lit niche holding a white-swathed cradle. A crucifix hung above it, Christ's arms stretched wide to welcome the children placed below him, a reminder that loving sacrifice had been made before.

She swallowed, looked down, pressed her lips together and closed her eyes, instinctively pulling the child tighter to her breast. *I'm so unlike Ye, dear Father. I ken only make this sacrifice kickin' and screamin' on the inside. I didna know he was such a bad'n. Give me strength, Father of Grace.*

The baby bleated a soft cry of protest and the woman's heart skittered. The last thing she needed was for one of the nuns to hear and come to see what was going on. Quickly she brought the babe's hand to her tiny mouth so she could find her thumb. A smile softened her face as the wee child spurned her thumb and settled for slurping on her two middle fingers.

Tears blurred her vision again, shattering the candle flames into glittering, twinkling, haloed-stars. Slowly, she stepped towards the cradle and laid the bundle of blessing inside. Trembling, she clasped the heart-shaped silver locket at her neck and slid it back and forth on the chain. *She's a right to be free from me mistakes.* The metal against metal zinged softly as she stared down at the babe, indecision furrowing her brow. *She's also the right to know.* After only a moment's hesitation she lifted the chain from around her neck and tucked it into the babe's blanket next to the note and the rag doll.

Looking up at the crucifix, she folded her barren arms. "Ye brought this child safe from me womb into this world. I give her back to Ye." The broken whisper sounded loud in the room. A sob caught in her throat as she touched the baby's cheek for the last time. "The Lord bless ye and keep ye, chil'. May He cause His face to shine upon ye. And give ye rest."

Turning she stumbled out into the darkness, leaving the babe behind.

Sister Josephine Claremont stepped into the vestibule the next morning, her hands tucked carefully into her sleeves. A slight rustling sound was her first clue that they had a new little one. Leaning over the side of the cradle, she peered down at the tiny babe. Lying on its stomach, eyes open, two fingers captured in its little mouth, the baby couldn't have been more than a day or two old.

"My, my, tiny one." She reached for the baby and snuggled it into the crook of her neck. "What hardships has our Good Lord rescued you from, eh?"

The baby shifted a wobbly head and slobbered all over its fist trying to find something to suck on.

"Now, now. That's not going to do you a bit of good, that fist is not. What say we get you a yummy meal of milk, hmmm?" Sister Josephine calmly walked upstairs to the nursery, even though her heart was pounding like the choir-boy who got carried away with his drum last Christmas. It never ceased to surprise her when a child was left here for them.

Sister Rose tsked when she entered the nursery. "Oh my, another one? Is it a boy or a girl?" Rose slipped a clean shirt over little Francy's head.

Five-year-old Anna stopped tracing on the slate and scampered over to see the baby. "Who's baby?"

"The Good Lord's, child."

Josephine laid the baby on its back and unwound the blanket around it. A thin onion-skin paper fluttered to the floor and Anna bent and picked it up. A silver locket and a small rag doll were the only other items with the child.

At the feel of the cool air on its body the little mite balled up its fists and howled.

"Hmmm! Good lungs!" Rose commented, handing Francy two wooden blocks.

Josephine reached for a dry diaper. "Girl," she pronounced in the middle of the procedure. "There now!" She cooed as she wrapped the blanket tightly around the little tike once more. "All done, and we'll get you a nice warm bottle of milk. How will that be? Hmmm?"

"Here's her letter." Anna held the paper up to Sister Josephine.

"I'll go get Mother Superior while you get her a bottle," Rose said.

Josephine looked down at Anna. "Thank you, child. I'm going to the kitchen for just a moment. I'll be right back and you can help me feed the baby. Mean time, watch Francy like a big girl."

Mother Superior and Sister Rose entered the nursery just as she was settling back down with the new little one and showing Anna how to hold the bottle.

Smoothing one palm down her habit, Mother Superior held out her hand for the letter. She scanned it and then lifted her head, eyes rounding. "We need to get this child on the next Baby Train. That's in two days. See to the task of outfitting her. I will look through our records for a suitable family."

Chapter One

Shiloh, Oregon. April, 1887

Victoria Snyder gasped and snatched the newspaper closer to her face. "Oh! Today of all days!" How had she missed seeing the ad until just now?

Mama rushed into the dining room, her hair still in rag curls. 'What is it, Victoria? I thought I heard you talking to someone?"

Victoria schooled her features, carefully folded the paper and set it aside. *Wedding planning. That's what's kept me from noticing it.* The last thing Mama needed to worry about on her wedding day was a couple more needy children. "It'll keep, Mama."

She stood and placed a kiss on Mama's cheek, hoping the wild pounding of her heart could not be heard. In her own ears it sounded like the thunder of a wild stampede. Her mind rushed over today's schedule. Would she make it to the train station on time? It would be tight, but she could make it. She *had* to make it.

She patted Mama's shoulders forcing her thoughts back to the present task. "You are going to be the most beautiful bride in Oregon today!"

Mama chuckled. "Well, not with these things in my hair!" Come help me take them out, would you? My arms get dreadfully tired, trying to untie them all."

Victoria grinned, delighted by her mother's excitement. She would think about getting to the train station, after the wedding. Right now she wanted to revel in Mama's giddiness. "Dr. Martin will be happy to take you as his wife any way he can get you! I think you should walk down the aisle with all those rags in your hair, just to see if he really loves you, or not!"

"Oh, Posh!" Mama waved away her joke with a flick of her wrist.

Victoria covered her mouth as Mama grinned and rushed

from the room in a flurry of frilled petticoats. She couldn't stop a little giggle at the thought of Mama actually showing up at the church with all her rag curls still in. *Wouldn't that give Julia Nickerson something to talk about at the next quilting bee!*

Lifting the skirt of her new golden-yellow gown, she followed Mama to help her finish getting ready. Entering the room, she glanced around and smoothed a hand down the front of her dress. Everywhere she looked Mama's touch was evident. From the colorful, hand-appliquéd floral quilt they'd sewn the year Victoria turned thirteen, to the braided rugs they'd just finished last summer – everything in this room would be a reminder of Mama. She fiddled with the pendant at her throat, unanticipated dread threatening to rob her of today's joy. After the wedding, Mama and Dr. Martin were going on a wedding tour to San Francisco, California. And when Mama got back she would move into Dr. Martin's little home above his office. Mama's trunks were already packed and waiting by the door.

Mama caught her eye in the mirror. "I'll just be across town, Ria."

Victoria forced a smile. "Of course you will. It'll just be different. I'll get used to it. And," she shook her finger, "don't think you are getting away from me, because I plan to visit you! Often!"

Mama chuckled. "You'd better, or I will come after you with my rolling pin! Now," she patted her hair and arched her dark eyebrows.

Victoria stepped up behind her and deftly began pulling the rags from her hair. She glanced up and compared their reflections. They were about as different as any two women could be. Mama's dark hair and coffee colored eyes graced a heart-shaped face with a smooth, clear complexion. It amazed her that anyone in this town actually believed she was Clarice Snyder's daughter. Even Papa had been blessed with dark hair and bronze skin.

Before Mama and Papa had moved to Shiloh they had lived in Nebraska. She could still vividly remember the taunts the children at school used to hurl at her. She swallowed and pressed away the memories. That was in the past. Still, she often wondered if she really did have vile blood running through her veins. Who were her people? Where had she come from?

"What are you thinking, honey?"

Victoria wrinkled her freckled nose at her red hair. "It's amazing that anyone in this town believes I'm really your daughter."

Mama's features softened. She reached up and patted Victoria's hand, meeting her gaze in the mirror. "You are as much my daughter as anyone of my own flesh and blood could ever have been, darling. The day the Good Lord brought you to Papa and me was the best day of our lives, and don't you be forgetting it. Just because I'm marrying again and moving over to the doctor's house, doesn't mean I don't love you."

"I know." Victoria made an effort to lift her shoulders and put a smile on her face. She would get through this. Mama certainly deserved this bit of happiness after all she'd been through.

Mama spun around on the stool and captured Victoria's hands. "Honey, I know I've told you this before, but I want to remind you again. You are special. Just because your parents gave you up, doesn't mean the Lord doesn't have great plans for you. I can't tell you the number of times that I've thanked the Lord for sending you to Papa and me." Tears pooled in her eyes. "When Jesus took Papa home, I thought I wouldn't be able to bear it, and you were such a source of strength to me."

Victoria pressed a handkerchief into Mama's hands, blinking back tears of her own. "Now, Mama. We can't have you looking all puffy-eyed on your wedding day."

Mama chuckled and dabbed at her tears. "Honey, I just don't want you to feel like I'm abandoning you."

Pulling her into a hug, Victoria rested her cheek atop the dark curls. "I know you aren't. Things are just going to be different. It'll just take a little while to adjust, is all. I'm so happy for you. And I'm really glad you are feeling so much better, lately. I don't know what I would do if I lost you, too." And that was the truth of it.

Mama patted her arm. "I'm not planning on skipping through

the pearly gates anytime soon, dear. I'm afraid you are stuck with me for a good long while yet."

Victoria chuckled. "Good! Now," she set Mama away from her and spun her back towards the mirror, "we need to finish getting you ready. Sky Jordan said he would be here to get you at ten and it's already a quarter past nine. We can't have you late to your own wedding!" She removed the last few rags from Mama's hair.

Grinning, Mama clasped a pearl necklace about her throat. "Doc said he'd come for me himself, if I was even one minute late."

"I can see him doing it, too." Victoria plucked the wedding dress off the bed and gestured for Mama to stand. Settling the gorgeous champagne satin over Mama's head, Victoria fluffed and fussed with the skirt until it lay in disciplined pleats over the voluminous petticoats. Stepping back she admired the ecru lace and pearls that graced the fitted bodice of the gown. "Oh Mama! You are so beautiful! Here." She gestured to the stool in front of the dressing table again and Mama sat. Victoria bent and began fastening the tiny satin-covered buttons that lined the back of the dress.

Mama cleared her throat and fiddled with something on the dresser top. "Rocky got back home this week."

Victoria's fingers stilled, her heart shying like a stung mare. Resuming the buttoning, she carefully kept any hint of emotion from her voice. "I heard."

"He stopped by Doc's last night while Hannah and I were there. Doc asked him to walk me down the aisle. I was hoping he'd get back in time."

"Before she went back to the orphanage last night, Hannah told me he was shot trying to help Jason apprehend a criminal."

"Mmmm, but Doc says he's going to be fine. It will just take a few weeks for him to fully recover the use of his arm."

Victoria fastened the last button and stood. Her lips pressed together, she reached for the brush and styled Mama's hair for the beautiful pearl combs. Nothing she said would keep the morning peaceful. Mama loved Rocky and had been gently pressuring Victoria in his direction for years – ever since Victoria had innocently proclaimed on her thirteenth birthday that she thought she loved him.

"Honey." Mama waited until Victoria met her gaze in the mirror. "I would much rather have had the few years I had with Robert, than to have never known what it was like to love him at all. Only the Lord knows the future. Don't rob yourself of happiness because you are afraid of what the future holds."

Victoria snugged the last comb into a wave of dark hair and rested the circlet of the veil on Mama's head, then bent and kissed Mama's warm cheek. "Alright, I promise not to rob myself of future happiness."

Mama arched a slim, dark brow.

Victoria gave her a cheeky smile, knowing she hadn't promised what Mama really wanted to hear.

"Ria, you know good and well what I mean."

Victoria sighed. "Mama, Rocky has not so much as ever even hinted that he thinks of me as more than a friend. But if he does, I promise you I will seriously consider him."

A gleam of satisfaction leapt into Mama's eyes and she nodded her acquiescence to Victoria's promise.

There. Now Mama could go through the day with a light heart.

And it wasn't like she was in any danger of having to follow through on her promise. Rocky was never going to pay attention to her in that way. So she would never have to worry about having a lawman for a husband – A lawman who could be killed in the line of duty anytime he went to work, or even stepped out his door to call in the dog.

And that would definitely ensure her future happiness.

ChristyAnne glared daggers at Jimmy Horn across the swaying train aisle. *Big bully*! She pressed her own half of an apple into Damera's tiny hands and sat back, folding her arms.

This time she would watch and make sure Mera got to eat it. Jimmy smirked, stuffed a huge bite of apple in his mouth and turned to look out the train window. *Hope he chokes on it!*

Mera tapped her arm. "Sissy, you can have yer apple. 'Sokay."

ChristyAnne smiled and used the sleeve of her dress to wipe away Mera's tears. "You eat it, Mera. 'S good for ya." Her tummy rumbled and she coughed, hoping Mera hadn't heard it. Raymond Thornton had taken Mera's biscuit at breakfast, so she'd given hers to her. *Least dumb 'ol Ray got picked at the last stop. Don't havta worry none 'bout him no more.*

She carefully wrapped the biscuit from tonight's meal in a scrap of cloth she'd saved and stuffed it into the top of her small valise. She and Mera could share it later. There wouldn't be any more food today and Mera always got hungry right before bedtime. A small snack usually helped her settle down and go to sleep. If they didn't get picked today, they'd at least have a bit of something to calm Mera's hungry tummy.

Since Jimmy was now busy drawing pictures in the dust on the seat in front of him she looked out her window. The train chuffed into a forest of tall trees that blocked out the sun and she could see her reflection pretty good in the dirty glass. She practiced her smile, the rhythmic chug of the engine in the background a monotonous reminder that they were moving farther and farther away from all they'd ever known. She adjusted her lips. Not too big a smile, but not too timid either. She'd tried big and timid both already. Those hadn't worked for her. Well… She sighed. Maybe they had. Someone at every stop had wanted to take her home with them, but no one, so far, had wanted Mera too. And she refused to be separated from her sister.

Miss Nickerson, the woman who worked for The Children's Aid Society, was getting desperate to find homes for the rest of them that were left. At the last stop, she'd made ChristyAnne go with an old woman and her husband who wanted a maid. ChristyAnne shuddered at the memory of that old woman dragging her out of the church by one arm while Mera screamed for her from Miss Nickerson's arms. Mama had always told her if she couldn't say anything nice not to say it at all, but the look on that woman's face when she'd told her she would break all of her fine dishes, rub dirt into her floor and even poison her well if she didn't take her little sister too, had almost been worth the whole ordeal.

ChristyAnne suppressed a giggle.

The woman's expression had reminded her of the time Raymond Thornton put that big ol' toad in the top of the lunch basket and it jumped out into Miss Nickerson's lap, because she looked just like Miss Nickerson had that day. Her mouth had dropped open and she'd sputtered several indecipherable phrases, then promptly marched ChristyAnne back inside the church to announce that she'd changed her mind about taking her. Miss Nickerson had been beside herself, but ChristyAnne had never been more relieved than at that moment. She had simply pulled the distraught Mera into her arms and rested her cheek atop her head, holding on tight.

The train lurched over a rough section of track and the whistle sounded. ChristyAnne reached over and clasped Mera's little hand. *No one is going to separate us*! Mera was all the family she had left in the whole wide world and nobody was going to take that from her.

The next stop was going to be the last on this trip. And if nobody picked them, ChristyAnne had determined that she and Mera would run away rather than go all the way back to New York. *I'm big for ten. Lotsa people think I'm older. I can get a job and take care of us*. She closed her eyes and rested her forehead against the glass. "I'm trying, Mama," she whispered. *I'm trying to take care of Damera like I promised you. But I miss you lots.* Hot tears pressed at the backs of her lids, but she didn't let them fall. She didn't want Mera to see how worried she was, and Miss Nickerson would just tell her to toughen up if she saw the tears.

Maybe at the next stop there would be a family that would want them both. Maybe.

Rocky gingerly slipped his arm into his Sunday-best, black

coat. Pain sizzled in jagged shards through his shoulder and down into his torso. He winced, closed his eyes and waited for the pain to pass. *Thank you, Lord that I'm still here to feel this pain.* It was the prayer he'd been repeating daily since his accident two weeks ago.

The scent of bacon and coffee wafted through his room. His stomach let loose with a rumble that could probably be heard in the next county.

Downstairs, someone knocked at the door and Dad answered it. "'Morning, Dad." That was Sky's voice – probably dropping off Brooke and Sierra, so Brooke could visit with Ma while Sky picked up the bride. Dad would be on his way out the door to head for the Sheriff's office. With all of them busy with the wedding today, Dad had said he would cover things down at the jail and to give Clarice and Doc his best wishes.

Rocky pulled a deep breath in through his nose and eased it out through his mouth. His tense muscles gave up some of their pull. So long as he didn't move his right arm the pain was tolerable. Thankfully Ma had pressed his shirt and suit last night, so he hadn't had to deal with ironing them this morning.

Using his left hand, he flipped his string-tie over one shoulder and fumbled to pull it around so he could tie it at the front.

Today he would have the honor of giving away Victoria's mother. Doc Martin had asked him yesterday, as he'd examined his arm, if he would be willing to do it. Rocky had never felt so privileged. Clarice Snyder was pure gold – one of his favorite people ever.

Her daughter's not so bad either. He grinned at that thought as he made an X from the two sides of the tie and tried to loop them together. His heart felt as light as Hannah Johnston's biscuits. Yesterday, Clarice had granted him permission to call on her daughter. Victoria hadn't been far from his thoughts recently – but especially since the accident. Yet the very reason for her occupying his thoughts, the fact that he'd almost lost his life, was the reason Victoria wouldn't want anything to do with him. He was a lawman. And her father had been a lawman. One killed in the line of duty.

He sighed and gave up on the tie, heading downstairs to where Ma could help him with it. All he could do was lay his heart bare before Victoria and hope she didn't trample it under her tiny booted heels. The irony in it all was that if he could get his hands on some nice horse-flesh and find suitable property in the area, he'd walk away from his tin star in a heartbeat. But he didn't see that happening any time soon. His savings would just have to sit in the bank a little longer.

Ma was in the front parlor, snuggling Sierra and cooing like only a granny could coo. "How is Grammy's baby, huh? Is Grammy's baby just getting to be *such a big girl?* Oh yes you are!" She smooched the baby's cheek loudly. Sierra slobbered happily on one fist, her gaze fixed on Ma's face. She didn't look too impressed with all Ma's commotion.

Rocky grinned at Brooke seated in the armchair to his right. "I see Ma's hands are full. Can you help me with this?" He gestured to the tie. "One handed bows are not something I've been practicing, lately. I'm bad enough when I have two."

Brooke smiled tiredly. "Sure." She started to rise.

Rocky reached out to stop her. "Just sit." Quickly, before she could protest, he bent down to a level that she could reach. "Sky tells me Sierra prefers to sleep during daylight hours."

"Yes. And last night was no exception." She grinned and deftly gave the tie one last adjustment. "There, you're all set. You look great."

Rocky gave a small bow. "Thank you. You don't look too bad yourself. I'd say green is definitely your color."

"Oh, yes. He's right, Honey," Ma pitched in. "Your red-blonde hair looks stunning with that green."

"Thank you. Sky picked this material out for me and had Mrs. Chandler sew it as a gift after Sierra was born. I thought that was very sweet of him."

Ma turned back to Sierra. "You have one smart Daddy. Yes you do!"

Rocky adjusted the sleeves on his coat. "Well, I better get on over to the church. Is Sky coming back for you ladies, or would you like me to walk you over now?"

Ma waved him on. "We have a few minutes yet. Sky said he would be back for us. Don't forget to grab yourself some bacon and eggs in the kitchen on your way out. Everything is made ready and waiting."

He grinned. "Thanks, Ma. My stomach could have been mistaken for T. Edgerton Hogg's Southern Pacific Railroad when I first smelled that bacon this morning."

Ma chuckled. "See you over there."

With a wave of his hand, Rocky headed for the kitchen, hastily sandwiched bacon and eggs between slices of bread, then hurried out the back door as he stuffed a huge bite in his mouth.

Bright sunshine warmed Shiloh. It was a good day for a wedding. A good day to start wooing Victoria's heart.

★

Chapter Two

In the small back room of the church Victoria sat with her mother. Mrs. Hollybough was playing the music Mama had picked out for the time before the ceremony, so the ushers must be seating people. Victoria glanced at Mama who sat on her chair, hands folded in her lap, eyes closed. Probably praying. Which I should be doing myself. Lord, bless Mama and Doc Martin as they join their lives today. Keep them safe while they travel to California and back and help me with all the adjustments I'm going to need to make in the near future. Her mind turned to the article she had read in that morning's paper. And help me know what to do about those children, Lord.

A tap at the door interrupted her prayer. Mama opened excited eyes as Victoria stood. They smiled at each other.

"Ready?" Victoria asked.

Mama laughed. "I've been ready since we walked in here and sat down."

Victoria opened the door. Rocky stood on the other side, looking more than handsome in his black Sunday-best suit.

She swallowed and glanced behind him towards the sanctuary. "Everything set?"

"They're ready for you." His gaze slid past her so that the words were directed straight to Mama.

A small sadness enveloped her and she bit her lip. This was the first time she'd seen him since he'd come home. And he'd spoken only to Mama. Barely even looked at her.

She brushed the disappointment aside. Right now she had to concentrate on making Mama's day the best it could be and she had no business being disappointed in anything Rocky did anyhow. She stooped and placed a kiss on Mama's cheek. "I'll be waiting for you up there. I love you so much!"

Mama returned the kiss and then Victoria pressed the bouquet of white daisies into her hand and brushed past Rocky, her own single daisy clutched against her like a lifeline.

Rocky stopped her with a touch to her elbow.

She turned towards him.

"Be sure and save me a dance, today." He smiled, his deep brown eyes softening.

Her heart forgot to beat, then suddenly remembered and set to beating extra fast as though to make up for lost time. She looked down at the Daisy. "Alright." He's a lawman. He's a lawman. He's a lawman. She glanced back up, forcing herself to meet his gaze.

For one moment they stood, transfixed, simply gazing at each other. Then Rocky ran his left hand down the front of his coat and focused on the floor. "Better get going." He looked back into her eyes.

"Yes. See you out there." His right arm, bent at the elbow, pressed slightly into his torso, as though to protect it from being jostled. "Is your arm okay?" Her gaze flicked to his shoulder.

He waved away her concern, again using only his left hand. "I'm fine. Don't worry about me."

Mama stepped out into the church entry and took Rocky's arm.

Quickly, Victoria fluffed out mama's train and then, stepping back around in front of her, preceded them to the aisle. Mama's best friend, Miz Hannah Johnston who ran the town orphanage, motioned to Mrs. Hollybough on the organ and the music changed. Clasping the daisy in front of her, Victoria started down the aisle, her steps deliberate and slow.

Doc Martin, who would soon be her third father but only the second one she'd ever known, stood at the head of the aisle nervously adjusting his cuffs. Pastor Hollybough smiled reassuringly as Victoria took her place and turned to face the family and friends gathered in the sanctuary.

Julia Nickerson's mother and father had managed to secure the seats right next to the one reserved for Rocky after he gave

Mama away. Where is Julia, I wonder? Come to think of it, she hadn't seen Julia around town for several weeks. She scanned the sanctuary surreptitiously and her brows arched in surprise. Julia never missed any social events in their small little town, but she wasn't here today. Victoria pressed her lips together and fixed her attention on the door as the bridal processional started and everyone stood. Why should it bother her that Julia's parents were obviously scheming to get Rocky to marry their daughter? It's not like you're planning on marrying him. Still, whoever he did marry, she hoped he was wise enough to stay a million miles away from the likes of the Nickersons, Julia in particular. With determination, she turned her thoughts elsewhere.

Mama radiated joy as she came down the aisle on Rocky's arm, creamy satin rustling and her gaze fixed solely on Doc.

Doc took an involuntary step towards Mama as she and Rocky stopped at the front of the church aisle and Victoria bit the inside of her cheek to smother the giggle that wanted to burst forth. He looked like a little boy on Christmas morning who'd been told he had to wait to open his presents for a few more minutes.

Rocky caught her eye and by the gleam in his own, she could tell he found it amusing, as well.

As she stood and watched Mama and Doc exchange vows her heart grew lighter and lighter. This was so right for Mama. After Papa's death, Victoria had feared she would lose Mama to poor health, but Doc had come by faithfully with a little of this powder and that herb. Probably his company, more than his medicines, was what had restored her health.

"I now pronounce you man and wife," Pastor Hollybough declared. "Doc, you may kiss your bride." Doc did so with relish and to the cheers of the audience.

Victoria grinned. She felt like she might burst forth into song as she headed back down the aisle. Lord, you are so good. Thanks for helping me to see once again how wonderful this is for Mama.

Rocky gritted his teeth and fisted his left hand. If Jay Olson asked Ria to dance one more time he might just have to go out there and cut in, pain be hanged. Couldn't she see what kind of a man Jay was? His arm encircled her waist far too tightly. Obviously the guy had only one thing on his mind! Ria laughed at something Jay said and Rocky stomped over to the punch bowl and snatched up one of the prefilled cut crystal glasses. He was going to have to have a talk with her about that man. Rocky took a big gulp of his punch. Even if she didn't want anything to do with him, the man she did marry needed to be four times the man Jay was!

Sky strolled up to him, Sierra tucked into the crook of his arm with her downy head lolling on his shoulder.

Rocky nodded a greeting, and tossed back another gulp of punch.

"Rock, you look like you did that time the big ol' bull stepped on your foot and then refused to budge."

The memory brought a pained smile to Rocky's face. "That bad, huh?"

Silently they watched Victoria and Jay twirl around the dance floor. "Why don't you ask her to dance?"

Rocky drained his cup and plunked it down on the table next to him. "Maybe another time." His shoulder felt like it was on fire. He pressed his lips together, refusing to admit that he was up and about too soon.

Jay leaned forward and said something into Victoria's ear. Her face burned scarlet and her jaw dropped for one second before it hardened and she stiffened in his arms.

Sky said, "Yeah. You're probably right. You should just stand back and let Jay woo her. That'd be best."

Rocky's whole body trembled with the self control it took not to march out onto the dance floor and lay Jay out with one well-placed fist. He reached for a chair and leaned his good arm into the back of it with a white-knuckled grip. What had Jay said to her?

The song ended and Victoria abruptly pushed back from Jay, said something to him, then lifted her skirts and stalked away.

Jay leaned back into his heels, slid his hands into his pockets and scanned Ria from head to toe as she stormed off. Turning with a smirk on his face, he met Rocky's gaze and stilled.

Rocky deliberately narrowed his eyes and stood erect.

Jay's smile faltered, then broadened into a challenge. He gave Rocky a two-fingered salute and then headed jauntily for the door, disappearing into the sunlight outside.

Sharyah stepped up beside Rocky and touched his arm. "What was that all about?"

Startled, he looked at his sister's worried frown.

Sky chuckled and adjusted Sierra on his shoulder. "Just a couple dogs struttin' around a tasty bone, Sharyah. Don't let it worry you. Rocky's gonna see any day now that if he wants that bone, he'd better stand up and start fighting for it." Sky pierced him with a look and arched a meaningful eyebrow.

"Really! Men!" Sharyah picked up her skirts and started off in a huff, tossing over her shoulder, "Victoria is much more than just a tasty bone and if Rocky can't see that then he doesn't deserve her!"

Rocky rubbed his jaw, angled Sky a glare, and headed over to say his congratulations to the new bride and groom. His shoulder had had enough of this day. He would have to talk to Victoria another time.

Clarice and Doc were talking with Miz Hannah Johnston. All three looked up as he approached.

Doc stood to his feet. "Well, speak of the devil!"

"Now, Dale! More like an angel, wouldn't you say?" Clarice pulled Rocky into a motherly embrace.

Rocky gritted his teeth against the shards of pain jostled loose by her squeeze and hoped his face looked normal as he stepped back.

"Well now, yes, I think you're right," Doc replied. But his attention never left Clarice.

Putting both her hands on Rocky's cheeks, Clarice looked up at him. "Honey, thank you for honoring me by walking me down the aisle. It means a great deal to me."

"Sure, anytime. The honor was all mine."

"Now," she stepped back, "we were just talking about you before you walked up. Would you mind helping Victoria get my trunks from the house into Hannah's buggy and then bringing them over to Doc's place?"

"Sure." He winced inwardly at the thought of having to lift anything heavier than a coffee mug, but the smile on his face never faltered. *So much for some rest.* "I'll head over there right now. You two have a good trip."

"I'll jus' go on with him," Miz Hannah said. "That way my buggy'll be right there an' he won't have to do no waitin'." She pulled Clarice into her plump ebony arms. "Doll, you go on and have yourself a wonderful time."

Clarice smiled. "You know we will."

Miz Hannah turned to him. "Come on, Darlin'. Let's go move some trunks."

As they approached Hannah's buggy Rocky's footsteps slowed, an uneasy feeling settling in the pit of his stomach. He had no desire to be driven across town by a woman. But if there was one unspoken rule in the little town of Shiloh it was this: No one touched Miz Hannah's buggy but her.

He cleared his throat. "I'll just walk on over and meet you there, Hannah."

Hannah threw back her big head and let loose with a laugh loud enough to draw the attention of several people down the street. "Honey chil', ain't nobody never died from being driv around by Hannah Johnston. You jus' climb on up there. I got somethin' needs discussin'."

Reluctantly, Rocky did as he was told. And Hannah set the buggy in motion with a smart snap of the reins and her characteristic, "Come on now!" call.

Rocky clenched his jaw and closed his eyes against the shooting pain. The consistent dull throbbing was much preferable to the stabbing shards that shot through him now.

Hannah huffed. "Honey, heaven knows you ain't gonna be liftin' no trunks, as much pain as you in. You do a good job o' hiding it, but I sees it. Not much gets by Miz Hannah. No sir, not much. Clarice woulda seen it too, 'cept for her head bein' in the clouds and all. But don't you worry none, I done sent Cade over already. He's gonna meet us there."

Rocky looked over at her. "He's back in town?"

"Yes. Said he done got a right smart price for them hosses. Right smart."

"That's good. Can you just drop me at home, then? I am about done for." He gave her a sheepish smile.

"Wisht' I could. Really I does. But I'm gonna need you to talk some sense into Victoria 'fore this day is through. 'Sides," she angled him a knowing look, "I was there last night when you asked her mama for permission to call. Ain't no time like the present."

Rocky frowned, wondering why she needed him to talk some sense into Ria. "What do you mean?" His mind flashed to Jay and heat surged through his chest. "What kind of crazy thing is she doing?"

"Don't get all het up, now. She ain't doin' nothin' what she ain't been doin' for the past several years. And that's goin' to the train station in Salem to pick up the straggler orphans what don't find no home."

He relaxed, easing back into the seat. About once a year an orphan train came through Salem. The children on it were from large cities back east, usually New York. Their parents were either deceased, or unable to care for them for some reason. Since Salem was one of the last stops on the route, any orphans who did not find a home here, had to travel all the way back to New York. Several years ago, Victoria had taken it upon herself to make sure every last child left at the end of the day would find a home. She met the train, and brought any unchosen children back to Shiloh, housed them in the orphanage, and worked tirelessly until she found good stable homes for them.

"She does that every year. What's different about this time?"

"What's different is, I don't gots no more beds down to the orphanage. Any chil' she brings home, ain't gonna have a bed to sleep in. I done tol' her she needs to leave things in the Good

Lawd's hands this time. Truth be tol' I was hopin' with the weddin' and all that she wouldn't notice the ad in the paper. But you know her and her obsession with helpin' them children. She's bound and determined to go."

"If she didn't listen to you, what makes you think she'd listen to me?"

Hannah bellowed a laugh and slapped her thigh. The horse twisted back his brown ears at the raucous sound and snorted, jangling the bit in his mouth. "Honey chil', she'll listen to you 'cause she cares right smart what you think."

Rocky didn't allow her words to take him down a path of hope. "Who does she have taking her to the train?"

Hannah angled him a look, chin tipped down, her widened eyes a stark white against the ebony of her face. "Usually she has Doc take her, but seein' as how he is indisposed today, she done asked Jay Olson to take her."

"Jay Olson?!" Rocky sat forward with a start.

Hannah gestured for him to calm down. "But he done somethin' she didn't like, though I don't rightly know what it was, and now she plans on goin' by herself."

"Well at least she has some sense," he muttered, settling back against the seat.

"I gots Elsa watchin' the children down to the orphanage whilst I come up to the weddin' but I cain't leave her alone long enough to run Ria down to Salem and back."

Even though it was most likely more sensible than having Jay Olson escort her, the thought of Victoria travelling the 20 miles to Salem and back by herself, sent a coil of frustration rushing through Rocky. Anything could happen to a woman alone on the trail these days. Especially with Salem growing like it was. He sighed. "I'll have a talk with her, but I can't promise you it'll do any good. You know how she gets when she has her mind set on something. Mules have nothing on her when it comes to stubbornness."

Hannah shook her head. "Ain't that the truth. Yes sir. Good Lawd's truth you just spoke."

A moment later she pulled to a stop in front of Victoria's house and Rocky wearily climbed from the seat. Hannah got down from her side of the carriage before he'd even thought of moving to help her and he gave her an apologetic look.

Hannah's face softened. "You's about done for. Want I should look at that shoulder?"

Rocky consciously relaxed his jaw as he started for the house. "My shoulder will be fine as soon as I get some rest. Thanks, though." He knocked on the kitchen door.

Victoria answered, a look of curiosity on her face. "Oh, hello. Since Cade stopped by, I didn't expect to see you here."

Rocky tried not to frown as he removed his hat. Had Cade compromised Victoria's integrity by going into her house while she was alone? Rocky clenched his fists at the thought of what something like that could do to Victoria's good name. Cade, of all people, should know what gossip fueled by a bit of truth could do to someone's reputation. But he was so easy-going, the gossip about him and his numerous courtships generally had about as much effect on him as rain did on a well-oiled slicker. On the other hand, the girls involved weren't able to so lightly dismiss the pronged tongues of the town's busybodies. Rocky had seen that on several occasions. And he didn't want Victoria facing similar backbiting through no fault of her own. *If Cade has thoughtlessly maligned her by his careless actions....* "Cade's inside?"

Victoria nodded and stepped back, motioning him and Hannah inside. "Yes, he stopped by with Sharyah several minutes ago. Said Hannah had asked them both to come by and help move Mama's things over to Doc's place."

Rocky eased out a breath of relief as he followed Hannah through the door.

Hanging her shawl on a peg, Hannah slanted him an amused look.

He smiled softly. Good ol' Hannah. She thought of everything.

Victoria smoothed her hands down the sides of her skirt. He most definitely liked her new dress. Somehow the yellow of it drew his attention to her red curls. Right now, he wanted to reach out and wrap the one caressing her cheek around his finger.

She blushed and glanced down, and he realized he'd been staring. He rubbed the back of his neck, looking at the floor. "Got any coffee?"

Hannah huffed and flapped her hands at him. "No coffee for you, now. You jus' go sit yourself down and I'll bring you some willow bark tea." She poured water in the kettle. "Ria, I ain't gonna hide nothin' from you. I done brung Rocky over here to talk some sense into you. So you jus' go on and have a talk with him. Cade, Sharyah and I, we'll take care o' Clarice's trunks." Victoria opened her mouth to say something but Hannah held a finger in her direction as she clunked the kettle down on the stove. "I mean it now. You and I done all the talkin' we gonna do on the subject."

Rocky suppressed a grin. Victoria was none too pleased at being dismissed from her own kitchen. She had a way of holding her mouth just so when she was about to let someone have a piece of her mind. He held his hand out towards the small sitting room. "Let's sit." He nodded his head, encouraging her to let it go.

With a tiny huff, Victoria complied.

"Cade!" Hannah bellowed as they left the kitchen. "Buggy's here!"

As Rocky and Victoria headed through the small dining room of the house, Rocky could hear a low-voiced conversation between Cade and Sharyah in the sitting room. Suddenly, the sound of a resounding slap cracked through the air.

Victoria darted him a glance, her mouth dropping open in surprise.

"Don't you ever say something like that to me again, Cascade Bennett!" Looking for all the world like she was running from a fire, Sharyah stormed out of the sitting room, skirts lifted. She bolted past them, tears streaming down her cheeks.

Rocky and Victoria watched her brush past Hannah, bang

through the kitchen door, and slam it behind her. The walls of the old house rattled with the force of her anger.

A moment later Cade stepped into the doorway, his serious blue gaze fixed on the closed portal, one hand thoughtfully rubbing his cheek.

Chapter Three

Victoria winced. Sharyah had been mooning over Cade Bennett for as long as she could remember. She wondered what he'd said to her to earn a slap. Sharyah wasn't the type to fly off the handle for no reason.

"Cade?" Rocky took a step towards him, anger radiating from every inch of his stance as he instinctively came to his sister's defense.

Victoria laid a hand on his arm. He glanced at her and she shook her head. Cade was still staring off after Sharyah. Maybe this would be what it took to make Cade realize how good Sharyah would be for him. Victoria sighed. Cade needed to settle down sometime, but she didn't want Rocky to lose his friend over a confrontation that could come to no resolve.

Whatever Cade had said to Sharyah, Victoria knew it couldn't have been anything inappropriate. He would never do that. Probably it was just an off handed comment that had hurt Sharyah's feelings. Cade was a good man. He would settle down, and sooner than later. But for now, she could sense he needed some space. "Cade, Mama's trunks are to the right of the door in the first room down the hall."

Cade dropped his hand to his side and headed back through the sitting room and down the hall without another word.

Rocky glared at his retreating back and spoke quietly. "If he were any other man…." A muscle in his jaw pulsed as he repeatedly clenched it.

"You know he wouldn't have said anything suggestive to her."

Rocky thought for a moment then seemed to relax. "Yeah, you're right." He pierced her with a look. "Speaking of which, what did Jay Olson say to you?"

Victoria felt her cheeks flame and led the way across the sitting room, gesturing to the settee.

He didn't sit. Instead, he studied her with his dark, long-lashed eyes slightly narrowed and a look of determination firming his jaw. He slid his hat through his hands, crimping the brim, and never looking away.

She glanced at the floor and squeezed her forehead with one finger and her thumb. "It was nothing." She flipped her hand as though batting away his concerns.

"It was enough of something to make you decline his offer to escort you into town."

"It wasn't so much what he said as the way he said it."

He made no comment, only waited, brow lifted, the unanswered question still on his face.

She sighed. "All he said was that he'd be honored to escort me into town. But there was something about the way he said it that made me feel... uncomfortable." *And the way he lowered his hand from my waist.* Uncomfortable was not a strong enough word to describe how *that* had made her feel. Repulsed was more like it.

Rocky seemed to relax a little and she thanked her good fortune that he didn't seem set on pushing the issue further.

"So Hannah wants you to talk me out of going to Salem today?"

Apparently taking the cue for a change of subject, Rocky eased himself down on the settee with a soft release of breath and tilted his head back against the seat, eyes closed. "Pretty much."

He must be in a lot more pain than he wants us to know about. Fear scurried through her veins. "Rocky, are you okay?"

He met her questioning gaze. "So tell me about this trip to Salem today. What is it all about?"

Not liking the way he'd dodged her question, Victoria sank into the wing chair and dusted at an invisible fleck on the brown velvet trim of her skirt. She shrugged. "It's the normal trip I take every time the orphan train comes to Salem. I just want to make sure that any children who are left there have a shot at finding a good home out here."

Rocky sat up and she noted that he was careful to keep his right arm pressed tightly against his torso as he moved. “You have a great big heart, Ria. But Hannah tells me there are no more beds at the orphanage right now. What are you going to do with the children?”

She lifted her palms by her sides, gesturing around her. “I can bring them here. There’s plenty of room here.”

“Hannah tells me she’s been having trouble finding homes for children through the orphanage. What are you going to do with them if you can’t find a home for them?”

She shrugged, swallowing down the pain of that thought. Not because she might have to take care of some children for a really long time, but because of how the children might feel if no one wanted them. “They’d be welcome to stay here indefinitely.”

Elbows planted on his knees, Rocky sighed, dropped his head down next to his left hand and squeezed the back of his neck. Just then, Hannah bustled in with a tea tray and pressed a large mug of steaming tea into Rocky’s hand. By the smell it was willow bark.

Victoria took up her own cup and sniffed it, happy to find that it was regular tea and she wouldn’t be forced to drink the bitter willow bark brew. She sipped quietly as Hannah hurried off calling directions to Cade on the loading of the trunks.

Rocky tasted his tea, his dark brown gaze meeting hers over the rim of his cup. “You know once you bring children into your home you’re going to fall in love with them and won’t want to give them to someone else.”

She waved a hand. “No. I’ve helped lots of children find homes before. I’ll be fine.”

He crossed the ankle of one foot over the knee of his opposite leg. “This will be different. You bring children here and you’ll be living with them day in and day out. You know you won’t want to part with them.”

A lump formed in her throat. “I’ll just have to deal with it. I obviously can’t take care of children on my own for long.”

“What are you going to do if they are all fifteen-year-old boys?”

She couldn't stop the smirk that tipped the corner of her mouth. "Then I'll invite them all back here and send them over to your parent's place to board in your room."

He grinned and leaned towards her speaking softly. "If our place gets too crowded, I might just have to see if any of the single ladies in town will have me. I've had my eye on a certain pretty red-head for quite some time."

Her eyes widened and heat rushed to her face as she looked down into her lap and rubbed a pinch of golden satin between her fingers. Rocky had never once flirted with her in the past. *He's a lawman*! The quelling reminder had little effect on her racing pulse. Surely she hadn't understood him correctly. There was a way to find out. She glanced back up with feigned innocence. "Saying something like that could get you slapped."

He chuckled softly. "Just give this willow bark a chance to get into my system first." He eased back and swallowed another mouthful of tea, never taking his gaze off her face. "Have I ever told you how beautiful you are?"

Victoria's heart lurched. She nibbled at the fingernail on her first finger, the heel of one foot bouncing up and down rapidly. She shook her head. He couldn't be showing interest in her like this now! Not when he'd just come home badly injured and she'd decided with such finality that a lawman definitely wasn't the kind of man for her. Forget his profession! Even if it weren't for that, she simply didn't deserve a man like Rocky.

Downing the last mouthful of the brew in his cup, he leaned forward and placed it on the tray Hannah had left for them. "Ria, getting shot has made me think through my life." He cleared his throat. "I was laying there on the floor with Jason and Cade leaning over me, both of them acting like I wasn't going to live to see the next minute, and I clearly remember I had one regret." He looked up at her. "So let me put that regret to rest." His deep brown eyes softened as they took in the lines of her face. "You are quite possibly the most beautiful woman I've ever seen."

Victoria realized she was holding her breath and let it go with a quick puff that came out on a nervous bit of laughter. She felt the burn as her face flushed crimson. She looked across the room, down into her lap, at his boots – anywhere but at his face. "Your one regret was that you'd never told me I was beautiful?" She peeked up at him, unable to resist the allure of his gaze.

"No." He shook his head. "It was that I hadn't ever courted you – gotten to know you better."

Victoria blinked. *He doesn't know that I'm adopted.* That reminder was like a douse of ice water on the flame of her beating heart. She took a calming breath. He at least needed to know that before he courted her. That might, after all, change his mind. Rocky didn't know where she really came from. *She* didn't even know her own lineage. What if she really did come from bad blood like Sarah Hollister had told her in the first grade? Rocky didn't deserve to get stuck with that.

"I asked your mother's permission last night to start courting you, and she granted it. Now I'm here asking you. Will you allow me the privilege to come calling?"

She pinched the bridge of her nose, then stood abruptly and paced the room like a corralled filly. She didn't know how to tell him. Victoria stared at the floor as she paced, arms folded, blinking back tears. Why was he doing this now? After all these years? Just when she'd promised Mama this morning that she would consider his offer? *Mama obviously knew what she was doing this morning when she extracted that promise!*

And what about her own feelings? She pressed her lips together, thinking of his shoulder wound. A few inches lower and he wouldn't be here to speak to her at all. What would she do if she agreed to allow him to court her, and then they ended up marrying? Part of her longed to agree. Oh! How she longed to agree. But life as a lawman was definitely dangerous, as proven by his recent near miss. What if later, perhaps after marriage and children, something should happen to him? She didn't know how she would live through something like that. She already cared far too much. Mama was right. It was already unbearable to think of something happening to him. She didn't want the hurt and worry to become worse. And she certainly didn't deserve a man like him.

Behind her, Rocky cleared his throat. "Ria?"

Raising one hand to stop his questioning, she said, "I can't talk about this right now. I'm going to miss the train if I stay here any longer." Picking up her skirts with a rustle of satin, she started out of the room.

He sighed. "I'm coming with you. Just let me get the buggy for you."

She spun around. "You can't come with me! You're already just about done in."

Tears still blurred her vision when he stepped towards her. "Ria." The word was a soft caress. He reached up, cupped her face, and traced her cheek with his thumb. "I know my job scares you."

She closed her eyes and forced herself not to tilt her head into his touch as she whispered, "I wouldn't be able to stand it, if… something happened and…." *If only that were all of it.*

He released a soft breath. "I don't have an answer for that except I know God is in control of the future, and I won't leave this world until it's my time to go." He paused and when she remained silent he continued. "Your words give me hope, though."

She looked at him, rolling her upper lip between her teeth.

He grinned. "I didn't know if you could care for me at all. Gives me hope that you wouldn't be able to stand it if something happened to me." He winked. "That's a start." His thumb caressed her cheek again, wiping away a tear that had spilled over. "Can you leave the future up to the Lord and at least give us a chance to get to know each other a little better?"

Silence filled the room. She didn't know how to tell him that she didn't think she could trust God with her heart. It was already in so many shattered pieces, she didn't know if even God could put it back together. "There's so much you don't know about me, Rocky."

"Mmmhmm. That's why I want to spend more time with you." He stepped back. "I'll go get the buggy and you can give me your answer when you are ready." Stopping at the door, he looked back. "I do know enough about you to know that everything I learn is only going to make me care more for you, not less."

Victoria watched him walk out of the room, then her eyes slid shut. If only she could believe that were true. Once Rocky found out her parents hadn't even wanted her, he might not want anything to do with her.

The train shuddered to a stop in the station with a huge puff of hissing sound. Miss Nickerson bustled down the aisle. "Come on children. Gather your bags. Quickly now." She clapped her hands twice.

ChristyAnne helped Mera hop off the seat and slip on her coat, then she climbed up to stand on the bench so she could reach their bags in the overhead compartment. Mera stepped out into the aisle and turned, waiting for ChristyAnne to hand her one of the small suitcases they'd each been given before the trip west.

A large man with a thick drooping mustache, barreled up the aisle. He wore a round bowler hat that looked oddly small on his large round head, and clouds of cigar smoke spewed from his mouth.

How could he stand the smell? She wrinkled her nose as a gray waft enveloped her.

Without so much as pausing, he smacked Mera's arm with his cane, pushing her aside as he hurried by, grumbling under his breath about the vile-blooded offspring of no-goods who couldn't' take care of their own children.

Mera rubbed her arm, large tears pooling in her big dark eyes as she watched him disappear out the door of the rail car. "That huht me!" Her lower lip pooched out.

ChristyAnne glared out the window as the fat man retreated and then handed Mera her little bag. "I'm sorry, Mera. I'll give it a kiss in a minute, but first we have to hurry off the train or Miss Nickerson is gonna get mad at us." She pulled her own case down. "Come on. Let's go." She hopped off the bench.

Mera toddled along in front of her, clutching her suitcase

with both hands up near her chest. A kind-looking man in a cap smiled and helped Mera down the train steps.

"Much obliged," ChristyAnne mumbled as she stepped down into the gravel of the train yard and adjusted her black sweater. She swallowed, pressing down her anxiety, and squatted in front of Mera to straighten her clothes. She had to make sure they both looked especially good.

Off to her right Miss Nickerson was admonishing the children to stay together, smile, be polite, speak only when spoken to, and the rest of the list of things they'd all heard at every train stop where they had been looked over since New York.

Mera's eyes were wide as she took in the hustle and bustle of the station, her small case on the ground beside her. In front of them was the depot building. A large round clock on the wall facing them proclaimed with bold black hands that it was five o'clock. Down the platform a ways, a boy about her age hawked newspapers and another offered to shine the shoes of anyone who passed his way. A man trundled by with a big stack of trunks and boxes on a rolling cart. One wheel needed some grease. It was squealing louder than Betty-Lou from back home had the time her arm got busted when she fell off the swing. The mean fat man in the bowler pushed the boy selling newspapers aside with his cane and tapped some of the ash from his cigar into the chipped, tin, change-cup of the shoe-shine boy.

"ChristyAnne!" Miss Nickerson jerked her hand in a motion to indicate she should pay attention and hurry-up all at the same time. The rest of the children were already in the single-file line headed for a small platform she could see just inside the depot doors.

Giving Mera's jacket one last dusting, ChristyAnne bent and kissed her little sister's arm, then captured her attention with a touch to her chin. "'Member to smile, 'kay?"

Mera nodded. "An' fold my hands." She mimicked the gesture ChristyAnne had taught her in hopes that their good behavior would win them a place to live. Together.

"Good. Now," ChristyAnne hefted both their cases, "come on."

Inside, the children all set their bags in a corner and climbed up onto the platform to stand in two rows facing a gathering crowd. ChristyAnne made sure she was standing directly behind Mera. Miss Nickerson began her remarks. She always said what wonderful hard-working children they were and that none of them would be any trouble, and if they were the Children's Aid Society would take them back, so ChristyAnne didn't pay attention to what she said. Instead, she scanned the crowd. Was there a new family waiting for her and Mera here? Off to one side of the crowd was a tall man in overalls. His wife stood beside him with a small frown on her face. They looked nice enough, but as soon as Miss Nickerson stopped talking they turned around and headed for the outside doors.

ChristyAnne sighed. That was the way of it. A lot of people just came out of curiosity to see what the orphan train was all about. Two men stepped forward. They looked like brothers. One bent and smiled at Jasper, one of the twins, while the other focused his attention on Jason. ChristyAnne swallowed. It looked like the twins were gonna be split up. But as Miss Nickerson gestured them over to the corner where her assistant would fill out the paperwork, ChristyAnne heard one of the men say, "We live on neighboring farms, so they'll be able to see each other often." She sighed. That brought some relief. At least the brothers wouldn't lose track of each other. She turned to scan the crowd once more and blinked. The fat, mean man with the mustache was talking to Miss Nickerson!

"Sure, a fine dairy ve haf as you know. I vas talking to your father, yust the other day, and he told me a yob you had taken vith the Children's Aid Society. Yes, my vife vould for some company be happy. Yust come out once you are done here. Ve vill look forward to haf you to dinner, ya!"

"Why thank you, Mr. Vandenvort." Miss Nickerson patted the hair at the back of her head and adjusted her flowery hat. "It has been an honor to help these children find homes, but I have to say it is very nice to be home! And I would be happy to come to dinner tonight."

ChristyAnne suppressed an eye-roll at her simpering tone.

The man nodded. "Good. The vife I will let know. Now, I need to vork in my dairy a strong young gal. Yust one." He blew a ring of smoke towards the ceiling and turned to scan them all with watery blue eyes.

"Well! I have just the one!"

Miss Nickerson turned and looked directly at her, and ChristyAnne's heart dropped with the speed of a stone.

If you would like to keep reading you can purchase Fair Valley Refuge here: www.lynnettebonner.com/books/historical-fiction/the-shepherds-heart-series/.

Also Available...

He broke her heart.
Now he's back to ask for a second chance.

Heart pounding in shock, Sharyah Jordan gapes at the outlaw staring down the barrel of his gun at her. Cascade Bennett shattered her dreams only last summer, and now he plans to kidnap her and haul her into the wilderness with a bunch of outlaws…for her own protection? She'd rather be locked in her classroom for a whole week with Brandon McBride and his arsenal of tricks, and that was saying something.

Cade Bennett's heart nearly drops to his toes when he sees Sharyah standing by the desk. Sharyah Jordan was not supposed to be here. Blast if he didn't hate complications, and Sharyah with her alluring brown eyes and silky blond hair was a walking, talking personification of complication.

Now was probably not the time to tell her he'd made a huge mistake last summer….

Two broken hearts. Dangerous Outlaws. One last chance at love.
Step into a day when outlaws ran free, the land was wild, and guns blazed at the drop of a hat.

Want to learn about other stories?

If you enjoyed this book...

...sign up for Lynnette's Gazette below! Subscribers get exclusive deals, sneak peeks, and lots of other fun content.

Sign up link: https://www.pacificlightsbookstore.com

ABOUT THE AUTHOR

Born and raised in Malawi, Africa. Lynnette Bonner spent the first years of her life reveling in warm equatorial sunshine and the late evening duets of cicadas and hyenas. The year she turned eight she was off to Rift Valley Academy, a boarding school in Kenya where she spent many joy-filled years, and graduated in 1990.

That fall, she traded to a new duet—one of traffic and rain—when she moved to Kirkland, Washington to attend Northwest University. It was there that she met her husband and a few years later they moved to the small town of Pierce, Idaho.

During the time they lived in Idaho, while studying the history of their little town, Lynnette was inspired to begin the Shepherd's Heart Series with Rocky Mountain Oasis.

Marty and Lynnette have four children, and currently live in Washington where Marty pastors a church.